Season for Love

The McCarthys of Gansett Island, Book 6

Marie Force

Published by HTJB, Inc.

Cover by Kristina Brinton

ISBN: 978-0615824376

marieforce.com

The McCarthys of Gansett Island

Book 1: Maid for Love

Book 2: Fool for Love

Book 3: Ready for Love

Book 4: Falling for Love

Book 5: Hoping for Love

Book 6: Season for Love

Book 7: Longing for Love

Book 8: Waiting for Love

Book 9: Time for Love

Who's Who in the McCarthy Family

Big Mac and Linda McCarthy are parents to:

- Mac McCarthy Jr., who is married to Maddie Chester McCarthy and father to Thomas and Hailey McCarthy
- Grant McCarthy, living with Stephanie Logan
- Adam McCarthy
- Evan McCarthy, living with Grace Ryan
- Janey McCarthy Cantrell, married to Joe Cantrell

Judge Frank McCarthy, brother to "Big Mac" McCarthy, father to:

- Laura McCarthy, cousin to Mac, Grant, Adam, Evan and Janey
- Shane McCarthy, cousin to Mac, Grant, Adam, Evan and Janey

McCarthy Friends & Family

- Owen Lawry, musician and best friend of Evan McCarthy
- Luke Harris, co-owner of McCarthys Gansett Island Marina
- Sydney Donovan, interior decorator, living with Luke Harris
- Ned Saunders, best friend to Big Mac McCarthy and Fiancé of Francine Chester, mother of Maddie McCarthy and Tiffany Sturgil
- Tiffany Sturgil, sister to Maddie McCarthy, daughter of Francine Chester, mother to Ashleigh Sturgil
- Bobby Chester, estranged father of Maddie McCarthy and Tiffany Sturgil, estranged husband of Francine Chester
- Jim Sturgil, estranged husband of Tiffany Sturgil, father to Ashleigh Sturgil
- Seamus O'Grady, hired to run the Gansett Island Ferry Company
- Dan Torrington, celebrity lawyer and friend to Grant McCarthy
- Charlie Grandchamp, stepfather of Stephanie Logan
- Blaine Taylor, Gansett Island police chief
- Slim Jackson, Gansett Island pilot
- David Lawrence, Gansett Island doctor
- Victoria, Gansett Island midwife

AUTHOR'S NOTE

Welcome back to Gansett Island for the long-awaited story of Owen Lawry and Laura McCarthy. Owen and Laura have been on "slow burn" status since book 4, Falling for Love. They met after her cousin Janey's wedding and formed an immediate friendship that has, over time, turned to love. How can you not love a guy who scrapes you up off the floor after a bout of morning sickness, especially when the baby isn't even his? Ah, Owen, how do we love you? Let us count the ways! Laura's estranged husband isn't going quietly, and some challenges from Owen's past will surface as well. Along the way, we'll catch up with all our favorite couples and catch a glimpse of some future romances in the making.

Next up are Tiffany and Blaine in LONGING FOR LOVE, followed by Adam McCarthy's story. I was going to call that LOOKING FOR LOVE, but looking and longing are a little too similar, so I'll be giving Adam's book a different name. More to come on that.

Writing about this family and their life on an island so much like my beloved Block Island has been the most fun I've ever had as a writer. Thank you for embracing my fictional family and for all the lovely reviews you've posted. I appreciate your e-mails and Facebook posts more than you'll ever know. I always love to hear from readers. You can reach me at marie@marieforce.com. If you're not yet on my mailing list and wish to be added for occasional updates on future books, let me know with an e-mail. Also, join us on Facebook at Marie Force

Book Talk (*www.facebook.com/groups/MarieForceBookTalk/*) where we chat about my books, other books we love and lots of stuff that has nothing to do with books! You can also join the fun at the McCarthys of Gansett Island Reader Group (*www.facebook.com/groups/McCarthySeries/*) where we cover important topics such as which of the Gansett Island men we wouldn't kick out of bed and what actors would play the McCarthy brothers in our fictional movie. When each new book is released, we form a separate group to dish about the new story. You can find the Season for Love Reader Group at *www.facebook.com/groups/SeasonForLove/*. Come join the fun!

While SEASON FOR LOVE is intended to be a stand-alone story, you will enjoy it more if you read MAID FOR LOVE, FOOL FOR LOVE, READY FOR LOVE, FALLING FOR LOVE and HOPING FOR LOVE first.

Thanks as always to my brilliant behind-the-scenes team: Linda Ingmanson edits for me, and Kristina Brinton does my beautiful covers. Thank you to my beta readers extraordinaire, Ronlyn Howe, Kara Conrad and Anne Woodall, as well as my writing buddy, Jessica Smith, who did a proofread.

This is the first book I've written in my new life as a self-employed author. I give thanks every day for all the readers who've made my new life possible. Thank you from the bottom of my heart.

xoxo

Marie

CHAPTER 1

Owen Lawry stood on the porch of the Sand & Surf Hotel to watch the last ferry of the day leave South Harbor for the mainland. He and his van were supposed to have been on that boat. With his obligations on Gansett Island over for the season, he'd planned to be heading for a two-month gig in Boston, the same autumn engagement he'd had the last five years. It paid well, and, after all this time, the club owners were friends.

His gaze was riveted to the ferry as it steamed past the breakwater into open ocean, where it dipped and rolled in the October surf. As the sun set on Columbus Day, officially ending another summer season on Gansett, Owen wondered what the hell he was still doing here when he was supposed to be on that boat, leaving for good-paying work on the mainland.

"You know why you're still here," he muttered, thinking of the blonde beauty who had him all tied up in knots. He was at the point where he wondered if a man could actually die from pent-up desire.

It might've been better for them both if he'd left as scheduled, if he'd taken the gig in Boston and gone about his carefree existence with the same lack of responsibility that had marked his entire adult life.

What was he doing here pining after a woman who was still married to someone else and carrying her estranged husband's child? What was he doing spending every waking moment with a woman who'd made it clear she was unavailable for all the things he suddenly wanted for the first time in his thirty-three years? He was driving himself slowly mad. That was the only thing he knew for certain.

Before he met Laura McCarthy, he was perfectly satisfied with his life. He spent summers playing his guitar and singing on the island—the closest thing to a real home he'd ever had—worked autumns in Boston and winters in Stowe, Vermont, playing to the ski crowd. In the spring, he headed for a few months off in the Bahamas. It was a good life, a *satisfying* life. Watching the last ferry of the day fade into the twilight, Owen had the uneasy sensation that he was also watching that satisfying life slip through his fingers.

He usually felt sorry for guys who allowed themselves to be led around by a woman. His best friends, Mac, Grant and Evan McCarthy, Joe Cantrell and Luke Harris, had fallen like dominoes lately, one after the other finding the women they were meant to be with. Only Adam McCarthy remained untethered and seemed happy that way.

Owen, on the other hand, was stuck in purgatory, caught between the single life he'd embraced with passionate dedication and the committed life he never imagined for himself. He wasn't *with* Laura, per se. He just spent all his free time with her. Weeks ago, they'd shared a couple of chaste kisses that had been hotter than full-on sex with other women.

Since then, there'd been nothing but an occasional hand to his arm or a brief hug here or there. He'd continued to collect her off the bathroom floor each day until the relentless morning sickness suddenly let up as she entered her fifth month of pregnancy.

As he leaned against the railing he'd recently replaced on the hotel's front porch, Owen realized he actually missed that time with her in the mornings when she'd been so sick and he'd been there to prop her up. "You're such a fool," he said to the gathering darkness.

The autumn days were shorter, the nights longer and the chilly air a harbinger of things to come. Shivering in the breeze, Owen questioned his decision to stay with Laura this winter for the millionth time. Did she even want him here? Did she want company, or did she want *him*? If she wanted him, she was doing a hell of a job hiding it. For a while there, he'd thought they were at the start of something that could've been significant for both of them. Now he wasn't so sure.

She treated him like a platonic buddy when all he did was fantasize about getting her naked and into his bed. Was he sick to be having such fantasies about a woman who was pregnant with another man's child? Probably. But as she rounded and swelled and glowed, he only wanted her more. At times, he even let himself pretend they were married and the baby was his.

"You're one sick son of a bitch," he said to the breeze. Sick or not, he wanted her with a fierceness that was becoming harder and harder to hide from her. One of these days, he was going to grab her and pin her against a wall and show her exactly—

"Owen?"

He sucked in a sharp, deep breath, ashamed to have been caught having such uncivilized thoughts about a woman he truly cared for. Making an attempt to calm himself, he turned to her. "Yeah?"

"Aren't you cold out there?"

Actually, he was on fire thinking about her, not that he could confess such a thing to her. "Not really. It's nice."

Laura tugged the zip-up sweatshirt of his that she'd "borrowed" around herself and joined him on the porch. Even though the oversized jacket swallowed her up, she was still his regal princess. She snuggled into his side, and it seemed the most natural thing in the world to slip his arm around her.

Resting her head on his chest, she let out a contented sigh. "It's so pretty this time of day."

His throat tightened with emotion, and his entire body ached from wanting her. "Sure is."

"It's pretty every time of day. I never get tired of our spectacular view," she said as a shiver traveled through her.

"You shouldn't get too cold."

"I'm fine."

"It's a good night for a fire." *Now where did that come from?* He'd no sooner said the words than he wanted to take them back.

"Oh, can we? I'd love that!"

Owen wanted to moan as he imagined how gorgeous she'd look in the firelight. With her around to look at all day, every day, he never ran out of ways to torture himself. "Sure we can. Mac inspected the chimney last week and declared us good to go." Owen had collected a ton of driftwood off the beach that had been drying on the porch for weeks.

"I got marshmallows at the store. We can have a campout."

Perfect, Owen thought. More torture. Her childlike glee at the simple things in life was one of the qualities he liked best about her and part of what made him want her with a burning need unlike anything he'd ever experienced.

"Will you play for me, too? You know I love listening to you."

Here, wrapped around him, was everything he'd never known he wanted. And wasn't it ironic that he couldn't have her. He would've laughed at the lunacy of the situation if his growing ache for her hadn't been so damned painful. "Absolutely," he managed to say. "Let's go in before you catch a cold."

Was she reluctant to step out of his embrace, or was that wishful thinking on his part? As he followed her inside, he took a last look at the horizon where the ferry was nearly out of sight and hoped he hadn't made a huge mistake by letting it leave without him.

Laura's alarm dragged her out of a deep sleep the next morning. Ever since she'd moved to the island right after Labor Day to renovate and manage the Sand & Surf Hotel, she'd been sleeping well again. That was a welcome relief following months of sleepless nights.

Discovering that her new husband hadn't quit dating after their May wedding had shocked the life out of her—almost as much as discovering she'd been married just long enough to get pregnant. Months of restless nights, mounting anxiety and relentless morning sickness had taken a toll. By the time she arrived to start her new job, she'd been a wreck.

A month later, she was restored, energized, loving her job and falling more into something with her sexy housemate with each passing day. She thought about the evening they'd spent together in front of the fireplace, roasting marshmallows and singing silly songs and laughing so hard she'd had tears rolling down her face at one point.

What would she have done without his steady presence to get her through these last few weeks? His care and concern had been a balm on the open wound her husband Justin had inflicted on her heart. And while she had no doubt Owen wanted more than the easy friendship they'd nurtured since they met over the summer, she didn't feel comfortable pursuing a relationship with him when they were on such vastly different paths. Not to mention, she was still technically married, which wasn't likely to change any time soon with Justin refusing to grant her a divorce.

With her baby due in February, her life would be all about responsibility for the next eighteen years. Owen's life was all about transience. He loved his vagabond existence. He was proud of the fact that everything he owned fit into the back of his ancient VW van. Other than the Sand & Surf, which his grandparents had owned and run for more than fifty years before their retirement, he had no permanent address and liked it that way.

His world simply didn't fit with hers, even if she liked him more than she'd ever liked any guy—including the one she'd married. Despite their significantly different philosophies on life, their chemistry was hard to ignore. She wasn't immune to the heated looks he sent her way or the overwhelming need to touch him that was becoming almost impossible to resist.

Standing with him on the porch last night, looking out over the ocean as the sun set, had been a moment of perfect harmony. They had a lot of those moments. Whether it was picking out paint colors for the hotel or discussing furniture options or reviewing advertising strategies, they agreed on most things. And when they disagreed, he usually said something to make her laugh, and she'd forget why she didn't agree with him.

She turned on her side to look out on the glorious view that was now a part of her everyday life. She'd loved the old Victorian hotel since she visited the island as a young girl after her mother died. Then it had reminded her of an oversized dollhouse. Those summers with her Uncle Mac and Aunt Linda had been the best of her life. They—and their island—had saved her from the overwhelming grief that had threatened to consume her. The island had saved her from the same fate earlier this year when she'd come for her cousin Janey's wedding and discovered a whole new life, thanks in large part to Owen.

With Justin fighting the divorce and still unaware he was soon to be a father, Laura should be spectacularly unhappy. As she got out of bed and dragged herself into the shower, she couldn't deny that the only reason she wasn't spectacularly unhappy was because she got to be with Owen every day.

She thought about that fact of her new life as she dried her hair and got dressed to meet her Aunt Linda for breakfast at the South Harbor Diner. Maybe it was time she and Owen had a heart-to-heart about what was really going on between them. But how exactly did one broach such a subject? Did she say, "Listen, I know you want me, and you know I want you, but that's where our similarities begin and end. We can't build a relationship based on chemistry alone." *Or could we?*

That question stayed with her as she went downstairs, where Owen was sanding the hardwood floors in the lobby. At some point over the last few weeks, her project of renovating the old hotel had become *their* project, which was fine with her. Everything was more fun with him around to share it with, and besides, his grandparents owned the place, so it seemed fitting to have him involved in the decisions.

Owen turned off the sander, removed his respirator mask and hustled her outside to the porch. "You shouldn't be breathing the dust."

When he was always taking care of her in one way or another, how was she supposed to remember they wanted different things out of life?

He took a closer look at her. "You look nice. What's the occasion?"

On regular workdays, she tossed her hair up in a ponytail and didn't bother with the light bit of makeup she'd applied to meet her always well-put-together aunt. "Breakfast with Linda, but I won't be long."

She felt guilty about leaving him to work when she was the one being paid to oversee the renovations. That reminded her she wanted to speak with his grandmother about getting him on the payroll. Since he'd given up his gig in Boston to babysit her this winter, it was the least she could do for him.

"Take your time," he said with a grin that made his eyes crinkle at the corners. "Believe it or not, I can manage on my own for an hour or two."

Looking up at him, she had to fight the ever-present urge to straighten the shaggy, dirty-blond hair that hung low on his brow. "Owen..."

Amusement and affection danced in his gray eyes. "What's on your mind, Princess?"

As a modern, independent woman, Laura knew she probably shouldn't love that nickname quite as much as she did. "We need to talk." They couldn't go on like this all winter without one or both of them incinerating from the heat that arced between them.

"Probably." He bent to press a soft kiss to her forehead. "But not when you've got somewhere to be."

The loving gesture took her breath away. She wanted to reach up, grab a fistful of that unruly hair and drag his sexy mouth down for a kiss that would leave him as breathless as he made her feel when he looked at her in that particular way. But then she remembered all the reasons why it was a terrible idea for her recently shattered heart to take a chance on a man who thrived on freedom.

She'd survived heartbreak once—barely. Why in the world would she set herself up for another trip down that hellish road? "Later, then," she said, her voice sounding as shaky as she felt. "We'll talk later."

"I'll be here."

Laura felt him watching her as she went down the stairs to the sidewalk. As much as she wanted to look back at him, she didn't. Rather, she took deep breaths to regulate her heart rate. The powerful effect he had on her was frightening. Nothing had even happened between them, and she already knew if he broke her heart, it would be way worse than the substantial damage Justin had done.

By the time she stepped into the South Harbor Diner, she'd almost gotten her heart to stop pounding, but the looming conversation with Owen had her vibrating with nervous energy.

Laura was surprised to find her friends, Grace Ryan and Stephanie Logan, along with her cousin Mac's wife, Maddie, sitting with her Aunt Linda in a corner table. Grace had recently gotten together with Laura's cousin Evan, and Stephanie was hot and heavy with Laura's cousin Grant.

Everyone around her, it seemed, was newly in love and glowing with happiness.

"Hi, honey," Linda said, rising to greet Laura with a hug. Linda's love and affection had helped to fill the awful void left in Laura's young life after her mother died. "You look so pretty. Come have a seat."

"I didn't realize we were having a party," Laura said, thrilled to see the others. Her new friends were also a big part of the reason she was so happy on the island. It was comforting to be around people who hadn't witnessed the thermonuclear meltdown of her marriage and didn't look at her with pity the way her friends in Providence did.

"Neither did we," Grace said, "and I'm kind of relieved to see you all. When Linda asked me to meet her, I thought I was in for a 'when are you going to marry my son' inquisition." She punctuated the comment with a cheeky grin for Linda.

"Don't be silly," Linda said. "I'd never ask such a question."

The others laughed at the ludicrous statement.

"*Right*," Stephanie said, dripping with sarcasm.

Propping her chin on her upturned hand, Linda zeroed in on Grace. "Since you brought it up, when *are* you going to marry my son?"

"Don't make eye contact," Stephanie advised Grace.

"You hush," Linda said to Stephanie, who she often said she would've hand-picked for Grant. "I could ask you the same thing."

"You're not the one who has to do the asking," Stephanie said, arching a brow meaningfully at her boyfriend's mother.

"Touché," Maddie said, laughing at her mother-in-law's shameless quest for information about her unmarried sons and their love lives.

Sydney Donovan came rushing through the door and made a beeline for their table. "So sorry I'm late," she said, also seeming surprised to see the others.

They scooted chairs around to make room for the newcomer, who was Maddie's close friend from childhood.

"Luke dropped me off on his way to see Dr. David," Sydney said. "Fingers crossed this is his last appointment for the ankle injury from hell."

"Oh, let's hope so," Maddie said. "At least he's finally off the crutches."

"And he's walking much better since the surgery," Sydney said as she accepted a cup of coffee from the waitress.

Laura shook her head when offered coffee. "Could I have decaf tea, please?" Oh how she missed coffee!

"And when are you two tying the knot?" Linda asked Sydney.

Sydney's cheeks flushed with color to match her strawberry-blonde hair. "Maybe soon."

"*Oh my God!*" Maddie said. "Have you been holding out on me?"

"Luke asked me a while ago, but I wasn't ready yet. I think I might be now."

"Oh, Syd," Maddie said, hugging her friend. "I'm so happy for you!"

After losing her husband and children in a drunk-driving accident more than a year and a half ago, Sydney had returned to Gansett Island earlier in the summer and reconnected with Luke, her first love, a part owner of McCarthy's Gansett Island Marina.

"I haven't told him yet," Sydney said, "so keep a lid on it for a few days."

"Our lips are sealed," Maddie said, and the others nodded in agreement.

"I'm thrilled for you both," Linda said, reaching out to pat Syd's hand.

"Thank you," Sydney said. "I'm rather thrilled myself."

"No one deserves it more," Laura said.

They talked wedding plans and hotel renovations and kids for a while before Linda tapped her spoon on her coffee cup to get their attention.

"The reason I invited you all to come today," Linda said, "is I have a project I need your help with."

"Sure," Grace said. "What can we do?"

"You've all heard about the new lighthouse keeper—Jenny Wilks?"

"I've heard she's living out there," Stephanie said, "but I've never seen her."

"Neither have I," Laura said.

"Mac told me she has her groceries delivered so she doesn't have to leave the lighthouse," Maddie said.

"That's what I've heard, too," Linda said. "Big Mac was on the search committee, and when she sealed herself off out there, he said we should do something. And that's where you all come in." She leaned in and lowered her voice. "Part of the application process was an essay about an event in their lives that made them who they are today. Hers is so heartbreaking. Listen to this..."

CHAPTER 2

"My name is Jenny Wilks, and I'm applying for the lighthouse keeper's position on Gansett Island," Linda read from a paper she pulled from her purse. "I currently reside in Charlotte, North Carolina, and the reason for my interest in the position dates back almost eleven years.

"The morning of September 11, 2001 began like any other Tuesday for my fiancé, Toby, and me."

"Oh God," Maddie whispered.

Sydney reached for Maddie's hand and held on tight.

Linda had agonized over whether to include Sydney when she called the women together. In the end, she hadn't the heart to leave her out. Now Linda hoped she'd done the right thing by asking Syd to come.

Linda cleared the emotion from her throat and continued reading. "We woke up in our Greenwich Village apartment, had breakfast, got dressed and left for work—me at an ad agency in midtown, and he as a financial services advisor at the World Trade Center's South Tower. I don't remember what we said to each other that morning. Probably the usual stuff about our plans for the day, what time we might be home, what we'd do for dinner. I so wish I could remember our exact words. I had no idea then how very precious they would be.

"We met at Wharton, survived the MBA program together and were due to be married that October. Toby was quiet and studious and destined for big things in his career. I used to call him my sexy nerd. While he tended to be shy with other people, with me he was easy-going, fun to be around and always making plans for our future. As we grappled with the stress of managing new jobs in New York while planning a wedding in North Carolina (where I'm from), his easy-going nature kept me sane.

"I was in a meeting when Toby called my cell phone that morning. We often sent texts back and forth but rarely called each other during the day. I was worried he might be sick or something, so I took the call despite the look of disapproval I received from my supervisor. I vividly recall getting up and starting to walk out of the room. I was about halfway to the door when the fear and panic in Toby's voice registered. He was saying things I couldn't comprehend. An airplane had hit the building, there was a fire and they were trapped. He told me they were going up on the roof, hoping to be rescued, but if it all went bad, he wanted me to know..."

Linda blew out a deep breath and shook her head as tears swam in her eyes. The first time she read Jenny's letter, she'd wept for an hour, imagining the horror of receiving such a phone call.

Stephanie gripped her free hand, a gesture Linda greatly appreciated as she summoned the fortitude to continue. She blinked back the tears and focused on the heartfelt words.

"He wanted me to know how much he loved me. Right around then, people in the office heard what was going on, and everyone ran to the windows where we could see plumes of smoke coming from Lower Manhattan. I started to scream. It couldn't be happening. I heard the words terrorists and Pentagon and hijacking and all sorts of things that didn't seem real. Toby was yelling at me over the phone. 'Jenny,' he said, 'are you there?' I snapped out of it and realized my entire body was cold. I was shivering uncontrollably. Toby needed me, and I had to pull it together for him.

"Somehow I managed to form words. I managed to tell him how very much I loved him, how certain I was that everything would be fine and we'd have a long and happy life together the way we'd always planned. Even though I was utterly terrified, I held it together until he started to cry. He told me he didn't want to leave me and that he was so sorry to do this to me. He said he wanted me to be happy no matter what, that my happiness was the most important thing to him.

"You all know what happened, so I won't belabor the point. His body was never recovered. It was like he went to work one morning and disappeared off the face of the earth, which is essentially what happened. For days, weeks, months afterward, I was a total zombie. My parents came to get me, and I went home with them to North Carolina. Toby's parents had a funeral in Pennsylvania that my parents took me to. I barely remember being there. My sisters quietly canceled the wedding I'd planned down to the last detail. Everyone was so very nice. Our money was refunded. People wanted to help in any way they could, but all the kind gestures in the world couldn't replace what I'd lost. The oddest part was I never cried. I didn't shed a single tear, even though every part of me hurt.

"I had nightmares for months over how Toby's life might've ended. It's a terrible thing to hope the person you loved most in the world had suffocated before other more horrific things could happen to him. I went to therapy and grief groups and all the things my family thought might help. A year went by without my knowledge, and it suddenly became critically important that I attend the anniversary ceremonies. My parents were adamantly opposed, but I needed to see it. I needed to see where he had died."

Linda put down the page to wipe the dampness from her face. The young women gathered around the table were white-faced and teary-eyed. "If I didn't think Jenny needed us so very badly, I'd never put you through this," Linda said softly.

"Please," Grace said. "Please finish."

The others nodded in agreement.

Linda cleared her throat and returned to the letter. "Minutes after I arrived at the place they called Ground Zero, a name I always hated, I broke down into the kind of heartbroken tears you see in the movies. Apparently, I made quite a scene. It's another thing I barely remember. My parents carted me out of there, and I'm told I cried for days. Once the tears stopped, I was finally, somehow, a little better. I didn't feel quite so numb, which was a good and bad thing because that's when the pain set in. I won't bore you with the details of that stage. Suffice to say it was ugly.

"After two years of barely functioning, I wanted my old life back—or as much of it as still remained. For all that time, my company held my job for me. Can you believe that? I still can't. That was a bright spot in a sea of gray. They welcomed me back with open arms. I found out my parents had paid the rent on our place in Greenwich Village, which was another bright spot. I went back to our home and wallowed in the comfort of being surrounded by Toby's things. After four years, I asked his parents to come take what they wanted and packed up the rest because it was no longer a comfort to be surrounded by his belongings.

"In the fifth year, I started dating again. That was a comedy of errors with one disaster following another. I felt sorry for the very nice guys my well-meaning friends fixed me up with. They didn't stand a chance against the fiancé I'd lost so tragically. Still, I went through the motions, mostly because it made the people around me more comfortable with my unending grief. I did what I could to make it better for them, because nothing could make it better for me.

"I became involved in the planning for the memorial, which was somehow cathartic when my rational self knew it probably shouldn't be. New York slowly recovered, the debris was cleared away and new construction began. Against all odds, life went on. I still had nightmares about how Toby died. I dreamed about the wedding we'd so looked forward to that hadn't happened. I went to work, I came home, I went to bed, I got up and did it all again the next day.

"As the tenth anniversary approached, I couldn't do it anymore. I couldn't stay in that city, in our apartment, in the job I'd had that day, with the well-meaning people who went out of their way to try to fix the unfixable. I started looking around for something to do that would get me out of the city, something that would get me off the treadmill my life had become. Two weeks before the tenth anniversary, I moved out of our apartment and went home to North Carolina. I couldn't stay for the dedication of the memorial or all the hoopla that would surround the anniversary. Leaving our apartment and our city for the last time was one of the most difficult moments in a decade of difficult moments.

"I've worked for the last year at a small PR firm in Charlotte. I saw your advertisement for the lighthouse keeper's position in the *New York Times* last weekend, and everything about it appealed to me. I have absolutely no experience running a lighthouse, although where one would get such experience I couldn't begin to imagine! I'm thirty-six years old, well educated in both the classroom and the school of hard knocks. I'm a reliable person looking for the opportunity to start over in a new place. I'd be honored to be considered for this position. Thank you for 'listening' to my story. I look forward to hearing from you. Sincerely, Jenny Wilks."

Linda folded the letter, returned it to her purse and used a tissue to dab at the moisture gathered in the corners of her eyes. The story hadn't been any easier to read the third time.

The others remained quiet and contemplative as they absorbed the letter. After a long moment of silence, Linda looked around at each of them. "We can't leave her out there all alone."

"Of course we can't," Laura said, mopping up tears.

"We can't descend upon her either," Stephanie said, pragmatic as always.

"True," Grace said.

"I thought if we put our heads together," Linda said, "we could think of a way—"

"I'll do it," Sydney said, her jaw set with determination. "I'll go."

"Are you sure you're up to that, honey?" Linda asked.

Sydney nodded. "Who better to make the first move than someone who's been there and done that?"

"No one," Maddie agreed, squeezing her friend's hand. "What'll you say?"

"I'll tell her I understand because I've been through my own hell. I'll let her know there's a wonderful, special community of people here who'd love to get to know her and make her feel at home."

"That sounds perfect," Linda said. "I had a feeling you all would know what to do."

"I don't know about the rest of you," Grace said, expelling a deep breath, "but I really, *really* need to see Evan right now."

"I was thinking the same thing," Maddie said. "About Mac, of course."

"Ditto," Stephanie said. "Grant."

"It's certainly a reminder that life is short and we need to make the most of every day we're given," Linda said. She noticed her niece still had tears rolling down her face. "Laura? Honey, are you all right?"

Laura reached for a napkin and dried her eyes. "I'm sorry. Jenny's letter brought it all back. That awful day when we didn't know where Adam was."

"Yes," Linda said. "It gave me some rough moments. I'm sure it did for Big Mac, too, which is why he didn't tell me about it until after he began to worry about her being out there all alone."

"Adam was in New York that day?" Maddie asked. "How have I never heard this?"

Linda nodded, her heart squeezing the way it always did when she thought of that nightmarish day when she'd thought for a few hours that her darling boy might be gone. "He'd just graduated from college and was working at his first job for a computer company in lower Manhattan. He'd only started the week before, so we didn't have any way to contact him there yet. His cell phone went right to voice mail for hours. Hours and hours."

"We found out much later that afternoon he wasn't even in the city," Laura said. "He was at a client's office in New Jersey. Cell service was nonexistent for days, but he finally managed to call around five o'clock. By then, we were so sure..."

"Best phone call of my entire life," Linda said, her voice catching as she relived a day she'd spent more than a decade trying to forget. That was another reason she'd been so determined to reach out to Jenny after she read the letter.

Laura wiped new tears from her face. "Listening to what happened to Jenny... I've been so caught up in my litany of troubles, but really, when it comes right down to it, I don't have any troubles. My life is blessed."

"I'm sure we all feel that way after hearing Jenny's story," Linda said as she drew Laura into a hug.

"She won't want our sympathy," Sydney said. "She's here for a fresh start, not to relive her nightmare with all new people."

"That's understandable," Linda said. "You'll let us know when you've seen her?"

"Of course."

"Thank you, honey," Linda said. "I appreciate your willingness to reach out to her."

"I'm not making any promises," Sydney said. "She might prefer to be alone. We can't force her out of her shell if that's where she wants to be."

"We forced you out of your shell," Maddie said with an affectionate smile for her old friend.

"That you did," Syd said, laughing. Looking around at the others, she said, "I have no doubt this peaceful place saved my life."

"Maybe it can save dear Jenny, too," Linda said.

"While I have you all here," Maddie said tentatively, "I wondered if you might be willing to help with another project."

"What kind of project?" Steph asked.

"I'd like to plan a benefit to assist the summer help who live here year round. With most of the hotels, restaurants, bars and marinas going dormant for the winter, there're a lot of people on the island who really struggle until the tourists come back in the spring. I used to be one of them."

Linda still experienced an occasional pang of shame whenever she thought about the unflattering rumors she'd once believed about her now-adored daughter-in-law. Maddie had made Mac so very, very happy. There wasn't much Linda wouldn't do for her. "What do you have in mind?"

"How about a big island Thanksgiving dinner where we supply the turkeys, everyone brings a side dish and we collect donations to go toward a fund for people in need?"

"How would the funds be distributed?" Grace asked.

"I haven't gotten that far, but I suppose we'd set up a system where they could request assistance and then we provide whatever we can to help out."

"I like it," Stephanie said. "I've worked tourist jobs for years myself, so I know how the off-season can be tough, especially in a high-rent place like this."

"Speaking of high rent," Maddie said with a shy smile, "I should also mention that I've petitioned the town council to use the property Mrs. Chesterfield left to the town as a site for affordable housing. I've contacted Habitat for Humanity about possibly building the homes."

"How do you have time to take care of a new baby and be an activist, too?" Sydney asked playfully. "You're amazing!"

"I couldn't agree more," Linda said. "What a marvelous bunch of ideas. I'll give Big Mac a heads-up about your petition so he's prepared to vote for it at the next council meeting."

"Only if he thinks it's a good idea," Maddie said.

"He'll love the idea. He's all about giving back to the community. I'm forever reining him in so he doesn't give away every cent we have."

"I can so see that," Laura said, smiling as she thought of her beloved uncle. "Let us know what we can do to help. I love all your ideas. I swing a pretty mean hammer, too."

"That's good to know," Maddie said. "I'll be recruiting everyone to help out if it actually happens. Mac has agreed to oversee the construction of the houses if we get approval."

"It's brilliant, honey," Linda said. "All of it."

"Thank you," Maddie said, clearly pleased by the approval. "I'll keep you posted."

CHAPTER 3

After breakfast, everyone scattered until only Laura and Maddie stood on the sidewalk in front of the diner.

Maddie checked her watch and frowned. "I have my six-week postpartum checkup with Dr. David in half an hour."

"Back in the saddle!" Laura said with a smirk.

"Believe me, we're both ready to resume normal programming. However, the idea of being poked and prodded by a doctor down *there* after all the poking and prodding of the last ten months doesn't hold much appeal."

Laura grimaced. "I feel your pain on that one. I've had more hands and eyes on my unmentionables since I've been pregnant than I ever could've imagined. You know you're getting immune to it when you hop up on the table and spread your legs like it's no big deal."

Laughing, Maddie said, "Exactly. By the time it's over, you won't have a shred of modesty—or dignity—left."

"Fabulous."

"So how are things with you? Mac and I have been worried about you since everything happened with Justin. I still can't believe it."

"Neither can I, but I'm hardly dwelling on it." She let her eyes drift to the Sand & Surf, two blocks away. "I've got much better things to be focused on these days."

"And much better *people*, too, if I'm not mistaken."

"Maybe," Laura said with a smile.

"If it makes any difference, your cousins adore Owen. Mac speaks so highly of him."

Laura stared out at the endless sea of blue that was glistening like diamonds in the autumn sunshine. "It does make a difference, it's just… I worry about getting too involved with him and then…" She met Maddie's steady gaze. "I'm afraid he'll get tired of being tied to one place—and one person—and want to leave."

"I can see why you'd be concerned about that with the way he's lived for so many years, but if you ask me, it's no small thing that he chose to spend the winter here."

"No, it isn't. Do you ever worry about Mac feeling antsy on the island? He used to hate it so much when he was a kid. He talked all the time about escaping to the 'real' world."

"He seems perfectly content with our life here, but he knows if the day ever comes when he isn't happy, we'll talk about our options."

"What's the secret to keeping him content?"

Maddie raised a brow and let out a hearty laugh. "Do I really have to spell that out for you?"

Laura smiled and shook her head. "It's really that simple?"

"He's a man. You do the math. Speaking of that… He's counting the minutes until we get the green light from David, so I'd better get going." She squeezed Laura's arm. "There're never any guarantees in life, but if you ask me, Owen Lawry is a pretty good bet."

"I tend to agree."

Maddie gave her a quick hug.

"Good luck at the doctor."

"I'll probably need the luck more when I get home to my husband. He's a little…pent up…at the moment."

Laura put her hands over her ears. "Lalala, too much information about my cousin."

Maddie left with a laugh and a wave.

Laura took her time wandering back to the hotel. She sat for a long time on a bench overlooking South Harbor and the breakwater, thinking about the conversation with Maddie as well as Jenny's story. The nine-thirty boat from the mainland pulled into port with a few passengers and four cars disembarking, much different from the frenzied arrivals in the summer months when the people, cars, bikes and pets flowed on and off the boats in a steady stream from sunup to sundown.

Tipping her face into the warm sunshine, she thought about what Maddie had said about Owen. Knowing he was at the hotel waiting for her filled her with an overwhelming sense of gratitude to have such a good man in her life. It was still too soon to gauge what might become of the bond they'd formed over the past few months. Nevertheless, he'd slowly but surely become one of the most important people in her life.

"Hmm," she said out loud. "How'd he manage that so quickly? Sneaky devil."

A flutter of movement inside made her gasp. Resting a hand on the baby bump, she waited breathlessly. "Do it again, baby," she whispered. "Do it again for your mama." She waited a full minute and was rewarded with a ripple that went from one side of the bump to the other. As she released a joyful laugh, her eyes filled with tears.

All at once, she wanted to see Owen, to tell him and show him what he'd come to mean to her. She wanted him to feel the baby move, too. Fueled by Jenny's reminder that life was short and time wasn't to be wasted, Laura got up from the bench and walked the short distance to the hotel at a brisk pace, anxious to be with him.

Carrying a rolled-up tarp, he came out the main door as she ran up the front steps.

"Whoa, Princess," he said, amused as he dropped the tarp and reached for her. "What's your hurry?"

Laura threw her whole self into the hug she gave him. "I wanted to see you."

Caught off-balance, he steadied them and returned the hug. "To what do I owe this unexpected pleasure?"

She took his hand and held it to her belly. "Feel this." As his palm heated her skin through the thin cotton top, she barely took a breath, hoping the baby was still awake.

"Oh, wow," he said when a little hand or foot thumped his hand. "Oh my God. That's amazing! Is that the first time you've felt him move?"

She nodded. "How do you know it's a him?" she asked with a teasing smile.

He flashed a sheepish grin. "Just a guess."

"I didn't say thank you," she said, breathless from the quick walk as much as the thrill of sharing her baby's first movements with him. Her heart was doing that pitter-patter thing it did whenever he was near.

His brows knitted with confusion. "For what?"

She looked up at him, meeting his steady gaze. "For staying. You stayed, Owen. Because of me. And I didn't say thank you. Thank you for staying."

He looked down at her for a long, charged moment before he dipped his head and kissed her.

Laura couldn't seem to care that they were probably starting a five-alarm Gansett scandal, as her Uncle Mac liked to say, by kissing on the front porch of the Surf in broad daylight. She linked her arms around his neck and combed her fingers through his shaggy blond hair. The kiss was soft and sweet and hot and tempting all at the same time. Weeks of restrained desire poured forth from both of them into a kiss that nearly blew the top of her head off.

"Wow," she whispered when they finally came up for air. "Where have you been hiding *that*?"

"It's been there all along, waiting until you were ready for it."

"I'm ready for it. I'm ready for you and for us."

"That must've been some breakfast with your aunt."

Laura tossed her head back and laughed.

He took advantage of the opportunity to rain kisses upon her neck and throat, turning her laughter into a moan.

"Owen."

"What, honey?"

"I want to... I want you."

His fingers tightened on her hips. "I want you, too. More than you could ever possibly know."

"Why do I hear a 'but' in there?"

Owen took her hand and guided her inside, away from the prying eyes of the town. He closed the door and turned to her, caging her in with his big body. While that same move from another man might be intimidating, being surrounded by Owen always made her feel safe. He ran his hands from her shoulders down to her hands. Gripping them, he raised them over her head and went in for the kill again, rendering her helpless against the full-body kiss. It went on for what felt like forever. Every time she thought he might he finished, he started all over again, destroying her with soft lips, an insistent tongue and the hard press of his big body against hers.

Only when the need for air trumped the need for deep kisses did he tear his lips free and turn his attention to her neck.

"I think," she said, tipping her head to give him better access, "that at least once in a lifetime, every girl should be pressed up against a wall and kissed stupid by a sexy man."

His chuckle rumbled from his chest. "You liked that, huh?"

She nodded, unable to take her eyes off him as she drank in every detail, appreciating him even more than she already had after hearing Jenny's story. How very lucky they were to have this moment in time together, however long it lasted.

"Did I kiss you stupid?"

"That you did."

"I like you smart, not stupid."

She wriggled her hands free from his grip and slid her arms around his waist. "In this case, and only this case, stupid is good."

His grin was so disarming. She wondered if he had any idea how ridiculously sexy he was when he flashed that grin and looked at her with devilish intent in his gray eyes.

"I believe that before you brought me in here and kissed me stupid, you were about to voice an objection to this new arrangement of ours."

"No objection," he said, pushing against her gently so she could feel what their kisses had done to him as he continued to leave hot, openmouthed kisses on her neck. "No objection whatsoever. Rather, I have a concern about timing."

"If you could stop kissing me for a minute, maybe we could talk about this concern of yours."

"Now that I've started, I don't think I'm ever going to stop kissing you."

All her female parts stood up and cheered at that news. "While I'd never want to discourage the kissing, especially now that I know how very good at it you are, I'd like to hear your concern." She gave his shoulders a gentle push, then grabbed his hand to lead him into the sitting room where they'd spent so much time together in recent weeks.

Groaning in dismay, he allowed her to pull him along.

"Sit."

"Will there be more kissing?"

"After we talk."

"Fine," he said, falling onto the love seat with a boyish pout on his sexy mouth.

"Now, tell me, what's on your mind."

As if he couldn't keep his hands to himself now that she had changed the rules of their relationship, he buried his fingers in her hair, stroking the long strands with intense purpose. Every time his fingertips brushed up against her scalp, they detonated a reaction that rippled through her entire body. She'd never been more sensitive to a man's touch.

"I want nothing more than to take you to bed and keep you there for days," he said. "Weeks. Maybe even months."

Laura swallowed hard and trembled, as much from his words as the feel of his fingers sifting through her hair. "But?"

"I'd really like the situation with Justin to be resolved before we go any further."

Laura's heart sank at that reminder of the standoff with her estranged husband. Justin had made it clear he was uninterested in a divorce and planned to fight her every step of the way.

"You also need to tell him about the baby. I know he hurt you and disappointed you terribly, but it's not right to keep the baby from him."

"I know," she said. "I've been thinking a lot about that, too."

"If it was my kid, I'd want to know, no matter what the situation was between myself and the mother. I'd want to know about my child."

"That's because you're upstanding and honorable. I wonder sometimes if he'll even care."

"He'll care. I can't imagine he's a total monster if you once loved him."

"No," she said, fiddling with a throw pillow. "He's not. He has a different idea about what it means to be married than I do."

"His ideas about marriage are different from most people's."

Pleased by his unwavering support, she looked over at him. "Where does this leave us?"

He took her hand and brought it to his lips. "On hold. Temporarily. Very temporarily."

"I'll take care of it. As soon as I can."

"And I'll be right here waiting to continue this 'conversation' as soon as you're ready." He held out his arms to her. "Come here."

She snuggled into his embrace, feeling relieved to have finally talked about the overwhelming attraction they'd been nursing for weeks, but also twitchy with restless desire. "Is kissing allowed during this temporary stand-down?"

"Absolutely. By all means. Yes."

"Are you sure?" she asked, making him laugh.

He cupped her face and gazed down at her, his eyes brimming with emotion. "I'm very, very sure." And then he sealed their deal with another of those amazing kisses.

CHAPTER 4

Mac held one end of a big sheet of plywood while Luke anchored the other side. Big Mac drove in the nails that would secure the wood over the windows of the marina gift shop. Winterizing the marina took about three weeks after the last boat left on Columbus Day. This year, in addition to the regular routine of boarding up buildings and shutting down the gas tanks, they planned to replace a big portion of the rotting planks on the main dock.

The work was a good distraction, Mac thought, as he waited to hear from Maddie. He'd been counting down to this day for weeks, since their adorable daughter arrived in the midst of Tropical Storm Hailey. Longer than that, actually. The weeks Maddie had spent on bed rest had also been torturous.

It'd been so long since he'd had sex—full-on, real-deal sex—with his wife that Mac couldn't remember the last time. Their daughter was absolutely worth the sacrifice, but he was ready, *more than ready*, to get back to normal. Maddie was ready, too, if the fooling around they'd engaged in recently was any indication. In fact, if they were any more ready, one of them might implode.

He took a deep, shuddering breath, trying to keep his mind on his work and not on his plans for later.

"So listen," Luke said. "I've been meaning to talk to you about this winter."

Grateful for the diversion, Mac said, "What about it?"

"You know how the International Yacht Restoration School people came over from Newport to look at some of my work this summer?"

"Sure do," Big Mac said, tugging the last of the nails from between his teeth.

Mac kept waiting for him to swallow one of them, but he'd learned to keep his thoughts about such things to himself.

"They want me to teach a class in January. I'd have to spend the whole month over there, but I could come back on weekends to help out on the hotel project. If I do it, that is. Nothing's been decided."

Mac tried to hide his surprise from his friend and business partner. Their construction business had a lot on its plate for the off-season, including the renovations to the Sand & Surf, a couple of kitchen upgrades and the possibility of the houses Maddie had suggested for the parcel of land left to the town by one of its most affluent residents. Losing Luke for a month would make it nearly impossible to get it all done before the spring.

"I know we've got a lot lined up for the winter," Luke said, seeming to read Mac's mind. "So I can take a pass, if need be."

"Don't be crazy," Mac said. "It's an amazing opportunity. You have to do it. We'll get by without you." Somehow.

"I could help out," Big Mac said.

"If you feel up to it, Dad."

Big Mac's scowl answered for him. "I'm back to normal after the accident, so you can quit your mollycoddling."

"Who's mollycoddling?" Mac asked, glancing at Luke, who shrugged. "Looks to me like you're pulling your weight just fine."

"Luke, for what it's worth," Big Mac said, "I think you should take this offer from IYRS. It's great to see you recognized for your amazing talent. I, for one, am very proud of you."

"Thank you," Luke said, seeming embarrassed by Big Mac's effusiveness.

Mac knew how he felt, having been on the receiving end of his father's effusiveness often enough. Still, it pleased him to know that his father had not only raised five children of his own but had been a huge influence in the lives of Luke and Joe, both of whom had grown up without their fathers.

"What does Syd have to say about it?" Mac asked.

"I haven't told her yet. I heard from them this morning, and I wanted to talk to you guys first. I'll tell her tonight."

"Do you think she'd go with you?"

"I suppose it'll depend on whether she'll be able to continue to work on the hotel project with Laura. She's really enjoying that."

"Whatever you decide," Big Mac said, "we're proud of you."

"Absolutely," Mac agreed.

"Thanks," Luke said. "That means a lot to me."

"Excuse me," a female voice behind them said.

Mac turned to find a young woman with light brown hair pulled into a ponytail. The hairstyle made her look younger than she was. He guessed mid- to late-twenties. She wore faded jeans and a rag wool sweater. "Hi there. How can we help you?"

"I'm looking for Mac McCarthy?"

"That'd be me," he and his father said in stereo.

"Junior," Mac said, extending a hand.

"Senior," Big Mac said, following suit. "This is our partner, Luke Harris."

"Nice to meet you all. I'm Kara Ballard, from Bar Harbor, Maine."

"Any relation to Ballard's Boat Builders?" Big Mac asked.

She grimaced slightly, but Mac saw it. "My family."

"Ah," Big Mac said. "I love your picnic boats. Gorgeous."

"Seriously," Luke said. "Beautiful lines."

Kara seemed embarrassed by their praise. "Thank you. They've done well for us." She cleared her throat. "The reason I'm here is I'd like to discuss a business opportunity with you."

"Sure," Big Mac said. "Let's get in out of this wind." He gestured for her to lead the way to the main building that housed the offices as well as the restaurant, which was now closed for the season.

Mac and Luke followed, and the four of them settled at one of the tables in the dining area.

She withdrew a brochure from her bag and opened it on the table. "You may be aware that Ballard's runs launch services in some of the bigger harbors in New England. We're in Bar Harbor, of course, Newport, Nantucket, Martha's Vineyard, and Hyannis. We use a smaller version of the picnic boats to transport passengers from the anchorages into shore."

"We sure could use something like that around here," Luke said.

"I was hoping you'd say that," Kara said, smiling at him. "My brothers oversee the other harbors. I've been tasked with setting up a launch service here on Gansett."

Big Mac was counting on his fingers. "You have *five* brothers?"

Mac laughed at his father's question. It was just like him to hone in on a detail like that.

Kara smiled indulgently. "Eight, actually, and two sisters."

"Wow," Luke said. "*Eleven* kids?"

"Those Maine winters are *long* and *cold*," Kara said with a spark of humor in her hazel eyes.

The comment drew a laugh from all three men.

"Are you oldest?" Big Mac asked. "Youngest?"

"Right in the middle. Number six. Anyway, we're in need of a landing place on Gansett. McCarthy's was our first choice." She handed them each another piece of paper that included projections of how many people would come through the marina as a result of the launch service. "You have the restaurant, laundry facilities, a well-stocked gift shop, showers and easy access to cab service into town."

"With the exception of the restaurant and gift shop, our facilities are for customers of our marina," Mac said as he studied the detailed projections. "We'd need bigger restrooms and more laundry facilities if we'd be serving the full anchorage."

His father nodded in agreement.

"We've been talking about making better use of the second-floor space above the restaurant," Luke said. "Maybe we can build some additional bathrooms and put in some more washers and dryers up there."

"Before next season?" Mac asked his friend and partner.

"We could do it," Luke said.

"What about IYRS?"

"It'll still be there next year."

"Luke—" Once again, Mac and his dad spoke in stereo.

Luke held up a hand. "We can talk about it later." To Kara, he said, "Proceed. Please."

"We'd like to rent a forty-foot slip, preferably on the outside row, where we would keep two launches for the season, which would run from May 1 to October 31."

Mac did some fast math in his head. "A forty-foot slip, at three bucks a foot is one-twenty a day times a hundred and eighty days is—"

"Twenty-one thousand, six hundred," Kara finished for him.

"You've done your research," Big Mac said, impressed.

"Like I said, your marina is our first choice. It has everything we're looking for—and then some. We also like that it's a family-owned-and-run business like ours."

"It'd cost us time and money to adapt our facilities to the increased traffic," Mac reminded her.

"Which is why we're willing to pay more than the dockage fees the first year. We'd revisit the fee structure after the initial season."

"How much more?" Mac asked.

"Forty thousand total?"

Mac exchanged glances with his father and Luke. "Forty-five," he said.

"Forty-two-five."

His father and Luke nodded.

"Done," Mac said, reaching out to shake on it.

Kara stared at him as she shook his hand. "That's it?"

Laughing, Mac sat back in his chair. "Were we too easy?"

"No, no. I figured it would take a few days to hammer out the details."

"One thing you'll learn pretty quick about my boys and me," Big Mac said, "is we don't dither over details. We know a good deal when we see one."

"He *definitely* doesn't dither over details," Mac said dryly. "That's my job."

"No shit," Luke muttered.

"I heard that," Big Mac said, playfully scowling at Mac and Luke.

Mac's phone chimed with a text from Maddie that said, "Green light." He got up so fast his chair fell over backwards. "I gotta go."

"Where?" his father asked.

"Home."

"Now? Why? Is everything okay?"

"Oh yeah. Everything is *just* fine. Kara, great to meet you. If you want to come back tomorrow, we can hammer out any additional details."

"Sure. I'm here for a week to get a feel for the island."

"Later," Mac said, bolting for the door. No doubt he'd catch flak from his dad and Luke for the way he'd run out of there when his wife summoned him, but so what? He'd been waiting months for this moment, and nothing would stop him from going to her. Right now.

Laura had known this phone call wouldn't be easy, but it had to be done. Never before had the idea of calling her dad filled her with such anxiety. Even telling him what had happened with Justin had been easier than asking for his help in getting rid of her scumbag husband.

It had always been important that she maintain her independence and not let her prominent father's connections make life easier for her. But this was no time for foolish pride. She needed to be free of Justin, and her dad could help.

Swallowing the knot of emotion that formed in her throat, Laura pressed send on the first number on her list of favorites.

"Hi, honey," he said. "I was just thinking about you."

Laura smiled, and her nerves melted away. Here was the one man who'd never let her down. She had no reason to be nervous about asking him for anything. He'd give her the sun and moon if he could. She heard the worry in his voice and hated being the cause of it. "Is that right?"

"I think about you all the time. After what Justin did..."

"I know, Daddy. I'm sorry you're worried about me."

"My brother tells me you're working hard and enjoying the hotel project."

"I love what I'm doing here. It's the most fun I've ever had." Of course Owen was a big part of why it was so fun, not that she was ready to tell her dad that part.

"Mac says you've made a new friend, too. The grandson of the hotel owners?"

Laura laughed. Leave it to her Uncle Mac to zero in on her burgeoning relationship with Owen. "Yes, his name is Owen Lawry."

"Do you need me to run a check on him? I can get one of my state police friends to—"

"No, Dad!" she said, laughing again. "Uncle Mac and Aunt Linda have known him since he was a kid. He's Evan's best friend."

"Well, I suppose that's as good an endorsement as we could hope to get." He paused, cleared his throat. "So, you like this boy, huh?" The question was poised in the same awkward fashion he'd used to extract information about her first teenage boyfriend.

"Yes," Laura said, amused by him as always. "I like him. He's been a very good friend to me through all of this."

"I'm glad to hear you're making new friends and putting the pieces back together."

"I'm trying."

"I wish I could say the same for your brother. He seems to have totally given up."

Laura hated to think of Shane's terrible heartache over his wife's addiction to prescription pain medication. "What's the latest?"

"Courtney asked for a divorce."

Laura winced. "That might be for the best, no?"

"Try telling him that. He's waited all this time for her to get through rehab, and now she wants out."

"Did she say why?"

"He says she's so ashamed of what she put him through that she can barely bring herself to look at him."

Laura's heart ached for her poor, sweet brother. He'd fallen so hard and so fast for Courtney, who'd hidden a raging addiction from him for more than a year before it blew up in her face—and his. "What will he do?"

"Once he finishes the job he's working on now, he's going out there to be with you for the winter. I think it'll be good for him to get some space from everything here and clear his head."

"We'll take good care of him. Don't worry."

"All I do these days is worry about both of you."

"I'm okay, Dad. I promise. But I do need a favor."

"Name it, honey."

"I have to tell Justin about the baby." It hurt to say the words. She was so utterly unprepared to see her philandering ex-husband again, but Owen was right. Justin deserved to know about the baby. "I expect he's going to give me a hard time. The more I think about everything that happened, it's clear to me that he was far more interested in forming a connection to you than he was in me."

Frank gasped. "That's not true! He was crazy about you. I saw that with my own eyes, which is why this is so hard to believe."

"You saw what he wanted you to see. He played us both."

"Why would he do such a thing?"

"Why else? To further his career, which is his first love. Being Judge Frank McCarthy's son-in-law furthers his career, which is the only reason he's fighting the divorce."

"That makes me sick. You don't think he'll want the baby?"

"I don't know what to expect there." The uncertainty terrified her, not that she would admit that to her dad and give him one more thing to fret about. Since her mother died when Laura was nine and Shane was seven, her dad had been both mother and father to them.

"What can I do, honey?"

"I'm coming over this week to speak to Justin. Would you mind terribly if I threw your name around a bit if it comes to that?"

"Of course not. Do whatever it takes to get that pond scum out of your life for good."

"He's going to be in my life for as long as we share a child." The thought of that was a hundred-pound weight on Laura's chest.

"I don't want you to see him alone."

"Owen will be with me." Laura knew without even asking that Owen would go with her.

"Are you sure that's a good idea? Won't it throw gas on Justin's fire if he sees you with someone else?"

"Owen will keep his distance unless I need him."

"If that son of a bitch has the nerve to get physical with you, I'll kill him myself."

"It won't come to that. I'll meet him in public. He's far too concerned about what people think of him to risk a scene."

"Will you come see me while you're here?"

"Absolutely."

"I want to meet your Owen, too."

Laura's face heated with embarrassment. "He's hardly *my* Owen."

"I'll be the judge of that."

Laura laughed at his pun. "You'd better behave, do you hear me?"

"So I can't ask his intentions?"

"Dad!"

Frank's guffaw brought a smile to Laura's face. "I'll be on my best behavior," he said.

"Love you, Dad," Laura said, her throat squeezing with emotion.

"Love you, too, sweetheart. Everything will be okay. I promise."

Since her dad had never once let her down, Laura chose to believe him.

Chapter 5

Maddie got home before Mac and made good use of the time. She changed into the white silk nightgown he'd bought her when they were first dating and covered it with the matching robe he'd given her for her birthday the following year. He'd given her everything, most importantly his love and devotion. Certainly, no woman had ever been so adored by her husband. He'd never been more attentive or solicitous as he'd been since she delivered their baby daughter in the midst of a tropical storm.

She brushed her hair until it hung in soft, shiny waves on her shoulders and smoothed on some of the strawberry-flavored lip balm that had been known to make her dear husband a little crazy. Who was she kidding? Everything about her seemed to make him a little crazy, and she loved every crazy, over-the-top thing about him.

The bang of the sliding door opening caught her attention. "*Madeline!* Where are you?"

"Showtime," she whispered in the mirror with a small, satisfied smile. At the top of the stairs, she looked down to find him on the sofa tearing at his work boots with hasty, fumbling movements.

"*Maddie!*"

She bit her lip to keep from laughing at him and went down the stairs to sit next to him on the sofa. "You beckoned?"

He turned to her, and when he saw what she was wearing, his eyes got big. His mouth opened and then closed. "You're stunning."

"You're dirty."

"I know. I'm sorry. I'll take a shower so fast I'll be back before I'm gone." He stole a quick kiss and headed for the stairs, stopping halfway up. "Where're my children?"

"With my mother and Ned until dinnertime."

"God, I love you so much."

Maddie laughed as he bolted up the remaining stairs and disappeared. She thought about going upstairs to meet him after his shower but decided it would be far more fun to make him come after her. Sure enough, he came flying down the stairs less than five minutes later, with a towel wrapped around his waist, his dripping-wet hair standing on end and a small spot of blood on his chin from where he'd nicked himself shaving.

"You're a mess," she said, laughing as she held out her arms to him.

Smelling of soap and sexy man, he came down on top of her. "I can't help it. Waiting for this day has made me nuts."

She combed her fingers through his hair, attempting to bring some order. "Good thing I love you even when you're a messy nut case."

That drew a smile from him. "So what did David have to say?"

"Everything looks good."

As she'd expected, he scowled darkly. "You're damned right it looks good. I hate the idea of that guy having his face…*there.*"

Once again, she held back a laugh at his ridiculousness. "He's a *doctor.* Seen one, seen them all."

"That's crap. Yours is way better than most. I should know. I did a lot of shopping before I bought."

"Mac!" She sputtered with laughter as she smacked his shoulder. "*Oh my God!* I can't believe you said that! You're *outrageous*. Don't forget 'that guy' saved your daughter's life."

"I'll never forget that, but it doesn't mean I want his face in my wife's hoo-ha."

She squished his lips together before releasing them. "You really need to stop talking now."

"Why? Is there something else you'd rather be doing?"

"Definitely." She kissed him fully, deeply, letting him know exactly what she'd rather be doing.

Mac pushed himself off her and held out his hand to help her up. He lifted her and headed for the stairs.

Maddie looped her arms around his neck and rested her head on his shoulder. She'd never felt truly at home anywhere until Mac McCarthy put his arms around her and refused to let go.

He put her down next to the gigantic bed he'd insisted they needed. That they occupied about three feet of it was a source of endless amusement to her. Sleeping in his arms had become as necessary to her as air and water.

For a long time, he only ran his hungry gaze over her, taking in every detail and heating her from within.

"I never get tired of looking at you, Madeline."

She released a nervous laugh and put her hands on his superbly formed chest. "I could say the same to you."

"I want you to know..." He combed his fingers through her long hair. "These last few weeks, watching you care for our baby, watching you feed her, you..." His voice faltered, and he rested his forehead on hers, collecting himself. "You take my breath away."

"Mac..."

He drew her in closer to him. "You positively glow when you're looking at that baby. Do you know that?"

"You should see yourself with her. So big and protective. She's a lucky girl to have you as her daddy."

"She won't think so when I refuse to let her date until she's thirty."

Maddie laughed. "I'll be around to manage you on her behalf."

He raised a rakish brow. "Manage me, huh? I could use some of your brand of management. I thought I'd die waiting for this day to get here."

She dragged her hand from his chest to his belly and pulled the towel off him, licking her lips as she tried to figure out where she wanted to kiss him first.

Mac let out an unsteady-sounding laugh. "You're going to finish me right off if you keep looking at me that way." He got busy removing her robe and nightgown in quick, well-practiced movements.

Maddie was always astounded at how competent he was at divesting a woman of her clothing. He'd had plenty of practice in his bachelor days.

"What are you thinking?"

Feeling guilty, she met his intense gaze. "About how you got so good at getting a woman's clothes off so quickly."

"The only woman whose clothes I want off—quickly—is the one I was smart enough to marry." He kissed her then, hot and sweet and full of the love and passion they'd shared from the day they met. His hands were everywhere, combing through her hair, smoothing a path on her back, cupping her bottom, coasting over her ribs to her breasts.

Maddie was mortified when the stimulation made her leak. She tried to pull back from him, but he let out a tortured moan and used the moisture to slide his fingers over her tender flesh.

She wrapped a hand around his throbbing cock, stroking him the way he liked, harder than she would've done without his guidance.

He stopped her. "Can't," he gasped. "I want to be inside you when I come."

"Hold that thought." She went to the bedside table and retrieved a condom leftover from their dating days. When she handed it to him, he moaned.

"*Seriously?*"

"I don't want to be pregnant again anytime soon."

"But you're breastfeeding. You can't get pregnant."

"That's a load of crap. Suit up or no nookie."

He took the condom from her. "Fine. Be that way."

"Want me to do it for you?" she asked with a coy smile.

"Absolutely not."

Maddie loved it when he pouted. He was so used to getting his own way that when he didn't, he acted like a petulant little boy—an adorably petulant little boy.

He rolled the condom on and reached for her. They landed on the bed in a tangle of arms and legs, lips fusing, tongues mating in a frantic, familiar dance.

He tore his lips free and bent to lave her sensitive nipples with his tongue.

"Mac… Wait, I don't want you to… Oh God." She wanted to die when her breasts tingled with the familiar sensation of milk letting down. "Mac. Don't. *Please.*" She worried about him being turned off by the flow of liquid, but it seemed to have the opposite effect.

"Wow, look at that." His tongue dabbed at the moisture on her nipple in a moment so erotically charged, Maddie knew she'd never forget it. The shocking intimacy, the reverent expression on his face… The images etched indelibly into the growing album of memories that made up their beautiful life together.

She wrapped her arms around him, holding his head to her chest. She'd spent most of her life hating her oversized breasts, but he managed to make her forget all about that with his worshipful treatment. "I love you, Mac. More and more every day. Just when I think I've reached the outer limit of how much it's possible to love you, you go and top yourself, and I discover there's even more."

When he raised his head to meet her gaze, she was stunned to see his shockingly blue eyes swimming with tears.

"That might be the nicest thing anyone has ever said to me." He pressed his lips softly to hers. "In fact, I know it is."

She combed her fingers through his damp, dark hair, leaving it mussed and sexy looking. "I mean every word of it."

"I know you do. And I feel the same way. I never imagined anything like this happening to me. I love you so much sometimes I feel like I could burst with it." As he spoke, he shifted so he was poised between her legs, his cock pressed against her, without demanding anything she wasn't ready to give. "Speaking of bursting..."

Laughing softly, Maddie cradled him between her legs and ran a soothing hand down his back. She cupped his muscular rear end and tugged, urging him to take her.

He let out a ragged groan. "I want you so bad, but I'm afraid of hurting you, babe."

"You won't."

"After what you went through..." A shudder rippled through him.

"Don't think about that, or you'll never want to have sex with me again."

Laughing, he kissed her with sweet reverence. "No chance of that." He reached between them and used his fingers to test her readiness. "Oh God," he gasped when he found her slick and primed for him. "Will you tell me to stop if it hurts?"

"Yes," she moaned when his fingers pressed on the tight bundle of nerves that pulsed with desire. "Mac, *please*. Hurry."

Moving slowly, he slid into her in small increments, giving her time to adjust and accommodate him. "Is it okay?" he asked through gritted teeth.

"It's divine," she whispered. "Nothing hurts. I promise."

That seemed to snap his control, and he surged the rest of the way in one thrust. "Oh shit, sorry. Sorry, I can't help it—"

She raised her hips in encouragement. "Love me, Mac. It feels so good."

Sweat beaded on his brow and back as he thrust into her, still holding back.

Aware of what it took to break him, Maddie grasped his firm ass and squeezed. As she'd know it would, that shattered his control. He let go, surging into her and taking them both to the place they could only go together.

For a long time afterward, he lay on top of her, heavy and solid and throbbing.

"I'm crushing you," he muttered.

"Don't go yet." She tightened her hold on him.

"I'm all yours, baby," he said, his lips soft against her neck.

His words only added to the glow of contentment that surrounded her.

"I'm sorry I was so rough," he said.

"You weren't. You were exactly what I wanted. I've missed this as much as you have."

"I don't know if that's possible." He raised his head and kissed her while gazing deep into her eyes. "I was like a horny teenager getting lucky for the first time. I skipped over all the preliminaries."

Maddie giggled at the look of disgust on his face. "Mom's not bringing the kids home until they wake up from their naps. You've got plenty of time to make it up to me."

"Have I mentioned lately how much I love your mother?" He withdrew from her and kissed his way down the front of her. "So much time to make up for."

As his lips left a trail of sensation on her belly. Maddie closed her eyes and gave herself over to him, body and soul.

After Mac and his dad left for the day, Luke spent a couple more hours at the marina, winterizing the fuel system, bleeding gas lines and securing pumps.

This time of year usually filled him with melancholy as the long, lonely winter stretched before him. This year, however, everything was different. Syd was back in his life, living with him, sleeping with him, filling his days and nights with her sweet love.

Nothing could've prepared him for the changes her presence had brought to his sparse existence. Whereas life without her had been satisfying in its own way, life with her was a vivid landscape full of endless possibility.

He snorted to himself as he tightened a bolt. "Look at you, spouting poetry." But that was what she did to him—what she'd always done to him from the time he was a boy in the throes of first love.

Over the last few months, he'd watched her blossom out of the fog of grief and into the land of acceptance. She would always miss and mourn the family she'd lost to a drunk driver, but she laughed more freely and more often now. She took pleasure in her work as an interior designer, and she gave herself to him with the kind of passion that left him speechless and humbled.

Thinking of the passion they shared had him closing up early and heading home to her. The only thing in the world he wanted now that he didn't have was a commitment from her to marry him. He'd asked her back in early September, after they attended the sentencing hearing for the guy who'd killed her family and they'd moved her out of her former house and into his island home.

His timing, he saw with hindsight, hadn't been the best. With the raw wound of her loss reopened by the court proceeding and the painful weeding out of her family's possessions, she wasn't ready to take the next step with him. He should've known that.

His intent had been to show her he was in it for keeps and to make her feel more secure in their relationship as they moved in together. He'd realized his strategic error when his marriage proposal had resulted in a stricken expression on the gorgeous face that had haunted his dreams for so many years. She'd told him then that she needed more time, and they hadn't spoken of it again. The unanswered question hung in the air between them.

Kara's arrival at the marina and the additional work their deal with her would generate in the off-season also cemented his decision to turn down the offer from the yacht restoration school. He and Mac had too much going on for him to leave the island for a month, and with Syd busy and happily engaged on the hotel project, this wasn't the time to uproot them. There'd be other opportunities to teach the class.

When he pulled into the driveway, he was relieved to see her Volvo parked in its usual spot. He had no doubt she was happy with him and their life on the island, but he wouldn't be truly satisfied until the one who'd gotten away had his ring on her finger.

It was old-fashioned, he knew, to think that way, but he needed to hear her say "I do." In the meantime, he kept waiting for something to happen that would screw it all up, and that was no way to live.

Reaching into the glove compartment, he withdrew the jeweler's box he'd hidden there more than a month ago. He'd bought the ring in Newport, the same day he'd gone to talk to the boat restoration people about the course they wanted him to teach. Syd had been too busy with the hotel project to come with him, so he'd taken advantage of the opportunity to shop for a ring.

The large emerald-cut diamond was housed in an elaborate antique setting that had seemed right for her. It was strong and fragile at the same time, like her. He wanted to put that ring on her finger in the worst way, but more than anything, he wanted her to want it as much as he did.

Even her father had given his blessing over beers on the Donovan's porch. Mr. Donovan had come right out and asked Luke if he planned to marry his daughter.

"*As soon as she's ready,*" had been Luke's reply. They'd come a long way from the time when Mr. and Mrs. Donovan hadn't thought he was good enough for their only child.

"*Good,*" Allan Donovan had said. "*She seems happy again since she's been with you. I like seeing that light back in her eyes.*"

"*So do I,*" Luke had said.

He couldn't risk extinguishing the light with another clunky proposal. He had to do it right this time. With that in mind, he reluctantly returned the ring to the glove box and locked it up until she was ready. He hoped he would recognize ready when he saw it.

Her dog Buddy came rushing out to greet Luke with sloppy, wet kisses to his face. "Hey, pal, did you have a good day?"

Buddy barked in response, which made Luke laugh. They had the same exchange every night when Luke got home from work, and it was another part of his new routine that he looked forward to each day.

He stepped into the living room that Syd had spent most of the summer redecorating. What had once been a dark and gloomy space had been painted a bright shade of cream. The new furniture was navy with maroon accents. Syd had removed the blinds on the windows to take full advantage of the sweeping ocean view. By letting in the light, she'd done the same thing for his home that she'd done to the rest of his life.

They planned to attack the kitchen next, and there was talk of eventually adding on to the house. He liked that she was making long-term plans for the place and took that to mean she planned to stay. Everywhere he looked, he saw her touch as he made his way to the back bedroom she'd turned into an office for her decorating business.

She was bent over a book of swatches, making notes in the sketchpad she carried with her everywhere she went. "*You never know*," she would say, "*when inspiration will strike*." Her strawberry-blonde hair was pulled back into a high ponytail that exposed the tender curve of her neck, one of his favorite places to kiss. He zeroed in on that spot and pressed his lips to her soft skin.

She gasped and then relaxed, tipping her head to give him better access. "You're home early."

"I was missing you."

"That's very sweet of you to say, but I hate to tell you, pal, you stink like gas."

He immediately pulled back from her. The stockbroker she'd married the first time around had certainly never come home stinking of gas. As soon as Luke had the thought, he regretted it. How pointless to be jealous of the dead man she'd chosen over him. That was ancient history, and it was better left in the past where it belonged.

"But that's okay," she said, turning to smile at him. "Because I was missing you, too."

"I'll grab a shower." He went into the laundry room and stripped off his work clothes, dumping them directly into the washer with a healthy dose of detergent. When Syd's arms came around him from behind, it was his turn to startle.

"I didn't mean to be insulting," she said, punctuating her words with kisses to his back.

"I know. I should've left the clothes outside." He turned to her and looped his arms around her, instantly aroused by her nearness. Studying her face, he ached with wanting her. He kissed her and rested his forehead against hers. "Let me take a shower, and then we can finish this conversation."

She replied with a mischievous grin and released him. "You're on."

Luke rushed through a shower and shave, emerging from the bathroom to find her reclined on the bed, waiting for him.

She held out a hand to him.

Knotting the towel around his hips, he took her hand and stretched out next to her.

She snuggled up to him, her head on his chest and her hand on his belly. "You worked hard today."

"Always do this time of year, getting the marina ready for winter." He took her wandering hand and brought it to his lips. "How was your day?"

"It was...interesting." She told him about breakfast with Linda and the girls and the letter from Jenny. When she mentioned what she'd volunteered to do, Luke immediately tensed.

"Why does it have to be you?"

"Why not me? I certainly understand what she's been through."

Luke chose his words carefully. "You're doing so much better. Is it wise to reopen that wound?"

She looked up at him. "I hear what you're saying, and I love you for being concerned, but now that I know she's out there and hurting, I have to see her. I can't explain why, but when I heard her story, I knew I had to do something."

As he thought about what she'd said, Luke combed his fingers through her hair.

"Can you understand that?"

"I think it's great that you want to reach out to her, but I want you to be careful you don't set yourself back in the process. You've seemed so much better lately. Happier, lighter."

"I have been happier," she said, caressing his chest. "So very happy. In fact, I wanted to talk to you about that."

"About how happy you are with me?" he asked with a teasing smile.

"Yes."

Luke all but stopped breathing while he waited to hear what she had to say.

"That question you asked me a while back..."

"I handled it all wrong. I know that now. You weren't ready."

She propped herself up on one elbow and looked him square in the eye. "I think I might be now."

"Really?"

She nodded.

He jumped up. "Hold that thought."

"Luke! Where're you going?"

"I'll be right back. Don't move."

Still wearing only the towel around his waist, Luke ran out to the truck. His hands were shaking as he unlocked the glove box and retrieved the ring. He went back inside and stopped himself in the hallway to take a deep, cleansing breath. When he had managed to calm down, he rolled his shoulders and returned to the bedroom.

Syd was sitting up on the bed with her legs curled under her. She eyed him warily.

With the ring box enclosed in his fist, Luke crawled up the bed to her.

She looped her arms around him and kissed him. "What're you up to?"

As his heart hammered, Luke drank her in. Sometimes he still couldn't believe that she'd come back to him, that she was here to stay, that the feelings of peace and joy she'd brought with her might last a lifetime.

"The last time, I did this all wrong. The timing was terrible. I didn't have a ring. You weren't ready. This time," he said, reaching for her left hand and bringing it to his lips, "I want to do it right. Sydney Donovan, undisputed love of my life, will you do me the great honor of being my wife?"

She blinked back tears as she placed her hands on his face and gave him the sweetest kiss he'd ever received. "Yes," she whispered against his lips.

Relief flooded through him, making him tremble. He pulled back from her to open the box and remove the ring.

She sucked in a sharp, deep breath as he slid it onto her finger. "Oh, Luke, it's *gorgeous*! I love it!"

"I love you, and I always will."

"I love you, too. Thank you for being patient with me."

"I would've waited forever for you."

With an exuberant squeal, she threw her arms around him. "We're engaged!"

Luke closed his eyes and held on tight, absorbing the moment as the fear finally released its grip on him. "When do you want to tie the knot?"

"Can I think about that and get back to you?"

"Whatever you want, baby. Anything you want."

Chapter 6

It took a couple of hours to work up the nerve before Laura sent Justin a text, asking if he could meet her at six on Friday at his favorite Providence restaurant. She said only that she needed to talk to him about something. Her hands were clammy by the time she sent the message. Placing the phone on her bedside table, she went into the bathroom to brush her hair and freshen up.

The phone chimed to indicate a new text. Her mouth went dry with anxiety when she picked it up to see what he had said. One word: *Fine.*

"Well," she said. "That's that." She rested a hand on the still-small baby bump and was rewarded with a ripple of movement that made her smile. The baby's tiny movements reminded Laura that her brief marriage hadn't been a total loss.

She went downstairs to see what Owen was up to and found him in the kitchen, standing watch over a pot on the stove. "That smells amazing! What did you make?"

"Sauce from scratch," he said proudly, lifting the lid for her to take a whiff. "My grandmother's recipe."

The combined aromas of garlic, basil and oregano had her taste buds standing up to take notice. "My mouth is watering," she said as she slipped onto a stool at the counter.

The review earned her a big grin from the chef. "I have to boil the pasta, and then we can eat."

They'd fallen into the habit of having dinner together every night. They took turns cooking, and some nights they went out, but it had become a standing date. One of the things she liked best about being with him was that it was easy. Neither of them had ever said the words, *let's have dinner every night*. It just happened. Everything with him was comfortable, except for one thing—the itchy, restless feeling that came with unfulfilled desire.

If she looked at him, she wanted him. It was that simple. But then she remembered what he wanted—a life free of encumbrances, which made her wonder why he'd want to get involved with her and her many encumbrances. She shook off those unpleasant thoughts. It was better not to think about the inevitable day when the freedom of the open road would beckon him.

She cleared her throat. "I didn't know you could cook like that."

"Neither did I. Don't get too excited until you try it. It might taste like crap."

"If it tastes anything like it smells, we've got a winner. Do you like to cook?"

"I haven't really had much chance, being on the road so much. I used to make a lot of grilled cheese sandwiches and pizza and stuff like that for my siblings, but I haven't done much cooking since then."

Since he so rarely spoke about his family or childhood, Laura was intrigued by the insight he'd shared. "Why were you cooking for them?"

"My parents were busy. They were out a lot, and I was in charge of the troops."

"How old were you then?"

"I don't know. Twelve, maybe."

"You were twelve years old in charge of *six* younger siblings?"

"Yeah, I guess."

"No wonder why you're so good at taking care of me."

"Am I good at taking care of you?"

"You know you are."

He poured the lemon-flavored sparkling water she favored into a wineglass and put it in front of her.

Laura smiled up at him. "Exhibit A."

Shrugging, he said, "Close your eyes and pretend it's chardonnay."

He was so adorable and so effortlessly charming. It never failed to touch her that he took such good care of her, as if it was the most natural thing in the world to him. He was always one step ahead of her, thinking of what she might need before she knew she needed it. A girl could fall madly, deeply and irrevocably in love with a guy who paid that kind of attention to her.

"What're you thinking about, Princess?" He puckered his lips in a mockingly serious expression that was so far out of character for him it made her laugh.

Because she couldn't very well scare the hell out of him by telling him she was thinking about falling irrevocably in love with him, she said, "Nothing much."

"Did you talk to your dad?"

She nodded. "He said to feel free to toss his name around with Justin. I hope it doesn't come to that." She looked up at Owen. "I'm meeting Justin on Friday at six in Providence."

"We'll take the three-thirty boat. I'll make a reservation for the car."

Laura was filled with relief. She hadn't even had to ask him. "You know you don't have to come."

"Yes, I do."

Her heart began to do that odd pitter-patter thing that often happened in his presence. When it first started happening, she'd chalked it up to pregnancy. Now she knew it had nothing to do with pregnancy and everything to do with him.

He put down the spoon he'd been using to stir the pot and wiped his hands on the towel he'd tossed over his shoulder. When he was satisfied that his hands were clean, he used them to frame her face, compelling her to look up at him. "I know I have absolutely no right to say this, but I don't want you to see him by yourself."

"You have every right to say anything you want to me." In an attempt at levity, she added, "I'd say you earned it after scraping me off the bathroom floor every morning for weeks."

"Which was entirely my pleasure."

"You're easy to please."

"You make it easy."

He stared into her eyes for a long, breathless moment as a hectic band of color slashed his cheeks, letting her know she wasn't the only one tormented by the attraction zinging between them.

When he looked at her in that particular way, Laura's mind went blank, taking with it all the reasons this was a bad idea. She reached up to link her fingers on the back of his neck, drawing him down to her.

"Laura..."

As she pressed her lips to his, she realized this was the first time she'd ever reached out and taken what she wanted from a man. And oh, how she wanted this man.

The kiss was chaste and sweet and even hotter than it had been earlier, which was saying something. When he would've pulled back from her, she tightened her hold on him. Their eyes met and held. He looked as undone as she felt, which was strangely comforting. Tipping his head ever so slightly, he kissed her again. This time, he slid an arm around her waist and drew her tight against him.

Laura melted as his nearness set off a riot of reactions that registered in all the most important places.

He brushed at her bottom lip with his tongue, coaxing his way into her mouth.

The moment their tongues connected, Laura forgot who she was, where she was and why this could lead to disaster if he suddenly decided he wanted to be somewhere else. She couldn't get enough, no matter how tightly she held him or how enthusiastically she met the thrusts of his tongue with her own answering strokes.

A growl rumbled through him that threw gas on her already out-of-control fire.

Her fingers burrowed into his hair and held on tight. In the far recesses of her mind where sanity lived, she wondered if she might be hurting him. Even farther off in the distance, she thought she heard someone call her name. Because investigating would mean stepping away from the most incendiary kiss of her life, Laura ignored it.

"Um, oh, sorry," the voice said, closer now.

Laura tore her lips free and turned to find her friend Stephanie standing in the doorway to the kitchen. Her face was bright red with embarrassment.

Owen kept his arms firmly around Laura and buried his face in the curve of her neck. His lips and breath sent a delightful array of shivers skirting over her sensitized skin.

"I brought the, um, book I told you about," Stephanie said as she put the book on the counter, "but I can see you're busy, so I'll be going now." She backed away from the doorway, flashed Laura a big grin along with a thumbs-up and was gone.

"That was embarrassing," Laura said.

As if she hadn't spoken, Owen raised his head, gazed into her eyes and kissed her again, softer this time but with no less urgency. Reaching behind him, he killed the flames under the pots.

Laura waited breathlessly to see what he would do next.

With his hands on her hips, he lifted her onto the counter, stepped between her legs and pulled her in tight against him.

When his erection snuggled into the V of her legs, Laura gasped and pushed against him. And then his hands were cupping her breasts, his thumbs sliding back and forth over her nipples that were feverishly sensitive thanks to the pregnancy.

"Owen," she said.

"Hmm?" His lips were busy on her neck, making her mind go blank again.

"I forgot what I was going to say."

He let out an unsteady laugh and pressed her hand against the hard bulge in his shorts. "That's what happens every time I lay eyes on you." Punctuating his words with kisses, he added, "Every. Single. Time."

Touched by his gruffly spoken words, Laura took advantage of the opportunity to explore the length and width of him, swallowing as he got bigger and harder under her hand. Since he was so tall and broad-shouldered, she wasn't surprised to discover he was big there, too. When she thought about how he would feel inside her, she shivered in anticipation.

As she squeezed him gently, his head fell back and his fingers dug into her shoulders.

"Until today, you never told me you wanted me like this," she said.

"Yes, I did."

"When?" she asked, continuing to stroke and caress him.

"When the last ferry left on Monday without me on it. Didn't that say it all?"

"I suppose that did make a statement."

He stopped the movement of her hand. "No more of that."

"Why? I quite like it."

"I quite like it, too. Far too much." He brought her hands to his shoulders. "Keep them there."

Laura's heart pounded as she waited to see what he would do. She noted the slight tremble of his hands as he unbuttoned her shirt and pushed it open. Her enhanced pregnancy breasts overflowed the cups of her white cotton bra, making her face heat with embarrassment. "I keep meaning to buy bigger bras."

"Don't," he said, his voice hoarse as he lowered his head and pressed his face into the valley between her breasts. "You're so sexy."

Laura arched her back, encouraging him.

He released the front clasp, and her breasts sprang free into his waiting hands. "Oh God, you're gorgeous."

Before she had time to prepare, his mouth was feasting on her nipple, hot and hungry. She clutched his hair, which was the only thing that kept her from sliding off the counter into a boneless pile on the floor.

"How many days until Friday?" he asked, his lips vibrating against her breast.

The question made her laugh, nervously. He was putting her on notice that the minute Justin knew about the baby, their relationship would shift to the next level. "Three."

He turned his attention to her other breast. "I'm not going to make it."

Laura's stomach chose that moment to let out a keening growl.

"Shit," he muttered. "I'm pawing you like a madman, and you're probably starving." He dipped lower to press his lips to the tiny baby bump.

Touched by his attention to the baby, Laura combed her fingers into his unruly hair, attempting to smooth and straighten.

He looked up at her, and the raw emotion she saw shining in his eyes was nearly her undoing. As she watched him pay homage to the child growing inside her, she realized that she no longer had to worry about the possibility of falling in love with him. It had already happened, probably quite some time ago as he was peeling her off the bathroom floor and making her tea and tending to her every need as if he'd been born to do exactly that.

With what seemed to be great reluctance, he stood up straight, tucked her breasts back into her bra and refastened the buttons on her top. When he was done, he rested his hands on her shoulders.

Laura tipped her forehead against his chest, gathering herself. She couldn't let him see that she'd fallen for him. The last thing she wanted was to make him feel trapped. If he felt trapped, he might run, and she really wanted him to stay. More importantly, she wanted him to *want* to stay.

"Let's get you and the little guy fed," he said.

Grant McCarthy was rarely intimidated, but Stephanie's stepfather, Charlie Grandchamp, intimidated the hell out of him. It had taken Grant days to work up the nerve to drive out to the small house Charlie had rented from the island's resident land baron/cab driver, Ned Saunders. The media attention following Charlie's release from fourteen years of wrongful imprisonment had driven him to the island, seeking peace and quiet—and the chance to be closer to the stepdaughter who'd been so relentless in her efforts to get him released.

Grant parked the motorcycle he'd borrowed from his brother Mac in the yard and took a deep breath for courage before walking up to the open front door and knocking.

No answer.

Great. I finally make it out here, and he's not around. Spotting the other man's small pickup truck, Grant walked behind the house to the barn that served as a workshop and garage. "Hey, Charlie?"

"In here."

Grant swallowed hard and stepped into the dusty space that smelled of dirt and mildew and other substances he didn't try too hard to identify. Charlie was bent over the workbench, sanding a block of wood. He was tall and muscular with a gray buzz cut and a piercing blue-eyed stare that Grant found unnerving—particularly since it was often directed his way. "Um, how's it going?"

"Fine."

Since his release, Grant had learned his girlfriend's stepfather was a man of few words, especially where Grant was concerned.

"Something on your mind?" Charlie asked.

"Ah, well, Stephanie, actually."

That got Charlie's attention. He spared Grant a brief glance before he returned his attention to the project on the bench. "What about her?"

"I, um, you know we've been together for a while now."

"Coupla months," Charlie said with a harsh chuckle. "Does that count as a *while* these days?"

Grant had no idea what to say to that. He decided to go with the truth. "She has a lot of insecurities because of everything that happened when she was younger. We tend to argue, from time to time, and to me it's part of the fun of being with her. For her, though, it's upsetting. More than it should be. I've been thinking about how I could make her feel more secure. About me. About us."

"And what've you come up with?"

"I'd like to ask her to marry me." Grant met that steely stare, determined not to blink. He almost succeeded. "Before you tell me why it's a terrible idea, let me assure you that we wouldn't get married right away. I want her to know I'm in it for keeps so she won't get that haunted look on her face whenever we disagree about something."

"I know that look."

It was the first thing Charlie had ever said to him that didn't make Grant feel like the guy hated him for being alive.

"What?" Charlie asked. "Are you surprised I know what you're talking about? I looked at that face every week for years when she came to see me in prison, and that line between her brows tore me up as much as it tears you up."

With that one statement, he tripled the number of words he'd said to Grant in their brief acquaintance. Grant cleared his throat. "I want her to know I'm not going anywhere without her. Not now. Not ever."

Charlie ran the sandpaper back and forth over the block of wood while Grant stood twisting in the wind, waiting for the other man to say something. Anything. Without looking at Grant, he finally said, "You love her? Really, really love her?"

"Yeah," Grant said. "I really, really do."

"What if she decides she doesn't want to live here on the island? What if she wants to go home to Providence and open the restaurant she's always talked about?"

She'd talked about a restaurant? To whom? Not to him. Stunned to hear that, Grant forced himself to focus. "We'll go to Providence, if that's what she wants. I can work anywhere." His failed relationship with Abby had taught him that much. "I want her to be happy."

"I want that, too. More than you know. She gave up a big chunk of her life trying to get my sorry ass sprung from jail."

"She'd do it again in a heartbeat. You know that."

"She's a good kid. She deserves better than what she got from her mother and me."

"From her mother, maybe. You saved her life. I don't think she feels you owe her anything."

"I owe her *everything*," Charlie said, his eyes flashing with a rare show of emotion. "She's the only one who gave a shit about whether I rotted in prison for the rest of my life. She deserves the whole world served up on a silver platter."

A knot of emotion lodged in Grant's chest. He couldn't agree more. "I want to give her that. If she'll let me."

"She'll fight you if you try to do too much for her."

"Believe me," Grant said with a shaky laugh, "I already know that." He forced a deep breath into his lungs. "Would I have your blessing?"

"Does it matter so much to you that an ex-con approves?"

"Yes, it matters. Very much so."

Charlie picked up a rag off the bench and wiped the dirt from his hands. "I'll give you my blessing if you promise you'll always be good to her, put her needs before your own and be faithful to her. Can you do all that?"

"Yes." He cleared his throat again. "Sir."

"In that case..." Charlie extended his hand to Grant.

Grant shook his hand. "Thank you."

"No, Grant," Charlie said, calling him by name for the first time. "Thank you. I'll never have the words to properly thank you for what you did for me—and for Stephanie."

Overwhelmed by Charlie's rare show of emotion, Grant said, "All I did was make a few calls." Charlie's fortunes had changed dramatically when Grant asked his celebrity lawyer friend Dan Torrington to take on the case. A call to Grant's uncle, Superior Court Judge Frank McCarthy, had also helped the cause.

"They were the right calls, and they made a huge difference." Charlie shook his head in disbelief. "I wake up every morning to the sound of the ocean and seagulls, and I still think I'm dreaming."

"I'm really glad it worked out—for your sake and Stephanie's." He paused before he added, "When you're ready, I'd like to talk to you about the movie."

"I'm not there yet."

"Whenever. I'd better get back before Steph starts to wonder where I am."

"When will you propose?"

"In the next few days. When the time is right."

Charlie nodded. "Good luck."

"Thanks. I'll see you." As Grant walked back to the motorcycle, he picked over the conversation in amazement. It was, without a doubt, the most substantial conversation he'd ever had with Stephanie's stepfather, who'd seemed wary and suspicious of him from the day they met.

He was puzzled, however, about why Stephanie had never mentioned her dream to open her own restaurant. He'd have to find a way to bring that up.

Riding the bike back home to her, Grant tried to think of the perfect way to ask her to marry him. It had to be as special as she was. Once she had his ring on her finger, maybe she'd stop worrying that what they had wouldn't last. Maybe they both would.

CHAPTER 7

After they enjoyed the delicious dinner he'd made, Owen and Laura settled in to watch a movie. Somehow, she ended up reclined with her feet in his lap and was treated to a divine foot massage. The last thing she remembered was the feel of his thumbs pressed against her arches. She awoke to him carrying her upstairs.

"Did I fall asleep again?"

"Yep. I can set my watch by it. Fifteen minutes—tops—and you're out."

Laura curled her arms around his neck, enjoying being pressed against his chest. "I'm not always this much fun. Only when pregnant."

"I'll have to take your word for that," he said in a teasing tone.

"Do you provide these services only for pregnant women?"

That drew a laugh from him. "I provide these services only for *you*."

Something about the way he said that filled her with a warm, cozy sense of security that, if she were being truthful, she'd never felt with Justin.

When Owen lowered her to the bed, she kept her arms around his neck. The position put his face very close to hers. Laura zeroed in on his lips. "Will you stay awhile?"

"Oh, um, sure." He pulled back from her and straightened to kick off his shoes.

"Only if you want to."

As he stretched out next to her on the bed, he reached for her hand and linked their fingers. "Of course I want to."

The bleat of a foghorn and the crashing waves against the South Harbor breakwater were the only sounds in the otherwise quiet night.

"This is a very odd situation we find ourselves in," Laura said after a long period of companionable silence.

"You could certainly say that," Owen said with a chuckle.

"I want you to know… I'd understand if you decided to leave. I know you have to work and—"

"I don't have to work."

"You don't?"

He turned his head and met her gaze. "Remember when I told you that living the way I do is pretty cheap?"

She nodded.

"I've socked away most of what I've earned over the years. I could safely take a couple of years off if I wanted to."

"Oh."

"Are you trying to get rid of me, Princess?"

"No! Of course not!"

"Are you sure?" he asked. "I don't want to be in your hair if you don't want me there."

"Owen, come on… I want you there."

"Why do I hear a 'but'?"

Laura rolled her bottom lip between her teeth as she tried to find the words.

"Laura? What's on your mind?"

"I don't want you to take this the wrong way."

"You can say anything you want to me. You should know that by now."

She did know that, and it was one of the things she loved about being with him. "I'm getting attached to you."

"Is that right?" A satisfied grin stretched across his face. "Then my campaign is working."

"Is that what this is? A campaign?"

He brought their joined hands to his lips. "I'm campaigning for a spot in your life, Princess."

"What spot would you like to apply for?"

His lips moved from her hand to the inside of her wrist. "The most important one."

She wondered if her pulse point was clueing him in to the rapid beat of her heart. Her mouth was suddenly dry and the palms of her hands damp. "Well," she said, attempting a playful tone, "there's a long list of qualifications for that position."

He added a touch of tongue to the sensitive skin on her inner arm, sending a sharp arrow of desire spearing through her that landed in a throb between her legs. "Name them."

She pulled her hand free. "I can't think when you're doing that."

"My apologies," he said, propping his head on one hand. His eyes were full of mischief as he waited for her.

Laura wished she possessed the quick wit to make her list of requirements funny and lighthearted, but nothing about this was lighthearted. Not anymore.

"Tell me about your qualifications."

"First of all," she said haltingly, "the candidate must want me and only me. No extracurricular activities allowed."

"Done. Next?"

Unnerved by his intense expression, she couldn't look away from him. "How do you know you won't change your mind about that in a couple of months or a year?"

"I suppose no one ever knows for sure about these things, but all I can tell you is I want to be with you—only you. It's really that simple."

"What do I do, after I take a big chance on you, if you decide you'd rather be somewhere else?"

He reached out to comb his fingers through her hair in a gentle caress that turned sensuous when his fingertips slid over her jaw and down her neck. "I wish I could assure you there's no chance of that happening, but I can't. I've been on the move my entire adult life, from one place to the next with no thought of the future or anything past the next gig." Leaning in, he kissed her forehead, her nose and then her lips. "Since I met you, I'm thinking about the future for the first time."

Seduced by his words and the emotion she heard behind them, Laura rested a hand on his hip. When he drew her in closer to him, she put her arm around him, tipping her face into his kiss.

"I know I'm not the best risk," he said between sweet kisses, "especially after what you've been through, but I care about you, Laura. I want to take a chance on us, but I'll understand if I'm not what you want."

"You are what I want. I'm just..."

"What, baby?"

"I'm scared."

"Of what?"

"That I'll take this huge leap of faith with you, and you'll stay because you said you would, not because it's where you really want to be."

He snuggled her in tight against him, keeping his lips on her forehead as his fingers continued to slide through her hair. "When I wake up in the morning, usually quite early even after a late gig, I lie in bed and look up at the ceiling wishing I was up here with you. I picture your gorgeous face and all your hundreds of expressions and how much I like to watch you sleep when you conk out on me. Sometimes, when I'm really lucky, I can smell your scent clinging to me because you hugged me the night before. I lie there wondering how long I have to wait until you come downstairs, all fresh-faced and pretty, full of excitement over whatever job you've got planned for the day. I want to hear how you slept, how you feel, if the baby is moving. I want to make sure you eat enough for both of you. I think about what we should do for dinner and if we might have time for a walk on the beach or if it's too chilly for you."

Laura barely took a breath as she listened to him.

"At night, after we've spent the entire day together, I go to bed and burn for you. I want to hold you and kiss you and make love to you and sleep with you in my arms. I want to feel your soft skin next to mine and have your hair tickling my face when I'm trying to sleep. I want to know the second you wake up, and I want my face to be the first thing you see every day."

All at once, Laura realized tears were rolling down her cheeks. "Owen..." She'd never in her life been more touched—or seduced.

"Now tell me, how in the world will I get all that if I'm not here with you?"

"I don't know," she said, wiping her face.

"No one knows anything for sure, Princess. All I know is I'm exactly where I want to be right now. I can no longer imagine a day without you in it. That's got to count for something, right?"

Despite all her worries, Laura decided she'd rather have a few months or a year with him than a lifetime with anyone else. "All right. You've convinced me. The job is yours for as long as you want it."

"Oh yay. Does this mean we're going steady?"

Laura laughed through her tears. "I guess it does."

"I'll do my very best not to let you down."

"I can't ask for much more than that."

He brushed the dampness from her face and cupped her cheek with his big hand. For a long, breathless moment, he looked into her eyes before touching his lips to hers.

Laura curled her hand around his neck and let go of the worry and the fear and gave in to the desire.

As if he sensed her capitulation, he tipped his head to delve deeper, teasing and flirting with his tongue until she opened to allow him in.

A low groan rumbled through him as he feasted on her as if he'd been starving for her.

Suddenly, Laura wanted to touch him everywhere. Her hands moved over his back, almost frantic in the quest for more of him. She found the hem of his T-shirt and pushed it up, flush with desire when her palms encountered warm, smooth skin.

Owen tore his lips free and let his head fall back.

"Are you okay?" she asked, surprised by his reaction.

"I'm way better than okay." He opened his eyes and kissed her softly, sweetly. "Feels so good to have you touch me. Finally."

"I wouldn't mind if you returned the favor," she said with a shy smile. Heat flooded her face, making her burn from the inside.

He traced a finger over her cheekbone. "I love the way you blush."

"It's so embarrassing. I've always hated it and gone out of my way to avoid saying or doing anything that would make it happen."

"Apparently, you're not worried about that anymore."

"Not with you."

"Good," he said. "I don't want you to ever worry about saying or doing the wrong thing with me. You hear me?"

"I hear you, and I want the same from you."

"You got it, Princess." His kisses were urgent, as if he was trying to make up for all the time they'd kept their distance. He kissed her as if he'd never get enough.

When Laura removed her hands from his back, he let out a tortured-sounding moan. "Take it off," she said, tugging at the T-shirt.

"Only if you do the same."

"Deal."

They disentangled only long enough to remove their shirts.

As his shirt cleared his head, Owen reached for her. He nuzzled his nose into the curve of her neck, which made her nipples pebble. "Your skin is so soft. So, so soft."

She squeezed her thighs together as the throb became harder to ignore.

He ran a finger down her neck to her chest, stopping at the front clasp to her bra. "Can we lose this, too?"

"Why not?"

His eyes lit up with boyish glee that made her giggle. He was so cute and so damned sexy, especially when he looked at her as if he wanted to have his wicked way with her. As he released the front clasp and pushed the cups aside, he said, "Do you suppose Stephanie has told the whole island that she caught us making out?"

"Maybe not the whole island. I'm sure she told Grant and Grace and probably Evan."

"We'll be in for it," he said as he kissed the slope of one breast while cupping the other.

"Do we care?"

"I sure as hell don't. Do you?"

"No, not really..."

He raised his head to make eye contact. "What?"

"I wonder if people will think I'm kind of slutty."

His face went slack with shock. "*What?* What the heck do you mean by that?"

"I married someone else in May. I'm pregnant with his baby but making out with you in October. It all happened kind of fast."

"It didn't feel fast to me." He rolled her extra-sensitive nipples between his fingers, drawing a gasp of pleasure from her. "It felt like pure torture, wanting you for weeks and weeks while having to keep my hands to myself."

Damn if that didn't make her blush again. Laura hated being the source of gossip. As Judge Frank McCarthy's daughter, she'd gone out of her way to lead an exemplary life and to stay below the radar so nothing she did would ever embarrass her father. Until her husband's post-marriage dating escapades, she'd never given anyone cause to gossip about her. "Still, people might talk."

"I don't think they will," Owen said. "The people who matter know what happened with your husband, and our friends know we've been hanging out for a while now."

"I suppose you're right."

"No one who knows you would ever think you were slutty."

She buried her fingers in his hair and tugged gently but insistently, bringing his attention back to her breasts and tilting her hips to press against his erection. "Maybe I want you to think I am."

All the air seemed to leave him in one big exhale. "Jesus," he muttered. "You never cease to surprise me. Please, by all means, be as slutty as you want with me. You'll never hear me object."

Laura laughed, thrilled with him and by him. Her laughter turned to moans when he zeroed in on her nipple, licking and sucking and rolling it between his teeth. Thanks to the pregnancy, her breasts were insanely sensitive, and the pressure between her legs continued to grow.

He seemed to know what she needed without her having to tell him. Shifting so he was cradled between her legs, he pushed against her, simulating intercourse as he continued to worship her breasts.

Even though he was driving her out of her mind, she still noticed he was careful to keep his weight off her abdomen. That he thought of her child, even in the midst of runaway passion, was another reason to love him.

She massaged her way from his shoulders to his waist, hesitating for a moment before she let her fingers wander inside his jeans.

He sucked in a sharp deep breath. "God, Laura, I want you so bad." Slowing the pace, he kept up the insistent press of his erection as he sucked hard on her nipple.

The combination had her crying out as the orgasm overtook her, leaving her quivering, pulsating and panting afterward.

"Wow," he said reverently. "That didn't take much."

Laura released an unsteady laugh. "I think it's the pregnancy hormones. It's not usually that easy." Even though she was sort of embarrassed by her unbridled reaction, she forced her eyes up to meet his. "Or maybe it's you and the way you make me feel."

"And how is that?"

"Safe, comfortable, amused, frustrated—"

His brows knitted. "Why frustrated?"

"You're not the only one who's been trying to keep his hands to himself the last few weeks."

The grin that stretched across his face made her heart do that pitter-patter thing. "Is that so?"

She nodded and reached up to frame his face with her hands. "I find you completely irresistible and ridiculously sexy."

"Oh. Well… Wow. I like that."

"I wish we weren't being so upstanding about the baby and telling Justin before we, you know…"

He rested his head on her chest, still breathing harder than usual. "Believe me, I know. But it's the right thing to do. I don't want anything to mess up what we have."

Laura put her arms around him, hoping to keep him right there with her. "Neither do I. Friday will be here before we know it."

He shifted his body to the side but kept his head on her chest. "If I live that long."

Laura fell asleep with her fingers buried in his hair and a smile on her face.

Grace finished brushing her teeth and took her long, dark hair down from the ponytail she'd worn for work. As much as she loved the challenge of running the pharmacy she'd bought in September, her favorite part of each day occurred when she finally got to crawl into bed with Evan.

It was ridiculous, really, how much time she spent thinking about him when she should've been thinking about work. Of course, when she was doling out prescription drugs, her focus was always on what she was doing. The rest of the time, however, she found herself staring off into space, thinking about him and, lately, worrying about him.

The poor guy had been so anxious since he found out the CD he'd spent nearly a year recording in Nashville was caught up in his record company's bankruptcy proceedings. There was a chance that megastar Buddy Longstreet would succeed in acquiring Evan's CD from the bankrupt company, but that was a long shot, and waiting to hear the judge's verdict was doing a number on Evan's nerves.

It made Grace sad to see him so unhappy, even if he went out of his way to hide his worries from her.

He was already in bed, shirtless and propped against the pillows, staring up at the ceiling the way he often did these days. He'd lost some of his sparkle as the waiting dragged on for weeks, and Grace would do anything to help him get it back.

She let her eyes wander over the muscular chest with the perfect amount of silky dark hair that played a starring role in her fantasies. As he did most nights, he'd showered and shaved before bed so his rough whiskers wouldn't mark her skin when they made love. He'd unofficially moved in with her in the loft above the pharmacy, and she loved having him and his guitars, surfboard and size-twelve sneakers underfoot.

But watching him suffer was making her suffer, too. He was so lost in thought that he didn't notice when she approached the bed—until she reached for the hem of her T-shirt and drew it up and over her head. That got his attention.

Grace couldn't get over how uninhibited she'd become since they'd been together. In the past, when she'd been extremely overweight, she'd hated being naked. Now she pranced around frequently in the all-together and had a man in her life who preferred her that way.

Evan extended his arm, inviting her to snuggle up to him.

Sometimes Grace still wanted to pinch herself because she got to sleep with him every night. She got to laugh and talk with him and make crazy love. The only things standing between her and total happiness were his unresolved career issues and her parents talking about coming to visit. The thought of that filled Grace with anxiety, especially since she'd failed to mention she was seeing someone or that he was living with her.

"Best part of the whole day," Evan said as she snuggled into his embrace.

"I was thinking the same thing. You've spoiled me forever for sleeping alone."

"That was my goal."

Grace left a trail of kisses on his chest as she made her way to his lips.

"Who was on the phone?" he asked.

"Stephanie. Apparently, she caught Owen and Laura in the middle of a big-time make-out session earlier."

"Well, it's about damned time. They've been on simmer for weeks now. I wondered when they'd boil over."

"According to Stephanie, they've definitely reached boil."

"I'm glad for them. I want everyone to be as happy as we are."

She brushed the hair back from his forehead. "That's sweet of you to say, but you haven't seemed too happy lately."

"I'm sorry. I don't mean to be a drag."

"You're not. Not at all. I only wish the situation would be resolved one way or the other so you're not stuck in this horrible purgatory."

"It's weird—I'm not even sure anymore what I want to happen."

"What do you mean?"

After a long pause, he said, "Whenever I think about the tour, I break into a cold sweat."

"Because of the stage fright."

"Yeah. It's so screwed up. Here I am on the brink of everything I've ever wanted, and when I heard about the bankruptcy, my first thought was, maybe I won't have to do the tour."

Grace propped her chin on his chest so she could see his face. "That's your gut talking. If the idea of being on stage in a big venue makes you break into a cold sweat, perhaps you shouldn't be doing it."

"Once I get past the initial panic, I love performing, but moving past it gets harder all the time."

"The bankruptcy could be a sign that you're supposed to be doing something else."

"But what? I'll have to do something soon. I don't want to burn through my savings, and there's not a lot I can do here, especially this time of year."

His words sent Grace's stomach plummeting. Of course she knew he'd have to leave the island at some point, but she liked to think that point was way off in the future. "I can take care of things until you decide what you want to do." Even though she'd sunk most of her money into the purchase of the pharmacy, she'd held some back in an emergency fund.

"That's very sweet of you, babe, but I'm not going to sponge off you any more than I already am by crashing here."

"It's not sponging. We're in a committed relationship, aren't we?"

"You bet your ass we are."

She loved his possessiveness, even if she'd never tell him that. "If I take care of you now, you can take care of me later. What does it matter? We take care of each other."

"I love you for that, Grace. I really do, but I need to make a plan—soon. I can't sit around and do nothing all winter."

"You're not doing nothing. You're writing songs—lots of them."

"That may or may not sell. I need something more solid than that."

"I have complete faith that you'll figure it out."

"You have to say that," he said with a small smile. "You love me."

"Yes, I do."

He curled a shank of her hair around his hand and gave a gentle tug to bring her close enough to kiss. "That's the only thing that's gotten me through these last couple of weeks. I hope you know that."

"We can get through anything as long as we have each other."

"I love you so much, Grace." He kissed her again and then hugged her. "So damned much."

She closed her eyes tight against the now-familiar rush of emotion she experienced every time he professed his love. Wanting to take his mind off his troubles, Grace wiggled out of his embrace and kissed her way down the front of him.

"Grace, babe, you don't have to—" When she took him in hand and ran her tongue over the head of his cock, he gasped and then moaned.

As she loved him with her hand, lips and tongue, she knew the second he stopped thinking about his career crisis and gave himself over to the pleasure.

CHAPTER 8

Joe Cantrell got out of bed and moved carefully so he wouldn't disturb Janey, who had an hour yet before she needed to get up for class. She'd been exhausted lately, so much so that he was becoming concerned about her. In the kitchen, he started the coffee and took his cell phone off the charger, anxious to hear how his mother's date had gone the night before. He opened the back door to let their menagerie of special-needs dogs out, and found his mother's number on his list of favorites.

Carolina Cantrell had been married at nineteen, a mother at twenty and a widow at twenty-seven. In all the years since Joe's father died in a car accident when he was seven, Joe had never known her to date—until last night. She'd finally given in and let one of her friends fix her up on a blind date. His mother had been ridiculously nervous when he spoke to her yesterday afternoon, and Joe had been anxious all night thinking about her out with some strange guy.

Her long-time friend Karen had done the fixing up, so at least it was with someone trustworthy. Or so he hoped. As the phone rang several times, visions of axe murderers danced in his head.

She finally answered on the third ring. "Hi, honey."

"What took so long?" he growled as his heart rate settled down to normal.

Her delicate laugh soothed and infuriated him. "Are you imagining axe murders and other horrors?"

She'd always known him far too well. "Don't be ridiculous."

"*Moi?* Ridiculous?"

"Fine. Whatever. I was worried. Call me crazy."

"You're very sweet, but you have nothing to worry about. He was a perfectly nice man, and we had a perfectly nice time."

"Sounds boring as hell."

"It was."

Joe winced. "Sorry. Are you disappointed?"

"Hardly. You know me. I couldn't care less about all this foolishness. I had my great love. I'm not silly enough to expect lightning to strike twice."

"Mom… Come on. You're only fifty-six. Don't talk like that."

"I know exactly how old I am, Joseph. Plenty old enough to know better than to walk around with girlish dreams. I had that once before. If that's all I ever get, it was more than enough."

Joe hated when she talked like her life was already over—or the best part of it, anyway. Losing his father had so devastated her, they'd been forced to leave their home in New York City and move in with her parents on Gansett Island. His grandparents' love had saved them both.

"Let's talk about something happier," she said. "How's Janey?"

"She's good. Tired, though. School is kicking her ass this semester."

"That doesn't sound like our Janey."

"I know. I'm kinda worried, actually. She's sleeping every chance she gets."

Carolina let loose with the delicate laugh that always reminded Joe of the sound wind chimes made.

"Why is that funny?"

"Is there any chance she might be pregnant?"

"What?" Joe felt like he'd been hit with an electric cattle prod. "No. There's no chance she's pregnant."

"You say that like the two of you aren't going at it every chance you get."

"*Mom!*"

"Oh, don't be a prude. I remember what it's like to be a newlywed, and I've seen you two together. You can barely keep your hands off her in a room full of people. It doesn't take much imagination to picture what goes on when you're alone."

"This is a very inappropriate conversation for a grown man to have with his mother."

"Since when have we ever been appropriate?"

Joe laughed at that. She'd taught him every swear word and filthy joke she knew by the time he was ten. Thanks to her, he'd been the first boy in his class to know the ins and outs of sex, information he'd happily shared with his peers.

"Remember the phone call from the school?" she asked, the merriment in her tone coming through the phone line.

"I was just thinking about that!"

They shared a laugh, remembering. "You were everyone's best friend that year."

"Yes, I was."

"I thought Linda would burst a blood vessel when Mac brought the info home to his younger brothers," she said with another laugh. "So is it possible your lovely wife is pregnant?"

Joe swallowed hard, imagining what Janey would have to say about being pregnant when she was only in her second year of veterinary school. "I suppose it's *possible*. If she is, she's going to kill me."

"Now, darling, remind her it takes two to tango."

Joe felt a little ill at the thought of raising the topic of pregnancy with his wife, who was stressed out enough with a full course load. But the idea of a baby, their baby... That filled him with the kind of giddy hope he'd only experienced once before, when he and Janey were first together.

"You might want to think about buying a test," his mother said.

"I'll talk to her."

"And, of course, I'll be the first to know if she is."

"Naturally."

"Don't let her kill you. I couldn't live without you."

"Don't worry. I think she loves me enough to let me live."

"Yes, she does. You're a lucky man."

"Believe me, I know that. I've never been happier in my life. I want the same for you, too."

"That's very sweet of you, but you know I'm happy."

"You're content. That's not the same as happy. Trust me, I know."

"I've decided to spend the winter on the island," she said, clearly not interested in pursuing the subject of her happiness any further.

"How come?" She lived in Connecticut but still owned the ramshackle island house her parents had called home. Other than the summer she'd spent in Tuscany the year he and Janey got together, she'd never missed a summer on Gansett but had given up on the winters after her parents passed away.

"Ever since I agreed to let Karen fix me up, all our friends want in on the game. I have no desire to be everyone's pet project. I'd rather go out to the island and get some work done." She designed jewelry and was happiest when she was hunkered down in her studio for hours on end.

"I hate to think of you out there all alone in the winter. Besides, there's only the one wood stove. You'll freeze your ass off." He remembered sleeping near that woodstove on many a cold winter night as a child.

"I'll be fine. I'll hardly be alone. I have plenty of friends still living there."

"I'll send Mac over to check on the stove and make sure the roof isn't leaking."

"You don't have to do that. He's busy with the new baby and his own family."

"I'm texting him the minute we hang up. Do me a favor when you get there and check in with Seamus. Make sure he's not running our business into the ground."

"Oh, I'd love to. He's such a sweetheart. You couldn't have hired a better steward to handle the ferries while you're in Ohio with Janey."

"He's been a godsend for sure, but he's full of big ideas on how we can grow the business. He exhausts me."

Carolina laughed. "You know you'll have to keep him on when you get back to the island. You'll break his heart if you let him go."

"I've already thought the same thing. It certainly doesn't suck to have someone competent to lean on so I can have a life, especially now."

"You've worked like a madman running that business on your own for your entire adult life. If anyone has earned a break, it's you."

"Thanks for that." She'd kept the books for years after his grandfather died, until Joe hired an accountant and freed her up to pursue her own passion. He'd retained her on the company's payroll and health insurance, however, a move that continued to be a point of contention between them. Since his grandfather had left the business to both of them, Joe wasn't budging on either of those things.

"How's the painting going?" she asked.

"Great. It's nice to have time to indulge, as you would say."

"And your class? How's that working out?"

"I love it," he said, still amazed that Janey had submitted an application for him to teach a first-year painting class at Ohio State and only told him about it when the school called about an interview.

"I bet you're a wonderful teacher."

"I don't know about that. It's fun, though."

"Good. Well, I need to run and start packing. The more I think of spending the winter on the island, the more excited I get. It's been years since I've been out there in the off-season. It used to be my favorite time of year there."

"I remember. We thought you were nuts."

"Sticks and stones, darling. Let me know how the pregnancy test works out."

"I will," Joe said with a sinking feeling. Janey wouldn't actually kill him, but he doubted she'd be thrilled to be pregnant with so much school still to go before she got her degree.

Owen came awake slowly, the sensual memories from the night before hitting him one after the other, each more exciting than the one before. Laura was pressed against him, sleeping soundly in his arms. He hadn't planned to stay, but when she fell asleep, he hadn't wanted to disturb her.

Keep telling yourself that, you opportunistic asshole. In truth, a team of mules and ten men couldn't have dragged him away from her lush softness. He took a quick inventory and realized her hand was tucked into the back of the jeans he'd left on out of sheer self-preservation. Her leg was between his, and her baby bump was resting against his belly.

The baby chose that moment to let him know it was awake, and Owen was breathless as he felt the ripple of movement against his skin. The miracle of it, the miracle of her, of what had been decided between them, was almost too much for him to process. He'd laid himself bare to her in a way he'd never done with any other woman. While he normally would've been embarrassed recalling the deeply personal thoughts he'd shared with her, he wasn't embarrassed. Rather, he was exhilarated and relieved that she finally knew the full depths of his devotion to her.

He'd stopped short of telling her he loved her. He was saving that for after she resolved things with her estranged husband. There would be plenty of time after that obstacle was cleared for declarations of love.

Unable to resist the opportunity to touch her, he ran his hand lightly over her back as he breathed in her sweet scent. When he reached the waistband of her yoga pants, he hesitated for a second before letting his fingers venture the slightest bit inside. He stopped abruptly when he reached the top of one cheek, knowing if he went any farther he wouldn't be able to resist taking more.

He withdrew his hand, and was startled by a mewl of protest from her. Even though her eyes were still closed, she tilted her hips to press her core against him, and he went hard as stone. A hiss of desire and frustration escaped from his clenched teeth.

"Don't stop," she whispered, rubbing herself against him with increasing urgency.

"Laura," he gasped.

She took his hand and returned it to her lower back. "Don't stop," she said again.

Did she think he was made of stone? That he could be tempted this way and not act? He'd tried to do the honorable thing by putting their relationship on hold until Justin knew about the baby, but she wasn't making it easy to remember his resolve.

Her hand moved over his chest as she continued to push against him in an increasingly provocative rhythm that was making him crazier by the second. Because she'd asked so nicely—and so insistently—he pushed his hand into the back of her pants again, this time cupping a sweet cheek that fit perfectly into his large hand.

"Yes," she whispered, her breath hot against his neck. She tugged on the button to his jeans, unzipped him and had her hand wrapped around his straining member so quickly he didn't have time to protest—not that he would have.

As if it had a mind of its own, his hand delved into the cleft between her cheeks until he encountered slick heat.

She moaned as he made contact with her clit and stroked him harder when he slid two fingers into her tight channel. When she raised her face, seeking his mouth, he kissed her with an urgency he'd never experienced so acutely before, as if he would drown or suffocate or die some other miserable way if she didn't save him. Tongues clashed and battled as the movement of their hands became more desperate.

"Owen," she panted, moving her leg to give him better access. "*Owen...*" She came hard around his fingers, triggering his own almost violent release as weeks of longing poured forth in the most intense orgasm he'd ever experienced. It left him panting and sweating and spinning as he came back down to find her watching him with bottomless blue eyes.

"Wow," she said, looking rather satisfied with herself.

"Yeah. Wow." As much as it had been, it wasn't nearly enough. He wanted to be inside her so badly he closed his eyes and shuddered when the need grabbed him by the throat, refusing to let go until he'd had all of her. The next few days were going to be hell on earth.

She caressed his face with her soft hand. "Are you okay?"

He nodded because he didn't trust himself to speak and having her touch him wasn't doing a thing to lessen the need. It only made it greater, if that was possible.

"You don't look okay."

He couldn't help but offer a small smile at the concern he heard in her voice. Opening his eyes, he met her worried gaze. "You demolished me."

Her eyes widened into an adorably innocent expression. "I did?"

"Totally."

"Is that a good thing?"

"It was a very good thing. But it's left me wanting so much more."

The hand that had been gently soothing his face stopped all of a sudden. "I want more, too. I've never experienced anything like this. I didn't even know..."

"Neither did I."

They were sticky and sweaty and the air smelled of sex, but he couldn't bring himself to let her go. Suddenly, he was afraid. What if he had waited his entire life to find this woman and he somehow managed to mess it up? What if Justin refused to give her a divorce and it turned into a big, protracted battle that took years to resolve? What if he never again got to hold her and touch her this way?

That couldn't happen. He wouldn't let it. One way or the other, he would make this work. He would make sure they both got everything they wanted—and then some. "We need a shower."

"Mmm." Her fingers had moved to his unruly hair, smoothing and combing. That was all it took to fire him up all over again. "In a minute."

Because he was afraid he might forget all about his honorable intentions and give in to overwhelming temptation, he attempted to zip his jeans over his still-hard cock, but the zipper wouldn't cooperate.

Laura laughed at his dilemma. "I thought we took care of that problem."

"I thought so, too," Owen said, grimacing as her laughter made the ache worse. "It's your influence. He can't get enough of you."

She trailed a finger down his neck to his chest, dragging her nail over his nipple.

"Is that supposed to be helping?" he asked, sounding strangled.

"We don't have to wait, Owen."

He stopped her hand before it could travel any lower. In the state he was in, if she so much as brushed against him, he'd detonate.

"I've filed for divorce. I'm single in every way that matters."

"You have to resolve the situation with the baby first. I don't know why that matters so much to me. It just does." He bent his head to kiss her, making sure to keep a tight rein on the desire to plunder her sweet mouth. It wouldn't take much to give in to the tremendous temptation. "We'll have all the time in the world once you get that worked out. We'll spend entire days in bed."

Laura laughed at that. "And what will your grandmother say when her hotel isn't ready for opening in the spring?"

Owen hovered above her, so close their lips were nearly touching. "She will say it was time very well spent. She's always wanted me to find someone special and settle down."

"Is that what you're doing with me? Settling down?"

He snorted out a laugh. "I'm hardly 'settled' around you. Agitated, horny, desperate, frustrated, needy, happy…"

She rolled her bottom lip between her teeth as she looked up at him. "Are you happy?"

"Very much so. Are you?"

Nodding, she said, "So happy. Who would've thought I'd be in the boat I'm in—pregnant and divorcing my cheating husband—but happier than I've ever been in my life? It's all because of you."

"I'll be happier when he knows about the baby and you guys have a plan for how you're going to handle custody." Owen rested his forehead against hers. "You do realize it'll be almost impossible to share joint custody when you're living out here and he's in Providence, don't you?"

"I'm almost certain he won't want joint custody. He's too selfish and career-oriented. He won't want to be responsible for the baby on his own."

"I don't even know him, but I already know that if he can find a way to make life difficult for you, he's probably going to do it." And that, Owen realized, was his greatest fear.

"My father can make life difficult for him, too. I plan to remind him of that on Friday, if I need to."

Owen hoped threats against his precious career would be enough to convince Justin to let her go.

Sydney stood in front of the mirror and gave her face a careful inspection. The sleepless night was obvious in the smudges below her green eyes. Thoughts of Jenny's story had kept Syd awake, thinking about how she should approach the other woman. What had seemed like such a good idea yesterday now had her wondering if Luke had been right to be concerned.

But she was determined to at least see Jenny and make her aware of the other women on the island who were anxious to meet her and make her feel welcome.

She glanced down at the ring Luke had given her the night before, struck again by its unique beauty. That he'd gotten her a ring she would've chosen for herself was further proof he was the one for her—as if she needed further proof. When she'd arrived on the island earlier in the summer after leaving the teaching job she'd once loved, she'd reconnected with Luke, and he'd helped her to put the pieces back together. His patience and tenderness had been a balm on the open wound on her soul. She thought of her late husband and children every day, but the memories were becoming easier to bear with the passage of time.

Being with Luke filled her with a sense of peace and tranquility she hadn't expected to find again after she lost her family. Her skin heated when memories of the passionate night with Luke played through her mind like an R-rated movie. Well, most of it was probably X-rated, she thought with a smile.

"What are you all smiles about?" Luke asked as he stepped into the bathroom and handed her a steaming mug of coffee.

"Oh, thank you." She rewarded him with a lingering kiss. "I have so much to smile about this morning."

He hugged her from behind and propped his chin on her shoulder. "It's nice to see you happy."

Sydney put the mug on the counter and turned to him, resting her hands on his shoulders. "I don't think I could've gotten to happy again without you."

"Yes, you would have. You were well on your way before we got back together."

"I was doing okay. I never would've gotten past 'just okay' without you. Without this." She went up on tiptoes to kiss him more intently. "Without us."

"You saved me, too, you know."

Syd raised a skeptical eyebrow. "How so?"

"I was destined for a life as a cranky loner who coasted along without experiencing the finer points."

"And do you feel like you're experiencing the finer points now?"

He moved his hands from her hips to her breasts, sliding his thumbs back and forth over nipples that responded to him instantly. "The finest of fine points."

She tossed her head back and laughed, which gave him permission to leave a trail of kisses on her neck. "Didn't you get enough last night?"

"Never enough," he said as he used his hand on her bottom to better align them so she could feel how much he wanted her.

"You have to go to work, and I've got a lighthouse keeper I need to see."

"You're really going to let me walk around all day in this condition?" He took her hand and held it against his rigid length. "Is that the kind of wife you plan to be?"

Sydney knew she should have some sort of witty comeback to an outrageous statement like that, but as usual, her brain turned to mush when he touched her. The combination of his fingers playing with her nipple and the pressure of his erection against her hand had her wavering. "What about work?"

"The McCarthys are always reminding me that I own the place." Sensing her capitulation, he tugged open her robe and his eyes heated with satisfaction when he found her naked underneath. "I get there when I get there."

"It can't be healthy to have as much sex as we do."

Luke laughed at that as he dropped to his knees before her. "It's extremely healthy. Keeps the stress level nice and low and does wonders for the blood pressure."

She fisted his hair and tried to stay upright when he squeezed her ass and nuzzled her belly. "My blood pressure is through the roof at the moment, and it's all gathering in one place."

"Mine, too, baby." He hooked her leg over his shoulder and lapped at her core, focusing on all the places that made her come apart, keeping it up until she shattered into a million pieces that only he could put back together. As she floated down from the incredible high, he scooped her up and carried her into the bedroom. Freeing himself from the jeans he'd put on for work, he came down on top of her.

Sydney wrapped her legs around his hips, urging him to take what she wanted as much as he did.

"Oh God, Syd," he whispered as he entered her. "I love you."

Raising her hips to meet his thrusts, she looked up to find him gazing down at her. "I love you, too."

"Always," he said, touching his lips to hers.

"Yes, Luke. *Yes.*"

They finished together in a burst of light and heat and energy that left her clinging to him, her anchor, her life, her love.

"What'll you tell Mac and Mr. McCarthy about why you're late?" she asked after a period of contented silence.

"I'll tell them something came up," he said with a dirty grin that made her laugh. "It was well worth the time." He kissed her once more, running his tongue over her bottom lip. "You're really going to marry me?"

"I really am."

"When?"

"As soon as we can."

"What do you think about a Christmas wedding?"

"Oh," she said, "I like that. I could use some new memories of Christmas. That's a tough time of year since the accident."

"We don't have to do it then if you'd rather not."

"No, I think it would be perfect."

"So it's a date?" he asked.

She kissed him. "It's a date."

CHAPTER 9

More than an hour after she'd intended to leave the house, Sydney was on her way to the Southeast lighthouse. As she navigated the winding island roads, she was glad she'd decided to bring her golden retriever, Buddy, with her. He was always good for breaking the ice, as few people could resist his overwhelming friendliness. She hoped Jenny liked dogs.

"How could anyone not love you?" she asked Buddy.

He took advantage of the invitation to nuzzle her outstretched hand. His coat was silky soft from the bath she'd given him the day before. Buddy was the only dog she'd ever known who actually enjoyed a bath. Any excuse to play with water.

Speaking of playing with water, her face burned when she remembered the shower she'd taken with Luke. He'd pressed her against the wall and made love to her again. His appetite for her was boundless, which was thrilling and exciting and overwhelming. She kept thinking that surely they would settle into a more typical relationship when the first blush of passion dimmed, but there was no sign of anything dimming between them. If anything, it got hotter and more intense all the time.

Syd drove around a curve and slowed when she saw a woman walking in the road. She wore a backpack, and her shoulders were hunched, which was why

Syd didn't immediately spot the telltale spiky red hair. She pulled up next to Stephanie. "What're you doing out here?"

Stephanie turned to her, and Syd was shocked to see that her friend's face was puffy and her eyes were red from crying. She gave Buddy a nudge to move him to the backseat. "Get in," she said to Stephanie. "I'll give you a lift."

"That's okay. I don't mind walking."

"Come on, Steph. You're clearly upset. Let me give you a ride."

Stephanie yanked the door open and got in, shutting the door with a slam.

"What's wrong?"

"What *isn't* wrong?"

"Did you and Grant have a fight?"

Stephanie released a harsh laugh. "We had *another* fight. All we do is fight. I can't take it anymore."

"Is it because of the screenplay?"

"For one thing. Everything is a battle. I grew up in chaos. I can't live like that anymore."

A car pulled up behind them and beeped for them to move along.

Sydney glanced in the rearview mirror before she accelerated. "Where're you headed?"

"To Charlie's."

"I'll take you," Syd said.

"You really don't have to. I don't mind walking."

"It's fine. I was heading out that way anyhow. Going to see Jenny."

"Oh." Stephanie stared out the window for a long time. "Here I am running away from my guy when she'd give anything for one more day with hers. Makes me feel kinda stupid."

"You're not stupid to take a breather if things aren't going the way you want them to."

"It's starting to register with me," Stephanie said slowly, "that there's a good possibility this thing with Grant isn't going to work out after all." As she said the words, she swiped at the tears that spilled down her cheeks.

"I don't think that's true," Sydney said. "I've seen you two together. He's wild about you. That's obvious to everyone."

"Maybe so, but what good is it if we drive each other crazy—and not in a good way?"

"There're bound to be bumps in any relationship. That's to be expected."

"Have you had bumps with Luke?"

"Sure we have. He was a terrible patient after he hurt his ankle—cranky as hell until I finally told him to knock it off or find a new nurse."

"Was he better after that?"

"Much. I'm lucky that he usually gets it the first time."

"You are lucky. Grant loves to beat the dead horse until it's a bloody pulp. The problem is, we both dig in and neither of us is willing to give an inch."

"Maybe writing the screenplay together wasn't the best idea."

"I'm beginning to think you're right about that."

"Talk to him. Work it out. You guys have a really great thing, Stephanie. Don't let this come between you."

"That's the turn."

Sydney drove onto the dirt road that led to Charlie's place.

Charlie was in the yard, splitting wood. He looked up with surprise when Stephanie waved to him from the car.

"Thanks for the lift, Syd."

Sydney leaned over to give Stephanie a hug. "Hang in there. I know you guys can work this out if you remember first and foremost that you love him."

Stephanie bit her lip as if trying to hold back more tears. "Don't say anything about it to anyone, okay?"

"My lips are sealed."

Stephanie nodded and got out of the car.

Syd watched her walk over to her stepfather and exchange a few words before she went into the house. He followed her. Satisfied that Stephanie was in good hands, Sydney continued on her way, reaching the lighthouse a few minutes later.

When she let Buddy out of the car, he bounded off ahead of her, romping his way across the open meadow that led to the red-and-white lighthouse. Sydney glanced up at the whirling beacon that alerted boaters to the island's craggy southern shoreline and was mesmerized until a whip of wind grabbed her hair and sent it flying. She secured it with the hair tie she wore like a bracelet.

"Well, here goes nothing," she whispered into the wind as she followed Buddy's barking around the base of the lighthouse to the other side, where she found him being loved on by a petite woman with shoulder-length blonde hair. "Hi, there," Sydney called. "Sorry to bother you."

"He's no bother. What's his name?"

"Buddy."

Buddy let out a bark at the sound of his name, making both women laugh.

"He's adorable."

Syd held out her hand to the other woman. "I'm Sydney Donovan."

"Jenny Wilks, the lighthouse keeper." She had friendly brown eyes, and her face was pink from the autumn chill. "Nice to meet you."

"You, too." Sydney took a long look up at the lighthouse and then back at Jenny. "What exactly is involved in keeping a lighthouse?"

Jenny's dimpled grin gave her the look of a college co-ed even though Syd knew she was well into her thirties. "Fortunately, not much. Other than recording the weather conditions and some other data for the Coast Guard each day, it's more or less an honorary position. You want to see the inside?"

"I'd love to, if I'm not putting you out."

"Not at all. Come on in."

Sydney whistled for Buddy to come with them and followed Jenny into what she referred to as the mudroom. Since Jenny kicked off her shoes, Sydney did the same and followed the other woman up a wrought-iron spiral staircase to a large, circular room that housed a galley-style kitchen and comfortable-looking sitting area. It had been updated with modern appliances and furniture she would've chosen for the space. The kitchen window looked out over the ocean, while the sitting room offered a sweeping view of the island that stretched all the way to the Salt Pond.

"Wow," Sydney said. "This is amazing! I've been driving past this lighthouse all my life and had no idea what was inside. It's so cozy!"

"I love it," Jenny said as she led Sydney up another flight of stairs to the bedroom and bathroom.

"Do you ever get lonely out here all by yourself?"

Jenny shrugged. "Sometimes, but I've been taking the opportunity to indulge in some hobbies I'd let slide." She gestured to the easel that was set up next to the bathroom window.

"May I?" Syd asked.

"Sure."

Sydney wandered to the easel for a closer look at the detailed painting Jenny was doing of the island. "This is really good!"

"Do you think so? I've been thinking it's total crap."

Sydney laughed. "I know that feeling. I've ventured into interior design in the last couple months. It's been a hobby up to now, and I'm finding it's a much different experience to create drawings of what a finished room might look like than it is to dabble with pillow placement."

"That actually sounds like fun."

"It is, once I get past the 'it looks like crap' phase of the process. This," she said, referring to the painting, "is definitely not crap."

"Well, that's good to know. To thank you for your opinion, I can offer you coffee, tea, soda or water. What's your pleasure?"

"Coffee sounds good. I never got my second cup this morning." She'd been too busy having mad, crazy shower sex with her fiancé. The word sent a flutter of excitement rippling through her.

"Right this way," Jenny said, leading Syd to the stairs.

Syd stole a glance at the photo of a smiling, handsome young man that sat on the table next to Jenny's bed. Sydney assumed he was Toby, the fiancé Jenny had lost on September 11. With Buddy on her heels, she followed Jenny down the stairs to the kitchen. "Are you sure I'm not keeping you?"

"Positive. It's nice to have the company."

"There's a whole town full of people who'd love to meet you, you know," Syd offered tentatively.

Jenny filled the coffeepot with water and turned to Syd. "Did they send you to find out if I'm antisocial or something?"

"Nothing quite like that. We were hoping you're doing okay out here all by yourself."

Jenny leaned back against the counter. "Did you read my letter?"

"Yes."

Jenny nodded. "So you know my story."

"Yes, and I'm sorry for your loss."

"Thanks."

Sydney swallowed hard and forced herself to say it, to give words to their common bond. "For what it's worth, I've been there myself. My husband and children were killed by a drunk driver almost two years ago."

"Oh my God," Jenny said. "God. How do you ever get past that?"

"The same way you've gotten past your loss—one day at a time, one foot in front of the other."

Jenny brought two steaming mugs of coffee along with cream and sugar to the sitting area. "How old were your kids?"

"Seven and five."

Jenny shook her head with dismay. "I'm so sorry."

"Thank you. It was a terrible time, and I miss them every day."

"I know what you mean. Not a day goes by..." Shrugging, she didn't finish the sentence. She didn't have to.

"There're some really amazing people who live here year-round," Syd said as she stirred cream and sugar into her coffee. "We have a lot of fun. If you're interested, I'd be happy to introduce you to everyone."

"As long as you're not talking about matchmaking, I might be game for that."

Sydney laughed. "Nothing like that. Most of the guys in our group are spoken for, anyway."

"And you?" Jenny asked, zeroing in on the ring on Sydney's left hand. "You're spoken for, too?"

Sydney felt her face heat with embarrassment. "Officially, as of last night." She held out the ring so Jenny could get a closer look.

"It's beautiful. Very unique. Mine had an antique setting, too."

The note of wistfulness in Jenny's voice had Syd regretting that she'd been so quick to show off her ring.

"Now, don't do that," Jenny said in a chastising tone.

"Do what?" Sydney asked, startled.

"Feel bad about showing off your ring. Naturally, you're very excited. I'm happy for you. After what you've been through, you certainly deserve it."

"Thank you. That's sweet of you to say."

"So who's the lucky guy?"

"Believe it or not, my high school boyfriend, Luke Harris. He was good enough to forgive me for leaving him for another man when I was in college. We reconnected earlier this summer, and now I can't imagine life without him."

"Does it feel weird to be in love again? I think about that sometimes... What it might be like. Would I feel disloyal to Toby? That kind of thing."

"It feels wonderful to be in love again, but I know what you mean about feeling disloyal. I went through that when Luke and I were first together—especially the physical part. I thought a lot about Seth, my husband, and what he would want for me. I like to think he would've wanted me to be happy, you know?"

Jenny nodded. "Toby would want that, too. I suspect he'd be appalled to know I'm still stuck in first gear. Even since I've been here. . . I have no idea how to move forward. Toby would probably give me a swift kick in the ass," she said with a laugh. "He wasn't one for sitting around feeling sorry for himself."

"I'm sure you haven't done that, Jenny."

"I've done some of that," she said with a smile.

"You've probably done the best you could, and that's all any of us can do in situations like ours."

"I suppose. I'm feeling ready to get unstuck, but I'm finding that's easier said than done."

Sydney rested a hand on the other woman's arm. "Let us help you. I promise our group of friends is very welcoming and supportive, and we'd love to have you."

"You make it sound so easy."

"It is. All you have to do is say yes. 'Yes, Syd, I'd love to come to your house for a small gathering on Saturday night to meet your friends.'"

"Yes, Syd," Jenny said, her eyes twinkling with mirth. "I'd love to come to your house on Saturday to meet your friends."

"Perfect."

Buddy let out a bark of agreement that made both women laugh.

Sydney drove away from the lighthouse a short time later feeling energized by her visit with Jenny. Reaching out to her had been the right thing to do. She was almost home when Luke called.

"How'd it go?" he asked without preamble, which told her how concerned he'd been.

"Better than expected. She's really very lovely. We had a nice chat."

"Well, that's good. I'm glad you didn't find it upsetting."

"I'm fine. Don't worry. And by the way, we're having a small gathering of our closest friends on Saturday."

"We can't have a 'small' gathering with our closest friends."

Sydney laughed. "I know, but I want Jenny to meet everyone, so I talked her into coming over Saturday." She paused before she added, "You don't mind, do you? It's bad enough that I've moved in and totally taken over your house—"

"It's *our* house, Syd. Whatever you want is fine with me."

"That's sweet of you to say. I'm very lucky to have such an accommodating fiancé."

"So am I," he said in a suggestive tone.

"Why do I get the feeling we're no longer talking about entertaining?"

"I find your accommodation *extremely* entertaining."

"*Luke!*"

His dirty laugh made all her nerve endings stand up and take notice. "Are you blushing?" he asked.

"Shut up, and go back to work."

"You're blushing. I know you are."

"Lalala, hanging up now."

"You did a nice thing, Syd, going to see her. I'm proud of you for doing that."

Touched by his praise, she said, "Thanks. Let's hope she still thinks so when she gets a load of our 'small' group of close friends."

CHAPTER 10

On Friday afternoon, Owen drove Laura's car to the ferry landing an hour before the three-thirty ferry to the mainland. He eyed the darkening sky and the frothy seas. "Gonna be a rough ride."

"That's okay."

"Are you sure? We don't have to go today. Another day or two won't matter."

"Yes, it will," Laura said. "I need to get this over with. I can't think about it anymore."

"Do you get seasick?"

"I never have before. What about you?"

"Doesn't usually bother me."

"Okay, then. We're going." She folded her hands in her lap and stared out the window. As the week had progressed and her date with Justin drew nearer, she'd become more and more tense and withdrawn.

She'd slept in his arms every night since the first night they spent together, driving him crazy with her nearness, her scent and her overwhelming allure. He couldn't wait until they were able to take their relationship to the next level. They had to get through today, or so he told himself. A sense of foreboding had sharpened with every passing day, ramping Owen's anxiety to previously unheard-of levels.

Laura's anxiety was also palpable. Her hands were so tightly linked in her lap that her knuckles had turned white. Owen reached over to rest his hand on top of hers.

She turned one of her hands up to press her palm to his.

They sat like that for a long time, until the ferry coming from the mainland appeared out of the mist, bobbing and rolling in the furious surf. He felt her hand begin to tremble under his. His heart hurt to know she was scared of taking the ferry but so determined to keep the appointment with her estranged husband that she was putting on a brave façade.

"Baby, why don't we wait? There's no need to—"

"I can't wait, Owen. I need to get this over with. Please."

He could deny her nothing when she sounded so undone. "Okay."

They watched the unloading of the arriving ferry, the passengers walking on watery legs as they disembarked—more than a few of them looking green around the gills. The ferry crew took fire hoses to the boat, probably to clean up the puke. Fabulous.

One of the employees rapped on the driver's side window.

Owen rolled it down.

"Rough ride today," the young man said. "We're issuing vouchers to anyone who wants to go another time."

"We have an appointment we need to keep," Owen said.

The kid shrugged. "Suit yourself," he said and moved on to the next car.

In the rearview mirror, Owen watched several cars drive away from the line. Even though his better judgment was telling him to do the same, Owen followed the hand signals of the ferry staff and backed the car onto the boat. With the car settled on the lower deck, he followed Laura upstairs. They had their pick of the benches and picnic tables. Laura dropped her purse on one of the benches.

Owen sat next to her. She had worn a black leather coat over a black turtleneck sweater and jeans tucked into boots. Her hair was piled on top of her head in a bun that made her look classy and sexy and untouchable. If he hadn't known her so well, that aura of refined class would've been off-putting to him.

Women who looked like her usually weren't interested in guys who played a guitar for a living or called an old van home. For the first time in his adult life, Owen wished he'd made different choices. He wished he'd been able to go to college and pursue a "real" career, so he would be the kind of man who deserved a woman like her.

The thought filled Owen with an overwhelming sense of insecurity. He'd never experienced anything quite like it. Imagining the suit-clad lawyer she'd married, Owen realized he'd never measure up to that. Not in this or any other lifetime. So what was she even doing with him? What did he have to offer her?

His stomach began to hurt as he imagined her seeing her fancy, successful husband and realizing she'd made a huge mistake replacing him with a guy who barely remembered to comb his hair most days.

The blare of the ferry's horn, signifying imminent departure, jarred Owen out of the increasingly disturbing thoughts.

"What's wrong?" Laura asked, tuned in to him as always.

"Nothing."

"That's not true. Your whole body is rigid, which is very unlike you."

"I lied," he said with a smile. "I do get seasick."

Her eyes went wide and her mouth fell open. "You do? Oh my God, Owen! You should've told me!"

He rested a finger on her sweet lips. "I'm kidding."

"Oh, good," she said, clearly relieved.

The ferry cleared the breakwater and took a precarious dip and roll that drew a gasp from Laura. She looked up at him with barely concealed fear marking her gorgeous face.

"It's okay." Owen put an arm around her and drew her in close to him. "They wouldn't have gone if it wasn't safe. Remember that."

"Gotcha."

The ferry slammed through the waves as it hugged the coast of the island. Once they cleared the bluffs at the north end, however, the seas got measurably larger without the protection of the island.

Laura moaned with dismay.

Shit, Owen thought. *We never should've done this.* The ferry crested a huge wave and sunk like a stone into a valley between waves. Across the way from them, a mother held a barf bag for her heaving child. Her gaze met Owen's, her fear palpable. Owen smiled at her, trying to reassure her as best he could.

The pounding went on for what felt like forever. While he'd never gotten seasick before, Owen's stomach was seriously unhappy with this ride.

Laura let out a whimper, and he released his hold on her so he could see her face. Tears filled her eyes, and her complexion had gone beyond pale to pasty.

"Are you okay?"

"I think I'm going to be sick," she whispered.

Owen released her. "Hold on to the bench." He got up and staggered to the case bolted to the wall that held barf bags and grabbed a couple before working his way back to her. In the short time it took him to get the bags, she had gone from ghostly to green.

She took a bag from him and bent at the waist, trying to breathe through the nausea.

As he rubbed a hand over her back, Owen glanced outside, hoping for signs of the mainland, but all he saw was mist and dark clouds and stormy seas. A glance at his watch told him they still had twenty minutes to go. *Christ, has an hour ever passed so slowly?*

"How're you doing, Princess?"

She shook her head and gave up the fight, heaving into the bag.

The same feeling of helplessness he'd experienced when she'd battled morning sickness assailed him. He did what he could for her, holding her shoulders as she retched. When she was done, he took the bag and handed her a new one, wishing he'd listened to his better judgment and insisted they postpone this trip.

He bobbed and weaved his way to the trash can and bought a bottle of water from the concession stand, which wasn't doing much business in light of the high seas. Wetting a napkin, he handed it to Laura.

She wiped her mouth and face.

"Do you feel better now?"

She shook her head.

"Do you think you could take a drink?"

"I'd be afraid to."

"We're almost there." Owen still couldn't see land, but surely any minute now...

The child across the way had exhausted herself and slept with her head in her mother's lap. The mom's face was pale and pinched as she fought her own battle with nausea. At one of the picnic tables, two young men were asleep with their heads cushioned on their arms, oblivious to the rough seas.

Must be nice, Owen thought as Laura got sick again.

Dry heaves racked her body, and Owen held her through it. Finally, a hint of the mainland appeared in the distance. "I can see the coast," he said. "Any minute now."

"Good," she whispered weakly, her head resting against his shoulder.

The pounding of the surf was relentless until the instant the ferry cleared the protection of the breakwater in Point Judith. Owen released a deep breath he hadn't realized he was holding as the water suddenly calmed and the ferry steamed smoothly into port.

An announcement summoned car owners to the lower deck to prepare to disembark.

"Do you think you can walk, honey?" he asked.

"I don't know." She attempted to stand, but her legs wobbled under her.

He hefted her bag to his shoulder and scooped her up.

"We've really got to stop meeting like this," Laura said as she let her head fall against his chest.

"Never," he said, kissing her clammy forehead. He hoped she bounced back in time for the meeting with Justin.

Owen walked down the metal stairs, deposited her in the front seat of the car and buckled her in.

She was asleep before they drove off the boat.

As they passed through the parking lot, Owen noticed Joe Cantrell's mother Carolina talking to Seamus O'Grady outside the terminal where they sold tickets. A sign posted in the window of the ferry office declared all boats canceled for the rest of the day. They'd gotten "lucky" to catch the last boat off the island. Owen's rumbling stomach contested the luck factor.

He pulled up next to them and opened the window. "No more boats, huh? Probably a good call."

"I hear it's bad out there," Seamus said.

"One of the roughest rides I've ever had." He gestured to Laura asleep in the passenger seat. "Poor Laura got sick."

"That's the worst," Carolina said. "Hope she feels better."

"Thanks. We're off to Providence. See you later." Owen used Laura's GPS to direct the car to "home," hoping that was her father's house and not the home she'd briefly shared with Justin, pulled out of the parking lot and headed for Providence.

His stomach took another sickening dip when he thought about what awaited them there.

"You really had to cancel the boats right when I wanted to go?" Carolina asked Seamus.

"Sorry, Miz Cantrell. But you heard what Owen said. This last trip was bad. 'Tisn't safe, I'm afraid."

As she had every time she'd been around the man her son had hired to run the business while he was in Ohio, Carolina decided she could listen to Seamus O'Grady recite the phone book and never get tired of his lyrical Irish accent.

If she were being truthful, she could also look at him for hours and never get enough of the rich auburn hair, devilish green eyes and mischievous grin that made her girlish heart stand up and take notice.

Too bad, she thought as she had before, *I'm old enough to be his mother.* Figures the one man who'd caught her attention since her beloved Pete died had to be roughly the same age as her son.

"Well, that puts me in a heck of a bind." She was terribly disappointed to postpone her trip to the island. "I guess I'll have to find a place to stay for the night."

"Balderdash!" Seamus said. "You'll stay at the house, of course."

Joe had turned his Shelter Harbor home over to Seamus to use when he was on the mainland.

"I couldn't impose on you," Carolina said.

"Don't be silly. It's your son's house, and there's plenty of room. I won't hear any objections. What would Joe say if he finds out I didn't take good care of his mama?"

Carolina rolled her eyes when she wanted to laugh like a schoolgirl. "You're so full of it, O'Grady."

"So you'll come and stay?" he asked. "No arguments?"

Since the closest decent hotel was more than twenty miles away, Carolina said, "Sure, why not?"

"Excellent," he said with a smile. "I'll grab us some fixings for dinner while you make yourself comfortable at the house."

"Don't go to any trouble on my account."

He bowed gallantly before her. "No trouble a'tall. Thanks to this nasty weather, I find myself with the rest of the day off. Perfect kind of day to whip up an Irish stew that'll make your mouth water."

Damned if her mouth didn't water just thinking about it.

"You've got a key?" he asked.

Carolina nodded.

"Okay, I'll see you there shortly."

"See you there." As Carolina returned to her car, she experienced a strange prickling sensation on the back of her neck. She ventured a glance over her shoulder and found Seamus watching her rather intently. Now what the devil was that all about?

Seamus told himself to breathe—in through the nose, out through the mouth. Damned if there wasn't something so incredibly sexy about Joe Cantrell's mum. Everything about her appealed to him, from the long blonde hair she wore in a braid down her back to the endless legs that filled out a pair of faded jeans to perfection. And then there were the grayish blue eyes that looked at him with feminine appreciation. Yes, he'd noticed that.

Seamus had been thunderstruck by her from the very beginning, not that he'd ever admit that to anyone. The first time she'd stopped in to "check up on him," as she'd teasingly said—more than a year ago now—Seamus had been so tongue-tied, he'd imagined her reporting back to Joe that he'd hired a complete idiot to run their family business. Seamus had waited for days to hear he was fired, but that call hadn't come.

Lusting after the boss's mother would surely lead to a termination phone call if Joe ever caught on to Seamus's fascination with her. Seamus liked this job. It was the best job he'd ever had, so he would do well to remember that and keep his eyes—and his hands—to himself while the entirely too appealing Carolina Cantrell was residing under his—or, well, Joe's—roof.

He let out a huff of aggravation and went into the office to get his jacket and keys. "I'm leaving for the day," he told the woman who was working the phones.

"See you in the morning," she said.

As he was driving to the grocery store, Seamus tried to figure out why, out of all the women he'd known, his boss's mother was the one who got to him. Why was she the one who turned him into a babbling idiot every time she showed up, usually out of the blue with no warning to prepare him?

All his legendary charm deserted him when Carolina Cantrell gave him the challenging look that let him know she wasn't buying what he was selling. Most women went stupid and giddy when he turned on his legendary Irish charm. Not Carolina. Oh no. She'd had his number from the first time they met, and there was nothing Seamus loved more than a good challenge.

"Joe would kill you for even thinking about her this way," Seamus muttered. Had he made a huge mistake inviting her to stay at the house? How would he hide his gigantic crush from her when they were staying in close quarters for the night? "Keep thinking about how Joe would dismember you if you so much as look at his mother, you stupid bloke."

He bought what he needed to make the stew and his grandmother's soda bread along with a couple of bottles of wine and some candles—in case they lost power. It wouldn't do to be unprepared for such an event, or so he told himself.

By the time he got to the house where Carolina's Jeep was parked in the driveway, Seamus was more nervous than a schoolboy before his first date. "Keep a handle on yourself, my man," Seamus said as he got out of the company truck and headed into the house.

The wind whipping through the trees made an eerie sound, and the rain was coming down in earnest now. He stepped into the mudroom, kicked off his boots and hung up his coat to dry. Grasping the bags of groceries, he stepped into the kitchen and got right to work on the stew. He popped open a beer and took several swallows, hoping to calm his nerves. His hands were so shaky he nearly lopped off a fingertip while slicing a carrot.

"Frickin' insanity, I tell you," he muttered. "Cook the food and stop acting like a dunderheaded nitwit."

"Do you always talk to yourself in the kitchen?" Carolina asked.

Seamus looked up quickly and found her leaning against the doorframe, holding a glass of wine. Her hair had been released from the braid and framed her face like wispy spun gold. A searing pain in his finger forced his gaze back to the cutting board, which was now covered in blood. Frickin' fabulous!

"Shit," he said as he headed for the sink to run the cut under cold water, praying it wasn't deep enough to require a hospital visit. He didn't want to waste any of his precious time with the lovely Carolina getting stitches.

"Let me see," she said, appearing at his side. With the bump of her hip against his, she shifted him to the side in a move that turned him on so completely he nearly swallowed his tongue.

She took hold of his hand and gave the cut a thorough examination.

The feel of her soft skin against his had him mesmerized, wishing the interlude would never end.

Sadly, she quickly completed her exam and held his finger under the cold water for another minute before releasing his hand. "I'm sure Joe has a first aid kit somewhere."

Seamus cleared his throat and batted his way through the cobwebs that had formed in his brain. While only a minute had passed, he felt as if he'd been under her spell far longer than that. "Under the bathroom sink," he said.

"Be right back."

He watched her walk away, because her fine rear in those faded jeans was a thing of beauty. The instant she was out of sight, Seamus released an unsteady breath and took a long look around the kitchen, as if he'd never before seen the modern appliances, intricate tile work and butcher-block countertop. His entire world had been turned upside down in the scope of a minute, the first time Carolina Cantrell officially touched him.

She returned with the first aid kit and directed him, with a hand to his arm, to take a seat on one of the barstools. The heat of her hand branded the skin of his arm, leaving him forever marked by the sensation of her touch.

All at once, it became vitally important to Seamus that she not touch him again. "It's okay," he said. "I can put a bandage on it."

"Oh, please, let me. It's my fault it happened in the first place. I startled you."

Taking his silence as consent, she took hold of his hand and dabbed at the cut on the pad of his index finger with antibiotic ointment that stung like a bastard.

He sucked in a sharp, deep breath.

"Sorry," she said with a wince. "I know it hurts."

If she kissed it better, he would die on the spot. Of that much he was certain.

Her scent surrounded him, a bewitching combination of earthy spiciness and sexy woman. Seamus wanted to lean in closer for a better whiff. When her hair brushed against his face as she bent over her task, he had to bite back a groan. It took every bit of willpower he possessed not to reach for a handful of silky blonde hair and bring it to his nose.

The second she had the bandage in place, he jumped up from the barstool and managed to crack his head against hers.

"Oh God," he said, stumbling through the words as he backpedaled away from her. "I'm so sorry. Are you hurt?"

Sending him a wry grin, she rubbed the tender spot on her forehead where his big noggin had connected with hers. "I'll survive." She studied him intently with eyes that seemed to see all the way through him. He certainly hoped that wasn't the case, for he'd be truly mortified if she were to have any inkling of his thoughts about her.

"You seem rather jumpy," she said. "Are you all right?"

"Of course." Heat infused his face in a blush so fierce he was reminded of his horrible teenage years when the sound of a girl's voice—any girl's voice—could make him blush and go hard, all in a fraction of an instant. That hadn't happened again since then, until the first time he met his boss's lovely mother—and every time since then.

He got busy again with the knife, watching his digits more closely this time. "I'm fine. I need a few more minutes to get the soup on and the bread in the oven."

"I'll start a fire," she said, wandering into the family room.

"Frickin' fabulous," he muttered again as he imagined how she'd look in firelight.

CHAPTER 11

Joe waited until Janey got through a week of midterm exams that had her stressed out and overwrought. When she arrived home from her last exam on Friday night, exhaustion clung to her. He met her at the door and took her coat.

"I'm going straight to bed," she said as she gave him a quick kiss and headed for the bedroom.

The dogs circled around her legs. That she gave them only perfunctory pats on the head was a sure sign of how tired she really was.

"Baby, wait. I know you're wiped out, but you need to eat. I made dinner. Why don't you have something to eat before you crash?"

He watched her eye the bedroom longingly before she turned her gaze toward him and nodded in agreement.

"Right this way." He held a chair for her at the table and served up the chicken piccata he'd made from scratch. One of the things Joe loved best about semi-retirement was having the time to try things he'd never done before, like cooking. That Janey praised his every effort as if it were fine French cuisine made it extra rewarding.

"So good," she said of the first taste of tender chicken.

"Glad you like it." He poured her a glass of the chocolate milk she loved and opened a beer for himself, needing some liquid courage for this conversation.

"Where did you learn to make this?"

"One of the women in my class made it for the art department potluck."

"Did you actually ask her for the recipe?"

Joe laughed at the face she made. "I actually did."

"I'm worried about what's become of you since I dragged you to the heartland."

"They'll never recognize me on the island."

"No, they won't. I need to remember this if I ever need blackmail. All I'd have to do is tell my brothers about you swapping recipes with girls on campus..."

"You wouldn't dare."

Janey laughed. "We'll see how you behave."

He shot her a playful scowl. "How'd the last exam go?"

"Good, I think. I'm never really sure."

"And yet somehow you manage to score As in every class."

"Don't jinx me."

"Wouldn't dream of it," Joe said with a smile.

They chatted about his class, his painting, their dogs and the latest gossip from the island, including his mother's plans to winter there.

"Are you sure that's a good idea?" Janey asked. "Her place out there is barely winterized."

"I tried to tell her that, but you know how she is when she makes up her mind about something. I sent Mac over to inspect the woodstove and the roof. He said everything looks fine, and he left her a cord of wood."

"Aww," Janey said with a warm smile. "My big brother is the best."

"Yes, he is. I felt better after he'd checked the place out. He also promised to keep in touch with her this winter. And you know your parents will, too."

"Absolutely. My mom will be thrilled to have her there." Though they were different as two women could be, Linda and Carolina had been friends as long as Mac and Joe had. "We'll see her when we go home for Christmas."

"Uh-huh." As Joe twirled spaghetti around his fork, he tried to think of a way to broach the pregnancy subject. It was so unusual to feel hesitant to talk to her about anything. He loved how they talked about everything and usually held nothing back.

"Hey." She nudged his leg with her foot. "Where'd you go?"

Joe looked up at her, surprised to realize he'd zoned out. "Nowhere. I'm here."

She nodded to the spaghetti he'd twirled into a tight mass around his fork. "Are you going to play with that or eat it?"

He pushed his plate away, too nervous to eat anymore. "I'm done."

"Do you mind if I finish it?"

"Go for it." Her increased appetite was another in a growing list of puzzle pieces Joe never would've put together on his own without his mother's insight. In addition to the sleepiness and appetite gain, her breasts were bigger and more sensitive, and she was often overly emotional, all of which, according to what he'd read, were indications of pregnancy.

"What're you thinking about?" she asked. "Is something wrong?"

"No, honey. Nothing's wrong. Finish eating, and then we'll talk."

She put down her fork and pushed the plate aside. "I'm done."

"Come here." He held out his hand to her and guided her onto his lap.

"What's going on, Joe? Are you mad about something? I know I've been a bit of a grouch during exams—"

He kissed the words right off her lips. "You haven't been a grouch. You've been busy and really, really tired."

"I know. It's crazy. I don't remember it being this bad last year."

Joe took a deep breath. "Is it possible that this year might be different because you're pregnant?" Because he was holding her so close, he felt her go rigid in his arms.

"I'm not pregnant. There's no way I'm pregnant! We've been careful, and I'm on the pill."

"And you've never forgotten to take it for a day or two because you were busy or preoccupied with school?"

He watched her closely as she thought back over the last few months.

Her mouth fell open and then snapped closed the instant before two big tears slid down her cheeks. "That's all it takes?" she whispered.

"That and nonstop effort," he said in a teasing tone.

"I can't be pregnant, Joe. I *can't be*. I have two and a half years of school left. How will I have a baby and manage school?"

Joe brushed away her tears and kissed her. "Easy—you'll manage school, *and* I'll manage the baby."

"How do you already have this all figured out?"

"I've had a couple of days to process the possibility. I told my mom the other day that you've been really tired, and she suggested you might be pregnant."

"How is it that she knew and I didn't?" Janey asked, piqued by the thought.

Joe laughed at the face she made. How could he not? She was so damned cute.

She scowled at him. "Hell of a vet I'm going to be when I can't even figure out that I'm pregnant without the help of my mother-in-law who lives a thousand miles from me."

"You're going to be the best vet ever, and I hate to tell you, we don't know for sure that you're pregnant."

"We need to get a test."

"I got three of them the other day. I was waiting for you to get through your exams before I mentioned it."

"Thank you for waiting. This would've taken me right over the edge this week, which, of course, you knew."

"So," he asked, his heart pounding with anticipation and excitement and more love than he'd ever felt in his life, "do you want to take one of the tests?"

New tears flooded her eyes as she nodded. "Is this why I've been crying over everything lately?"

He took her by the hand and led her into the bathroom. Under the sink, he retrieved one of the tests he'd stashed there. "Maybe so."

"I suppose it's better to be pregnant than to be having a nervous breakdown over school."

"Much better," he said, laughing. He took the test out of the box and handed it to her. "Pee goes here." When he started to leave the room to give her some privacy, she called him back.

"Stay. We did the rest of it together, why not this part, too?"

He smiled at her logic and leaned against the wall while she took care of business.

She placed the innocuous plastic stick on the sink, and they watched in stunned amazement as a blue plus sign appeared a few minutes later.

"Well," she said, "your mother was right." She turned to him, looked up and met his gaze. "I'm sorry I wasn't more careful."

"Please don't say that. Everything happens for a reason, and when you think about it, this might be the perfect time for us to have a baby."

She raised a brow in the skeptical expression that was so Janey. "How do you figure?"

"If we wait until you finish school, I'll be almost forty. That's getting sort of late if I want to have any energy left for Little League coaching and football playing and wrestling, not to mention tea parties and fashion shows and Girl Scouts."

Janey laughed through her tears and hugged him.

"It's all going to be fine," he whispered into the silky softness of her blonde hair. "I promise. It might not be how we planned it, but life is what happens when you're busy making other plans."

"Or when you're busy making love like sex-starved lunatics."

"That too," he said with a laugh. He slid his hands down her back to cup her bottom, lifting her into his arms.

She curled her arms and legs around him as he carried her to their bedroom. The menagerie collected around their feet, and Joe nearly tripped over them.

"Goddamn it," he said when he'd recovered his footing. "I'm carrying very precious cargo here, people."

"Don't swear in front of the baby."

He was relieved she'd taken the news better than he'd expected and so excited to be a father, a thought that suddenly filled him with fear.

"What?" she asked. "Why did your brows go all furrowy?"

He deposited her on the bed and crawled in next to her.

She snuggled up to him as she did every night.

"I barely remember what it's like to have a dad. What if I'm no good at it?"

"Oh, Joe! You'll be a great dad! This baby will be so lucky to have you. You're already thinking about tea parties and football practice."

"You're awfully sure I'll be good at it."

"I'm positive." She kissed his neck and then his jaw before finding his lips in a kiss that quickly spiraled into passionate need. Her arms tightened around him as her tongue flirted with his, making him crazy with desire.

"Love me, Joe," she whispered.

"I love you love you more than anything, Janey Cantrell." Joe added the second "love you" as they always did and peppered her face with kisses before taking her mouth again. Without breaking the kiss, he tugged at their clothes until all the important parts were revealed. He entered her carefully, without the usual abandon that marked their lovemaking.

"*Joe*," she moaned in protest. "Come *on*."

"I don't want to hurt you—or the baby." Everything was different now that he knew their child lay between them, precious and fragile.

"You won't." She arched into his thrust and clutched his backside, keeping him buried deep inside her.

He drew her nipple into his mouth, sucking and tugging, sending her into a powerful orgasm that finished him off in record time. "Sorry," he said, panting in the aftermath of the explosive climax.

Her hands were soothing on his back. "For what?"

"For not lasting longer."

"You lasted just long enough. I can barely keep my eyes open, and what if I fell asleep in the middle of, you know..."

"You'd better not fall asleep in the middle of *that*."

Janey chuckled and held him close enough that he could hear her heart beating fast beneath his ear.

After a long moment of contented silence, he said, "I promised my mother I'd tell her as soon as we knew for sure."

"Can it be our little secret for tonight? We can tell her and my parents tomorrow."

Joe closed his eyes against the rush of emotion. He couldn't remember a time when he'd been happier. "Sure, baby. Whatever you want."

"I have everything I want." She tightened her arms around him. "Everything I could ever want."

And that, Joe decided as he followed her into sleep, was all that mattered to him.

CHAPTER 12

Grant spent two days hoping he would hear from Stephanie before his friend Dan Torrington clued him in.

"She's not coming back," Dan said.

"How do you know that?" Grant asked Dan, who was visiting for the weekend and thinking about spending the winter on the island to pen the book he'd been planning to write for years. He'd fallen in love with the island on an earlier visit.

"Grant, my friend, let me tell you something about women."

"I can't wait to hear this," Grant muttered.

"They are sensitive, delicate creatures."

Grant didn't want to be around when Stephanie heard herself described as a sensitive, delicate creature.

"They require tremendous amounts of attention."

"I give her tremendous amounts of attention. Hell, she has practically *all* my attention."

"Maybe that's the problem. You're spending too much time together."

Grant, who used to go months between visits when he was dating Abby, now couldn't imagine a day without Stephanie in it. He couldn't picture his life without her front and center, irritating him and loving him. The pain he'd carried in his breastbone since she stormed out of their house two mornings ago had intensified when he began to fear that he might've lost her for good this time.

"You could be right," Grant said.

"I usually am."

Grant rolled his eyes at his friend's arrogance.

Dan gestured for Chelsea, the bartender at the Beachcomber, to bring them two more beers.

The pretty young bartender set down the bottles with a friendly smile for Dan.

"Thank you, sweetheart," he said.

"My pleasure. I have to ask you—are you related to the Baldwin brothers?"

"Nope," Dan said. "I get that a lot, though. People think I look like Billy Baldwin."

"You really do." Based on the dreamy look on her face, Chelsea was quite fond of Billy Baldwin.

Dan flashed her the dimpled grin that had made him famous. "Thanks for the beers."

"You're going to get sued calling women 'sweetheart,'" Grant said when Chelsea moved on to other customers.

Dan scoffed. "Puleeze. She loved it. You heard what she said. 'My pleasure.' Would she have said that if she were offended? Hell, she thought I was Billy Baldwin! Maybe he can play me in your movie."

Grant rolled his eyes. "You're more famous than he is, not that she knows that."

Dan brushed off the reference to his fame, as he always did. He'd made a career out of freeing prisoners who'd been wrongly convicted. Stephanie's stepfather was the latest in a long string of successes. "Take it from me. Chicks like to be *charmed*. They need to be *wooed*."

"That's what I've been doing with Steph, and look at where it's gotten me."

Dan had the audacity to laugh at that. "You haven't been *wooing* her. You've been driving her crazy with your vision of her story. So take a step back from the screenplay for a while, work out the relationship issues and see where you are."

"What do you know about relationship issues anyway? Your idea of a relationship is dinner and a hotel room."

"And that's bad how, exactly? You don't see me mooning around for two days because my girlfriend told me to screw and moved out."

"She hasn't moved out. Yet." The thought that maybe she had struck another note of fear in Grant's chest. He wondered if he might be having a heart attack. "You're not helping."

"What happened anyway?"

"I have no idea. We were arguing about this one part of the screenplay we've gone over a hundred times and she got all pissed and left."

"Grant." Dan waited until Grant spared him a glance to continue. "She's not coming back. If you want to fix this, you have to go to her."

"I'm not the one who left. Why do I have to do the chasing?"

Dan shook his head with dismay. "I have so much to teach you, my friend."

While Grant wanted to object to that statement, he couldn't. Stephanie was his second serious girlfriend, and he'd screwed up the first one rather royally. As much as he'd cared for Abby, he truly *loved* Stephanie. If he had to beg and grovel, he would. After two days without her, he'd discovered he had no pride where she was concerned.

He tossed a twenty on the bar and stood.

"Where're you going?" Dan asked.

"You know where I'm going."

Dan turned to face him, brushed a hand over Grant's jacket and adjusted the collar, patting him on the shoulder when he was satisfied. "There. Now you can go."

"Thanks, Mom."

"Call me tomorrow. Let me know how it goes."

Grant's stomach hurt when he imagined the many ways this could go wrong. "I will. You're here for a few more days, right?"

"At least. I'm due in court in LA next Friday, and then my schedule is clear until after the first of the year."

"It'll be nice to have you around this winter."

"It'll be nice to be here, if you're not pouting the whole time." Before Grant could respond to that, Dan gave him a gentle push. "Go get your girl, and don't screw it up."

"I'll try not to." As Grant made his way to Mac's motorcycle in the parking lot, he thought of the many ways it was possible to screw this up. Maybe he already had by waiting two days to go after her. His stomach started to hurt in earnest at that thought. He'd never wanted anything more than he wanted to be with her, but nothing had ever been more difficult. How was that possible?

On the way to Charlie's place, where he'd heard she was staying, Grant tried to remember what had caused the fight. Try as he might, he couldn't recall the specific exchange. There had been many of them over the last couple of months, since they'd begun to collaborate on the screenplay about Charlie's unjust incarceration and Stephanie's relentless campaign to free him.

When Grant pulled into the driveway, Charlie was washing his pickup truck. He stopped what he was doing and gave Grant that blank look he did so well as Grant parked the bike and walked over to him.

"Is Stephanie around?" Grant asked, discovering in that moment he had a shred of pride left, and it was seriously dented by having to ask her stepfather where she was.

"Yep."

"Could I see her?"

"I'd say that's up to her." Charlie studied him for a long, uncomfortable moment.

Grant resisted the urge to squirm under the heat of the other man's stare.

"I take it you never got around to asking her the question we talked about the other day?"

Grant shook his head and crossed his arms over his chest, his left hand resting on the ring box in his coat pocket. He'd carried it with him for weeks, hoping for the right chance to ask her.

"What happened?" Charlie asked.

"I think maybe it was one spat too many for her."

"So what's your plan, hotshot?" This was asked with a hint of amusement that was so shocking coming from the normally stoic Charlie that Grant was temporarily rendered speechless. "I, um, was thinking I'd apologize for whatever I did that made her so mad."

"Good place to start." Charlie pointed his chin toward the path that led to the beach. "She went for a walk a little while ago. You might catch her on the way back."

Grant's heart lurched at the thought of seeing her. Two days was too damned long. "Thanks."

"Good luck," Charlie called after him.

Grant waved to let the other man know he'd heard him and headed down the well-worn path. As he got closer to the bluffs, the smell of the ocean assailed him, reminding him, as it always did, of home. But now that he'd met Stephanie, fallen in love with her, lived with her… She was his home, and he'd be positively lost without her. "You should probably tell her that," he grumbled to himself. "For a guy who's supposed to be rather good with words, you need to find the right ones, and you need to do it fast."

He traveled about a half mile down the path before he found her sitting on a rock that overlooked the Atlantic. Her arms were stretched out behind her, and her face was tilted into the late afternoon sun.

His heart contracted painfully at the sight of her. He ached for her but was reluctant to say or do anything that would make things worse.

She must've sensed him there because she turned and met his gaze. Surprise registered on her expressive face before she shuttered herself, the way she had so often lately. He hated when she did that. It left him feeling closed out and closed off from her, two places he never wanted to be where she was concerned.

Grant walked the final thirty feet to her, feeling as if his entire life would come down to whatever transpired here. "You look like a sun goddess sitting on your stage waiting for the gods to show up to worship you."

"Looks like it worked," she said with a small smile that warmed the cold places inside him. She held out a hand. "Now come worship me."

Grant took her hand and joined her on the rock. He wrapped his arms around her and pressed his lips to her sun-warmed face. "Steph, I—"

"Shhh. Don't say anything. Just hold me."

Because there was nothing he'd rather do, he did as she asked. He had no idea how long they sat there, wrapped up in each other as the sun dipped lower toward the horizon.

"I'm sorry," he finally said, softly so as not to break the magical spell.

"So am I." She ran her hand over his hair and down to cup his face.

Her touch sent a shiver of longing through him.

"I've had some time to think," she said.

That quickly, the longing turned to dread. Something about the way she said the simple sentence terrified him. "And?"

"This…" She took a moment to compose herself, which only added to his growing anxiety. "This isn't working."

The words and the pain he heard in her voice as she said them hit Grant like an arrow straight to the heart. "That's not true."

"Wait," she said. "Hear me out."

"I don't want to hear you say you're leaving me. I can't hear that."

"You can't possibly be happy with the way things have been."

"In our worst moment, I'm happier with you than I've ever been before."

"Grant…" Tears rolled down her face, every one of them breaking his heart. "I love you so much. You know I do. But after the way I grew up, the constant upheaval, the fighting, the sick feeling in my stomach, always worrying when the bottom was going to fall out… I simply can't live like that anymore."

Every one of her words hit him like poison arrows filled with pain serum. It occurred to him all at once that he'd done a terrible thing to her by letting the passion they shared in bed spill over into the other areas of their life together. She was absolutely right. After her tumultuous childhood, she needed calm stability, not high drama.

"You're right." Grant bit back the tidal wave of panic and focused on what he needed to do to fix this, because losing her was not an option he was willing to consider. "You're absolutely right, and I understand that the way it's been between us doesn't work for you—and I get why. But that doesn't mean we can't make some changes to make it work better in the future."

She eyed him warily. "What kind of changes?"

"For one thing, we'll no longer work together. That's not good for us."

"No," she said, "it really isn't."

"The screenplay is my job. I bought the rights from you and Charlie, and I'm asking you to trust me to do justice to your story."

"No pun intended," she said with a smile that gave him the first shred of hope that they might get through this crisis.

"No," he said, amused, "no pun intended." He took her hand and linked their fingers. "Do you trust me to tell your story with dignity and grace and courage and humility and all the other words that come to mind when I think of what you went through alone for so many years?"

"Yes," she said, her voice heavy with emotion, "of course I trust you to do it right. If I didn't, I never would've given you the rights."

"Then you have to take a step back and let me do it."

She nodded, even as tears threatened again.

He brought their joined hands to his lips. "And you, my love, need to take the money I paid you for the rights to your story and open that restaurant you've always dreamed of. Here or in Providence or both, if that's what you want."

Her eyes went wide with surprise. "How do you know about my restaurant?"

"I have my sources."

"Did Charlie tell you that? Who else would know?" She waited a heartbeat. "Why did Charlie tell you? *When* did he tell you?"

"He told me the other day when I came over to see him."

Her mouth fell open in shock. "You came to see Charlie? By yourself? I thought you were scared of him."

Grant snorted with laughter. "I didn't say I was *scared* of him. I said he's intimidating and looks at me like he wants to kill me in my sleep."

"You also mentioned that he'd probably learned a few ways to do that while he was in prison," she reminded him.

"Okay, maybe I was a *little* scared of him, but I had something I needed to ask him, so I had to man up and come talk to him."

"Wow," she said, truly amazed, "I would've liked to have seen that. What did you have to ask him?"

"I can't tell you that. It's guy stuff. You wouldn't understand."

She rolled her eyes at that. "Was he nice to you?"

"Yes."

She crooked the famous brow that let him know she wasn't buying his bullshit. "Really?"

"He warmed up as the visit unfolded."

That made her laugh, which filled Grant with wild, foolish hope. When it was good between them, there was nothing better. He made a silent vow to work harder to make sure it was good between them all the time going forward. Nothing was more important than her happiness, not even the damned screenplay he'd let come between them, a thought he decided he'd better share with her so she'd understand that he truly got it.

"I thought I'd learned my lesson after what happened with Abby."

"What lesson is that?"

"That nothing is more important than you are. Not the screenplay or my career or my family. Nothing."

"I know how important the screenplay is to you, Grant. You shouldn't make light of that."

"If someone told me I'd be the most successful writer in Hollywood for the rest of my life but I couldn't have you, I'd say thank you very much, Hollywood. It's been a lovely ride, but I'm done now. I have something far more important in my life than any movie will ever be. I've got the real thing, the love story of a lifetime, and there's nothing in this world that will ever be more important to me than she is." He shifted his body off the rock so he was on his knees before her, keeping a firm grip on her hands. "Stephanie, you're the love story of my lifetime, the one I can't live without."

Every emotion she possessed skirted across her expressive face as she waited breathlessly to hear what else he had to say. In all of Grant's thinking about this moment, it had never occurred to him that she might say no to his question, but now he wasn't so sure. He pushed that unsavory thought aside to focus on saying the right thing. Words were his business. He'd never needed them more than he did right now.

"I know it's been rocky at times, and it's apt to be again once in a while, but I promise I'll do everything in my power to make you happy, to give you the family you've always wanted, the life you've always wanted and the security you've never had. You'll never have to wonder where I am or who I'm with, because I'll always want to be with you more than I want to be with anyone else. There's nothing in this world I wouldn't do for you, but I need you to do one thing for me first."

"What?" she asked, sounding breathless now, too.

"Marry me." He released her hands to retrieve the ring box from his pocket and opened it to reveal a simple square-cut diamond. He knew her well enough to suspect that anything flashier would've been wrong for her.

She gasped, and her hand covered her mouth.

He *loved* that he'd taken her completely by surprise.

Her eyes darted from the ring to his face—possibly to gauge his sincerity—and back to the ring.

"Stephanie Logan, I'll love you every day for the rest of my life. Will you marry me?" Grant thought his eyes were deceiving him when he saw her nod. "Is that a yes?"

The word "yes" got caught on a sob, but he heard it. Loud and clear. He slid the ring onto her finger and reached for her.

She came right off the rock and launched herself into his arms. They landed on the sand in a clutch of arms and legs.

"I've got you, baby," Grant said, running a hand over her back as she continued to cry. He hoped they were happy tears. "Are you okay?"

She nodded and clung to him.

"That'll learn you not to try to break up with me."

Sobs turned to laughter, which turned to passion the instant his lips met hers. "I love you," he said when they came up for air. "Only you."

"I love you, too."

"And do you promise to never try to dump me again?"

"I may try, but I'm sure you'll find some smooth, sweet words to talk your way out of it like you did today."

"Speaking as a reviewer, tell me, what did the trick?"

She rolled her eyes at him. "As if you don't know."

"I really don't."

In one of her signature moves, she brushed the hair off his forehead and ran her fingers through it lovingly. "The love story of a lifetime was a pretty good line."

"Just pretty good?"

"Extremely memorable. The security I've never had was a close second."

"I thought you might like that."

"When you marry a writer, you ought to get a proposal for the ages."

His eyes went wide at what surely had to be one of the finest compliments he'd ever received. "Is that what this was?"

"Absolutely," she said, kissing him again.

"How about a marriage for the ages to go with it?"

"I'm all for that. Is this what you had to talk to Charlie about?"

Nodding, he said, "I couldn't ask you without his blessing."

"And he gave it?"

"With some assurances."

That made her snort with laughter. "I hope he made you work for it."

"Oh, trust me. He did." His lips found the tender underside of her jaw, one of his favorite places to kiss her. "Steph?"

She tipped her head to give him better access. "Hmm?"

The setting sun cast her skin in a warm glow. "Why didn't you tell me about the restaurant?"

"I don't know. I figured I'd get around to it eventually."

"Are there other things you want that I don't know about?"

She shook her head. "You covered all the high points in your proposal."

"I want you to know—I get what you said about how you grew up. Things will be different from now on."

"Thank you for listening—and for hearing me."

"Any time I don't do that, give me a kick in the ass. Promise?"

"Yes," she said, laughing. "It'll be my pleasure to kick you in the ass. Can I spank you sometimes to mix things up?"

"Whatever you want, babe." The suggestion was all it took to get Grant thinking about officially sealing their deal. "Speaking of your pleasure..." He extricated himself from her embrace and stood, offering her a hand up. Drawing her into his arms, he held her tight for a long time before he let her go, slung an arm around her shoulders and directed her to the path. "Let's go home."

An hour after they left Point Judith, Owen followed the GPS directions to Providence's tony East Side, still hoping he was heading to her father's house. Laura hadn't stirred once during the ride, and her face remained ghostly pale.

He got his answer about the address when they reached a two-story white colonial with black shutters, nicely trimmed bushes and the name McCarthy on the mailbox. Owen pulled into the driveway and parked next to a silver Cadillac sedan. He tried to decide his next move. Did he wake her up or let her sleep awhile longer? He wanted to let her sleep but didn't think it was appropriate to sit in her father's driveway for half an hour without letting him know they were there.

Frank McCarthy solved the problem for him by coming out of the house to greet them.

Owen emerged from the car and stopped short at the sight of Laura's dad, a shorter version of Big Mac McCarthy. Whereas Big Mac was all rough edges and relaxed cool, Frank was tailored and urbane in a light blue dress shirt, dark dress pants and black wingtips. While Big Mac's gray hair was often wild and unkempt from the wind that whipped through the docks, Frank's was combed into a tame style suitable for a courtroom. He wore a concerned look in the blue eyes he shared with his brother, daughter and nephews.

"I trust you're the Owen Lawry I've heard so much about," Frank said as he approached Owen with his hand extended.

While Owen digested the fact that Laura had told her father about him, Owen shook the older man's hand. "Yes, sir. I can't believe our paths haven't crossed before now. I've been close to your brother's family since I was a kid."

A flash of regret registered on Frank's face. "I've not been able to spend as much time on the island as I would've liked to over the years." He glanced at the car. "Did she get sick? I wondered if she would. The ferry has always made her queasy even on the best of days."

"Is that right?" Owen said, surprised to realize she'd lied to him about never getting sick. He took that as an indication of how badly she'd wanted to keep the appointment with Justin. "She did get pretty sick, and it wiped her out."

"Poor baby." He glanced at the gold watch on his wrist. "You've got about forty minutes until you need to head out to meet he who shall not be named."

In that moment, Owen realized he was going to get along famously with Laura's dad. Laughing, he said, "I like that."

"Thought you might." Frank opened the passenger door. "Let's get her inside."

"Allow me," Owen said.

Frank stepped back to let Owen unclip the seat belt and scoop Laura out of the front seat.

She woke up when they were halfway to the door. "Oh, hey, are we here?"

"You're home, honey," Frank said. "Everything's okay."

"Hi, Daddy," she said with a weak smile. "Sorry to show up in rag-doll condition."

"I figured it might be a tough crossing today."

"That's one word for it," she said. "You met Owen?"

"I sure did," Frank said, leading the way into the house.

In a low tone that was for her ears only, Owen said, "We'll discuss the fact that you lied to me about getting seasick later."

"Sorry," she said sheepishly. "I couldn't think about this meeting with Justin anymore. I need to get it over with."

"I get it, honey. I'm kidding."

"Here you are carrying me around again."

"It's a terrible hardship," he said, kissing her forehead before he put her down on the sofa in what looked to be a formal living room.

"What can I get you, Laura?" Frank asked. "Some of that lemon tea you like? Will that settle your stomach?"

"That'd be great, Dad. Thanks."

"Coming right up. Owen? Ready for a cold beer?"

"I wouldn't say no to that. Thank you."

"Be right back."

Owen sat next to Laura and took her hand. "Do you feel any better after you slept?"

"A little. Sorry to be so high maintenance. I hate that you've seen me puke at least ten times by now and we haven't even slept together. Yet."

The word "yet" sent a shiver of anticipation dancing down his spine as he thought of the hotel room he'd booked at the Westin. "I hate to remind you that we *have* slept together."

A heated blush added some much-needed color to her cheeks. "You know what I mean."

"Don't talk about it with your father in the next room," he said in a low growl that betrayed his ragged emotions.

Her soft laughter filled him with anticipation and love. So much love. At some point, he'd fallen so damned hard for her and couldn't wait to have the chance to tell her—and show her—what she meant to him.

Frank returned with their drinks and turned his focus on Owen.

Owen tried to release her hand, but she only held on tighter.

"Daddy," Laura said with a note of warning in her voice. "Don't even think about it."

"What?" Frank asked, all innocence. "What'd I do?"

"If the word 'intentions' comes out of your mouth, I won't be responsible for my actions."

Owen couldn't contain a chuckle at Laura's attempt to "manage" her father. He realized Frank shared his brother's ball-busting sense of humor, which made Owen like him even more than he already did.

"I don't know what you're talking about," Frank said. "All I was going to say is that it's nice to finally meet him. Am I allowed to say that?"

"Yes, but nothing else."

To Owen, Frank said, "She was always such a nice girl. I'm not sure where I went wrong."

"She's still a nice girl," Owen said with a warm glance at her. "The nicest girl I've ever known."

The compliment earned him a smile from Laura.

"On that we agree," Frank said. "So what's the plan for he who shall not be named?"

At the reminder of why they were in Providence, Laura lost some of her sparkle. She put the teacup on a side table. "I'm going to tell him about the baby and try to convince him that our marriage may be over, but we've got a child to consider."

"I'm very concerned about him getting physical with you," Frank said.

"He never would, Dad. He's far more likely to come at me with words, but I'm ready for him with a few words of my own."

"That's my girl."

Owen was proud of her determination, but the hollow feeling in his gut was a reminder of all the many ways this could go horribly wrong for her—and for them. Whatever happened, he decided as she visited with her father, he'd be there for her. They were in this together.

CHAPTER 13

"Do you think he knows what we've got planned for later?" Laura asked as they left her father's house a short time later. He'd offered them a place to stay for the night, but Laura had told him they'd made other plans.

"I sure hope not," Owen said.

"I bet he knows."

"I can't think about that, let alone talk about it, until we get past part one."

Her pensiveness had him reaching for her hand. "I'll be right across the room, watching every second. No matter what happens, it's going to be okay."

"I hope you're right." Laura wanted to believe it was all going to be fine, but she knew Justin and wasn't convinced he'd let go without a fight, especially once he found out about the baby.

"I gotta ask you... I mean, it's none of my business, but..."

"You can ask me anything. You know that."

"What'd you ever see in this guy? He sounds like a world-class dick."

Even though she sensed he hadn't meant to be funny, Laura laughed. "I suppose he does from what you've heard of him. But no one's all bad or all good."

"You are. You're pure goodness. You don't have a mean bone in your body."

Touched by his sincerity, she said, "You haven't seen me when I get mad. Watch out."

"Spare me, killer. I'm not afraid of you."

"You say that now…"

"I'll have to take your word for it."

The amusing banter was exactly what she needed to stay calm and focused.

"You still haven't told me what you saw in him."

"He was handsome and charming and ambitious."

"Everything I'm not," Owen grumbled.

"How can you say that? You're all of those things—and then some."

"I'll give you the handsome and charming," he said to her laughter, "but how do I rate ambitious when I call an old van home?"

"You're living your life on your own terms and no one else's. You do what you want, when you want, and make a damned good living doing it. Not to mention, you're doing something you love. What's not to respect about that?"

"Hmm, I hadn't thought of it that way. Still, I'm not exactly a lawyer."

"Thank God for that. I've been around lawyers my whole life. You're a refreshing change of pace."

Out of the corner of her eye, she watched him mull that over. Even as he drove the car, taking directions from her, she could see his wheels turning a mile a minute. "I can tell you're dying to say something else. Why are you suddenly holding back on me?"

He looked over at her, seeming surprised by her insight.

"What is it?" she asked.

"I, um, I wonder if the refreshing change of pace can hold your interest long-term."

"Owen," she said, flabbergasted. "I can't believe you'd say that! I can't wait for us to be together—truly together without my estranged husband and divorce hanging over us. I think about that all the time." She took his hand and held it between both of hers. "You believe me, don't you?"

"I want to. Tell me this—am I the first guy you've ever dated who called a van home?"

Laura smiled. "Yes, you are."

"I bet every other guy you've been with has an Ivy League education and a Brooks Brothers wardrobe."

"Those things don't matter to me. Not anymore."

"I knew it!"

"So I might've had a type in the past. That was then." She held on tighter to his hand. "This is now. I want you. I want to be with you."

"I want you, too, Princess. But I'm not looking for a fling. Been there, done that. I'm ready for something more."

"I am, too. That's what I thought I was getting when I married Justin."

"I'm worried that you haven't given yourself enough time to get over what happened with him."

"I remember asking Janey about that when she got involved with Joe so soon after she caught David with someone else. She said when you find out the man you love has been unfaithful, all the love you once felt for him disappears as if you never loved him at all. That's what happened to her—and it was the same for me. After my friends told me what he'd done, I couldn't even look at him without feeling sick. All the good feelings were gone, and there's nothing he could say or do to ever bring them back. They're gone. I was over him the minute I knew he still wanted other women. Some women can forgive that kind of transgression. I'm not one of them, and neither was Janey."

Owen was quiet for a long moment as he thought about what she'd said.

"Do you believe me?"

"I want to, but I've been around the block enough to know that it's not always that simple."

"Sometimes it's exactly that simple."

"I hope you're right."

"I usually am," she said with a cocky grin, hoping to lighten the mood. She wished there was something she could say or do to set his mind at ease and let him know he was exactly what she wanted and needed. No one, other than her dear dad, had ever cared more about her than Owen seemed to. She'd never been more in tune with anyone, and she couldn't wait to see what the future held for them. The thought strengthened her resolve to get through this encounter with Justin and get on with her life with Owen.

"Thanks for coming with me," she said as he pulled into a parking space across the street from the restaurant.

"No problem. I'll be watching the whole time. If you need me, tug on your earlobe, and I'll be right there."

"You've been watching too many spy movies."

He stopped her from getting out of the car with a hand to her arm. "Promise me you'll do it if you need me."

Because he seemed to need it, she nodded. "I promise."

"Whatever happens, it's nothing you can't handle. Remember that."

"I will. Let's get this over with."

Owen sent her in ahead of him, promising to follow in a minute so they wouldn't be seen together.

The maître d' greeted Laura by name. She'd been called "Mrs. Newsome" only a couple of times before it all went bad. Fortunately, she hadn't gotten around to legally changing her name. "Your husband is already here. Follow me."

"Here we go," Laura whispered to herself. She held her head up as he led her to Justin's usual table in the far corner, where he'd once told her he could see everyone in the place. Justin was all about seeing and being seen, which was why he stood up to greet her. She was counting on the fact that the Justin she knew would never be anything other than gracious and polite in public.

She'd worn the oversized black sweater intentionally so he wouldn't notice her pregnancy until she was ready to tell him. At the sight of the face she'd once planned to wake up to for the rest of her life, her entire body went on alert against imminent danger. Her reaction to him was so powerful she nearly took a step backward in self-defense. Because he'd never given her the slightest reason to be afraid of him, she forced herself to take the final steps to the table.

Justin put down the vodka cocktail he'd been nursing and leaned in to kiss her cheek.

She had to force herself not to cringe or pull away from him as his lips brushed against her skin.

"It's good to see you." He made sure to keep his voice low so the maître d' wouldn't hear as the older man settled Laura into her chair and handed her a menu. It occurred to her right then that her back would be to Owen, which only added to her growing anxiety.

Justin wore one of the custom-made suits he paid a thousand dollars apiece for, with a crisp white shirt and burgundy tie. As always, his dark hair was immaculately styled and his brown eyes were shrewd as he took a long, measuring look at her.

Laura did her best not to wilt under his intense scrutiny even as she tried to remember what she'd ever seen in him. He'd once been charming and amusing and romantic, with grand gestures she now realized were all for show. It'd been all about wooing Judge Frank McCarthy's daughter and had nothing at all to do with her. Unfortunately, she'd fallen for his game like a lovesick fool. Being picked up off the bathroom floor after a vicious bout of vomiting was her idea of romance these days.

"Your server will be right with you," the maître d' said.

"Ask him to give us a few minutes," Justin said.

"Of course."

The moment they were alone, Justin's charming smile turned into a satisfied smirk. "I knew you'd come around in time. You'll be glad to know I've decided to forgive you."

Laura was stunned. "For what?"

"Like you don't know. Let's start with giving up a primo apartment and having all my stuff sent to my mother. Thanks for that, by the way. I needed to deal with a thousand questions from her like I needed a hole in the head."

"I didn't know where you're living."

"You could've asked me."

"I didn't wish to speak to you."

"Clearly you've changed your mind about that. You're here, aren't you?"

"Only because we have some things we need to discuss."

"I've already told you there isn't going to be a divorce, so if that's why you're here, you're wasting my time—and yours."

She fought to keep her voice even so he wouldn't know how upsetting and difficult this was for her. "That's not the only thing we need to talk about."

He sat back in his chair and took a sip of the cocktail, looking arrogant and smug, which put her on even higher alert—if that was possible. "There's nothing you can tell me that I don't already know."

Laura sat up a little straighter. "What's that supposed to mean?"

"I know you're living on Gansett Island, working at the Sand & Surf Hotel. The owners have charged you—someone with absolutely no experience in such things—with the task of restoring that dump. I know you've taken up with the big dude with the shaggy hair who's over there staring daggers at me." He nodded toward Owen. "A *homeless guitar player*? Really, Laura? Gone slumming, have you?"

"He's worth a thousand of you," Laura shot back before she could stop herself. Angering him wouldn't accomplish anything.

"I get it—you're paying me back for what you think I did to you, which was nothing, by the way. Great, we're even. Now it's time for you to get your ass home and honor your marriage vows."

"That's not going to happen."

"Yes, it is."

"I know it's hard for you to imagine that someone might say no to you, but I'm not coming home—not now or ever. My home is on Gansett, and that's where I plan to stay."

"Even after you have my baby? Were you planning to tell me about that?"

Laura's mouth fell open. "How do you... When did you..."

"There's nothing a good private investigator can't find out for the right price."

Appalled and horrified to know he'd had her followed, she had to dig deep to recover her composure. "I was going to tell you. That's why I'm here."

He waved a hand dismissively. "Here's how this is going to go. You're giving up the island, the hotel, the guitar player, the whole thing and coming back where you belong, or I'll make sure you never see that baby. Your rebellion is over. You've made your point."

Anger whipped through Laura like a wildfire. "Who the hell do you think you are? You can't tell me what to do or where to live."

He leaned in closer to her, his dark eyes flashing with fury and what might've been hurt, not that she cared about that. Not anymore. "I'm your *husband*, and that's my kid you're carrying. At least I think it is."

Once again, Laura acted without thinking as her hand connected with his face in a loud slap that had everyone in the place looking at them.

His face flushed with rage.

Before he could say a word, she stood and propped her hands on the table, leaning in so he could hear her. "Listen to me, and listen good, you miserable son of a bitch. The biggest mistake I ever made was marrying you. You'll sign the divorce papers—*immediately*—or not only will I make sure you never see this kid you're not sure is yours, I'll also see to it that my dad does everything within his considerable power to ruin your precious career. Do I make myself clear?"

As she'd known it would, the threat of Frank McCarthy's wrath had the color draining from his face.

"I *said*, do I make myself clear?"

He took another sip of his drink and eyed her hatefully. "I'm not surprised you're already shacked up with someone else. You have no idea how to be without a man. Poor little daddy's girl can't be alone for five minutes."

Even though his words struck a direct hit to one of her deepest insecurities, she refused to show him that. "Sign the papers, Justin, or we'll make your life a living hell. I may be a daddy's girl, but there's absolutely *nothing* he wouldn't do for me. You'd do well to remember that."

Laura didn't wait to hear whatever he might have to say to that. For the first time in her life, she didn't care that she was making a scene that would be talked about for days to come. All she cared about was getting out of there—as quickly as possible. She was aware of Owen getting up from the table he'd occupied and chasing after her, but she didn't stop moving until she reached the car. With nowhere left to go, she leaned against the car, breathing heavily as her hands began to shake.

He'd had her followed. He knew about Owen. About the baby. For a brief, horrifying moment, she wondered if she was going to be sick again, right there in the parking lot.

Owen caught up to her and reached for her.

She stopped him by putting her hands up. Every nerve in her body was on fire. If he touched her, if anyone touched her, she'd scream.

"Jesus Christ," Owen said, his face flushed from running after her. "What the hell did he say?"

Laura reached for the door handle, fumbling with it, frustrated when it refused to open.

"Wait, honey. Let me unlock it." He held the door for her until she was inside before closing it and going around to the driver's side. "Are you going to talk to me?"

"Later. Please. Let's go."

"Where do you want to go?"

"Anywhere but here." She caught a glimpse of Justin emerging from the restaurant in time to watch them drive away. His expression was impassive, but his eyes were sharp as always.

"I want to know what he said to you."

"It doesn't matter. He'll sign the papers."

"Laura, honey—"

"I can't talk about it. I just can't." Her mind raced. In addition to having her followed, he'd implied the baby wasn't his. If it hadn't been so insulting she might've laughed. Except nothing about this was funny. She'd married an egotistical, sadistic asshole. How had she not seen that? Had she been so desperate to be married that she'd failed to notice he was a heartless bastard? The wedding had been only six months ago, but it might as well have been years, for she simply couldn't remember for the life of her why she'd ever thought she loved him.

The queasiness returned with a sudden fury. She rolled down the window to let in the cool air, which helped to combat the nausea.

To his credit, Owen didn't say a word as he drove them to the Westin. Because it was one of the taller buildings in the city, she didn't have to tell him how to get there. As he grabbed their overnight bags from the trunk and checked them into the hotel, Laura tagged along like a docile child. Justin's ugly words about how she couldn't get by without a man in her life rang through her mind like a refrain from a song that got stuck on replay. Over and over and over again.

They rode the elevator to the sixth floor in the silence that followed them into the room. When she thought about the plans they'd made for this night, she again felt sick. She went over to the window and stared out at the city she'd called home for most of her life, seeing nothing but the look on Justin's face when he'd implied that the baby wasn't his.

If she were being honest with herself, she'd known about Justin's mean streak before she married him. She'd known he was capable of doing whatever it took to win on behalf of his clients and had cringed on more than one occasion when he'd laid out his trial strategy to her. "*You can't argue with results,*" he'd said proudly when she questioned his tactics. But until he'd aimed it at her, she'd truly had no idea how deep the mean ran or how low he would stoop to advance his agenda.

Owen came up behind her and rested his hands on her shoulders. "What can I do?"

"I...I need some time to myself." Her voice wavered, betraying the emotion she was trying so hard to contain. The last thing she wanted was to suck him into the vicious storm of her divorce.

His hands fell away from her shoulders, his disappointment palpable. "Sure. Whatever you need."

As she heard him moving around the room, she hated herself for dragging him on the emotional roller-coaster ride with her. He deserved so much better.

"I'll be back in a while," he said. The hotel door clicked shut behind him as he left the room.

Laura's legs gave out under her, and she slid down to the floor, still leaning against the big window with the panoramic view of the city. The baby chose that moment to deliver a resounding kick that broke open the floodgates. Tears spilled down her cheeks, and sobs shook her body.

Rattled by Laura's withdrawal, Owen took the elevator to the lobby. He wanted to go find Justin Newsome and beat the shit out of him. But because that wasn't an option, he withdrew the business card Frank McCarthy had slipped him before they left his house earlier and called the cell number Frank had scrawled on the back.

"What happened?" Frank asked when he answered.

"I have no idea. All I know is he said something that made her slap his face."

"Is that right? Well, good for her. She should've done that a long time ago, if you ask me. So what did he say?"

"That's the thing. She won't tell me. It's like she's folded into herself and shut me out. She's right there, but she's a million miles away. It's kind of scary, actually."

"Oh no. Damn it. That's what I was afraid of. She did the same thing when her mother died. Scared the hell out of me. She'd look at me and answer me when I asked her a direct question, but it was almost as if no one was home."

"Yes, that's it. Exactly. When I put my hands on her shoulders, I could tell she was trying not to recoil away from me."

"That, too," Frank said. "Same thing. She couldn't bear to be touched for weeks after Jo died."

"What do we do?" Owen asked with growing desperation.

"For one thing, it's time I had a talk with her *husband*. I'd promised her I'd stay out of it unless she asked me to get involved, but enough is enough."

"I agree. If you can get him to sign the divorce papers, I think that would help."

"I'll do what I can. In the meantime, you'll be with her?"

"Every minute that I can. She wanted some time to herself, so I came down to the lobby."

"Don't leave her alone too long."

"I won't."

"You love her, don't you?"

"Yes," Owen said, his voice gruff with emotion and fear and confusion. There was also relief to admit to someone—even her father—that he was in love with Laura. Sometime soon, he hoped he could tell her, too.

"Good." Frank sounded relieved. "Don't give up on her. She's going through a rough time right now, but we'll get her through this, and then you two can make some plans."

"I hope you're right." Based on what Owen had seen since they left the restaurant, he had good reason to fear that nothing was going to work out the way they'd planned.

"I'll do everything I can to make sure she gets what she wants," Frank said. "Will you head back to the island tomorrow?"

"Yes, we're on the ten-thirty boat. We're supposed to go to a party tomorrow night. But after this… I don't know if she'll be up for it."

"The island is good for her. It always has been. After my wife died, I was so out of my element with two grief-stricken kids on summer vacation. I had to get back to work, but I was torn, needing to be in two places at once, you know?"

"I can only imagine."

"When my brother and Linda offered to take them for the summer, I jumped at the chance to give them some stability and the distraction of five cousins who were about their same age. But I was frightened by Laura's withdrawal and reluctant to leave her, even for a little while."

"What happened?"

"With Mac and Linda's support, I gave it two weeks and went out to the island to see them for the weekend. She wasn't quite back to her old self by any means, but she was better than she'd been. By the end of the summer, she'd come back to us almost all the way. Neither of my kids were ever quite the same after we lost their mom, but I never again saw the scary withdrawal that happened right after."

"Until now."

"When it happened the first time, the psychologist I consulted with told me it was her coping mechanism. By withdrawing into herself, she could keep the bad stuff out and postpone the emotional firestorm for that much longer." Frank paused for a moment and softened his tone. "Linda told me they all went out for ice cream one night toward the end of the summer. God bless Mac and Linda. They had seven kids underfoot, but they made that summer so fun for my kids. Anyway, apparently Laura dropped her cone on the ground outside the ice cream shop and broke down. Linda realized she was finally allowing the grief to come out and sent Mac home with the other kids. She and Laura sat on the seawall for two hours while my poor baby cried her heart out."

Owen ached as he pictured nine-year-old Laura coming to terms with her mother's death.

"It was a tough time for all of us, but she was a little better after the summer on the island."

"I'm glad you told me this. It makes me feel better to know that she's doing what she needs to do to get through this. I wish she wasn't shutting me out, though."

"Be patient. When she's ready, she'll let you back in."

"I can do that."

"Will you call me if you need me? If she needs me?"

"Of course."

"In the meantime, I'll do what I can to dispose of him."

Owen released an unsteady chuckle. "Legally, I presume."

"Unfortunately, yes."

"It was really great to meet you, sir. Laura talks about you so fondly."

"That's nice to hear, but please call me Frank. I have a feeling we'll be seeing a lot of each other."

"I sure hope so."

Owen ended the call and forced himself to give her another half hour before he couldn't stay away any longer. He let himself into the room, which was dark and quiet. As his eyes adjusted to the darkness he saw her curled up on the bed.

"Laura?" he said in a whisper.

When she didn't reply, he hoped it was because she was asleep. He pulled the throw blanket from the foot of the bed and spread it over her. Feeling weary but wired at the same time, he took a shower and shaved. Then he stretched out on the bed next to her, wanting to be nearby if she needed him during the night.

It took him a long time to fall asleep.

CHAPTER 14

Carolina knew it was probably wrong to be so fascinated by a much younger man. But listening to Seamus tell her about his childhood in Ireland, his parents, the brothers he'd caused such mischief with and the grandmother who'd done her best to set him straight, she was utterly captivated.

"I'm sorry," he said. "I'm going on and on, and you're probably bored stiff."

"On the contrary. I love to listen to your stories. And that brogue…" She fanned herself. "Lovely."

His entire face flushed with heat, and he became very interested in watching the flames dance in the fireplace.

"What're you thinking about?"

He shook his head, letting her know he didn't want to say.

"*Now*, you're going to hold out on me? After I heard about the frog you put in the nun's habit? What could be worse than that?"

He let out an inarticulate grunt, got up, gathered their dishes and headed for the kitchen.

Perplexed, Carolina went to help with the dishes.

"That's okay," he said when she headed for the sink. "I've got it."

"Let me help."

"I said I've got it."

Surprised by his sharp tone, she took a step back and put up her hands in surrender. "Sorry."

"No, Jesus, I'm sorry. I, uh…" He looked positively dumbfounded.

Confused, Carolina moved toward him, drawn by an attraction stronger than she'd experienced in a very long time.

"Please, don't," he said, stopping her progression with a pleading look.

"Did I do something wrong?"

"God, no," he said with an ironic laugh. "It's not you. It's me."

Her brows knitted with consternation. She'd never seen him so undone. He was usually all cool confidence and cocky charm. "What is?"

"You…" He swallowed hard. "You're beautiful."

Of all the things she'd expected him to say, that hadn't been one of them. Her entire body heated as the realization registered. He was interested in her. As a woman. *Oh my…*"Thank you," she was finally able to say. "That's very sweet of you to say."

"'Tis the truth," he said, pulling up the sleeves of his shirt to do the dishes. He seemed almost angry as he washed and rinsed the bowls and silverware, banging around the kitchen with barely contained energy vibrating off his muscular frame.

"Seamus."

He spun around, seeming almost surprised to see her still standing there. "Yes?"

"Come here."

"No, thank you. I don't think that would be a good idea."

She held out a hand to him. "Please?"

He eyed her hand as if it was a stick of dynamite before he reluctantly reached out to fold his hand around hers.

Carolina had no idea what she was doing when she led him into the living room and urged him to join her on the love seat in front of the fire. Without releasing his hand, she compelled him to meet her gaze. "Talk to me. What's going on?"

He released a sound that fell somewhere between a groan and a laugh. "You're the last person I can talk to about this. No, wait, that's not true. *Joe* would be the last person I could talk to about this. In fact, if he knew the thoughts I've been having about his dear, sweet mum, he'd cut me up and feed me to the sharks."

Carolina's mouth fell open. She quickly closed it and tried to process what he'd said. "You've been having...*thoughts*... About me?"

Looking sheepish and maybe ashamed, he gave a brief nod.

"For how long?"

"How long ago did we first meet?"

"You're kidding."

"I'd never joke about something like this," he said, clearly offended by the insinuation.

"I'm sorry. I didn't mean to imply that you were joking. I'm surprised. That's all."

He tried to tug his hand free, but she wouldn't let go. "Let's forget about it," he said. "I never planned to say anything about it."

"Why not?"

Staring at her as if she were crazy, he said, "Because! For one thing, your son would *kill* me. I like my life—and my job. He trusted me to run his company, and I take that very seriously. He shouldn't have to be worried about his employee having impure thoughts about his mother."

The more agitated he got, the thicker his brogue became. He was sexy as hell, and she wanted him more than she'd wanted any man since she lost her husband. Right in that moment, it didn't matter that he was eighteen years younger than her or that he worked for her son. For once, she wasn't thinking of Joe or anyone other than the sweet, sexy man sitting beside her.

"Well, say something already," he said with a huff that nearly made her laugh.

Rather than speak, she caressed his face.

He sucked in a sharp, deep breath and tried to turn his face away. "Miz Cantrell..."

"I think," she said as she dragged her fingers lightly along his whisker-roughened jaw, "that you should probably call me Carolina, or I'll feel like a dirty old woman."

"No. I couldn't." He took hold of her wandering hand. "This can't happen."

"Why?"

"Joe would—"

"Joe is my son, and I love him dearly, but I don't need his approval."

"I do. He's given me a wonderful opportunity, and I wouldn't do anything to disappoint him."

It was a matter of honor to him, she realized, and how could she not respect that? "Of course," she said, withdrawing her hand. "I apologize."

"That's it?" he asked with a glint of devil in his eye and a healthy dose of disappointment. "You're giving up, just like that?"

Carolina stared at him, uncertain of what he meant. "But you said—"

"Don't listen to me. I'm full of blarney. Everyone knows it."

"You're confusing me."

"Am I? Let me be clear then: You're the sexiest woman I've ever met, and I've wanted you fiercely since the first time I laid eyes on you." He framed her face with his hands and brushed a light kiss over her suddenly sensitive lips. "You'll tell him I tried to be upstanding, won't you?"

Astounded and aroused and amused and filled with anticipation, Carolina managed a nod. "I'll tell him you didn't stand a chance against his cougar mother."

That made Seamus laugh—hard. His green eyes were still dancing with amusement when he kissed her again, with much more intent this time. "I can't believe this is happening," he whispered against her lips. "I've imagined it so many times."

"I didn't know. You never said..."

He focused his attention on her neck, sending a torrent of sensation zipping through her. "I tried to resist. I swear I did."

Before she knew what was happening he had them off the small sofa and was stretched out over her on the floor. The firelight cast a warm, cozy glow over them as they devoured each other with hungry eyes.

"Has there been anyone else?" he asked.

Carolina knew he meant since her husband. She shook her head. "Occasional dates, but no one I cared enough about to sleep with."

"Ah, my poor lass," he whispered as he kissed her again. "It's been such a long, lonely time for you. I have no right to want you the way I do."

"Why do you say that?"

"My thoughts about you are downright indecent."

Ridiculously flattered, Carolina linked her hands around his neck. "Is that so?"

Nodding, he lowered his head for another soft, seductive kiss.

"Seamus?"

"Hmmm?" He was sprinkling kisses on her face with immaculate attention to detail.

"If we do...*this*..."

That drew a chuckle from him.

"I want you to know..."

"What, love?"

"It can't be anything more."

He stopped short and stared down at her, his eyes heated and intense. "Why do you say that?"

"You're so young," she said, sliding her hands over his shoulders. "Your whole life is in front of you. You'll want a family and children—"

He stopped her with another kiss, this one deep and hot. "Don't tell me what I want," he said softly but firmly. "I'm a grown man who knows himself as well as it's possible to know oneself."

Surprised by the kiss as much as what he'd said, she fumbled to find the words.

Before she could say anything, though, he was kissing her neck and she was squirming beneath him, needing more. Much, much more.

"And what I want," he said, the sweep of his breath on her sensitive skin causing goose bumps to erupt on her arms and legs, "what I've wanted since the first time I saw you, is this." He settled between her legs, pushing the hard column of his substantial erection into her heated core.

Carolina gasped and arched into him.

Suddenly, he stopped, pulled away from her and stood. He extended his hand to help her up. "There's a nice, soft bed in the other room. Will you come with me, lovely Carolina?"

She stared at that outstretched hand as all the many reasons this might be a very bad idea fled from her mind. Linking her fingers with his, she let him lead her from the room. When he took her past her son's bedroom and into the guest room, the gesture had Carolina realizing with crystal clarity that she could very easily fall in love with this kind, thoughtful, charming, *sexy* Irishman—and that would probably be a disaster for both of them.

Evan woke to relentless banging on the door. Grace was long gone to work, and he was in no rush to get up, so he snuggled in deeper to the pillow, hoping whoever it was would take the hint and go away.

More pounding. "I know you're in there, boy. Open up!"

Ned? What the hell?

Evan dragged himself out of bed, pulled on a pair of boxers and ran his fingers through his unruly hair as he made his way to the door and tugged it open to face his father's best friend.

Ned scowled at him. "Waddaya doin' still in bed at ten o'clock?" He wore a ratty old sweater over faded jeans and boat shoes held together with duct tape. To look at him, you'd never know he was one of the wealthiest men on the island. His mane of white hair had been somewhat tamed, and his blue eyes were sharp as he took in Evan's disheveled appearance.

"I was up late last night." Evan decided it was better not to think about what he'd been doing with Grace until the wee hours, or he might embarrass himself. "What're you doing here?"

"I wanna talk to ya." Carrying a tray with two cups of coffee and a white bag, Ned pushed past him into the loft. "Put some pants on, fer Christ's sake."

"Come in, why doncha?" Evan said, annoyed and amused at the same time.

"Don't mind if I do."

Evan closed the door, reached for a pair of discarded jeans on the floor and put them on, leaving the button undone. He gratefully accepted the coffee Ned handed him and took a sip. "Mmm, that's good."

"Cream and two sugars, right?"

"You got it." His stomach growled. "What's in the bag?"

"Blueberry muffins. I sure do miss my marina donuts in the off-season."

"I'm sure your heart doesn't miss them."

"My heart is in perfect working order."

"Is that Francine's doing?" Evan asked with a grin.

Ned blushed like a schoolboy. "That ain't none a yer damned business."

Evan hooted with laughter at Ned's embarrassment. "When are you two going to make it official?"

At that, Ned's expression darkened. "We can't get rid of her dirtbag ex-husband. He's demanding to spend time with the girls. Tiffany did it, but Maddie ain't up fer it, and we got no intention of forcing her. Far as we're concerned, it's already official."

"Sorry to hear that about the ex. He sounds like a real winner."

"Don't get me started."

Evan broke the top off the still-warm muffin and devoured it in two big bites. "To what do I owe the honor of this visit?"

"I got a business proposition fer ya."

"Is that right?"

"Yep. I'm gettin' sick of watchin' ya mope around waitin' fer news from Nashville."

Evan sat up straighter. "Now, wait a second—"

"Hear me out, boy," Ned said in a gentler tone. "It's hard on all of us watchin' ya suffer. Yer mama and daddy are worried aboutcha, yer brothers, Grace."

"I don't want anyone worried about me," Evan said, losing interest in the muffin.

"Too late." Ned put down his coffee and leaned in, elbows propped on knees. "Here's what I think we oughta do about it. I think we oughta open our own recording studio right here on the island."

Flabbergasted, Evan stared at the older man who'd been like a second father to him. "You wanna run that by me one more time?"

"You and Owen, ya know a lotta people in the business, people like the two of ya who've been performing for years but never caught a break. I've been readin' about a coupla singers who got real lucky posting their stuff to that iMusic and You Movie and found an audience."

Evan held back a laugh as Ned butchered the names of the sites.

"So I gets to thinkin', why can't the boys do that right here? We set up the studio, you guys bring in the talent, record yer own stuff and post it out there fer people ta buy."

Evan continued to stare at the older man as if he'd lost his mind. "Do you have any idea how much it costs to set up a recording studio?"

"About two hundred fifty grand or so, if my research is correct."

"And where do you propose I get two hundred fifty grand to open this so-called recording studio?"

"I'll give it to ya."

"*What?* Have you totally lost what's left of your mind? You can't give me a quarter of a million bucks like it's lunch money."

"Why not? Yer gonna get it after I'm gone, so why can't I give it to ya now, when ya need some direction in yer life, and I can watcha make somethin' of it?"

"Get it when you're gone? What does that mean?"

"Who do ya think my heirs are, ya nitwit? I ain't got no kids of my own. So you, yer brothers, yer sister and now Francine, Maddie and Tiffany will get it all. And there's a lot to get." He shrugged self-consciously. "This is somethin' I wanna do. It's somethin' I think you and Owen can make a go of. It'd keep ya here on the island with yer lady—where I think ya wanna be—and it would keep ya off the stage, where ya don't wanna be."

Evan had no idea what to say. How did Ned have this all figured out when Evan couldn't even get himself out of bed in the morning? And how the hell did he know about the stage fright? Evan had told only Grace about that, and she'd never repeat it. He and his siblings had long suspected the guy was psychic or something, and this was further proof. "I, um, have no idea what's involved with recording music. I do the singing."

"Doncha know people who do? Couldn't ya get 'em out here to teach ya?"

Running his fingers through his hair, Evan got up to pace the small kitchen.

"Well, doncha?"

"Yeah, I suppose I do."

"And doncha know all kinds of singers and musicians who never got a break who might be interested in tryin' something new?"

Evan nodded as a spark of interest and excitement began to take root inside him.

"Y'all could create one of them"—Ned waved his hand as he searched for the term—"artist communities right here on the island."

"I don't know, Ned. You're talking about a huge investment of time."

"And do ya got so many better things to do at the moment?"

Hands on his hips, Evan met Ned's challenging gaze.

"Well, do ya?"

"No."

"All right, then."

"I can't take that kind of money from you."

"Ya ain't *takin'* it. Think of it as an investment. We'll be partners. I'll be silent, of course."

Evan raised an eyebrow.

"What? I *will* be silent."

"I'll believe that when I see it."

"Believe whatcha want. If yer interested in this, I'll finance it. If you ain't interested, no harm, no foul."

"I'll need to talk to Owen."

"I'd expect ya would."

"Can I get back to you?"

"I ain't going nowhere." Ned got up and put his empty coffee cup in the trash.

"Ned?"

"Yeah?"

"Thank you. I'm truly overwhelmed that you would've given this so much thought and come up with such an…*intriguing*…idea."

Ned patted Evan's face affectionately. "I wanna see ya back on track, boy. It ain't nothin'."

"Yes, it is."

Ned shrugged off the praise. "Let me know whatcha decide."

Evan walked him to the door. "I will." He watched Ned bound down the stairs with the pep of a man half his age. He drove off in his cab with a toot and a wave.

Evan closed the door and leaned back against it, his heart racing with adrenaline and excitement and a healthy dose of skepticism that kept him from getting too far ahead of himself. Could they really make something like this work?

Pushing off the door, he headed for the shower, anxious to get cleaned up and go find Grace. He needed to know what she thought of the idea before he did anything else.

Laura awoke with a start. She'd been dreaming about falling, spinning through space with nothing to break her fall. All at once, she became aware that she was sleeping in Owen's arms. His familiar scent and the steady beat of his heart under her ear calmed and soothed her. Then she remembered what had happened the night before, and she started to pull away from him.

"Stay," he whispered. "Just for a minute."

Reluctantly, Laura returned her head to his chest but couldn't seem to relax into his embrace the way she usually did. At what point during the night had she moved across the bed to him? Justin was right. She couldn't do anything by herself. Even sleep. The thought disgusted her.

Owen ran his hand over her back in a soothing rhythm. "What're you thinking about, Princess?"

The nickname she'd once loved now rankled. "Nothing."

"Come on. I know better than that. You're always thinking about something."

Laura wished that wasn't the case. She wanted to turn off her brain and forget about the ugly encounter with Justin. The desire to unsubscribe from her thoughts reminded her of the weeks after her mother died when she'd been desperate to stop the merry-go-round of painful memories. She'd learned then that there was no way around these things, only straight through them to the other side, as painful as that might be.

"I'm sorry about last night," she finally said. "I totally punched out on you."

"Don't be sorry, honey. I don't want you to worry about me. Let's focus on what you need right now, okay?"

"You're too good to me."

"We're good to each other. That's what it's all about."

His kind words brought tears to her eyes. She closed them, trying to contain the flood.

"Whatever he said to you," Owen continued in a soft, soothing tone, "it doesn't matter. *He* doesn't matter and neither do his opinions. If you let him get to you, he wins."

"I know." She brushed at the dampness on her face. "I need to call my dad. He'll be wondering what happened."

He nudged her hand out of the way and finished the cleanup job for her. "I talked to him last night. He said to tell you to call whenever you're ready."

"Thank you for thinking of that."

"No problem." Owen's lips were soft against her forehead. "Do you want to talk about it? Maybe if you let it out, you can let it go."

Laura didn't want to talk about it—now or ever—but Owen had been so good and so patient. She couldn't allow her mess to cause him unnecessary pain. "He… He implied the baby wasn't his."

Owen's entire body went rigid. "*What?* I hope that's when you smacked him."

Laura couldn't help but laugh. "You saw that, huh?"

"Um, the whole place saw it—and heard it."

"Good. It was the least of what he deserved."

"What an awful thing to say. I'm sorry you had to hear that, honey."

"He had me followed. He knew all about the baby, the island, the hotel. And you."

"Shit." He released a long, deep breath. "Will that screw up the divorce?"

"No more than it already is. He made all sorts of threats and demands until I mentioned my father would make his life a living hell if he didn't sign the papers. That seemed to get his attention."

"Whatever it takes."

"It's pathetic."

"What is?"

"I am. I'm thirty-one years old and still relying on my dad to get me out of scrapes."

"This isn't your garden-variety scrape, and there's nothing wrong with taking advantage of your connections to solve a problem. That's what anyone would do."

"I guess." She wriggled free of his embrace and sat up, propping the pillows behind her.

Lying on his side, Owen rested his head on his upturned hand and studied her. "What else?"

"That was it."

"No, it wasn't."

Glancing at him, she found gray eyes watching her keenly. "What do you mean?"

"I think he said some other stuff that has you suddenly thinking our relationship is a bad idea."

Stricken by his insight, Laura looked away from him.

"Ah-ha, just as I suspected." He surprised her when he sprang to his knees, straddled her legs and reached for her hands. "Tell me."

Laura bit her lip and shook her head.

With his hands on her face, he compelled her to meet his gaze. "Did I ever mention I was so good at getting secrets out of my brothers and sisters that they got together and made a pact to never lie to me, because the punishment wasn't worth it?"

A hint of a smile found its way to her lips. "No, I don't think you mentioned that."

"I should warn you that my tactics are underhanded and dirty and involve tickling and other forms of torture."

"That sounds quite frightening."

"My skills are not to be trifled with. It would be easier—especially for you—if you tell me what I want to know so I don't have to get rough with you."

Knowing he never would, knowing she was safer with him than she'd ever been with any man, Laura looked up at him. "While I'm not one to give in to intimidation tactics, I do have the baby to think about."

"That's right. So you'd better start talking."

Reluctantly, Laura said, "He implied I can't function without a man in my life."

Owen was so startled he went completely still. "Wanna run that by me one more time?"

"In a way, he's right. I've always had boyfriends. Before him, I lived with a guy for a couple of years. Before that, I lived with my dad."

"You're a gorgeous, sexy, adorable woman. It's no surprise to me that you had a lot of boyfriends." Pausing, he added, "And why does knowing that make me insanely jealous?" He looked away from her, as if contemplating the question, before he returned his attention to her. "So let me get this straight… Because your douchebag soon-to-be-ex-husband implied that you can't get by without a man in your life, you're thinking you should take a step back from me to prove something to him. Do I have that right?"

"Something like that," she said sheepishly.

"You're a dope."

"Hey!" She never imagined she'd feel so lighthearted this morning after what had transpired the night before. Leave it to Owen.

"Listen to me." He glared down at her. "Are you listening?"

"Do I have any choice?" she asked, amused by him.

He shook his head. "You are, without a doubt, the strongest, ablest, sexiest, cleverest, funniest, *sexiest*—did I mention sexiest—woman I've ever met in my life. There is nothing, absolutely *nothing*, you couldn't do or handle on your own if you had to. It's no sign of weakness that you choose to have people you care about in your life. Anyone who implies otherwise does so because *his* life is empty and meaningless, and he knows what a treasure he's losing."

Even though she was moved by his heartfelt words, Laura said, "You don't have to say that stuff to make me feel better."

"If you imply I'm blowing smoke up your skirt, you'll make me mad."

The sinister scowl he attempted made her laugh.

Owen bent to kiss her neck, drawing a surprised gasp from her. "We had some big plans for this hotel room."

"I'm sorry I messed things up."

"You didn't mess anything up."

As his lips left a trail of heat on her neck, Laura arched into him, drawing him down to her. Filled with desire for him, it occurred to her that she'd intended to push him away. Leave it to him to not let her get away with that. Maybe Justin was right. Maybe she didn't know how to be without a man. While that might be true, it was becoming more impossible by the day to imagine her life without *this* man.

CHAPTER 15

Owen felt her yield beneath him and was finally able to take a deep breath. She'd planned to push him away because that asshole Justin had taken a crack at her. Owen couldn't let her do it. She meant too much to him to let anything come between them, especially a guy who'd basically called his wife a slut.

He knew he should stop kissing her and let her up, but her skin was so soft and her natural fragrance so alluring. She was everything, *everything* he'd ever dreamed of and more. He wanted to tell her and show her what she'd come to mean to him. His lips moved from her neck to the V of her T-shirt, to the plump rise and fall of her breasts. He was driven by the need to cement their bond, to make her his in every way that mattered.

"Owen," she gasped when he found her nipple through the thin layer of cotton and rolled it between his lips. Her fingers in his hair tightened. "Owen, wait..."

Summoning every bit of control he could muster, he looked up at her. "What, honey?"

"I just... I need..."

"You're not ready."

As she shook her head, her bright blue eyes shimmered with tears. "I want to be, but I'm still trying to process it all."

"I'm sorry. I'm an insensitive clod. You've been through a major ordeal, and all I'm thinking about—"

She stroked his hair and then his face. "I'm thinking about it, too. Believe me. When it happens, I want it to be the right time for us. I don't want it to be about you comforting me. Does that make sense?"

"Of course it does, and you're right." He touched his lips to hers. "Absolutely right."

She seemed to sag in relief that he understood.

He gathered her close to him and knew his own relief when her arms encircled him.

They stayed like that for a long time before he reluctantly released her. "Let's grab showers and breakfast and head for the ferry. Maybe we can get back to the island a little sooner than planned."

"That sounds good."

"I'm telling you now, though, if it's as rough as it was yesterday, we're not going. Got me?"

"I gotcha."

"Good."

As he headed for the shower, the lingering fear that she might succeed in pushing him away after all stayed with him. *No*, he thought. *I won't let that happen*. He'd wait it out until she was ready, and then he'd tell her—and show her—how much he loved her.

Carolina woke with strong arms wrapped around her from behind and a muscular, hairy leg between both of hers. She wanted to purr like a kitten—a very satisfied kitten. It'd been so long since she'd been in bed with a man that she'd forgotten how amazing it could be. And she'd never suspected any man could ever make her feel the way her Pete had.

Seamus's hand moved from her belly to cup her breast, rolling her nipple between his fingers.

Carolina let out a moan and pushed back against his erection. How was it possible, after the night they'd shared, that she wanted him again? She started to turn toward him, but he stopped her.

"Stay," he said gruffly. "Like this." He drew her leg up over his hip, and as he continued to play with her nipple, the blunt head of his cock nudged at her tender opening. "Are you sore, love?"

"No," she said breathless with anticipation. The position was new to her. And now that she knew the ecstasy they were capable of achieving together, she'd never admit to a tiny bit of soreness.

His hand shifted from her breast, coasting slowly over her belly, down to where they were joined by the most tenuous of connections.

Carolina thought she'd go mad as he slowly rocked his hips, entering her in small increments as his fingers found the heart of her desire. Her skin heated, her breath caught. She pushed back against him, seeking deeper penetration, but he wouldn't be rushed.

"Easy, love," he whispered against the tingling skin on her neck. "Nice and easy."

He kept up steady pressure on her clitoris as he rocked into her, deeper with each stroke. Only his harsh breathing told her this slow seduction was affecting him every bit as much as it was affecting her. By the time he smoothly shifted them so she was on her knees and he was entering her fully from behind, Carolina was so primed, she exploded in the midst of his first deep thrust.

Seamus rode out her climax and continued to pump into her.

She couldn't believe it when she came again. This time he went with her, straining against her until they fell together in a boneless, gasping heap on the bed.

"Lord, woman," he said, his lips vibrating against her back. "You're amazing."

Carolina, who was focusing on drawing air into her lungs, couldn't seem to form a coherent thought, the same reaction she'd had the other three times. His gifted hands had wrought astonishing reactions, reactions she wouldn't have thought she was still capable of at this age. The pulsing aftershocks in the place where they were joined were proof that she was more than capable, which was a revelation in and of itself.

Floating on a cloud of contentment and satisfaction, Carolina allowed herself to doze for a few minutes. And then she'd have to drag herself out of this heavenly bed and go home to the island with the memories of a one-night interlude with a sexy Irishman to sustain her during the long, cold winter.

She woke a short time later when her cell phone rang in the kitchen.

Seamus kissed her shoulder, finally withdrew from her and got up. "Don't move. I'll grab it for ya, love."

Without his body to warm her, Carolina dove deeper into the flannel sheets and down comforter she'd helped Joe choose for his guest room. She was on her way back to sleep when Seamus returned.

"It was Joe. I didn't get there in time."

At the mention of her son's name, Carolina was instantly awake and instantly guilty. She sat up and tucked the covers under her arms to cover her breasts. She took the phone from Seamus without meeting his gaze but let her eyes travel over his finely muscled chest, rippling abs and below to—

The phone rang again, and Carolina's face burned with embarrassment.

"I'll make some coffee while you talk to your boy." He walked out of the room, treating her to a view of his finely shaped posterior, which bore the scratches she'd inflicted the night before.

Horrified by the proof of the fiery passion they'd shared, she cleared her throat, hoping she wouldn't sound guilty and suspicious while talking to her son. "Hi, honey," she said, smoothing the comforter with her free hand.

"Hey, where were you?"

"I didn't hear the phone," she said, swallowing the huge lump that suddenly formed in her throat.

"Did you make it to the island?"

"Not exactly." She was sick with guilt. What in the world had she been thinking going to bed with a man only two years older than her son? Somewhere across the ocean in Ireland was the mother who'd given birth to Seamus, and Carolina couldn't help but wonder what she'd have to say about what her son had been up to during the night.

"Oh no?" Joe said. "What happened?"

"The weather was awful. Seamus called off the ferries after the three-thirty boat from the island had a particularly rough crossing." She nearly choked on the name of the man she'd taken as a lover, the man who worked for her son. *What the hell was I thinking?*

"Sounds like a good call. So where'd you stay last night?"

When her eyes burned with tears, she closed them. "In your guest room."

"Everything all right, Mom? You sound kinda funny."

Alarmed, Carolina said, "Oh, sure, everything's fine."

"I hope Seamus took good care of you."

Carolina's entire body heated when she thought of how well Seamus had taken care of her. "Yes, of course he did." She very nearly choked on the words. "He was very...hospitable." Cringing, she closed her eyes. Desperate to get the focus off her, she said, "So, what's going on?"

"Well, it turns out you were right. Janey's pregnant. Congratulations, Grandma."

As the word "grandma" registered, Seamus appeared in the doorway, still naked as the day he was born. He leaned against the doorframe, sipping a mug of coffee and watching her intently.

"Mom? Are you there?"

"Yes, honey, that's wonderful news! How did Janey take it?"

"Better than expected. It probably helped that I was clearly elated over it."

Forcing her eyes off the hunk of man in the doorway, Carolina pictured her son's handsome face and forced herself to focus on the significant conversation. She imagined his elation over the baby was similar to his sheer joy on the day he married the love of his life. "I'm so happy for both of you. You'll be wonderful parents."

"Thanks. We're excited, to say the least."

"I'll bet you are. I want to hear all about it—every detail."

"You got it. We're going to the doctor next week to find out how far along she is, due dates. That kind of stuff."

"I can't wait to hear."

"Me, too. So what time are you heading to the island?"

"I guess that depends on whether the ferries are running."

Seamus gave a thumbs-up to let her know he'd already checked, and they were good to go.

"Text me when you get there," Joe said.

"I will. Give Janey my love, and tell her congratulations from me."

"Will do. Talk to you soon."

"Love you."

"You, too."

Carolina ended the call and bobbled the phone between her hands. She was filled with nerves and morning-after regret.

Seamus came to sit next to her on the bed and handed her the mug.

Grateful for the distraction and the badly needed caffeine, Carolina tried to focus on the coffee—anything to keep her eyes off the tempting sight of him.

"I take it congratulations are in order." His eyes sparkled with mirth. "Grandma."

She choked on the coffee.

He took the mug from her, put it on the bedside table and patted her back. "Okay?"

Nodding, she shrugged off his embrace, wishing he would catch the hint and take his big, naked body elsewhere so she could get up and grab a shower. Even after what they'd shared during the night, she wasn't prepared to prance around naked in front of him.

Apparently, he had no such hang-ups, but he was eighteen years younger. Her eyes were drawn to the penis that hung large between his legs even when he wasn't aroused. Remembering the first time he'd pushed that big member slowly into her tight channel made her mouth water with desire. She tore her gaze off that part of him and sought a safer place to plant her eyes.

When she looked up, she found him watching her carefully, waiting for her to make eye contact. Damned if he didn't seem amused over her visual tour of his body.

"What's got you all worked up, my love?"

"I'm not your love. Don't say that."

He curled a lock of her hair around his finger and brought it to his nose. "I sure would like you to be."

"That's not going to happen! Did you hear what my son just told me? I'm going to be a *grandmother*!"

He had the audacity to laugh! He actually *laughed*!

"What the hell is so funny?"

"You are," he said, leaning in to nibble on her neck. "Congratulations, by the way. Sexiest grandma I ever met."

She swatted at him, but that didn't deter him. "Stop that! Have you heard a word I've said?"

"Uh-huh." The neck nibbling continued as if she hadn't spoken. "I heard every. Single. Word." He punctuated his words with more kisses and the slide of his tongue over her sensitized skin. "And every moan and sigh and scream, too."

Mortified by the reminder of how completely she'd come apart in his arms, Carolina tried to push him away, but he wouldn't be pushed. "Please, Seamus. I enjoyed last night. I really did. But I can't do this. I just can't."

He tugged the covers free of the iron grip she had on them, exposing her breasts. Her nipples reacted instantly to the cool air and the heated promise in his gaze. His attention shifted from her neck to her chest to the valley between her breasts. While his lips were busy on the front of her, his hands slid down her back to cup her ass and arrange her under him. The man, she'd discovered during the night, was a master multi-tasker.

"Did you hear what I said?" she asked, breathless from the tug of his lips on her tender nipple.

"I heard ya, love."

"Then why—"

He sucked hard and stole the words right off her lips.

Her back arched as her body betrayed her yet again. Before she had a chance to figure out how she'd so thoroughly lost control of the conversation, her fingers were buried in his hair to hold his head to her chest, and her legs were wrapped around his hips as he made love to her yet again.

By the time he finally let her out of bed to take a shower an hour later, Carolina was royally screwed—in every possible way.

Maddie made chocolate-chip muffins and coffee in preparation for her meeting with the ladies who'd agreed to help plan the Thanksgiving dinner to benefit the island's summer employees. She used to be one of the struggling year-round residents who relied on the tourists for income, before Mac McCarthy came along and changed her life in every possible way. Now that her fortunes had improved so dramatically, she was anxious to give something back to the people she'd once worked and commiserated with when times were tough.

Her sister Tiffany came through the sliding door from the deck a few minutes later. Maddie had asked her to come early because she was anxious to talk to her. Tiffany hadn't been herself in recent weeks, and Maddie was concerned about her baby sister.

"Hey," Tiffany said.

"Hi, honey." Maddie crossed the big, open great room to greet her sister with a hug and kiss. "How are you?"

"Good." Tiffany tossed her denim jacket on a chair. "Busy."

"How's the store coming along?"

"Fine."

Maddie poured coffee for both of them and slid onto a barstool next to Tiffany. "When do I get a sneak peek?"

"When it's ready," Tiffany said, as she always did when Maddie asked about the store. She was dying of curiosity to see what Tiffany was doing with the former location of Abby's Attic, but so far Tiffany had kept the details to herself.

"How's Ashleigh liking preschool?"

"She loves it as you well know. You see her every day when you drop off Thomas."

"They both love it." Maddie stirred some cream into her coffee. "So, have you seen Dad?" Their father had recently resurfaced more than thirty years after he left his family on the island and never looked back.

"Once. He said he'd call, but I haven't heard from him. What about you?"

"He's left me a couple of messages, but I'm not ready to talk to him. I hate that I'm the only thing standing between Mom and Ned getting married—"

"She doesn't expect you to do anything you don't want to do. She and Ned seem perfectly thrilled to be living together."

"Yeah, they do."

Tiffany reached for one of the muffins and pulled the top off.

"I'm worried about you," Maddie said. "You've been very distant lately."

"Have I?"

"What's going on, Tiff? You know there's nothing you can't tell me."

Tiffany focused on her coffee and muffin for so long, Maddie suspected she wasn't going to say anything. "Something happened." The words seemed to burst out of her in a rush of air and relief.

Instantly on alert, Maddie said, "What?"

"Blaine."

"*Ohhhhh*," Maddie said, instantly relieved and desperately curious. Since Blaine Taylor was the island's police chief and Mac's good friend, Maddie knew that whatever happened had most likely been a good thing. "Well? Are you going to tell me?"

Tiffany's face turned bright red. "We...um, well... We kinda kissed. And stuff."

Maddie, who had never before seen her fearless sister blush, stared at her, astounded. "What kind of stuff?"

"The good kind of stuff, but not *the* stuff. If you know what I mean."

"Huh," Maddie said, still nearly speechless. "When was this?"

"A while ago. Early September."

"Why didn't you tell me?"

"I haven't told anyone."

"So, like, did you run into him or something?"

"Or something. I got arrested."

"*What?*"

Tiffany held up a hand to keep Maddie in her seat. "It was no big deal. I snuck into Jim's place, wanting to talk to him, and he accused me of breaking and entering."

"That bastard!"

"You don't know the half of it. Anyway, Blaine showed up and told Jim it doesn't count as B&E if the door is unlocked."

"Then how did you end up arrested?"

Tiffany averted her gaze, looking ashamed. "I might've slashed the tires on Jim's precious Mercedes on the way in."

Maddie rocked with laughter. "Oh, that must've pissed him off!"

"Seriously. It was well worth getting arrested."

"Why wasn't any of this in the paper?"

"I guess Blaine decided not to file a report. He did me a huge favor."

"Good for him." Maddie had always liked the sexy policeman, but now she *really* liked him. "So when did the kissing—and stuff—happen?"

"When he drove me home."

"Oh."

"It was…"

Maddie reached for Tiffany's hand and was shocked to find it freezing. She rubbed it between both of hers. "What, honey?"

"*Insane.*"

"In what way?"

"It was like…we were possessed or something. He made me. . you know… in my kitchen."

"Oh," Maddie said, fanning herself. "Wow."

"Yeah." Tiffany focused intently on her muffin.

"So did you…return the favor?"

She shook her head. "Unfortunately, he got called away to an accident before I could. I haven't seen him since."

Hearing that, Maddie experienced a profound sense of disappointment, as if she'd been the one to have an explosive encounter with a man she'd never seen again.

"It's just as well," Tiffany said with a shrug. "Nothing good could come of that in the midst of my ugly divorce. He'd be crazy to want to be involved with me right now."

"Sweetie," Maddie said, clutching Tiffany's hand, "he'd be crazy *not* to want you. Look at you! You're a walking, talking sex kitten." Maddie had always envied her sister's lean, lithe dancer's body and silky dark hair. "I've seen how he looks at you like a hungry tiger."

"Meow," Tiffany said with a weak smile.

Maddie laughed. "It's not that he doesn't want you."

"Then why haven't I heard from him since the most explosive sexual-encounter-in-which-no-one-actually-had-sex of my life?"

"Could be anything, but I doubt it's because he doesn't want you. He was as into it as you were, right?"

"Ah yeah. You could say that."

"Do you want me to have Mac talk to him and see if he can gather some intel?"

"God, no! Jesus, don't breathe a *word* of this to Mac. I'd never be able to look at him again. Promise me!"

"I promise, but I hate to tell you Mac is aware that you've had sex."

"He doesn't need to know I had near-sex with his friend."

"Relax. I won't say anything if you don't want me to."

"I don't."

Maddie sipped at her coffee as she studied her sister.

"Why are you staring at me?"

"I'm wondering why you haven't sought him out. It's not like you to hold back when you want something."

"Because."

"Oh, okay. I see now."

"Stop being a smart ass!"

"Can't help it. It's in our DNA."

"I can't go chasing after him. The whole thing was too…intense. I was a disaster for days afterward."

"Why, honey? Was he rough with you?"

Tiffany blushed again. "Kinda, but I loved it."

"So then why were you upset?"

"Because! If I'd stayed with Jim, I would've lived the whole rest of my life without knowing *that* is possible. I had no idea. If that's what you have with Mac, I'm in awe—and envy."

"Oh, baby, come here." Maddie gathered her sister into a tight hug. "That's what I want for you—the kind of all-consuming passion that you forget your own name in the midst of it."

"Is it like that for you guys?" Tiffany asked, her voice muffled by Maddie's hair.

"Yeah."

"*Every* time?"

"Uh-huh," Maddie said, laughing.

"How do you *survive* it?"

Maddie released her sister but kept her hands on Tiffany's shoulders. "I don't just survive it, I *crave* it." She smoothed Tiffany's hair back from her face. "There's no chance of anything else happening with Blaine?"

"Not right now. Not with the divorce moving so painfully slow."

"I thought Dan Torrington was helping you with that."

"He is, but Jim is fighting every step of the way. It's draining. Dan suggested arbitration. Apparently, it's quicker than waiting on the courts, but Jim is fighting that, too."

"I'm sorry it's such an ordeal."

"It's fine," Tiffany said with a sweep of her hand. "At the end of it, I'll be free of him and have primary custody of Ashleigh. That's all I care about."

"I hope you'll also get a boatload of money that you richly deserve for putting his ass through law school while you worked two jobs—and carried his child."

"Dan is working on that, too. Naturally, Jim is fighting that part the hardest. He cares more about his goddamned money than he does about his own daughter."

"I know it seems hard to believe now when everything is so chaotic, but someday soon the divorce will be final, and you'll be free to do anything you want. Including our oh-so-sexy police chief."

Tiffany stuck her tongue out at her sister. "Very funny."

"You won't be laughing when you're naked and horizontal under him."

Tiffany shook her head and put her hands over her ears. "I can't even think of that, or I'm apt to spontaneously combust."

Maddie laughed at the tortured expression on her sister's face. "Mark my words, your day is coming. The two of you are going to incinerate the entire island when you finally get together."

"Whatever you say."

What Maddie was about to say was lost when Linda McCarthy came breezing through the sliding door. "Good morning, ladies. I brought chocolate-covered strawberries!"

"Do I have the best mother-in-law ever?" Maddie asked her sister. Once Linda had found out chocolate-covered strawberries were one of Maddie's favorite treats, she'd made them often for her daughter-in-law.

Knowing Linda had been anything but friendly to Maddie when she first started dating Mac, Tiffany rolled her eyes at Maddie when Linda looked away. "The best ever for sure."

"Did you hear that Sydney had the loveliest visit with Jenny out at the lighthouse?" Linda asked Maddie. "She's coming to the party at Luke and Syd's tonight."

"I did hear. Syd said Jenny is terrific." Maddie offered one of the strawberries to her sister. To Tiffany, she said, "Jenny lost her fiancé in the World Trade Center."

"Oh God. How awful."

"I'm so glad we reached out to her," Linda said. "I can't wait to get to know her better. Now, as for the fundraiser, I was thinking we can open the marina restaurant for the occasion."

"That's what I had in mind," Maddie said.

"Maybe we could even make it an annual tradition," Linda said.

Maddie hugged her mother-in-law. "Even better."

"I only wish I'd thought of it sooner. Of course the folks who support the summer economy struggle in the off-season after the tourists leave. Why didn't we ever do this before?"

"All that matters is we're doing it now, and that we do whatever we can to take care of them in the future."

"You and I need to talk at some point about getting you back to work, young lady," Linda said.

Maddie had thought long and hard about her position as head of housekeeping at McCarthy's Gansett Island Inn and had dreaded this conversation with her mother-in-law—and boss. "About that…"

Linda raised a brow in inquiry.

"Mac and I have talked about it, and I've decided to stay home with the kids while they're little. Maybe when they're older, I could come back to the family business?"

"As much as I hate to lose you, I completely understand. Of course you want to be with my precious grandbabies while they're small. I can hardly blame you for that. And there'll always be a place for you in the family business. Heck, you and Mac and Luke will be running the whole show before too much longer."

"I'd like you to consider Daisy to replace me."

Linda seemed startled by the suggestion.

"Before you discount her, she's very smart and capable."

"She hides that rather well behind her skittish, deer-in-the-headlights personality."

"She hasn't had an easy life. Trust me when I tell you she could more than handle the job. I'd make sure of it."

"I'll certainly consider it."

"Thank you. Now, how about some coffee?"

"I thought you'd never ask."

CHAPTER 16

Other than a quick phone call to assure her father that she was fine after the ugly confrontation with Justin, Laura stayed quiet on the much smoother ride back to Gansett. Though it was dark and rainy and cold, the wind had died down, making for smaller seas. Her thoughts were jumbled and confused as she continued to think through what had transpired on the mainland.

To his credit, Owen didn't push her to talk when it was obvious she didn't wish to.

The baby was particularly active today, as if he or she was aware of its mother's agitated state. It wasn't good for the baby for her to be upset. She knew that, of course, so she tried to focus her thoughts on the upcoming tasks at the hotel. Mac and his team would begin rebuilding the deck in the coming week, and she had a meeting with Syd on Monday to go over some decorating ideas for the third-floor suites. Also on Monday was the appointment and ultrasound with Victoria, the midwife, at which she'd have the option to learn her baby's sex. She hadn't yet decided if she wanted to know or not.

Laura had plenty to do, plenty to keep her mind occupied with productive, proactive thoughts. There was absolutely no need to dwell on the things—and people—she couldn't change. Determined to proceed with grace and forbearance, she leaned her head on Owen's shoulder and tried to decide how she should proceed with him.

He'd done so much for her, had been there during some of the darkest days of her life, had been a friend, a confidant and almost-lover. On top of all that, he'd changed his plans to spend the winter with her. What more could she want from any man? What more did he have to do to prove his devotion to her? Absolutely nothing, she decided. He was right—if she let Justin's bitterness spill into their relationship, she'd be risking her best chance at the kind of love that lasted a lifetime. She could tell she surprised him when she reached for his hand and closed her fingers around his.

He squeezed her hand and cradled it between both of his. "Feeling okay, Princess?"

She nodded. "I'm feeling great, actually." The closer she got to her beloved island, the more her burden seemed to lift, freeing her to pursue the many things that interested her now, including the handsome man sitting beside her.

"Is that right?"

"Uh-huh."

"And what brought this on after the twenty-four hours you've had?"

"You did."

He looked down at her, seeming perplexed. "What did I do?"

"Nothing and everything."

"You're talking in circles, sweetheart."

She smiled at him. "Am I?"

"You know you are."

"It means so much to me that you came with me on this trip, that you held my head—again—when I was sick, drove me to my dad's, came to the showdown with Justin and put up with my mood last night."

"I didn't mind doing any of that."

"I appreciate it, and I don't take it for granted."

He put his arm around her and pressed a kiss to the top of her head when she snuggled into his embrace. "I seem to be a lovesick fool where you're concerned," he said. "I'd rather be holding your barf bag than doing anything else with anyone else."

Her heart literally skipped a beat. "That's the most romantic thing anyone has ever said to me."

Owen snorted with laughter. "You're also rather easy to please, which is another thing to love about you."

She ventured a glance up at him. "You're throwing an awfully big word around there, buddy."

His gaze met hers, steady and true. "I know." He cupped her face and bent to kiss her.

Reaching up to smooth his perpetually messy hair, she said, "That's something we should probably talk about at some point."

"We've got all the time in the world to talk about everything."

She wrapped her arm around him and rested her cheek on his chest. His heart beat faster than usual, letting her know he wasn't unaffected by the conversation. "Owen?"

"Hmm?"

"Things are apt to be a bit…messy…for a while yet, but I want you to know…"

"What, honey?"

"That I want to be with you. I want to make this work. I want…everything with you."

The next thing she knew, he had pulled her onto his lap, and his strong arms were tight around her. Fortunately, they had their corner of the ferry cabin mostly to themselves as two other nearby passengers slept through the crossing. "I want that, too. More than you know." He rested a hand on the baby bump. "I can't wait to meet this little person and have him or her change both our lives forever."

Overwhelmed by his softly spoken words, Laura nestled into his neck, breathing in the familiar scent of him and nuzzling his warm, soft skin.

A tremble rippled through him, and he tightened his arms around her.

She loved knowing she could make him tremble, make him *want.* "When we get back to the hotel, do you think maybe we could, you know, pick up where we left off this morning?" she whispered in his ear.

"Your bed or mine?"

Laura laughed, feeling happier than she had in longer than she could remember. The situation with Justin was out of her hands. He knew about the baby and knew she wanted a divorce. She was never going back to him, so there was nothing stopping her from moving forward with Owen. "Yours is closer to the door."

"I like how you think." His hand tunneled under her jacket and sweater, seeking skin.

Laura wriggled on his lap, encouraging his touch.

"You might want to sit still, or you'll damage my most important parts—and we'll be needing them later."

Her laugh died on her lips when his hand moved from back to front, sliding over the baby to cup her breast. When he tweaked her nipple, she let out a ragged moan.

"Shhh," he whispered, his lips close to her ear, reminding her of where they were.

"How much longer?"

He twisted his head around to look out the window. "Just passing the bluffs. A few more minutes."

"Good," she said, feeling a sudden sense of urgency after months of significant moments leading to this one.

"Feeling anxious?" He played with her nipple relentlessly, making Laura hot and tingly and needy.

"Very." She ran her hand over his chest, shivering when she remembered how his rough chest hair felt against her extra-sensitive breasts. "Pregnancy is known for ramping up the sex drive, so I've got five months of bottled-up frustration I need to expend. If you're up for it, that is."

Using her hair to muffle his groan, he pushed his straining erection against her bottom. "I'm definitely up for it."

Laura giggled at the tortured sound he made.

"Has this damned boat ever taken longer?"

She kissed the scowl off his face. What she'd intended to be a quick tide-me-over kiss quickly became a heated, sensual duel, each of them straining to get closer until he finally pulled away.

"Gotta stop before I forget where we are."

She wrapped her arms around his neck and breathed him in during the endless minutes before the ferry crew called car owners to the lower deck to prepare for landing.

Owen was on his feet in a flash, giving her a second to land, before he grabbed her hand and tugged her along behind him to the stairs. Once in the car, while they waited for the signal from the crew to drive off the boat, Owen tapped his fingers impatiently on the wheel.

Watching him out of the corner of her eye, she linked and unlinked her own fingers, over and over and over again until she thought the tension would literally burst from her chest.

"Do we need condoms?" he asked after a long, charged moment of silence.

"You tell me."

"I've never had sex without one. I have a physical every year, and I'm healthy."

"In that case, since pregnancy isn't a worry, I don't see why we'd need one."

"And you're sure it's safe? For the baby?"

"Perfectly safe."

He blew out a choppy breath. "I think it's very possible I might be having some sort of cardiac incident."

Laura smiled and reached over to cover his hand, hoping to calm him.

He turned their hands and pressed hers palm-down to his throbbing cock, drawing a tortured groan from both of them. "What the hell is taking so goddamned long?"

"There were a couple of trucks that came on last." Laura had a better view of the action from the passenger seat. "They're unloading them."

After what seemed like an endless wait, one of the crewmembers waved at them to proceed off the boat. Five minutes later, they were pulling into the parking lot behind the Surf.

"I'll come back for the bags later," he said as they got out and met in front of the car. He took her hand and propelled her up the back stairs to the hotel, fumbling with the key and swearing under his breath when the lock fought back.

"It's all in the wrist," she said, pushing his hand out of the way.

"Very funny."

When the door swung open, he half dragged her in behind him, slamming the door shut and pushing her up against it. He devoured her mouth in deep, searching kisses that made her legs weak and her heart race.

"Laura, Laura, Laura, my sweet Laura," he whispered, turning his attention to her neck, kissing and licking and nibbling. "God, I want you. I've wanted you for so damned long."

She clutched his shoulders, needing him more than she'd ever known it was possible to need anything. "I've wanted you, too, for just as long and just as much."

And then he scooped her up and carried her through the kitchen, across the lobby and into his suite.

In what had become their pattern when he was picking her up off the bathroom floor after a bout of morning sickness, she looped her arms around his neck and rested her head on his shoulder.

He put her down next to his bed and started pulling at clothes with barely restrained urgency.

With their clothes in a pile at their feet, he yanked at the bed covers and urged her in ahead of him. He was right behind her, reaching for her.

Laura decided that the heat of his skin against hers was about the best thing she'd ever felt.

"I've dreamed about this moment." His hand slid down her back to her bottom, tugging her in tight against him. "And it's better than anything I could've imagined."

"Mmm, so much better."

She couldn't stop touching him—his chest and belly, caressing him until he groaned in frustration. Curling her hand around his cock, she stroked him the way he liked, hard and quick.

His eyes closed, and his hips pushed against her hand, urging her on.

Empowered by his reaction, she kissed her way down the front of him. Since his eyes were still closed, he didn't realize her intention until she'd taken him into the heat of her mouth.

His eyes flew open, and his fingers gripped her hair so tightly it was almost painful. "*Laura*," he said in a choked tone. "I can't take that right now."

"Yes, you can." She ran her tongue down the length of him and below, paying homage to his most sensitive parts. "What did you say last night? You take care of me, and I take care of you?" As she spoke, she kept her lips close to his shaft. "I've got a lot of taking care of you to do if I'm going to even things up between us."

"You don't have to..." He nearly levitated off the bed when she dipped her tongue into the slit at the top. As he released an inarticulate sound, his hips surged, pushing his cock into her mouth.

Laura took him deep again, as deep as she could, and lashed at him with her tongue. She looked up to find him watching her with feverish eyes. His hands had fallen to his sides, giving her complete control.

"Mmm," she said, making sure her lips vibrated against his sensitive skin.

"Baby, stop. *Stop*."

Rather than stop, though, she sucked on him and cupped his balls, squeezing gently.

With a harsh cry, he erupted into her throat.

Feeling a sense of power unlike anything she'd ever experienced, she licked him clean as he quivered and trembled beneath her. She kissed his belly and chest, tongued his nipple and drew another sharp cry of surprise from him.

As she stretched out on top of him, his arms encircled her. "You…that was… you're amazing." He turned them so he was on top but kept his weight off the baby. "I've never felt anything like that." He kissed her. "Ever." His eyes glinted with humor and devious intent. "My turn."

Her entire body hummed with anticipation that surged into a sharp tingle between her legs.

He worshiped every inch of her, paying particular attention to nipples made extra sensitive by pregnancy. By the time his broad shoulders pushed her legs apart, she was already on the verge of an explosive release. The first touch of his tongue on her throbbing clitoris was all it took to set her off. His fingers slid into her slick channel, riding the wave of her climax. "Again," he whispered as he set out to drive her mad a second time.

Laura would've sworn she couldn't do it twice, but she'd learned not to underestimate him. He took his own sweet time leading her up and leaving her hanging at the precipice three times before he took her over in a second wave that was more powerful than the first.

On his knees, he spread her legs even farther apart and wrapped his hand around his hard cock, stroking himself. Keeping his gaze fixed on hers, he aligned their bodies and began to push into her.

She was so primed his entry should've been easy, but he was big, and he had to work his way in slowly.

He held himself up on his arms when he dipped his head to kiss her with sweeping, insistent strokes of his tongue over her lips and into her mouth. All the while, he kept up the slow, steady push and pull.

Needing to breathe, Laura broke the kiss and gulped in greedy breaths. She smoothed her hands over his sweat-slicked back, curving them over the rounded globes of his ass. She squeezed, encouraging him to keep going.

"Does it hurt?" he asked.

"No, no. Feels so good." She arched her back, wanting more, wanting everything he had to give her.

"For me, too, Princess. Nothing has ever felt so good." He pressed his lips to her neck, which made her shiver.

"It's because you don't have to wear a condom."

He shook his head, gazing down at her with love and affection and desire in his eyes. "It's you. You make all the difference." Glancing down to where they were joined, he said, "About halfway there."

She let out an unsteady groan. "*Seriously?*"

He laughed softly. "You can do it."

"I'm not sure I can."

Sliding a hand under her, he turned them in a smooth move that startled and stirred her. Somehow he managed to remain lodged within her. "You do the rest," he said, his hands on her hips guiding her as she straddled him. "Relax and let it happen." He flattened his palm on her belly to steady her before moving both hands up to cup her breasts. Under her, he shifted slightly to sit up a bit. The new position sent him deeper into her and put his mouth in direct proximity to her breasts. He rolled her nipple between his lips and dropped one hand to the V of her legs, teasing the firm nub of her clit between his fingers.

The combination made it easier for her to slide farther down on him.

"Two more inches to go," he said as he dabbed her nipple with the sharp point of his tongue.

"You're lying."

He took her hand. "Feel."

Sure enough, a good two inches remained. "You got way more than your share, mister."

Laughing, he said, "Never heard any complaints before."

"I'm not complaining," she said as a fine sheen of sweat coated her skin from the effort to relax and allow him in. "Exactly."

"Come here." He put his arms around her and brought her in tight against his chest, capturing her mouth in a heated kiss that was all slick lips and eager tongues. His fingers dug into her hips to stop her from moving as he once again kissed her stupid.

Her entire body throbbed, but the epicenter was between her legs where he remained wedged. And if she wasn't mistaken, he was getting bigger.

She moaned against his lips. "You've got to be kidding me."

"Sorry," he said sheepishly. "He has a mind of his own."

"He thinks an awful lot of himself."

He flashed that devastating grin that got to her every time. "He does have a rather healthy ego." Cupping her ass, he squeezed and teased as his hungry mouth went to work on her other nipple. "We'll have to practice a lot so it becomes routine for you."

She choked out a shaky laugh. "I don't think *he* will ever become routine to me."

"Do you want to stop?"

"If you stop, I'll kill you."

That made him chuckle softly as his fingers delved deeper into the cleft of her ass, leaving no part of her untouched or unexplored.

Laura let her head fall back as a riot of sensations bombarded her. Suddenly, she needed to move and squirmed against his tight hold. His hands moved to her hips, but he let her set the pace and gasped when she finally took all of him.

She cried out when he rolled her clit between his fingers while he flexed his hips, pushing deeper and touching a spot inside her that had never been touched before. Losing herself in the intense spasms that rippled from the soles of her feet to her scalp and every pressure point in between, she came hard. One wave followed another, stealing the breath from her lungs along with any remaining doubts that this man was the one meant for her. When she returned from the heavenly ride, he was poised above her, looking down at her in amazement.

"Wow," he said reverently.

How had he turned them over again without her even knowing? "Yeah." Still breathing hard and throbbing at all her pressure points, she brought him down for a kiss. That was when she realized he was harder than ever and still buried deep inside her. "You didn't..."

Smiling, he shook his head. "Wrap your legs around my hips."

Tentatively, Laura did as he asked.

"Ready?"

Biting her bottom lip, she nodded, not entirely sure what she was agreeing to but trusting him implicitly.

"Hold on to me, baby." He reached beneath her and gripped her bottom, the position opening her to him even more than she'd been before. Slowly, gently, he began to move in steady strokes.

Even though the pressure was intense between her legs, her entire body was on fire for him. She'd never had sex like this—all-consuming, full-body sex.

"You're so beautiful," he said against her lips as his tongue dipped into her mouth, teasing and withdrawing before she could catch it. He looked her square in the eye. "I love you, Laura. I wanted to be deep inside you, with your arms and legs wrapped around me, the first time I said those words to you. I've loved you for almost as long as I've known you."

Tears filled her eyes as her heart pounded in time with the steady, unrelenting motion of his hips. "I love you, too. I'm so glad you stayed here with me."

He rested his forehead on hers. "Best thing I ever did." Tipping his head, he took her mouth again in a series of deep kisses that left her breathless and on the edge of yet another release, which was certainly a first. Everything about this encounter was a revelation to her. "You got one more for me, babe?"

"Maybe."

"That's my girl. Does anything hurt?"

She shook her head and gripped his backside, wanting to keep him buried deep. Arching into him, she contracted her internal muscles, which drew a deep, tortured groan from him.

"Do it again," he said, his breathing harsh and erratic.

She dug her fingers into his ass and bore down hard on his cock.

He gripped her bottom so tightly she wondered if there'd be bruises—not that she cared in the least—threw his head back and came with a strangled sound that dragged her right along with him in a climax that seemed to go on forever.

Rolling them to their sides in a smooth move, he collapsed next to her, still throbbing inside her.

"That was incredible," he said many minutes later. "Unlike anything I've ever known."

"For me, too," she said, nuzzling his chest hair and planting kisses on his chest.

"I had a feeling it would be kinda awesome with you, but that…" He ran his fingers through his unruly hair. "I don't think they've invented the word for that yet."

Laura laughed at his befuddlement. Never would she have expected to feel so light and free after the nightmare she'd endured the day before. As long as she was with him, she could expect more days like this one. Maybe even a lifetime of lightness and freedom and laughter and contentment. Maybe it was okay to hope for such things again, knowing everything about this was different from anything that had come before.

"I can hear that big brain of yours working overtime," he said, tapping lightly on her forehead.

She looked up at him. "I'm thinking that at one of the worst times of my life I found you, and what a lucky, lucky day that was."

"Luckiest day of *my* life when I found *you* standing in the wind and rain, staring wistfully at my family's broken-down hotel. You were so cute and waiflike wearing that huge old raincoat with the hood that practically swallowed up your incredible face. When you looked at me, I felt the impact like a punch to the belly."

"You never told me that."

"When did you start to, you know…"

"Love you?"

He nodded, boyish and adorable as he waited for her.

Laura didn't even have to think about it. "Remember the tropical-storm party at Mac and Maddie's?"

"Uh-huh."

"We were on the deck, and you gave me your jacket. I was so numb from everything that'd happened with Justin that I didn't even realize I was cold. Somehow, I'd managed to survive the wedding the day before and being Janey's bridesmaid. Don't get me wrong. I've always loved Janey like a sister, and I was so happy for her and Joe. They obviously belong together."

He smoothed his fingers over a strand of her hair and tucked it behind her ear.

"Watching them open their gifts, seeing their joy... It was too much. I went outside to get some air, and there you were with your warm coat, your job offer and the perfect amount of empathy when I told you what'd happened with Justin. You were the first person I told out here. And then Evan called you inside to play. You asked if I had any requests, and I said anything by James Taylor. You played 'You've Got a Friend.' Smiling at the memory, she rested her hand over the steady beat of his heart. "You've been my friend—my best friend—ever since."

"Being your BFF has been the most fun I've ever had."

Delighted, she looked up at him and said, "You know what that second F stands for, don't you?"

Nodding, he held her gaze as he brought her in closer for a kiss. "I know exactly what it means. I'm afraid you're stuck with me, Princess. You've ruined me for all other women."

She rested her head on his chest, grinning foolishly. "Then my work here is finished."

"Your work here, my love, is just getting started." To prove his point, he rolled her under him and made love to her all over again.

Chapter 17

Seamus carried Carolina's overnight bag to the Jeep, mourning the loss of the closeness they'd shared during the night. She hadn't said more than ten words to him since the call from Joe reminded her that she'd been fooling around with a man roughly her son's age. It didn't seem to matter that the man in question didn't give a fig that she was older than him or had a son his age or was about to be a grandmother. Even after having her, he wanted her more than he'd ever wanted anyone else. He'd be damned if he'd let her walk away like what had transpired between them hadn't rocked him.

"Ya can't fool me, love," he said when they were standing beside her Jeep with nothing left to do but say their good-byes. He'd called the office to get her car on the one o'clock boat. He was captaining the five o'clock boat, or he might've gone with her and spent all day trying to convince her to give him a chance.

"What's that supposed to mean?" she asked testily.

With his hands on her hips, he brought her in close to him and watched her eyes dart nervously around as if concerned the neighbors might see them. "I know you enjoyed yourself last night. Some things can't be faked."

Her face flushed with color, which was all it took to make him hard as a rock for her. "I didn't fake anything, and I never said I didn't enjoy it."

"Then why can't ya bring yourself to look at me?"

"I looked at you."

"You looked at my dick. You took a good long look and licked your lips because you want more of it. But ya can't seem ta bring yourself ta look at my eyes. Why is that? What're you afraid of, love?"

She raised her chin and met his gaze, her blue eyes heated with anger and desire. By now he certainly recognized the desire. "I'm not afraid of anything."

He framed her face and kissed her, hard and long and deep. At first, she fought him, her attempts at protest opening her mouth to his insistent tongue. He kissed her until she stopped fighting him, until her arms were wrapped tight around his neck and her core was pushed even tighter against the thigh he'd wedged between her legs. "If you're not afraid of anything, you'll see me again."

"I told you, I'm not interested in a relation—"

He kissed her again, harder and longer and deeper than before, pressing his leg against her in pulsing movements that had her pushing back just as insistently. By the time he broke the kiss, they were both breathing harshly. "Don't lie to me, and don't lie to yourself, Carolina."

"I'm not lying to anyone." She tugged free of his tight embrace and wiped a trembling hand over her kiss-swollen lips. "I had a lovely time last night, but I told you before, that's all it can be. I refuse to take up with a man nearly twenty years younger than me, who works for my son. What would people say?"

He hadn't realized he'd given her the power to hurt him. Staring at her, he hoped to shame her into taking it back. "You disappoint me, lovely Carolina. I thought you were made of more courageous stuff than that."

"You don't understand—"

"No, I really don't, but I'm hardly going to beg. I had a grand time. Best sex of my whole damned life." He took her hand and brought it to his lips, leaving a tender kiss on the back before he released her. "I'll never forget it."

Opening the car door, he held it while she got in. He reached for the seat belt and leaned in to buckle it, drawing a gasp from her when he brushed against her. As he retreated, he stopped when his face was an inch from hers. "Worries about what other people would think or say won't keep you warm during a long, cold winter. Not as warm as I could keep you." He caressed her face and gave her one more soft, sweet kiss. "You know where ta find me if you change your mind."

"I won't."

Shrugging, he said, "Okay."

The Jeep's tires made a squealing sound as she tore out of the driveway. Watching her go, Seamus hoped he'd played it right. He could've bowled her over with romance, but until she realized how good they could be together and got past her hang-ups about being with a much younger man, all the romance in the world wouldn't matter.

No, she had to make the next move. And when she did, he'd be ready.

Big Mac McCarthy was working with his son and Luke, replacing some rotted planks on the main pier, when Linda came flying into the parking lot in her little yellow Bug, skidding to a stop and tooting the horn. "What the heck has gotten into her?"

"Since she's your wife, we'll let you go find out," Mac said with a cheeky grin.

"Thanks, pal."

"Go on now before she comes after you."

Luke chuckled at their banter as he continued to pound nails into a pressure-treated plank.

Scowling at his son, Big Mac headed up the pier to meet his wife. "Who put bees in your britches, sweetheart?"

She surprised the heck out of him when she ran to him and launched herself into his arms. They'd had a rough couple of months after he was injured in an accident at the marina earlier in the summer. But right around Labor Day, they'd patched things up, and since then… Well, he was reminded of the first year they were married. The gal couldn't keep her hands off him, not that he was complaining. Nope, no complaints. He tightened his arms around her and spun her, noticing that Mac and Luke were watching them.

Stopping the spin, he made sure his back was to the nosy nellies down the dock. "What'd I do to deserve this?"

Glowing with delight, she linked her hands around his neck. "I just got off the phone with Janey, and she had the most amazing news." Linda moved her hands to his face and kissed him.

Out of the corner of his eye, he noticed Mac and Luke had gone back to work, which made him chuckle to himself. *Eat your hearts out, boys. Mom and Dad still got it.* "Are you going to tell me the news?"

"You're going to be a grandpa again!"

Big Mac's mouth fell open in shock.

"Don't feel bad," Linda continued. "Apparently, they were surprised, too. They'd planned to wait until Janey finished school, but she forgot to take her pill—"

He used a kiss to stop her from sharing too many details about his daughter's sex life—a sex life he still liked to think was nonexistent despite significant evidence to the contrary. Returning his wife to terra firma, he kept his hands on her shoulders. "Is she feeling okay?"

"She's been terribly tired, which is what got Joe to thinking something was going on."

"He must be thrilled. He'll be a wonderful father."

"I said the same thing. Although, apparently, he's worried. His own father has been gone so long he barely remembers him. He's afraid he won't be any good at it."

"That's ridiculous. He'll be a natural."

"Yes, he will," she said, caressing his face. "He's had you, and you showed him how fatherhood is done. That baby will be very lucky to have him as its dad and you as its granddad."

"That's nice of you to say, babe." He guided her around the corner of the gift shop, out of the view of Mac and Luke, and bent his head to kiss her more thoroughly. "How about we call it a day a little early?" He waggled his brows to let her know what he had in mind.

Her cheeks flushed with color. "I'd love to, but I need to go see Carolina. Did you hear she's come back to the island for the winter?"

"Mac mentioned that he went out to check her woodstove and roof."

"Oh, he's such a good boy. I'm sure Joe appreciated that."

"I hate to think of her out there all alone in that old house."

"She won't be all alone. She has us and lots of other friends."

He nibbled on her neck, hitting the spot that got her attention every time. "So that's a 'no' on the go-home-early plan?"

"Give me an hour?"

"I suppose I can do that. Don't forget, we've got Luke and Syd's party later, too."

"I haven't forgotten. I'll see you at home in an hour."

He slapped her on the fanny. "Don't be late."

She left him with a kiss that made him wonder how he'd last an hour. "Tell Mac and Luke I'll see them later."

After she drove off, he walked down the dock to rejoin the boys.

"Everything all right, Romeo?" Mac asked.

"I should've spanked you more often as a child." He picked up his hammer and grabbed a fistful of nails. "It so happens that I'm going to be a grandfather again. Congratulations, Uncle Mac."

"Who? Evan or Grant? Or Adam? Not *Adam*. He doesn't even have a girlfriend."

"Stop getting all excited thinking one of your brothers f'd up. Your *sister* is expecting."

Mac's hammer froze in midair as he gaped at his father. "They were going to wait until she finishes school! I thought I had years to get used to the idea before I'd have to see my baby sister knocked up!"

Big Mac shrugged. "Finding out where the plan went wrong would require details I can't handle."

Mac nodded, his eyes big. "Right there with ya."

"You two are ridiculous," Luke muttered. "Absolutely ridiculous."

Carolina had brought the last load of boxes from the Jeep into the house when a horn tooted in the driveway. As she went out to see who was there, Linda McCarthy jumped out of her cute yellow car, swinging a bottle of champagne over her head.

Carolina smiled at her old friend. Apparently, Linda had heard from her daughter.

"Congratulations, Grandma!" Linda said as she enveloped Carolina in a hug.

"Same to you!" She put an arm around Linda to walk her inside. The two women were polar opposites. Linda was petite and polished and classy and always well put-together. Carolina, who had at least four inches on Linda, preferred torn jeans to tailored suits, and a messy braid was her idea of doing her hair.

While they might've been polar opposites, Linda was also one of her closest friends. Big Mac and Linda McCarthy and their gaggle of kids had been family to her and Joe for longer than she could remember. Actually, it'd been since the first day of kindergarten, when Joe came home talking about his new friend Mac McCarthy. That was how far back the two families went. And when Joe married Janey earlier in the summer, they'd made their unofficial family status official.

"Can you even believe it?" Carolina asked. "I thought we'd have to wait years for this news."

"So did I. Apparently, Janey was forgetful with her pills during a crazy semester."

"Secretly, I'm glad it happened now before Joe gets too much older."

"Yes, he's positively ancient," Linda said, grinning.

"Sorry for the mess. I literally just got here. I think I probably have some tea I can offer you."

"The heck with the tea. Let's break out the bubbly!"

Linda managed to blow the cork off the bottle without breaking a window or taking out an eye, but it was a close call on both counts.

Carolina found some wineglasses from the cabinet and washed out the dust that had gathered since they were last used.

When they each had a glass of champagne, Linda held hers up to make a toast. "To our kids and our grandbaby, who is incredibly lucky to have a couple of young, saucy chicks as his—or her—grandmothers."

Delighted by the idea of sharing a grandchild with Linda and Mac, Carolina touched her glass to Linda's. "Hear, hear."

They collapsed into kitchen chairs to enjoy the bubbly.

"You've got a bit of a rash on your face," Linda said, pointing to her own cheek to show Carolina where it was.

"Do I?" Carolina got up and went into the bathroom to take a look. *Oh God. Oh my God. I'm wearing my secret shame on my face.* As she returned to the kitchen, her face burned with mortification. "It's not a rash."

Linda raised a brow. "No?"

Carolina shook her head and took her seat. "I did a bad, bad thing."

Instantly interested, Linda leaned in. "Do tell."

She couldn't bring herself to look at Linda. "I had sex."

"Well, it's about damned time!" Linda smacked her hand on the table, making Carolina jolt. "So what we've got, ladies and gentlemen of the jury, is a case of razor burn to the face and possibly other areas as well."

Carolina crossed her legs, trying not to think about what other parts of her might bear the mark of Seamus's whiskers.

"Are you going to tell me who it was?"

"Never."

"It's someone I know?"

Carolina had never been more ashamed of herself. She'd slept with a man roughly the same age as their sons.

"Who's been telling you for *years* that you need to get back on the horse?"

If the soreness between her legs and her aching thighs were any indication, she'd gotten back on the horse in a big way.

"I can't believe you're clamming up on me. Tell me this much: why was it a bad, bad thing?"

"Because." Carolina fiddled with the stem of her wineglass. "He's younger than me."

"So what?"

She met Linda's gaze. "A lot younger."

"It wasn't one of my sons, was it?"

"Shut up! Of course not. They're like my own children, for God's sake."

"That's a relief."

"See? That's exactly what I was thinking this morning as the mother of a man roughly the same age as the one I slept with. What would *his* mother think?"

"So you slept with a guy Joe's age."

"No! He's two years older than Joe."

"Thank God for those two years." Linda attempted to cover her laughter with a hand over her mouth. "Now, who do I know who's thirty-eight?"

"Stop! Do *not* do that!"

"So it *is* someone I know."

"*Linda!*"

Linda reached across the table for Carolina's hand. "Was it good?"

"It was…stupendous."

"And do you like this man?"

Miserably, she nodded. She *sooooo* didn't want to like him.

"And does he like you?"

"He likes me too much. He won't listen to me when I tell him he needs to find someone his own age and get married and have babies. What in the world does he want with an old cougar like me? It's so wrong!"

Linda choked on her champagne. "What the hell is a cougar?"

"Oh, come on! You know."

Linda shook her head. "I've been living on this island for nearly forty years. I'm not exactly up on the hip lingo."

"A cougar is an older woman who preys on a younger man."

"And did you *prey* on this younger man?"

"I was certainly willing, if that's what you mean. I wasn't ashamed until this morning when Joe called to tell me the news while I was naked in bed with… *him*." God, she'd almost said naked in Joe's guest room, which would've told Linda exactly who her too-young lover was.

"You didn't do anything wrong, Caro. As long as there were two consenting adults in that bed, it doesn't matter that you're older than him."

"It would matter to Joe."

"I wouldn't be so sure. If you ask me, he'd want you to be happy. Pete's been gone such a long time."

"Thirty years this summer," Carolina said. Sometimes it still felt like yesterday; other times, it was like she'd dreamed him, and he'd never really existed. She had only the son who was the image of his father to remind her that Pete had indeed existed, and she'd once loved him more than life.

"In all that time, there hasn't been anyone else. Isn't it time?"

"Not with someone who has his whole life in front of him, who should have a family of his own."

"What if that's not what he wants?"

"He says he wants me and doesn't care about having kids."

"You should listen to him, Caro. A man of thirty-eight certainly knows what he wants out of life—and what he doesn't."

Carolina shook her head. "I can't get involved with him. It wouldn't be right."

Linda touched a finger to the razor burn on Carolina's cheek. "Seems to me you're already involved."

"It was a one-time thing." A beautiful, unforgettable one-time thing.

"I'm sorry to hear you say that. I hope you'll think some more about it before you decide anything for certain. In the meantime, you're going out tonight."

Startled, Carolina said, "Where am I going?"

"To a party Luke and Syd are having for the new lighthouse keeper, Jenny Wilks. She lost her fiancé in the World Trade Center on nine-eleven."

"Oh my. That poor girl."

"She's had a hard time jumpstarting her life after her loss. I think you ought to meet her. The two of you have a lot in common."

"I'm not in any mood for a party, and besides, I wasn't invited."

"I'm inviting you. For goodness sakes, you know we don't stand on formality around here. Put some makeup on that 'rash.' Mac and I will pick you up at seven." She stood and planted a kiss on Carolina's cheek. "I have to get home and have sex with my husband before the party."

Carolina put her hands over her ears. "Too much information."

"I may try this cougar thing on him."

"It won't work because he's older than you, but go get 'em, tiger."

"Don't mind if I do."

"Linda?" Carolina stopped her friend at the door. "You won't tell anyone, will you?"

"Of course not, honey. But I'm going to badger you about keeping your options open."

"Cougars and tigers and badgers, oh my."

Laughing, Linda walked out the door. "See you at seven, Granny."

Owen left a trail of kisses on Laura's back, hoping to rouse her out of a deep sleep. "Time to wake up, Princess." He felt sort of guilty for wearing her out so thoroughly that she'd slept for hours after the second time they made love. The sex had been so damned good, better than anything he'd ever imagined possible between two people. Apparently, love made all the difference. Who knew?

Keeping up the kisses until she finally stirred, Owen told himself he should let her sleep, but after a couple of hours without her, he missed her. What a fool she'd made of him.

"Mmm," she said, making him smile.

He added more kisses to her lower back. "*Laura*, are you in there?" Only when he gave a light pinch to her bottom did she open her eyes.

"Ow."

"Sorry, but I've been trying to wake you up for ten minutes."

"You're not sorry."

"No, I'm not. I got to play with your awesome bum. Did I ever tell you your bum is awesome?" As if to prove his point, he cupped a cheek and squeezed. "It's a really, really *good* bum."

"I should hope so after all the *years* I've spent in yoga class."

Owen's brows lifted straight up to his hairline. "Yoga?"

She bit her lip as if trying to hold back a laugh and nodded. "I'm *super* flexible."

He swallowed hard. "I may need a demonstration of said flexibility. Very, very soon."

As if he were a naughty schoolboy, she patted his face. "If you behave."

"Behaving is no fun," he said, kissing her neck and then her lips. With one arm around her, he snuggled her in close and was rewarded with a nudge to the belly from the baby. "I think he likes me."

"Do you think you'll like him?" she asked, looking up at him with bottomless blue eyes.

"I know I will. He's part of you, and I love every part of you."

"It might be prudent to wait and see on this one, Owen. It's a big deal, and I wouldn't blame you—"

He stopped her with a deep kiss full of all the love and longing he'd spent so many weeks trying to hide from her.

She pulled back and held him at arm's length. "Don't try to change the subject."

With frustration rippling off him in great waves, he sat up and ran his fingers through his hair. "I know it's a big deal, Laura. I get it. Trust me on that."

"It's a lot to ask anyone to take on. Everything between us is so new, and who knows how you'll feel in a couple of months when it all becomes very real?"

He stared at her, incredulous. "You still think I'm going to bolt, don't you? After all we've already been through together, you're waiting for me to cut and run."

Gripping his arm, she stopped him when he would've left the bed. "I don't think you're going to bolt. Honestly, I don't. But it's really important to me that you know if the day comes when it becomes too much for you, all you have to do is say so."

How could she say that? Especially after what had just transpired between them. "Duly noted."

"You're mad."

Scrubbing his hands over his face, he took a deep breath and forced himself to look at her. "Not mad. Frustrated, I guess." Taking her hand, he brought it to his lips. "When I say I love you, I mean it. I really do."

"I know you do. You've shown me that every day for months."

"I've gone out of my way to avoid words like 'love' and 'forever' because I wasn't willing to make the commitment that goes with them. Now I am."

Her eyes went soft and misty, which made him want her all over again. "And I love you for that. More than you could possibly know. All I'm saying is it's one thing to make a commitment to me. It's another thing altogether to commit to a baby who isn't yours."

He bit back a flash of anger. "When is your next doctor's appointment?"

She seemed surprised by the question and his unusually sharp tone. "Um, I'm seeing Victoria, the midwife, on Monday for an exam and ultrasound. Why?"

"Can I come?"

Her eyes got very big, and she started to say something but stopped herself.

"Well, can I?"

"Y-yes, I suppose, if you really want to."

"I really want to. What about the classes? The ones they show in the movies with all the huffing and puffing."

Biting back a laugh at his description, she said, "Childbirth preparation?"

"Yeah. Who's going to that with you?"

"I was going to ask Grace—"

"I'll do it."

"Oh." She seemed momentarily speechless. "You know that means you also have to be in the delivery room as my labor coach, right?"

"Duh." He knew he sounded like a bratty ten-year-old, but damn it, she'd pissed him off by questioning his commitment. And as fast as he'd worked up the head of steam it dissipated. He supposed it was only natural that she'd be concerned about whether he would be as committed to her child as he was to her. "Sorry. That was uncalled for."

Laura held out her arms to him. "Come here."

Under no circumstances could he resist her when she looked at him that way. Even though he was still annoyed and agitated, he slid into her warm embrace. Being in her arms was like coming home, only better. As a military brat, he'd never been truly at home anywhere, except for the summers he'd spent at the Surf with his grandparents. How ironic—and fitting—that the hotel should serve as the backdrop for this new chapter in his life.

"I'm sorry." She kissed his cheek and ran a soothing hand over his back. "I didn't mean to question your commitment. That's not fair after everything you've done for me."

"It's not about what I've done for you. I only do exactly what I want to—nothing more, nothing less. Being with you, doing things for you, it's the most natural thing in the world to me."

She tightened her hold on him. "Owen..."

"What, honey?"

"Do you really want to be my labor coach?"

"Hell, yes. I want to be there when the little guy takes his first breath. I want to be there for his first steps. I want to be there for everything." When his gaze met hers, he was surprised to find her eyes swimming with tears. "What?"

"You're amazing. I have to be the luckiest girl on the face of the earth."

Touched by her words and the emotion he heard behind them, he said, "Just because he isn't mine doesn't mean I won't love him, Princess. As much as I love his mother."

She wrapped her arms around his neck and clung to him. "Thank you. For that and a million other things. I love you so much. So, so much."

With his face buried in soft, fragrant hair, his hands full of soft, fragrant skin, and his heart full of her soft, sincere words, Owen had never been happier or more content. If only the nagging worry about what Justin might do or not do wasn't hanging over them, everything in his world would be perfect. "We need to get going to Luke and Syd's."

"In a minute." Her mouth found his in a kiss that said more than words alone ever could about the deep bond they'd formed.

"Keep that up, and we're going to need more than a few minutes."

"I don't mind being late," she said with a saucy grin that got his motor running all over again. "Do you?"

He slid his leg between hers and tugged her closer to him. "I don't mind at all."

Chapter 18

Sydney had asked Jenny to come early so she could meet Luke and get settled before the masses arrived. As the day of the party had drawn closer, Sydney had become nervous about how many people they'd invited.

"So you know how I mentioned this would be a small gathering?" Sydney said as she handed Jenny a glass of chardonnay and shooed Buddy away before he got dog hair all over Jenny's dark jeans.

Jenny's eyes sparked with amusement. "Did it mushroom?"

"Since there's not much to do around here this time of year, word gets out about a party, and next thing you know..."

"It's not a small party anymore. Just like high school."

"Exactly! Does that freak you out?"

"A year or two ago, it would have, but I'm doing better now. Like I said the other day, it's time to get unstuck. I may as well meet everyone at once."

"They're all so nice and truly looking forward to meeting you."

"I'm sure they're nice if they're your friends. I appreciate that you reached out to me, Syd. I was thinking after you left the other day that it took some gumption, knowing what we had in common."

Syd sat on the sofa and let Buddy rub up against her. She'd long ago given up on the dog-hair battle. "When I first came back here earlier in the summer, I was s tuck, too, so I know what you mean. Everything that's happened since then has been nothing short of miraculous."

As if on cue, her own personal miracle came into the room wearing faded jeans and a navy-blue sweater. His hair was still damp from the shower, and his handsome face was freshly shaven. He was positively gorgeous and all hers. "Luke, honey, come meet Jenny."

"Hi, there." He extended a hand to Jenny. "It's great to finally meet you. We've been wondering about our mysterious new lighthouse keeper."

She shook his hand. "After Sydney's visit, I figured it was time to come out of hiding before y'all started making up stories about me," Jenny said, a hint of North Carolina in her voice.

"So the crazy cat lady rumor isn't true?" Luke asked, making Jenny laugh.

Syd smiled at him, appreciating his effort to be sociable when his usual tendency was to hang back and take it all in.

"No cats," Jenny said with a good-natured grin. "Yet."

That earned a smile from Luke. "You want a glass of wine, babe?" he asked Sydney.

She'd been running around all day making preparations and was more than ready for a drink. "Don't mind if I do."

"Stay there. I'll get it."

As he left the room, Jenny fanned her face. "H-o-t," she whispered. "Good for you, girl."

Laughing, Syd was pleased to realize that Jenny would fit right in with their group.

A short time later, the house was filled to overflowing. The new arrivals were friendly and accepting of Jenny and full of congratulations for their newly engaged hosts. Several bottles of champagne were presented to Luke and Sydney. Everyone brought appetizers, bottles of wine and six-packs of beer. The guys had gravitated to the kitchen, and the women gathered in the living room.

"I love what you did with this room, Syd," Linda McCarthy said. Along with her famous artichoke dip, she'd brought Joe's mom Carolina, who was back on the island for the winter.

"Thank you," Syd said. "I was happy with how it came together."

"I need you to do something fabulous with my living room," Maddie said. "It's sort of blah."

"It's not blah," Syd said. "It's functional, which is what you need with young kids underfoot."

"Functional," Maddie said, making a distasteful face. "There's a stylish word."

A young woman Sydney didn't recognize poked her head in the door.

"Come in!" Syd called to her as she walked over to welcome the newcomer. "Hi there, I'm Syd."

"Kara Ballard. Mac and Luke mentioned that I should stop by tonight and meet some people."

"Oh yes! You're their new business partner. Luke told me about your launch service. I think it's a great idea."

"I'm glad you think so. They've been great about helping me figure out the logistics. So you're Luke's fiancée?"

The word still brought a thrill several days after he put the ring on her finger. "That'd be me."

"He was really excited telling me how he got engaged," Kara said with a hint of wistfulness that caught Syd's attention. "Could I see your ring?"

"Oh, of course! I love showing it off."

Kara took a close look at the ring. "It's gorgeous. Congratulations."

An aura of sadness clung to the pretty young woman that made Syd curious. She slipped an arm around Kara and escorted her into the kitchen where Big Mac, Luke and Mac greeted her warmly.

"What can we get you to drink?" Big Mac asked.

"A light beer would be great."

"Are you old enough to drink?" Big Mac teased.

"Very funny," Kara said with a laugh. "I'm older than I look."

"One beer coming right up," Luke said.

Mac introduced Kara to his brothers, Grant and Evan, as well as Ned, Seamus O'Grady, Blaine Taylor and Dan Torrington, who'd tagged along with Grant.

"Nice to meet you all," Kara said, thanking Luke when he handed her an open bottle of beer.

"I can't leave you in here alone with them," Syd said, tugging Kara along with her. "Too much testosterone."

The comment earned her groans and wads of balled-up napkins aimed at her head.

Kara seemed more than grateful to leave the men for the safer gathering of women. Syd introduced her to Maddie, Tiffany, Francine, Linda, Carolina, Grace and Stephanie.

"Where're Laura and Owen?" Grace asked.

"I don't know," Syd said. "She told me they'd be here."

"Did they make it back from the mainland?" Stephanie asked.

"I haven't heard," Grace replied. "Evan tried to call him a couple of times this afternoon, but the calls went straight to voice mail."

"I hope everything is okay," Stephanie said. "Laura was anxious about the meeting with her ex."

For the sake of Jenny and Kara, Syd said, "Laura is Mac, Evan and Grant's cousin. She's been hired to oversee the renovations and redecoration of the Sand & Surf Hotel in town and to manage the place when it reopens in the spring."

"Oh, I love that old place," Jenny said. "Every time I drive by, I imagine the stories it has to tell."

"It's been on that corner for a hundred years," Linda said. "My husband told me this is the first time it's been fully renovated since it was built."

"I believe it," Syd said. "It's fallen into disrepair, especially since Owen's grandparents retired and moved to Florida."

"When I was a kid, I used to dream about owning the Surf," Maddie said. "I'd imagine grand tea parties and ladies in fancy dresses on the big porch."

"I think Laura said something about offering tea parties," Stephanie said.

"We should have one there," Maddie said, "all of us, when the Surf reopens."

"That'd be fun," Syd said. "What do you think, Jenny?"

"Sounds good to me. I'm a tea-party regular. I have nieces."

Syd suddenly remembered the tea parties in her own past. Her daughter Malena had been a big fan of the tea party.

Maddie sent her an empathetic smile, seeming to know exactly what Syd was thinking.

"So you're not the only one who got engaged this week, Syd," Grace said, nudging Stephanie.

Linda let out a most unladylike shriek. "*Grant McCarthy! I'm going to kill you!*"

That set the other women into a gale of laughter as they cajoled Stephanie into showing off her new ring.

Jenny and Kara exchanged wide-eyed glances at the goings-on.

"What'd I do?" Grant asked as he came into the living room to face his mother.

"You got *engaged* and didn't tell me?"

"You didn't tell your mother?" Stephanie asked, incredulous.

"I, uh, well, I was going to."

"Idiot," Stephanie muttered as she accepted a hug from her future mother-in-law. "He's an idiot."

"I have no doubt you can fix the mess I made of him," Linda said.

"I'm afraid it'll take the rest of my life."

"I'm right here," Grant said. "And I can hear you."

"Good," Stephanie said. "Now go tell your father before he hears it through the grapevine, too."

"Dad, Mom and Stephanie are being mean to me," Grant said as he went back into the kitchen where much celebrating and backslapping ensued after Grant shared his news.

"That's not all the news," Mac said. "Luke, do you have a speakerphone handy?"

"Sure, let me get it."

Everyone was focused on the kitchen as Mac punched in a long-distance number and set the phone on speaker.

"Hey, brat," he said, signaling to the others to stay quiet.

"You've got the wrong number," Janey said.

"What're you all grumpy about?"

"I'm not feeling very good. And why are you calling me from Luke's house?"

"Because a few of us got together tonight, and we were sharing some good news. Did you hear Grant and Stephanie got engaged?"

"No way!"

"And Luke and Syd."

"Wow! That's fabulous news. Congrats, you guys. Joe says congrats, too."

"Thanks, Janey," Luke said.

"We hear you have some news of your own to report."

"Mom has a big mouth."

"*I can hear you*, Jane Elizabeth McCarthy Cantrell," Linda said.

The gathering tittered with laughter.

"Hi, Mom," Janey said meekly.

"So what's your news?" Mac asked.

"You already know."

"But everyone else doesn't."

"It appears that somehow I'm pregnant."

The news was met with whoops and hollering.

"Yay, Janey!" Maddie said. "I'm so glad Thomas and Hailey will have another cousin close in age. But I thought you were going to wait until you finished school."

"So did I. That's a whole other story."

"She can't keep her hands off me," Joe said.

That got everyone laughing again.

"Congratulations, you guys," Evan said. "I'm going to be an uncle! Again!"

Grace went to him and gave him a celebratory hug.

"Who's going to be an uncle?" Owen asked as he came in holding Laura's hand and yet another six-pack of beer.

"I am," Mac, Grant and Evan said together.

"I'm pretty sure it's not Adam, so that leaves Janey?"

"You got it," Janey said. "Knocked up while still in vet school."

"Oh, Janey," Laura said, leaning toward the phone. "That's so exciting!"

"See?" Joe said. "That's what I said, too."

"Of course it's great for you," Janey said to her husband. "You're not the one slogging through vet school while knocked up."

"Why don't we let you two have this argument in private?" Mac said, grinning at the others. "Congratulations, brat. And Joe."

"And stop using the words 'knocked up,'" Big Mac said to his daughter. "I can't bear it."

Amid much laughter, shouts of love and congratulations, Mac ended the call with his sister.

"I'd say all this good news calls for some champagne," Big Mac said. When everyone had a glass, he raised his. "To love."

"Hear, hear."

Sydney snuggled into Luke's embrace as Grant hooked an arm around Stephanie and hugged her tight against him.

"To love," Luke whispered in Sydney's ear.

Sydney smiled up at him, at peace with her past, content in her new life and excited about the future.

***

"He's looking at you," Maddie whispered to Tiffany.

"Huh?"

"Blaine. He keeps stealing glances at you. Every chance he gets." Maddie gave her sister a nudge. "Go talk to him."

"I can't."

"Of course you can. Don't be ridiculous."

"You don't understand."

"What don't I understand?"

Tiffany turned away from her sister.

Maddie poked her the way she used to when they were kids and she wanted to get a rise out of her younger sister. "Go. Talk. To. Him."

"Shut. Up."

"You shut up."

"No, you."

Maddie laughed at the familiar exchange, also a holdover from childhood. "What have you got to lose?"

"Only my dignity. When I think about what happened with him…"

"You want more of it?"

"That's not what I was going to say!"

"So you don't want more of it."

"I didn't say that either."

"I hate that Jim did this to you," Maddie said, shaking her head.

That got Tiffany's full attention. "Did what?"

"The Tiffany I know and love wouldn't think twice about going after something she wants. My Tiffany took notice of Jim Sturgil in high school and set out to make him hers. She started a dance studio when she was barely a kid and made a go of it. When she had a baby and needed a job while her husband was starting his practice, she started a day care business that was also a huge success. My Tiffany goes after what she wants. She doesn't sit in the corner wishing things were different."

"I know what you're doing."

"What am I doing?"

"You're trying to piss me off so I'll march over there and do something stupid that I'll regret tomorrow."

"You won't regret it."

Tiffany shook her head, and Maddie was astounded when Tiffany's eyes filled. "I'm sorry." She put her arm around her sister and pulled her close. "It's none of my business."

"You're right. I've become a total wimp. I'm afraid of my own shadow."

Maddie couldn't stand to see Tiffany so defeated and hated her ex-brother-in-law for what he'd done to his wife's self-esteem. "I shouldn't have said anything."

"I really want to talk to him. I do. Not here, though. Not with an audience."

"Why don't you go out on the deck to 'get some air'? I bet he'd follow you."

Tiffany shook her head. "Too obvious."

"I could go in there and tell him you'd like to talk to him."

"And that's not obvious?"

"I'm having flashbacks to high school here."

"I know. It's ridiculous. Don't worry about it. If it's meant to be, it'll happen on its own."

"If you say so."

Carolina should've brought her own car. She realized her strategic mistake the second she stepped into Luke and Sydney's cozy home and came face-to-face with the one man she most wished to avoid at the moment, especially with Linda "Hawkeye" McCarthy at her side.

"Miz Cantrell," he'd said in that annoyingly sexy brogue as he bowed gallantly over their joined hands. "How lovely to see you. I didn't know you were on island."

As a jolt of electricity traveled from his hand up her arm, she wanted to wipe that smug I've-seen-you-naked smile off his face.

"Nice to see you, too, Seamus." She pulled her hand free. "How's business?"

"Excellent. Even in the off-season, the people keep coming and coming and *coming*."

The reminder of how many times he'd made her come the night before paralyzed her. "Th-that's good to hear."

His smile told her he knew his comment had struck a bull's eye. "And how's Joe?"

"As you well know, since you speak to him several times a week, he's just fine."

His amusement at her discomfort was apparent in the devilish glint in his eyes. Fortunately, Linda had been distracted as she greeted Evan, Grace, Grant and Stephanie and hadn't noticed the tension between Carolina and Seamus.

"Knock it off," Carolina hissed at Seamus.

"Knock what off? What'd I do?"

"You know exactly what you're doing."

"Let me drive you home."

"Not happening."

"You know you want to."

Before she could think of a suitably dismissive comment, Linda had come back to claim her. Carolina managed to steer clear of him after that, but she was acutely aware of his every move—and the fact that he hardly took his eyes off her. Every time she glanced into the kitchen, her gaze met his. Each time, she immediately looked away, but her nipples tightened, her sex ached and her face burned with mortification.

She had to get herself under control before Linda tuned into what was going on. That was the last thing she needed. Linda was already curious enough about Carolina's young lover. If it ever got back to Joe that she was sleeping with the man he'd hired to run the business in his absence... The thought of it made Carolina want to die on the spot.

Good lord, what had she been *thinking*? Letting her mind wander back twenty-four hours, it was clear with hindsight that she hadn't been thinking at all. She'd been under the influence of Irish charm. That was the only possible explanation for her actions.

"Are you all right, honey?" Linda asked, squeezing Carolina's arm.

"I'm fine but in need of the restroom." She had to get out of there before she burst into tears or did something equally embarrassing, such as grab Seamus O'Grady by the arm and drag him out of there so she could have her wicked way with him. Again. "Be right back."

She kept her head down as she wandered into the hallway to find the bathroom, which was occupied.

"Feel free to use the one in our room, Carolina," Syd said, pointing to the last room on the left.

Desperate for a private moment to recover her composure, Carolina thanked Sydney. Her heart raced as she rushed through the dark bedroom to the adjoining bathroom and closed the door, leaning back against it to drag deep breaths into her straining lungs. This was utter madness! She couldn't be in the same room with him without getting hot all over. She'd lived without sex for thirty years! How was it that one night with a randy Irishman had her panting like a bitch in heat?

Mortified by her thoughts, she splashed cold water on her face and studied her reflection in the mirror. Nothing on the outside had changed, but her insides resembled the aftermath of a tornado. The more agitated she became, the madder she was with Seamus for doing this to her. She'd said *one* night. One damned night. What about that didn't he understand?

"You need to make him understand, before it's all over the island that you're sleeping with your son's employee," she whispered to her reflection. "Get it together!"

After a few more deep breaths, she felt ready to rejoin the party. Hopefully, Mac and Linda would be up for an early night. She opened the door and gasped with shock when Seamus pushed her backward into the small bathroom and closed the door. The sound of the door locking echoed like a gunshot.

"*What're you doing?*"

He grabbed her hips and yanked her into him. "This." His lips came down on hers, hard and determined.

Carolina intended to push him away, but her arms didn't get the memo. They looped around him as she returned the kiss with a frantic urgency to match his.

Cupping her ass, he pushed his erection against her and had her on the verge of explosive release in a matter of seconds.

The fear of knowing they could be discovered at any second made the whole thing even hotter, if that was possible. If she'd been looking for proof that she'd taken leave of her senses, here it was, wrapped around her.

When he tugged on the button to her jeans, Carolina realized he intended to have sex right there in Luke and Sydney's bathroom. Turning her head to break the kiss, she said, "Stop." With a hand to his chest, she pushed him back. "Stop."

"Let me take you home." His voice was raspy as his lips burned a trail on her neck.

"No."

"Please, Carolina. Tell them you don't feel good, and I'll offer to take you home."

"I can't. Everyone will know why we're leaving."

"No one will know anything other than your son's employee is giving you a ride home."

"I told you this isn't going to happen."

His fingers dug into her hips as he pushed his hard cock against her throbbing core.

Remembering how he'd stretched her almost to the point of pain made her whimper with the need for more.

"It's already happening."

"Seamus, *please.* I can't do this."

"Can't or won't?"

Her head dropped onto his chest as her fingers gripped his belt loops.

"If you mean it, love, you might want to let me go."

He paused for a heartbeat, giving her a chance to release him.

Almost against her will, her fingers tightened their grip on his jeans.

He chuckled as his lips moved over her neck.

"Don't get all full of yourself," she snapped, annoyed by how easy she was with him. "This doesn't change anything."

"It makes me so hot when you're bossy. Like last night when you told me to fuck you harder. *So hot.*"

Furious with herself as much as him, Carolina let him go, reached around him and opened the door to a rush of cooler air. "Leave me alone."

With her hands trembling and her heart beating so hard it felt like it might burst, Carolina took a minute in the hallway to pull herself together before she rejoined the party.

Linda pounced immediately. "Are you all right? Your face is all red."

"I feel like I'm coming down with something. Would you mind terribly if we left early?"

"I'll give you a ride," a voice behind them said in a lilting Irish brogue. "I was getting ready to leave myself. I'm on the eight o'clock boat in the morning."

Carolina closed her eyes, seeking forbearance. She couldn't whack him—or murder him, for that matter—in a room full of people.

"Are you sure you don't mind, Seamus?" Linda asked. "I don't mind taking her."

"I'm going right by her place on the way to the Beachcomber," Seamus said with a crafty grin.

Her place was in the complete opposite direction from the Beachcomber, and he knew it. Since Linda had been looking forward to the gathering, Carolina hated to drag her away early. "Thank you," she said to Seamus through gritted teeth. He was so going to pay for this, except that was exactly what he wanted.

"If you're sure," Linda said, giving Carolina a speculative glance.

"No trouble a'tall," Seamus said. "Shall we, Miz Cantrell?"

If looks could kill, he'd be so dead.

His decadent mouth curled into the charming smile that'd gotten her into this mess in the first place.

"I'll call you tomorrow to check on you," Linda said, giving Carolina a hug.

"I'll be fine. I'm sure it's just a bug that's going around."

"Of course it is. What else would it be?"

Carolina left Linda's question unanswered. As she and Seamus said good night and thank you to their hosts, Carolina plotted his imminent demise. She was going to slice him into tiny pieces and ship him back to his homeland in a shoebox. And then she was *really* going to hurt him.

Chapter 19

"Where the heck have you been all day?" Evan asked Owen.

"I was…busy. Why?"

"I've been trying to call you. I need to talk to you."

Owen took a drink of his beer and fixed his gaze on Laura, who was huddled across the room with Grace and Stephanie. He wondered if she was spilling their secrets to her girlfriends. In the past, women who kissed and told bothered him. In this case, however, he wanted the whole world to know that she was his and he was hers and they were officially together. For keeps.

"Hello? Owen, are you listening to me?"

"Sorry, what were you saying?"

"What the heck is *with* you, man?"

"Same thing that's been with you since you got together with Grace."

Following Owen's gaze to Laura, Evan scratched at the stubble on his jaw. "Is that right?"

"Uh-huh."

"You and my cousin. Who'd a thunk it, huh?"

"Not me, that's for sure. But now it's all I can think about."

"I know that feeling," Evan said with a laugh. "I like you guys together."

"I do, too. So what'd you want to talk to me about?"

"A business opportunity." Evan outlined Ned's plan for a recording studio on the island. "What do you think? Could we make a go of it?"

"You could. That'd be right up your alley."

"But not yours?"

"Sounds like a lot of work."

"It would be, but I really think we could do it."

Owen was pleased to see Evan excited about something again. Watching him wait to hear what would become of his hard-won career in Nashville had been difficult on everyone who cared about him.

"Think about all the musicians we both know, people like you and me who've never gotten a break. There's so much talent out there looking for an outlet."

"You're excited about this."

"Yeah, kinda, but I was hoping we could do it together."

Owen chose his words carefully, not wanting to put a damper on Evan's enthusiasm. "I think I've found my calling at the hotel."

"Doing what?"

"Whatever needs to be done," Owen said with a shrug. "Once the renovations are finished, Laura will manage the hotel, and I'll help her. It'll always need constant care and feeding. I'll have more than enough to keep me busy. I've discovered I enjoy puttering around the old place."

Evan's eyes had bugged out of his head. "Are you *listening* to yourself? Since when are you Mr. Fix It? You're a *musician*. That's who you've always been."

"People change, Ev. Things change. I'll always be a musician, but there's other stuff I want to do, too. My grandparents ran that place for half a century. I like the idea of keeping it in the family."

"How does Laura fit into that?"

"If I have my way, I'll be keeping her in the family, too."

"You're really not interested in the studio?" Evan asked, looking crushed.

"I'm very interested in seeing the amazing things you're going to do with it. I can't wait to buy your first record."

"But you're not going to be part of it."

"I'm sorry, but no."

Evan rested his hands on his hips, seeming a little lost. "I wasn't expecting you to say no."

"Sorry to let you down."

"You're not. I'll have to rethink the plan. That's all."

"I have no doubt you can take this opportunity and run with it. You've already got everything you need to make it a huge success. You don't need me."

"I'll need you later tonight. Luke asked us to play after a while. Did you bring your guitar?"

"Never leave home without it."

Evan nodded. "Good."

"You're not pissed are you?"

"Nah. Surprisingly enough, I get it."

"You've always had more ambition than I did. I was happy playing covers in bars, while you were writing songs and chasing the big deal."

"For all the good that did me," Evan said bitterly.

"Everything happens for a reason. Maybe you were meant to venture down this new road."

"Grace said the same thing."

"So she's in favor of the studio idea?"

"Hell, yeah," Evan said with a grin. "It'd keep me here on the island with her. She's thrilled."

"Give her time. She'll wise up."

"Very funny."

Owen's cell phone rang, and he was surprised to see Frank McCarthy's number on the caller ID. "I gotta take this," he said to Evan.

"Go right ahead."

Owen walked outside to take the call. "Hi, Frank."

"Owen, I'm glad I caught you."

"We're at a party. Is everything okay?"

"I had a conversation tonight with the son-in-law who shall not be named."

Owen's gut clenched with anxiety. "And?"

"I convinced him that it's in his best interest to sign the papers and give Laura primary custody of the baby. He agreed to a visitation schedule of occasional weekends and vacations, two weeks in the summer and alternating holidays."

Owen released a deep breath he hadn't realized he was holding. "That's great. Laura will be thrilled."

"I'm not so sure."

"Why's that."

"He has a condition."

Owen's stomach began to hurt. "What condition?"

"He wants her to end it with you."

He'd received actual gut punches that hurt less than those words did. "What right does he have to dictate who she spends time with?"

"None whatsoever, but try telling him that. I'm having lunch with the senior partner at his firm on Monday. We went to high school together. I'll feel him out and see if he's willing to lean on his wayward associate on my behalf."

"Will you keep me posted?"

"Of course. I called you because I didn't want to upset Laura any more than she already is. Will you tell her about this?"

Owen closed his eyes and pictured her gorgeous face as she told him she loved him earlier. "If you're seeing the partner on Monday, I suppose I can wait until then to mention it to her but not much longer. I don't want to keep things from her."

"As my father would say, I like the cut of your jib, young man."

Owen thought of his own father, who'd never approved of a thing about him. "Thank you. That's nice of you to say."

"I'll be in touch," Frank said. "Take good care of my girl in the meantime."

"I will."

Reeling, Owen stashed the phone in his pocket. What the hell was he supposed to do now?

"Tell us everything," Stephanie said as she and Grace dragged Laura to a quiet corner in the living room. "What happened with the ex? And Owen! That was one heck of a kiss I walked in on the other day."

"Sorry about that," Laura said, mortified.

"Don't be sorry! Spill the beans!"

"You first," Laura said. "I want to hear all about the proposal. Was it so romantic?"

"He did a good job," Stephanie said with a soft glow in her eyes. "Especially since I was trying to break up with him when he asked me."

"*What?*" Grace said. "Why?"

"We were constantly at odds. It was too much for me. I lived like that for years with my mother, and I can't do it anymore."

"How did he change your mind?"

"How else? Words. The man is gifted. In more ways than one."

Grace let out a snort. "I bet it was quite something."

"Unforgettable," Stephanie said.

Laura took a closer look at Stephanie's ring. "I wouldn't have pictured the traditional engagement ring for you."

"Grant said he debated something eclectic but decided to go traditional because I'd never had that before. Turns out I kinda dig tradition."

"Oh," Grace said. "How sweet is that?"

"I know. He definitely has his moments."

Laura hugged Stephanie. "I'm so happy for you. No one deserves to be happy more than you do."

"Thanks. I'm so happy it's not even funny. Not only do I get a lifetime with Grant, my dad is free and clear and figuring out what's next. His battle was at the center of my life for so long that some days I can't believe I don't have to think about it anymore."

"It must be such a relief," Grace said. "I can't even imagine what that was like."

"It was a fourteen-year nightmare."

"It's all in the past now, and you can do anything you want," Laura said.

"I know," Stephanie said with a gleam in her eye. "That's why I'm finally going to open the restaurant I've always dreamed of."

"Open it in the hotel," Laura said. The words were out of her mouth before the thought was fully formed.

Stephanie's confusion showed on her face. "Huh?"

"Adele—Owen's grandmother—and I agree that we need a top-shelf restaurant in the hotel. We've got the space and a huge kitchen and everything you'd need. We'll renovate it to your specs—whatever you want."

"You're serious."

"I'm dead serious."

"I love that idea," Grace said. "You guys would make a great team."

"I totally agree," Laura said, more in love with the idea with every passing minute. "You'd have carte blanche over the restaurant. It'd be totally yours."

"Wow. I don't know what to say."

"Say yes," Laura said. "Let's work together to bring the Surf back to its former glory."

"It does have everything I want—an ideal location in town, a spectacular view of the water and built-in foot traffic," Stephanie said. "It sounds perfect, but I'd need to take a closer look at the kitchen and dining room before I decide for sure."

"Come by in the morning and look to your heart's content."

"I will. Thank you for the amazing idea. If it works out, this could be terrific for both of us."

"Yay," Grace said, clapping her hands. "Now let's hear about what happened with the ex—and Owen."

Laura filled them in on the highlights—or lowlights as they were—of her conversation with Justin.

"So where does it stand now?" Stephanie asked, still scowling over Justin's comment about the baby's paternity.

"I'm waiting on him. I left there convinced he would sign the papers, but part of me suspects he's not done fighting."

"What did he say about the baby?" Grace asked.

"He already knew."

Stephanie's brows narrowed. "How?"

"Apparently, he had me followed. He knew all about the hotel, the baby, Owen."

"So creepy," Grace said with a shiver. "I dislike this guy more all the time."

"No kidding," Stephanie said. "What does Owen say about it?"

"He's been amazing," Laura said. "So supportive and understanding. Get this—he asked if he could be my childbirth coach. Can you believe that?"

"He loves you," Grace said. "The whole time he was talking to Evan just now, he was watching you."

"Was he?" Laura asked, smiling.

"Couldn't take his eyes off you," Grace confirmed.

"He's. . . wonderful. I hope Justin signs the papers and sets me free before Owen runs out of patience with the situation."

"He's not going anywhere," Stephanie assured Laura. "Any man who'd willingly volunteer to witness childbirth must have a big, bad thing for you."

"No kidding," Grace said. "If that's not a measure of his devotion, I don't know what is."

The baby chose that moment to send a rippling wave across Laura's stomach. She took that to mean the baby agreed with her friends.

"So what's her story?" Dan Torrington asked Grant.

"Whose story?"

"Rebecca of Sunnybrook Farm over there." Dan nodded to Kara, who was chatting with Big Mac and Linda.

"No idea. Hey, Mac," Grant said to his brother. "Come here."

"What's up?" Mac asked when he joined them.

"Dan wants the skinny on Kara," Grant said.

"I don't know her all that well except that she's from Maine and number six in a family of eleven kids."

"*Eleven?*" Grant asked. "Jesus. I thought our family was big."

"Imagine twice as many of us plus one," Mac said with a grin.

"No, thanks," Grant said. "I've got all I can handle with four siblings."

"What's she doing on Gansett?" Dan asked, his gaze riveted to Kara, who was making Big Mac and Linda laugh with an animated story. For some strange reason, he desperately wanted to hear what she was saying.

Mac told them about the launch service Kara had proposed for the Salt Pond and the role McCarthy's Gansett Island Marina would play in the plan.

"Why didn't we think of that?" Grant asked.

"Dad and Luke have talked about it over the years, but that's as far as it got," Mac said. "This is even better for us because we get the benefit of increased foot traffic for the restaurant and gift shop—and possibly new customers for the marina when they see how great our place is—but none of the headaches of running the launch service ourselves. Win-win."

While Grant talked business with his brother, Dan continued to watch Kara. She wasn't even his type. He went for built-like-brick-shithouse blondes, not buttoned-down, wholesome country girls. She wore Levi jeans, for Pete's sake. Though they did amazing things to her excellent ass, he couldn't remember the last woman he'd known who wore plain old Levis.

It was hard to tell through the bulky sweater if she had anything going on up top, and from what he could gather from a distance, she didn't wear a lick of makeup on her fresh-faced complexion. *She wouldn't last a day in LA*. For some reason, the thought pleased him.

"How long is she here?" Dan asked Mac.

"She's heading back to Maine on Monday, but she'll be back in March to get ready for the season."

For some strange reason, Dan felt oddly deflated to know she was leaving. Soon.

"What're you up to, Torrington?" Grant asked when Mac went to find his wife.

Startled out of his thoughts, Dan said, "Nothing."

"Why're you staring at her? You're going to creep her out."

"I'm not staring at her."

"Don't tell me you're interested. You're way too old for her, and she's hardly your type."

"Funny, I was thinking the same thing. And yet..."

"What?"

"There's something about her. Look at her. She's pure as the driven snow."

"Which is why you need to stay far, far away."

Dan rested a hand over his chest. "I'm wounded."

"You'll survive."

"Introduce me."

"I don't know her either," Grant protested.

"I believe you know the people she's talking to, don't you?"

Grant rolled his eyes. "I've met them once or twice."

"Come on then."

"Why do I have the sinking feeling I'm going to regret this?"

"Be a pal, McCarthy. Remember that favor I did for you when your girlfriend's stepfather was unjustly incarcerated?"

"How long will I have to pay for that?"

"I'll let you know in a decade or two when the debt is repaid. In the meantime..." He gave Grant a gentle nudge to get him moving.

"Fine. Let's get this over with." Grant crossed the kitchen to where his parents were talking to Kara. "Having a good time, everyone?"

"Kara Ballard," Big Mac said, "this is our idiot second son, Grant, who got engaged and forgot to tell his parents for two days."

"I was busy," Grant said, shaking hands with Kara. Waggling his brows, he added, "Celebrating."

Kara's cheeks went pink at Grant's mention of celebrating, and Dan became even more intrigued. *Pure as the driven snow,* and *she blushes. Too good to be true.*

"Kara, this is my friend Dan Torrington."

"Nice to meet you." When she met his gaze, he noticed her eyes were brown with flecks of gold. And were those...*freckles*? Her shy smile was right out of a toothpaste ad. Good God, she was too cute for words, and as Grant had said, probably far too young for him.

"Nice to meet you, too," Dan said. "I hear you're in the boat business."

"Her family has a big outfit in Bar Harbor," Big Mac said.

"What do you do?" Dan asked.

"Business development, mostly, but as of next summer, I'll be running the launch service in the Salt Pond."

Dan would've bet his sizable fortune that she'd been the smart girl in school who'd ruined the curve for guys like him. He wondered if she ever let down her ponytail and got a little wild. He'd sure like to know.

"And you, Mr. Torrington? What do you do?"

Grant guffawed at the "Mr. Torrington," earning him a swat and a glare from his mother.

"Call me Dan, please. I'm a lawyer."

"Oh," Kara said, barely hiding her contempt. "That's...nice."

Dan's face lifted into a half grin as he bit back the instant urge to ask what she had against lawyers.

"Stephanie is beckoning us," Grant said to his parents. "I hope I'm not about to hear the words 'wedding plans' come out of her mouth."

"Oh, I can't wait to plan another wedding!" Linda said, leading her husband and son into the living room.

"Fabulous," Grant muttered as his mother tugged at his arm.

Dan laughed at his friend's dismay. "The poor bastard has no idea what he's in for."

"What's that supposed to mean?" Kara asked.

Surprised by her tone, Dan chose his words carefully. "Wedding planning isn't for the faint of heart."

"Are you married?"

"Nope."

"Then what do you know about wedding planning?"

The memories flooded over him in a wave of pain that caught him off guard. How was it possible that it still hurt so badly? "Came close once."

"What happened?"

"Why Ms. Ballard, we've just met," he said with the effortlessly charming smile that had served him well with women his entire life. "I don't know if I'm ready to start spilling *all* my secrets." The instant the words were out of his mouth he regretted them. What he'd intended as teasing had clearly embarrassed her.

"I'm sorry. You're absolutely right. It's none of my business."

"Hey, I was only kidding." He bent his head to look into her eyes. "Seriously, kidding. The engagement didn't work out." His shrug belied the ongoing pain of finding his fiancée riding his best man two days before the wedding. Two losses for the price of one. "It was one of those things."

"Well, it must've been a difficult time. I'm sorry you had to go through that."

"Shit happens."

She became intensely interested in her beer bottle. "Yes, it does," she said in a world-weary tone that told him she knew all too well what he meant.

Dan had an urgent need to know what kind of shit had happened to her. Wanting to keep her talking, he gestured to her beer. "Can I get you another?"

"No, thank you. I'm heading out soon."

"Not before you tell me what you have against lawyers."

Her startled gaze shot up to meet his. "What makes you think I have anything against lawyers?"

"The giveaway might've been the oh-so-polite 'that's nice' when I said I am one."

"I don't have anything against lawyers. They serve a useful purpose."

"Is that so?"

"You would know better than me. Are you useful?"

He thought of the three-dozen people who were now walking free thanks to his efforts to overturn unjust convictions. "I'd like to think so."

"There you have it."

She was absolutely adorable and absolutely wrong for him, but he was absolutely intrigued, nonetheless. "I'd like to take you to dinner tomorrow night."

She stared at him as if he'd told her he wanted to take her on a vacation to the moon. "You… I…"

"It's a simple question: Will you go out with me tomorrow night?"

"I…" He could see that she wanted to. How could he miss the flash of longing that crossed her expressive face? With every passing moment, he became more interested. "No, but thank you for asking."

"There's nothing I can do to change your mind?"

"No."

Well, didn't that beat all? Dan couldn't remember the last time a woman had said no to him. About anything.

"I have to go now," she said. "It was nice to meet you."

"You, too."

She scurried off as if someone had told her the house was on fire. As she said her good-byes to Mac, Big Mac, Luke and Sydney, Dan once again noticed the fine things those faded Levis did to her sumptuous ass. The second before she went through the door, she glanced into the kitchen to find Dan still watching her intently. The wistfulness he saw on her expressive face had him standing up straighter. For a brief instant, he thought about going after her.

But he stopped himself before he could act on the impulse. If she wasn't interested, neither was he.

"Keep telling yourself that," he muttered.

"That didn't take long," Grant said when he rejoined Dan in the kitchen.

"What?"

"I've never seen a woman run away from you so quickly. Are you losing your touch?"

"I wouldn't say that. However, it does occur to me that it might be far more interesting to write my book here in the spring than over the winter."

Grant eyed him suspiciously. "What are you up to?"

"Nothing. Yet..."

Tiffany didn't step onto the back deck because Maddie had suggested Blaine might follow her. No, she needed some fresh air and a moment alone. She'd give everything she had for a cigarette, but she'd given them up a couple of months ago and was sticking to her resolve for Ashleigh's sake.

But honestly, if she had to spend one more second surrounded by newly in love couples who couldn't keep their hands to themselves, she was going to scream. They were all so freaking *happy*. It made her want to barf. She'd once been exactly like Grace and Stephanie and Laura and Sydney and even Maddie, smug in her conviction that she'd found the love of her life. She'd married Jim when she was twenty and had been so certain their love affair would last a lifetime. But at some point, it had all gone wrong, and she still had no idea why.

She wanted to warn her friends to be careful. She wanted to tell them that sometimes things didn't work out the way they were supposed to. She wanted to tell them that they could devote their whole heart and soul to a man only to be rebuffed for no good reason.

However, she doubted any of them would want to hear it. Hell, she hadn't wanted to hear it, even when it became obvious that her husband had checked out of their marriage. It had taken him moving all the furniture out of their house for her to finally get a clue that it was over between them.

Deep-seated loneliness pierced through the layer of cynicism and bitterness she hid behind. As much as she wanted to disdain the outbreak of happiness in her circle of friends, she couldn't deny that she was envious. When would she get her happily ever after? Even her mother was stupid in love with Ned and happier than Tiffany had ever seen her. No one deserved it more after what Francine had endured, raising two kids on her own after her husband abandoned the family, but Tiffany was jealous of her own mother!

Shaking her head with disgust, she was about to return to the party when a dark shadow fell over her. Tingling awareness had her entire body standing up to take notice. He didn't have to say a word. She knew who he was by the way her body reacted to his nearness. Her nipples pebbled, and the ache between her legs reminded her of the incendiary incident in her kitchen and the single most amazing orgasm of her life.

"I've thought of you," he said without preamble. The rough, sexy texture of his voice sent shivers dancing down her spine. "A lot."

Tiffany cleared her throat and jammed trembling hands into the pockets of her jeans to ensure she wouldn't do anything stupid like grab him and kiss him. "I've thought of you, too."

Memories of that night came flooding back—handcuffing herself to Jim in a desperate attempt to get him to talk to her. Her body burned with the mortification of remembering him calling the police and how Blaine responded to find her naked and handcuffed to her husband. Had any plan ever gone so wrong?

"Are you still married to the douchebag?"

The question drew an unsteady laugh from her. Jim's histrionics that night had earned him no favor with Blaine. "Unfortunately, yes. But not for much longer."

"Good."

Her brain froze on the single, gruffly spoken word. "Why is that good?"

He moved closer, and Tiffany stepped back, encountering the rail that encircled the deck. In the dark, she could barely make out the chiseled features she'd committed to memory. Her heart pounded with excitement and anticipation and a tiny bit of fear. She barely knew this man and already understood that he had the power to demolish her in a way that Jim never could have.

Blaine's work-callused finger landed on her chin and slid down over her neck and throat, leaving a trail of fire between her breasts and hooking on the waistband of her jeans.

Tiffany was so startled and aroused she'd all but stopped breathing, until he tugged on her jeans, shocking her out of the stupor.

"The minute you're free of him, the very same *second* it's final, you're going to call me."

"Oh, I—"

He brought his face in so close to hers that the hint of his whiskers against her cheek and the mild, masculine scent of his cologne made her tremble madly.

Closing her eyes, she imagined his sun-bleached hair, golden-brown eyes and the hard, muscular chest he'd pressed against her breasts during the explosive encounter in her kitchen.

"You're going to call me," he said, "and we're going to pick up where we left off. Are we clear on how this is going to go?"

Tiffany didn't know whether to be relieved to know there'd be more with him or outraged over his dominant tone. No one told her what to do!

When she didn't answer him, he gave the waistband of her jeans a firmer tug that threw her off balance and caused her breasts to mash against his chest.

She gasped when her sensitized nipples made contact with hard muscle.

"I *said*, are we clear?"

While she wanted to protest his high-handedness, she was so aroused all she could manage was the briefest of nods. It was a shock to realize high-handedness turned her on.

"I didn't hear you," he growled in her ear.

"Yes," she whispered. "We're clear."

"Good." He released her so suddenly she nearly stumbled. Only his hands on her shoulders kept her from falling. And then his palm was on her face in a tender caress that stole the breath from her lungs.

She tipped her chin in invitation, needing his kiss more than she'd ever needed anything.

But then he dropped his hand and stepped back. Before she could register her disappointment, he was gone.

For a long time afterward, Tiffany stood on the deck taking deep, gulping breaths of cool autumn air. When the trembling finally subsided, she went inside to find Dan Torrington. It was time to get this divorce finalized.

CHAPTER 20

Carolina was so angry that it didn't occur to her to ask how Seamus knew where she lived. *Whatever*, she thought, it saved her from having to speak to him as he drove his company truck along the island's winding roads. When she thought of the way he'd totally manipulated the situation, she wanted to scream.

"What part of the words 'one-night stand' don't you understand?" she asked after many minutes of tense silence.

"The one-night part."

"Are you being intentionally obtuse?"

"I love when you get all stern with me. It makes me hot."

Apparently, everything made him hot. "Answer the question!"

"I've forgotten what it was."

Oh my God! He is impossible! "I'd like to walk the rest of the way."

"That's not happening."

"This island is perfectly safe. Now stop the truck, and let me out."

"It is not perfectly safe for anyone, let alone a gorgeous woman, to walk on these dark roads—alone—at night."

Oh, that voice… It ought to be licensed as a deadly weapon! All he had to do was talk, and she forgot about being mad with him.

"What I don't understand is why a wise, mature, independent woman such as yourself would give a flying fig about what anyone else thinks of her."

"No, you wouldn't understand."

"Make me understand, Carolina. Tell me why we can't have something we both want."

"I don't want it! I told you that!"

"You do want it. You won't allow yourself to have it. There's a difference."

"Now you're splitting hairs."

"There's a difference," he said again, more forcefully this time.

They rode in silence for ten more minutes before he pulled into the dirt lane that led to her home.

"How do you know where I live?"

"When something interests me, I pay attention." Reaching for her hand, he brought it to his lips. "And you, lovely Carolina, interest me."

She tugged her hand free and got out of the truck. "Thanks for the ride."

When she heard his door slam, she spun around, intending to tell him not to even think about following her. She encountered the broad wall of his chest and uttered an unconvincing squeak of protest when he put his arms around her, cupped her ass and lifted her onto the hood of the truck.

Shocked and aroused, the heat of the engine was nothing compared to the heat that zipped through her veins as he leaned over her.

"Give yourself permission, Caro," he whispered, his gentle tone in sharp contrast to the rough way he'd handled her. His use of her nickname twisted her insides into knots. "Take what you know you want." He flexed his hips and pushed the hard column of his erection into the V of her legs. "Take it."

"I can't," she said, thinking of Joe and the family Seamus would someday want. Burying her fingers in his thick auburn hair, she tugged him in for a searing kiss. "I want to," she said many minutes later when she had no choice but to come up for air. "I won't deny that."

"Don't deny *us*, Caro." His fingers dug into her bottom as he throbbed against her. "We could be so great together."

"Until you wake up one day and realize what you've sacrificed. I won't take that away from you."

"You're not taking anything I'm not freely giving, love. I want you. I've wanted you from the first time I laid eyes on you. I've never wanted anyone the way I want you."

Carolina couldn't deny that she was seduced, as much by his heartfelt words as the rocking motion of his hips.

"What would your mother say?"

At that, he froze, looked down at her in the faint moonlight and let out a deep, ringing laugh. "What in the name of Jesus, Mary and Joseph does my dear sweet mum have to do with this?"

"*If*, and I use that word very, *very* rhetorically, this were to happen, someday, I might have to face her."

"She'd think the world of you, love. She'd have all the respect in the world for a woman who was widowed far too young and raised a fine son all on her own while helping her parents run a successful business. What's not to respect about that woman?"

"The part where she's eighteen years older than the dear sweet mum's precious son and having wild sex with him?"

His lascivious grin almost drew a smile from her. "It was rather wild, wasn't it?"

With her hands on his face, she said, "Focus."

"I'm very focused." He turned his attention to her neck and made her whimper when he nibbled his way from her ear to her throat. "It's really quite simple, love." His breath on her sensitive skin touched off an outbreak of goose bumps. "I want to be with you. I want to sleep with you and eat with you and talk with you and wake up with you and fight over the TV with you and go to bed with you." His teeth closed on her earlobe. "I want to make wild love with you every single day."

Carolina blinked back tears. She was so far out of her league with this man and so powerfully charmed by him. "How can you possibly know that will make you happy?"

"I can't possibly know for sure, but I have a sneaking suspicion it could make us both happy." His lips found hers in the dark for one of those long, deep, wet kisses he specialized in. By the time he drew back from her, she was quivering and on the verge of an explosive release. "I know you're worried about what Joe might say, and to tell you the God's honest truth, so am I. I think the world of him and would never want to disappoint him."

As he spoke, he smoothed the hair off her forehead. "But he's found his love, and he's as happy as any man could ever hope to be. I can't imagine the man I know and respect would want anything less for the mother he loves so dearly." He kissed her again, softly and sweetly this time, and then lifted himself off her. The cool night air was a shock after the heat of his body. With both hands, he helped her down from the truck.

Carolina was caught off guard by his unexpected retreat. Reeling, she stumbled, and he caught her.

"It's okay, love." He kissed her forehead. "Go on in now. You think about what I said, and when you're ready, you come to me."

She started to walk away but turned back to him. "It's not about whether I want you, Seamus."

"I know that."

With a nod, she went inside and closed the door, leaning against it until she heard the truck start up and pull out of the driveway. Then she slid down to the floor and sat there for a long time, thinking about what he'd said and wishing things were different. Oh, how she wished things were different.

Owen and Evan tuned their guitars in a ritual as old as their friendship. They'd been playing together since they first met when they were in high school. That was why it had pained Owen to say no to Evan's business proposal. At one time, he might've been intrigued by it. But now he was intrigued by the idea of living and working with Laura. Funny how things changed.

With a fire burning in the hearth and most of his favorite people gathered around him, Owen should've been more at peace than he'd ever been in his life. But Justin's demand weighed heavily on Owen as he let Evan lead the way through the first set.

Evan, who'd been plagued by worse than usual allergies this fall, signaled for Owen to continue without him when a relentless bout of sneezing sent him from the room.

As Owen strummed his guitar, he sought out Laura, almost willing her to look at him. When her gaze met his, he felt the impact from the top of his head to the bottom of his feet. What a lucky, lucky bastard he was to have found her. Now that he had her, there wasn't much he wouldn't do to keep her close. He wondered if Justin had any idea how determined they were to be together. Well, he'd soon find out if he chose to make an issue of their relationship.

He smiled at Laura and played the opening chords to George Harrison's song "Something." Playing for her and only her, he put everything he felt for her into the song, letting her know something about her made her different from every other woman in the world.

At first, only Laura realized he was sending her a love letter in the form of a song, but by the time he hit the second chorus, everyone else had tuned in to the moment unfolding between them. *I guess we've gone public*, he thought, satisfied that their friends were in on the secret they'd been keeping.

Laura sent him an intimate, loving smile that warmed him all the way through. He couldn't wait to go home with her, to debrief the party, to sleep wrapped up in her. He couldn't wait for everything with her.

The door swung open to admit Slim Jackson, Luke's good friend and the island's number-one charter pilot. He was tall and muscular with dark hair and eyes and an easy, relaxed manner. His grandfather had tagged him with the nick name when he was a gangly kid, and it had stuck, becoming funny when Slim grew into a well-built man.

"Hey, you made it," Luke said to Slim as Owen finished the song to enthusiastic applause.

Slim said something to Luke that had him turning to signal Owen.

He put down his guitar and went over to see what was going on. Shaking hands with Slim, he noticed the other man seemed uncharacteristically rattled. "What's up?" Owen asked.

"I just flew your mom over from the mainland."

Owen hadn't spoken to his mother in a couple of weeks, and she'd never mentioned a trip to the island. "Really? What's she doing here?"

"She didn't say, but she's in rough shape. Her face was all red like she'd been crying, and it seemed like she was in pain or something. When we landed, she cried out from the impact. I tried to talk her into letting me take her to the clinic, but she insisted I drop her at the hotel."

A red haze of rage blinded Owen as Slim's words registered. He knew what must've happened, because it'd happened before.

Laura came up to him and rested her hand on his back. "Is everything okay?"

"We need to go." Owen's calm tone belied the uproar going on inside him. "My mom is here."

"Did you know she was coming?"

He shook his head, not trusting himself to say anything more. Crossing the room, he put his guitar in the case and closed the latches with fumbling fingers. He was aware of Laura saying good-bye to the others, but he focused on breathing through the rage. He could only imagine what must've happened this time. Had she finally left him? Owen refused to entertain a hope that had been dashed so often in the past.

"Yo, O, are you okay?" Evan asked quietly. He crouched next to Owen and rested a hand on his shoulder.

"Did you hear what Slim said?"

"Yeah." Evan was the only person on the island who knew the truth about Owen's upbringing with the rigid army general who'd beaten the crap out of his wife and children every chance he'd gotten. "What can I do for you?"

Owen didn't know what he wanted. He was tempted to run and hide the way he'd done as a young child when his father's rages would overtake him. Owen had run away and hidden until he was old enough to get between his father and the victim of choice. Running and hiding wasn't an option with his mother possibly hurt and waiting for him in town.

Evan seemed to sense Owen's indecision. "I'll give you and Laura a ride home, and we'll see what's up, okay?"

"Thanks, Ev."

"Come on, let's go."

Evan smoothed the way with the others for a quick escape.

Owen settled Laura in the front seat of her car, stashed his guitar in the trunk and took the backseat, thankful for Evan's offer to drive. Owen had no idea what to expect when they got to the hotel, and the sick feeling in his stomach brought back memories he'd run from his entire adult life. Images ran through his mind like a horror movie, snippets from the past he'd tried so hard to forget. Sometimes he suspected the reason he'd kept moving from one place to another was because he was afraid of what would happen if he ever stood still for too long.

Laura turned in her seat and extended a hand to him.

He closed his cold hand around her much warmer one and held on. "There are things I should tell you… Things you should know…" He wondered if she'd be angry that he hadn't told her before now.

Evan glanced at the rearview mirror and met Owen's gaze.

"The most important thing right now is whatever your mom needs," Laura said. "Don't worry about me, okay?"

He gave a small nod, loving her for understanding.

"Whatever it is, I'll be right there with you," she added.

"Me, too," Evan said.

Owen's throat tightened. How could he tell his two closest friends that he didn't want them there? He didn't want them to see what his father had done to his mother. He didn't want them to know. But he could hardly send them away when neither of them would think of leaving him.

They weren't like the transient people he'd encountered growing up in the military who were quick to turn the other way at any sign of trouble, especially in the family of a high-ranking officer. These people truly cared about him, and they wouldn't let him go through this alone.

He wanted to thank them for their support, but he couldn't seem to form the words. They'd left the porch light on, which was how Owen saw her sitting on the front stairs, leaning against the rail. "Stop."

When the car slowed, Owen jumped out and jogged the last two blocks to the hotel. "Mom?" Her chin-length blonde hair hid her face, so he couldn't tell if she was asleep or unconscious.

Mindful of her injuries, he rested a hand carefully on her shoulder. "Mom."

Her puffy blue eyes opened and immediately filled with tears when she saw him.

"What're you doing out here?"

"The hide-a-key was missing."

Crap, Owen thought, remembering that they'd taken it with them. "What happened?"

She waved a hand, weary with defeat. "You know."

"Do you need a doctor?" He was aware of Evan and Laura standing behind him, waiting to hear what they could do to help.

"I don't know."

"Can you stand up?"

"I think so." But when she tried, her cries tore at Owen's guts.

"Evan, go get David Lawrence. Hurry."

Laura materialized on the other size of his mother, and between the two of them, they managed to get her inside. Of course, none of her injuries were visible, because his father had learned a long time ago to avoid faces, lest someone discover their family's dirty secret.

"How did you travel all the way from Virginia in this condition?" he asked through gritted teeth.

"I wanted to be here, at the hotel. I wanted to see you." She broke down into sobs that shattered his heart. He would kill that son of a bitch for doing this to her. He should've killed him years ago and spared them all the nightmare he'd inflicted upon them. Choking back the rage, because it wasn't what his mother needed and it certainly didn't change anything, he tried to stay focused on getting her settled on his bed.

Laura found a throw blanket and helped him cover her.

"Laura, this is my mom, Sarah. Mom, this is Laura McCarthy. She's my..." Owen didn't know what word would be appropriate. He looked to Laura for guidance.

"I'm his girlfriend," Laura said with a loving smile that filled him with gratitude.

Sarah looked up at him, the pain making her eyes heavy. "You never said..."

"I hadn't gotten around to telling you, but I was going to. Soon. Laura is the manager Gran hired to get the hotel open again."

"Oh, Mother mentioned you."

"I'm a big fan of your mother's," Laura said, speaking as if they were meeting at a cocktail party rather than in the aftermath of violence. In that moment, he appreciated her more than he ever had before. "I'm looking forward to meeting her in person." She tucked the blanket around his mother's feet. "Is there anything I can get for you, Mrs. Lawry? Some water or tea maybe?"

"No, thank you, honey. I'd like to close my eyes for a minute. I'm so tired."

"You rest, Mom," Owen said, bending to kiss her forehead. "The doctor will be here soon to fix you up."

Sarah released a deep breath and was asleep within seconds.

Laura took Owen's hand and led him into the sitting room. Turning, she put her arms around him and held on tight.

Woodenly, Owen returned the embrace, even as his mind raced with questions and worries and rage. Always lurking right below the surface was the rage he'd fought so hard against. It would've been so easy to become like his father. Choosing the alternate path had been a lifelong struggle. In the past, he wouldn't have allowed anyone to touch or comfort him. Allowing Laura into his nightmare seemed as natural as breathing, even though he was so ashamed, too. He'd lived with the shame almost as long as he'd lived with the fear and pain.

"What can I do for you?" she asked after a long moment.

"Just this," he said, tightening his hold on her. "I can't figure how she managed to get here from Virginia when she can barely move."

"She was fueled by determination."

He held on to her until they heard the main door swing open.

Evan rushed into the sitting room with David Lawrence following him.

"Thank you so much for coming, David."

The island's only doctor shook Owen's hand. "No problem. Evan said you suspect domestic abuse?"

Gritting his teeth, Owen nodded.

"You understand that I'm a mandatory reporter," David said, "meaning that if I suspect a crime has been committed, I'm required to report it to the proper authorities."

Laura's hand on Owen's back propped him up in more ways than one.

Owen had lost count of the many times the authorities had tried to intervene on behalf of Sarah Lawry and her children. Each and every time, they'd been steamrolled by the general. Not this time, Owen decided. This time would be different. "I understand." He gestured for David to follow him. "She's in here."

David asked Owen to leave him alone with Sarah.

Owen hesitated, unsure of what to do.

Again, Laura took his hand and drew him out of the room. "It's okay," she said. "Let him examine her and see what she needs."

He reluctantly allowed Laura to lead him back to the sitting room.

She urged him to sit next to her on the love seat and never let go of his hand.

Evan took one of the chairs.

Owen appreciated that neither of them said a word while they waited a long time for David to emerge from the bedroom. When the door opened, Owen jumped up. "Is she okay?"

"She will be, but it'll take some time. She gave me permission to tell you that among a litany of other bruises, she has severely injured ribs. Tomorrow, I'd like to have her come in for an X-ray. Until we know if any of the ribs are broken, she needs to take it very easy. With broken ribs, there's a danger of piercing a lung. I wanted to take her in tonight, but she refused."

Owen forced himself to meet and hold David's steady gaze when he wanted to look away. Even at thirty-three, he was still embarrassed by the nightmare of his family. "Did she say how her ribs came to be injured?"

"She said her husband punched and kicked her." His tone lacked judgment or condemnation, though Owen wouldn't have blamed him for either.

Owen's entire body pulsed with tension at the confirmation of what he'd already known.

"I need to call Blaine," David said.

"Does she know you're doing that?"

David nodded. "I explained what would happen. Blaine will report the incident to the authorities in Virginia, who will arrest her husband. We'll document her injuries, and Blaine will take the report."

Owen tried to imagine his father being arrested in Virginia and the fury that would unleash. He shuddered at the thought. "She may change her mind about pressing charges in the morning," Owen said, his voice faltering.

Once again, Laura's hand on his back and her steady presence gave him the courage to proceed.

"That's the pattern," Owen added.

"So it's happened before?" David asked.

Owen nodded. *Too many times to count.*

"Because there was no sign of a head injury, I gave her a shot for the pain that should ensure that she sleeps through the night. I'll see her at the clinic in the morning."

Of course there was no head injury, Owen thought. *The general was strategic about where he aimed his blows so no one would ever know they were there.* "Thank you, David. Send me the bill."

"Don't worry about it. I'm happy to help." He handed Owen a card. "My cell number is on there. Call if you need me during the night."

Overwhelmed by the support, Owen said, "I appreciate that."

Evan walked David out and returned a minute later.

"Is there anything I can do, O?" Evan asked.

"Go on home," Owen said. "Thanks for your help."

"Are you sure? I don't mind hanging out."

"There's nothing you can do."

"Take my car, Ev," Laura said. "I'll get it tomorrow."

"No worries," Evan said. "I can walk. It's not far to the pharmacy." He crossed the room to give Owen a hug and then turned to hug his cousin. "Call me if you need anything."

"I will," Owen said.

When they were alone, Owen glanced at Laura, knowing he should at least try to explain.

"Not tonight," she said firmly. "Not ever, if you don't want to."

The sudden surge of tears took him by surprise. He would've thought he'd exhausted his lifetime supply many years ago.

She wrapped her arms around him and held on tight until he had expended decades' worth of grief and helpless rage. And then she urged him to stretch out on the sofa and snuggled up to him.

Embarrassed to have broken down in front of her, he rubbed his face as bone-deep weariness set in. “You should go up to bed. You need your rest.”

“I’m not going anywhere without you.”

“I have to stay down here in case she needs me.”

“I know.”

“Laura—”

She rested a finger on his lips. “Shh. I’m not leaving you alone. Not now, not ever. Close your eyes and try to get some rest.”

“I’m nothing like him. I’d never—”

“Owen! My God, do you honestly think you have to tell me that?”

“I wanted you to know because of the baby.”

“Owen, *please…*”

The brush of her lips against his neck registered at the same moment he felt new dampness on his face. He hated that he’d made her cry.

“You could never hurt me or the baby,” she said softly. “Never.”

“I’m sorry to drag you into this. I didn’t want you to know.”

She turned his face, forcing him to meet her gaze. “I love you. I love everything about you. Everything.” Her sweet, gentle kiss was nearly his undoing. “Close your eyes. It’s okay. I’m here, and I love you. Always.”

Owen closed his eyes and tried to relax. Wrapped in her love, he was able to quiet his mind and sleep.

CHAPTER 21

Grace was asleep when Evan got home. Sitting in the dark for a long time, he downed two beers before he felt calm enough to crawl into bed beside her. He lay awake for a long time, staring up at the ceiling as he tried to process everything that had happened. Filled with tension, he'd about given up on sleep when Grace turned over and snuggled up to him.

Evan put his arm around her and drew her in close, taking comfort from her presence.

"What's wrong?" she whispered.

"I don't get it."

"What, honey?"

"How a guy can beat the shit out of the woman he supposedly loves."

"Oh no. Owen's mom?"

Evan nodded. "Apparently, it's been going on for years with her—and the kids when they lived at home. Owen grew up in the midst of a nightmare."

"Did you know about it when you guys were younger?"

"He only told me recently."

"Poor Owen. He's such a nice guy."

"How does a man do that to the people he loves? I'll never understand it."

Grace's lips were soft and sweet on his chest as she kissed her way to his lips. "You can't understand because Big Mac McCarthy was your father, and he raised you and your brothers along with Joe and Luke to be the kind of men who worship the women they love."

"I'm ashamed to admit that I never knew how truly lucky I was to grow up the way I did until recently. Knowing what Owen went through, and you and Stephanie and Maddie... We were so very blessed."

"Yes, you were, and now some very lucky women are benefitting from the most excellent way Big Mac McCarthy raised his boys."

He could feel her smile in the dark as she continued to rain kisses upon his face.

"I want to help Owen, but I don't know how."

"Be there for him. That's all you can do. Take your cues from him."

She was right, as usual. "Owen's not interested in the recording studio," Evan said as he arranged her on top of him and closed his eyes, absorbed in her sweet love. He had no idea how he'd ever survived without her.

Focusing her attention on his eyelids and then the tip of his nose, she said, "You don't need him to do it. I have no doubt you can make a huge success of it all by yourself."

He ran his hands over the silky skin on her back. Until he met her, he hadn't known skin could be so soft. "You have such faith in me, Grace. It humbles me. It truly does."

"There's nothing you can't do if you set your mind to it," she said as her lips finally reached his mouth.

Anchoring her with his hand buried in her hair, he devoured her with his lips and tongue.

Shifting her hips ever so slightly, she nudged at his erect cock and sank down on him, making him gasp from the pleasure that zinged through him. For someone so new at sex and love, she was damned good at it.

"Love you so much, Gracie," he said, his voice raspy as he fought a losing battle against the seductive movements of her hips.

She bent over him, sending her hair cascading over his face in a silky rain shower. "I love you more."

Gripping her hips, he rolled them over in a smooth move that took her by surprise. "Not possible," he said as he thrust into her with increasing urgency.

She wrapped her arms and legs around him and held on tight for the ride. "Let's call this one a draw."

"You got it, baby."

Laura woke to the sound of quiet moaning. At some point, Owen had arranged her so she was sleeping on top of him with his arms wrapped tightly around her.

Moving carefully so as not to disturb him, she worked her way free of his embrace.

He muttered in his sleep but didn't wake up.

She smoothed a hand over his hair and kissed his forehead before she went to check on Sarah.

With the light from the hallway to guide her, Laura approached the bed. "Sarah?" When Owen's mother didn't answer, Laura realized she was murmuring and weeping in her sleep. Heartbroken for her, Laura took a tissue from the box on the bedside table and wiped the tears from Sarah's cheeks.

Owen came into the room a few minutes later. "Is she okay?"

"I thought she was awake, but she's dreaming."

"Nightmares, no doubt," he said gruffly.

The pain she heard in his voice hurt her, too. "Let's leave her be," Laura said. "David said the medication would ensure that she sleeps all night."

They returned to the sitting room, but Owen stopped her from proceeding to the sofa. "I have an idea." Using the pillows from both sofas, he built them a bed on the floor in front of the fireplace.

While he lit the fire to warm the room, she went upstairs to get another blanket and some pillows. She took advantage of the opportunity to change into pajamas and brush her teeth. With her hands braced on the sink, she took a brief moment to gather the fortitude to see him through this crisis.

She was still coming to grips with what she'd learned about him and his family. *No wonder he rarely speaks of his childhood.* The thought of what he'd endured had her on the verge of tears, but she fought through the emotion, wanting to be as strong for him as he'd been for her.

"Whatever he needs," she whispered. He'd been there for her in every possible way in the months they'd known each other, and she wanted nothing more than to return the favor.

Carrying the blanket and pillows, she went downstairs to find that he had changed, too, into a pair of flannel pajama pants that hung low on his lean hips. The firelight cast a warm glow on his chest, giving the light dusting of hair a golden hue.

He took the pillows from her and helped her spread the blanket over the sofa pillows. With the bed made, they stretched out together and pulled a second blanket over them. He reached for her, and she settled into his embrace as if they'd been sleeping together forever.

She ran her hand over his chest and belly, hoping to soothe and comfort.

He released an unsteady laugh and stopped the movement of her hand.

"Oh, sorry."

Bringing her hand to his lips, he pressed a kiss to the back of it. "Don't be sorry. I love when you touch me. I love it a little too much, if you catch my drift."

Laura smiled and turned her face up to kiss him.

"If you weren't here, I'd be going crazy right now," he said. "Whenever this happens, I fight my own battles with rage."

"That's only natural, Owen. Of course you're angry. Anyone would be."

"It goes so far beyond angry. I hate him. I want him to die in some awful, painful way. When we were kids, he would drag us all to church every week and knock us around afterward if we dared to move during the service. I used to pray that he would die. I prayed he'd get hit by a car or get cancer or get shot when he was deployed. But none of that happened, and after a while, I stopped believing in God."

Listening to him, she ached for the boy he'd once been and the man he was now, still so full of pain.

"I was five the first time he hit me. I said something he didn't like. I think it was about lima beans, and he slapped me right across the face at the dinner table. I went flying out of the chair, and my head hit the wall. That's my very first memory. I was in kindergarten and had to stay home from school for a week because my face was bruised. After that, he got smart about hitting in places that were less visible."

Laura blinked back tears, imagining the shock of a five-year-old when one of the two people he trusted to love and care for him betrayed him so completely. "What did your mother do?"

"Nothing."

Astounded, Laura tried to find the words. "I don't understand. How could she do nothing when he *hit* her child?"

"I didn't understand for a long time either. It took years for me to get that she was terrified of what he'd do to her if she dared to question him. By then she had three children, me and three-year-old twins, and no way to support us without him. We were living in Washington, DC, at the time, far away from her family in Ohio. She had no way out, so she kept her mouth shut, tended to the surface wounds and focused on surviving each day. It took a very, *very* long time for me to understand that pretending it wasn't happening was her way of coping."

Laura wanted to tell him to stop, that he didn't have to put himself through this, but she sensed he needed to get it out, so she kept quiet and let him talk.

"By the time I was ten, I was getting between him and my siblings, who continued to arrive on a regular schedule. I got so I could tell when he was about to blow. A vein in his forehead would bulge, and that was my signal to get the other kids the hell out of there."

"So you took the beatings for them."

"As often as I could. Sometimes I wasn't home…"

He blamed himself for the times he'd been unable to protect the others. "It wasn't your fault, Owen."

"I know that now. Took years of therapy to get me there, though."

The spark of humor she heard in his voice was a small comfort, knowing his father had failed to break his spirit entirely.

"No one ever stepped in to help you? Surely, people knew what was going on."

"Everyone knew. But he was a rising star in the army and outranked most of the people who knew. No one wanted to get on his bad side, so they kept quiet. It wasn't like it is now with mandatory reporting and teachers on the lookout for abused kids. Back then, people turned away from things they didn't want to see. The closest we came to going public was when I was in tenth grade, and he broke my arm."

Laura gasped. "Oh God. Owen… God."

"He made up a big story about me falling off the top bunk. I could tell the doctor didn't believe him. He managed to get me alone when we went for the X-ray, and he asked me, point blank, if someone had hurt me. He was a young officer in the medical corps. I remember him vividly, as if it was yesterday. I wanted so badly to tell him, but I didn't believe he stood a chance against my father, who could squash him like a bug."

Owen released an ironic laugh. "I was concerned about ruining his career before it got started, so I told him it happened the way my father said it did. I've thought so many times about what might've been different for all of us if I'd had the guts to tell that doctor the truth."

"You were a frightened child navigating a nightmare," Laura said. "You can't hold yourself responsible for not stopping it."

"Again, I know that now, but at the time, I felt like the biggest coward on the face of the earth. And my father tuned into that. He knew that doctor had his number, and he knew I'd been too afraid to tell the truth. He got off on that."

"Sick, sadistic son of a bitch," Laura said.

Owen laughed and hugged her tighter, his lips brushing her forehead. "If we weren't talking about him, I'd think my princess's dirty mouth was insanely sexy."

"I'll share some of my other naughty words with you at a more appropriate time."

"I'll look forward to that." He ran his hand over her back in a gesture that comforted and soothed her. Wasn't that just like him, to worry about comforting her while reliving his own nightmare? "The only respite we ever got was the summers we spent here with our grandparents. Gram could never understand why we cried for days when it was time to go home."

"So even she didn't know?"

"He warned us about talking about our family's business to 'outsiders' and the dire consequences our mother would face if we 'talked out of school.' That was one of his favorite expressions. Since she was stuck at home with him while we were here, we kept quiet. Now we know Gram had her suspicions something was off, but after it all came out later, she said if she'd known how far off it really was, she would've shot him herself and borne the consequences."

"From the little I know of her from our phone calls, I have no doubt she would've done it."

"Oh, I know she would've. She loves us like nobody's business. If it weren't for her and Gramps and those summers we spent here we'd all be in the loony bin."

"It must've been so tough to go home at the end of the summer."

"It was horrible. We had this period of total normalcy every year, and we lived for it. Other than his deployments that got more infrequent the higher up he got, it was our only break from the insanity." Owen's fingers slid through her hair absently, as if he needed to touch her. "I was offered a couple of scholarships to college, and my father wrangled me an appointment to West Point."

"I thought you didn't go to college."

"I didn't. I refused to go, which led to his never-ending belief that I'm good for nothing, along with another violent confrontation. But I wasn't a little kid anymore. I'd grown into a man when he wasn't paying attention, and I laid him out flat. Knocked him right out cold."

"Oh my God. What did he do?"

"He called the cops and pressed charges against me."

Laura sat right up and looked him in the eye. "Are you fucking kidding me?"

Smiling at her choice of words, he said, "I wish I was. I was eighteen at the time, so I was charged with felony assault, which was later whittled down to a misdemeanor, but it's still on my record. He saw to it that I spent a few nights in jail, too. I lost my appointment to West Point, which further infuriated him. Of course he took no responsibility whatsoever for his own role in the incident."

Laura had never heard anything so outrageous in her life. "What about the scholarships?"

"As much as I wanted out of there, I turned them all down."

"*Why?*"

His small smile conveyed a world of meaning.

"Your siblings," she said as understanding dawned on her. She resettled her head on his chest. "You couldn't leave them."

"Righto. I did what I could for them until he kicked me out of the house when I was twenty. He was getting tired of not being able to pound on anyone because I was always interfering. After I knocked him out, he knew better than to screw with me. I took my sisters, Julia and Katie, with me. They're the twins, and they were eighteen at the time. We got jobs and our own place, and the others spent as much time with us as they could. We thought about reporting him to the authorities, but we were always afraid he'd wriggle out of it because of his standing in the community and then things would be even worse for the others. So we kept quiet and did what we could for the younger ones. When he was transferred to Ft. Hood in Texas, we went with them, doing everything we could for the four still stuck at home. Our imperfect system was working pretty well until the youngest one, Jeff, tried to kill himself when he was fourteen."

"Jesus," Laura said.

"Long story short, he made it very clear he would try again until he was successful unless we got him out of that house. That's when we finally told my grandparents what'd been going on. They retired and moved to Florida. My father fought it tooth and nail, but Jeff went to live with them, and the rest of us were finally free. Everyone except my mother, that is."

"With all of you out of the house, why didn't she leave him?"

"Ahhh, isn't that the question of the ages? We did everything we could to try to convince her to leave. We offered her money and places to stay and anything she could possibly need. Every time we thought she'd finally had enough, she went back for more. Eventually, we quit trying. After one of these incidents, the child of choice patches her up and listens to her swear this was the last time. And then they come home from work to find her gone again. It's happened at least a dozen times in the last ten years. She's never come to me before. It's always one of the others."

"It's because she knew if she came to you, she'd have to face her own conscience for what she allowed you to endure for all those years."

"Too bad I didn't meet you sooner. You could've saved me a small fortune in therapy. That's exactly what my therapist said."

"Maybe the fact that she's here is a sign that she's finally had enough."

"I've learned not to get my hopes up."

They were quiet for a long time as his fingers continued to spool through her hair.

"Now you've heard the whole ugly story. I can only imagine what you must be thinking."

Laura rested her chin on his chest and met his gaze. "I'm thinking that you are, without a doubt, the most amazingly heroic man I've ever had the pleasure to meet."

"Oh *please*, Laura," he said with a groan. "Don't pin me with that. I missed so many opportunities to put a stop to it."

With a hand on his face, she forced him to look at her. "If I want to think you're heroic, I'm allowed to. You were very brave, and you stood up for your younger siblings, protecting them from the worst of it. You sacrificed your own chance to escape to be there for them. If that's not heroic, I don't know what is." She kissed the protest off his lips. "I hate to think about what you went through for so long. I wish I could've been there for you."

"I wouldn't have wanted you anywhere near it."

"If your mom hadn't come here, would you have ever told me?"

"I suppose I would've had to explain at some point why I have nothing to do with my parents other than an occasional call to my mother to make sure she's still alive."

"Where are your brothers and sisters now?"

"Julia and Katie still live in Texas. Julia is an office manager, and Katie is a nurse. I'm really proud of both of them. They lived through the worst of it with me and came out on the other side happy and productive."

"Are they married?"

He shook his head. "None of us are. I'll let you dissect the deeper meaning of that."

"It doesn't take a shrink to figure out why the institution doesn't hold much appeal to any of you."

"My brother John put himself through college with some help from me and my grandparents. He's an engineer living in Tennessee. Cindy stayed in Texas, too. She cuts hair at a salon outside of Dallas, and does really well. Josh is a cop in Virginia, fortunately not in the town where my parents live, so he won't have to be the one to arrest my dad." This was said with a chuckle that belied the deeper pain he had to be feeling as decades of violence came to a head.

"And Jeff?" Laura was almost afraid to ask about his youngest sibling.

"He had some issues with drugs for a while. My grandmother waged war, got him into a top rehab and nipped it in the bud. Now he's in college and doing really well. Fingers crossed."

"You know, I thought the world of her before tonight, but now..."

"She's amazing," he said simply. "We never would've survived without both of them."

"I wonder..." Laura stopped herself, not wanting to delve too deeply into things he might consider private.

"What, honey? After all I've told you, there's nothing you can't ask me."

Laura chose her words carefully. "I don't know Adele all that well, but I have a sense of her as a strong, capable woman from our frequent phone calls. And now, after hearing what she did for you and your siblings, I admire her even more. So I can't help but wonder how a daughter of hers ended up in this situation."

"Gram and I have had many a conversation about that," Owen said. "Apparently, my mother fell hard and fast for my dad at a dance when she was in college. Her parents had him tagged as verbally abusive and passive aggressive from the get-go, but there was no reasoning with her. After a while, Gram said it became a matter of pride to my mom. She refused to admit they'd been right."

"Pride goeth before the fall."

"Exactly."

With her hand on his face, she kissed him with all the love and passion she felt for him. "This doesn't change anything between us, so don't add that to your list of worries. I was already head-over-heels in love with you, and after this, I love you even more than I did before."

"Laura..." He cupped the back of her head and brought her in for another sweet kiss. "I love you, too."

The kiss took on a new urgency as need overtook them. Before she had time to register his intent, she was under him, clinging to him as he kissed her with deep, sweeping strokes of his tongue.

Even though it was the last thing she wanted to do, she turned away from him to suck in greedy breaths and to gather her sanity. "We can't do this with your mother in the next room."

"Yes, we can." His lips were hot on her neck as his erection throbbed against her core. "We'll be so quiet." He rolled the tendon at the base of her neck gently between his teeth, setting off a wave of reaction that went all the way through her.

She bit her bottom lip to keep from crying out from the intense burst of longing and pushed hard against him.

"I knew I could convince you."

Her unsteady laugh drew a smile from him. "You think you're so clever." She hooked her feet around his legs, giving in to his passionate persuasion.

All at once, he stopped moving and dropped his forehead to her chest, drawing in deep breaths.

Confused, Laura combed her fingers through his hair. "What is it?"

"I have something else I need to tell you." He raised his head and looked into her eyes. "Your dad called earlier."

Surprised, Laura said, "Why didn't you tell me? Did he want to talk to me?"

Owen shook his head. "He wanted to tell me that he'd talked to Justin."

"And?" Laura asked, sensing she wasn't going to like this.

"Justin agreed to the divorce and the custody arrangement you wanted for the baby."

She gasped. "*Are you serious?* Why didn't you tell me?"

"Because it came with a condition."

A sense of dread overtook her. "What condition?"

"You have to give me up, and greedy bastard that I am, I didn't want to tell you because I need you so damned much. Especially right now."

"I'll never give you up! He's crazy if he thinks he can blackmail me that way."

"You need to think of what's best for you—and the baby."

"That's exactly what I'm doing. *You're* what's best for us."

His eyes went soft at her pronouncement. "Your dad is talking to the senior partner at Justin's firm on Monday. Apparently, they're old friends."

"Yes, they went to Mount St. Charles together."

"Your dad didn't want to upset you any more than you already were yesterday, which is why he called me. He's hoping his friend will agree to exert some pressure within the firm."

"Let's hope it works. I've had about enough of Justin Newsome."

"What if he won't give you the divorce?"

"Then you and I will live in sin for the rest of our lives, and I'll fight him with everything I've got for custody of a baby he doesn't even want." As Owen's mouth curved into a sensuous smile, she let out a huff of aggravation. "Why is that funny?"

"It's not funny," he said, kissing her again.

"Then why are you smiling like a crazy fool?"

"Because you're so fierce and sexy when you're pissed. I'll have to remember to make you mad as often as possible."

Before she could form a response to that outrageous statement, he had captured her mouth in another sensuous kiss. His hand found its way under her pajama top to roll her nipple between his fingers, drawing a response from her despite her reluctance to make love with his mother in such close proximity.

"Take this off," he said, tugging on her top and lifting to give her room to move.

"Owen… What if your mom wakes up?"

"She won't."

"What if she does?"

"We'll hear her."

He helped her pull the top over her head. "God, I love the way you feel." Rubbing soft chest hair over her nipples, he made her whimper with the need that coursed through her.

She couldn't believe they were doing this, but before she could make another feeble attempt at protest, he was tugging at her pajama bottoms as well as the thin bit of lace that covered her.

"Owen..."

"Shhh. It's okay. I need you so much, Laura. So damned much."

"I'm here," she said, surrendering at last. After all he'd shared with her and all he'd been to her, there was nothing at all she wouldn't give him. She pushed her hands into the back of his flannel pajama pants to cup the muscular globes of his ass.

His groan became a tortured moan when she shifted a hand to the front to stroke him. Remembering how it had felt earlier to take him into her body had her straining against him, wanting him desperately.

"Easy, baby," he whispered, his breath against her ear setting off a whole new series of shock waves. "Nice and easy." He entered her slowly, stretching her almost to the point of pain before torturing her with his retreat. "Are you sore from before?"

Unable to form words, she shook her head and squeezed his ass again, hoping to encourage him to move faster.

He took the hint and entered her fully on the next stroke, drawing tense gasps from both of them. "Nothing has ever felt so good," he said, his raspy, sexy voice telling how deeply affected he was by their lovemaking. Remaining buried in her, he throbbed and pulsed as he kissed her senseless.

"*So* much more than your share," she said as she moved her legs farther apart and struggled to accommodate him.

His soft laughter rocked them both, sending him deeper into her.

All their problems faded away, and Laura was consumed by the heated glide of their skin where they were joined, the friction of his chest hair against her nipples, the scent of his appealing cologne and the dip and dive of his tongue into her mouth, mirroring the movements of his hips.

They came together in a moment of perfect harmony that left her heart pounding and her body throbbing.

"Thank you," he whispered after a prolonged period of charged silence.

She knew he was talking about far more than their explosive lovemaking. Tightening her arms around him, she closed her eyes and let sleep claim her.

Chapter 22

The next day passed in a blur of activity that included a trip to the clinic where David determined that Sarah's ribs weren't broken, only badly bruised. After they returned to the Surf, Blaine came to take Sarah's statement. Laura had ceded to Owen's wishes that she not be present to hear the dirty details.

An hour after he and the police chief had entered the bedroom, Owen emerged abruptly from the room.

Laura, who'd busied herself going over Sydney's proposed designs for the second-floor guest rooms, got up and went to him and was shocked when he brushed her off.

"I can't right now," he muttered on his way to the front door. It slammed behind him a minute later.

Filled with indecision, Laura stared at the door. Should she go after him?

Blaine came out a minute later.

"Is she all right?" Laura asked of Sarah.

"I suppose she will be, but she's got a long road ahead of her."

"Is she going forward with the charges?"

"Yes."

Laura nodded. "Good. It's about time."

"On that we agree. I'm going to get things moving. Tell Owen I'll be in touch."

"Thank you, Blaine."

Even though she wanted to go after Owen, she knew he needed some time to himself. Laura took a deep breath to settle her nerves and went into the bedroom to check on Sarah.

From the bed, she was staring out the window, watching the latest ferry steam through the South Harbor breakwater.

"Mrs. Lawry? Can I get you anything?"

"You could call me Sarah," she said with a small smile.

Laura was astounded by the way the smile took years off Sarah's face. In it, she also saw a hint of Owen. "If you'd like."

"I would." She patted the bed. "Come and sit for a minute."

Laura perched on the edge of the bed, careful not to jostle the injured woman.

"Owen seems quite taken with you."

"As I am with him. He's an exceptional man, but I probably don't have to tell you that."

"No, you don't," Sarah said, "and it's no thanks to me that he turned out the way he did."

Laura had no idea how to respond to that.

"He hadn't told me about you or the baby."

"I, um—"

"I don't mean to make you uncomfortable. I'm surprised, that's all. I'd given up on him settling down and having a family."

"I should tell you that I was briefly married, and the baby's father is my soon-to-be ex-husband."

Sarah's face fell with disappointment. "Oh."

Laura couldn't tell if that single word conveyed a world of judgment or understanding.

"I thought you and Owen—"

"We are," Laura said, blushing. "Very much so. Owen has been such a good friend to me during a difficult time."

"He's a caretaker. Always has been."

"He's very good at it."

"Yes." Sarah tugged at a string that had come loose on the quilt. "Unfortunately, he had no choice but to become good at it when he was far too young for such responsibilities."

"He doesn't blame you," Laura said. The words were out of her mouth before she could stop them.

"He should."

"Well, he doesn't."

"I don't deserve him or any of them. Somehow, they all turned out beautifully despite me."

"It's absolutely none of my business, but..." Laura stopped herself, debating whether she should finish the thought. Her situation was hardly comparable to what Sarah was dealing with.

"Please, speak freely. I have very little pride left."

Hearing her say that broke Laura's heart all over again. "Six months ago, I was on the verge of marrying the man I thought was the love of my life. Nothing since then has turned out like I'd expected, but somehow I seem to be exactly where I belong. And all of the pain and disappointment led me to Owen. I can't help but hope the same thing might be possible for you."

Sarah attempted a smile, but it turned into a grimace when her ribs protested the small movement. "What happened with your husband?"

"He failed to give up his dating life after we were married."

When Sarah raised an eyebrow, Laura again caught a glimpse of Owen in the familiar expression. "Is that right?"

"Uh-huh."

"How'd you find out?"

"He made a date online with one of my bridesmaids. She'd noticed his profile was still active, so she started talking to him, to see what he would do. One thing led to another, and he made a date with her. She went to the restaurant to see if he'd have the nerve to actually show up, and there he was waiting for her."

"My goodness. How shocking that must've been for you."

Laura could vividly remember the moment her two best friends from childhood had come to her new apartment to tell her what they'd learned about her new husband. "It was…awful."

"You were lucky to find out early on before things got worse." She glanced at the window, lost in her own thoughts. "I was too bullheaded. I didn't listen to my parents or my friends who told me they didn't like the way he talked to me. If he talked to me that way in front of people, they'd say, what will it be like when you're alone?"

Laura stayed quiet and let her get it out.

"He was charming and persuasive and ambitious. I fell so hard for him. It didn't take long to realize I'd married a monster. Back in those days, women with children and no way to support them didn't leave. We stayed and did the best we could with what we had." She returned her gaze to Laura. "I admire the courage it took for you to leave him."

Laura covered Sarah's cool hand with her much warmer one. "You have that same courage inside of you."

Sarah closed her hand around Laura's. "I'm not going back this time. I'm not sure what I'll do, but I can't go back to him. If I do, eventually he'll kill me."

"You'll stay right here with us for as long as you like. This hotel is much more yours than it'll ever be mine, and there's a place for you here for however long you wish to stay."

Tears sparkled in the gray eyes that were so much like Owen's. "I can see why my son cares so deeply for you."

"It's going to be okay," Laura said, squeezing Sarah's hand before releasing it. "Get some rest, and call me if I can get you anything."

"Thank you, honey."

Laura got up to leave the room and was startled to find Owen standing in the doorway. She was relieved to see some color in his cheeks after the time outdoors. Her heart gave a pitter-patter at the intense way he looked at her as she moved toward him.

He stepped aside to let her by and tugged the door closed behind her.

"Are you okay?" she asked.

His shrug didn't tell her much, but the pain she saw in his eyes told the true story.

She didn't know if he'd welcome her touch, but she couldn't contain the need to hold him and kiss him and care for him the way he'd cared for her. Tentatively, she wound her arms around his waist and rested her head against his chest.

A long moment passed before his arms came around her in a looser than usual embrace. She realized he was so used to dealing with the pain on his own that he had no idea how to accept her comfort.

"I'm here, Owen," she said softly, not wanting to disturb the fragile peace. "Whatever you need, whenever you need it, I'm right here. You don't have to do it alone anymore."

He released a deep breath, and with it, some of the tension began to leave his big frame. His forehead dropped to her shoulder, and his nose nuzzled her hair.

Laura ran her hands over his back, wishing there was something she could say to make it better for him.

"It was about an undercooked chicken," he said many minutes later.

At first, Laura didn't understand what he meant, and then it dawned on her. The undercooked chicken had sparked his father's rage.

"It's going to be different this time," Laura said, hoping she was right. If she raised his hopes only to see them dashed, she'd never forgive herself. "She seems determined to leave him."

"She has been before."

"Have the police ever been involved?"

He shook his head. "She's always managed to evade them and never filed a report before."

"It's a good sign that she's taking that step."

"I hope you're right."

"Have you talked to your siblings yet?"

"I wanted to wait until she saw David and Blaine took the report."

"Why don't you go on out to the porch and call them now? I'll stay close by in case she needs anything."

He drew back from her but kept a firm grip on her hands. "I was on the beach just now thinking about everything that's happened, and it occurred to me that maybe you'd be better off taking a step back from me. Things are bound to get ugly with my father, and the situation with Justin—"

With her heart aching at the thought of losing him, she shook her head. "I'm going to pretend you didn't say that."

"Think about it, Laura. Justin won't give you the divorce as long as we're together, and with everything that's going on in my family—"

"We need each other more than ever," she said firmly. "I told you I love you. Do you think that means *I* cut and run the first time things get a little difficult?"

He stared at her, incredulous. "A *little* difficult? Do you have any idea how my father is going to react to being *arrested*? If it goes to court, we'll have to testify. All of us—possibly even you, too, if you stick around, since you saw her in this condition. It's going to be a whole lot more than a little difficult for a long time."

"If I stick around?" She made a huge effort to keep the panic out of her voice. She told herself he was reacting to the emotion of the situation, and it had nothing to do with them. "Where exactly would I go?"

He ran his hands through his hair, frustration rippling off him in waves. "I'm not suggesting you go anywhere. I'm suggesting that maybe this isn't the time for us to be together."

"When would the right time be? Can you tell me that?" Since he had no ready answer to that question, she bit back the panic and pressed on. "Our timing has been off from the very beginning, but that didn't stop us from becoming friends or falling in love or making a commitment to each other."

"Laura—"

"I'm holding you to that commitment, Owen. You made promises to me. You said you love me and that you'd love my baby." Even though tears threatened to derail her, she forced them back, knowing she needed to be strong for both of them. "Didn't you mean that?"

"I did." He sounded so wounded and so desperately unhappy, and she knew that neither had anything at all to do with her. "You know I did."

"Don't let him take something else from you. He took your childhood and your sense of security and your chance to go to college. Don't let him take me, too." She stepped toward him to close the yawning chasm he'd tried to build between them and rested her hands on his chest. Under her palms, his heart beat hard and fast. "Don't let him win, Owen."

"It's going to get so ugly, Princess. You have no idea."

"It's nothing I can't handle if it means I get to be with you."

"You say that now—"

"I'll say that forever."

He leaned his forehead on hers. "You're too damned stubborn for your own good."

"You love that about me."

"Yes, I do." His arms came around her in the fierce embrace she'd grown accustomed to. "I love you so goddamned much. I don't want you anywhere near the ugliness."

"I want to be wherever you are—good, bad or ugly."

"How'd I get so lucky to find you?"

"We both got lucky, and if we hold on tight to this precious love we have between us, there's nothing we can't get through together."

"I'm going to take your word for that."

"Good," she said, relieved and overwhelmed to know that no matter what the future might bring, they'd face it together.

EPILOGUE

"One more big push, Laura," said Victoria, the midwife, from her perch between Laura's legs.

Behind Laura, Owen propped her up and wiped a cool cloth over her forehead as he had for hours now.

"So tired," Laura said, panting between contractions.

"I know, honey," he said, "but you're almost there. I know you can do it."

His calm, steady support had gotten her this far, and she'd be damned if she'd let him down now. As a blizzard howled outside the warm confines of the clinic, Laura bore down on the next contraction. The pain was unlike anything she'd ever experienced, and for an instant, she wondered if the baby was capable of splitting her in half.

"That's it!" Victoria said. "You did it!"

The baby screamed in protest as it emerged into a world of bright lights and frightening noises.

"You've got a gorgeous baby boy," Victoria said as she quickly cleared his airway and cleaned him up. "With all his fingers and toes." She wrapped him in a receiving blanket and handed him to his exhausted mother.

"Oh, a boy," Laura said as she took her first look at the scrunched-up face and the tiny mouth that formed a perfect O to express his outrage. She was so glad now that she'd waited to find out what she was having until he arrived. His head was covered in glossy dark hair that reminded Laura of Justin's. She blinked back the torrent of tears that spilled from her eyes so she could see every detail of the little face.

"My God, look at him," Owen said reverently. "He's beautiful."

"I'd say he's pretty close to nine pounds," Victoria said. "Well done, Mom."

"We'll give you a minute to get acquainted, and then I'll be back with David to check on both of you," Victoria said.

"Thank you," Laura said, unable to tear her gaze off her newborn son.

Owen's hand covered hers as she held the baby. With his free hand, he used a tissue to mop up her tears and then grabbed a second one to deal with his own.

"It's true what they say."

"What's that?" he asked.

"The minute you see the baby, you forget all about what you went through to have him."

"I don't know if I'll ever forget it. You were amazing, honey."

"So were you." She tipped her head back for a kiss. "I never could've done it without you."

He caressed her face. "Yes, you could have."

Victoria popped her head into the room. "We've got some anxious grandparents and an uncle out here waiting to meet the new arrival. Mind if I show them in?"

"Please do," Laura said.

Her father and brother escorted Owen's mother into the room a minute later.

"Oh, let me see him," Frank said, leaning over the bedrail for a closer look at his new grandson. "He's beautiful."

"Your daughter was amazing, Frank," Owen said. "A true warrior goddess."

"I have no doubt," Frank said, kissing Laura's cheek. "She always has been. Are you okay, honey?"

"Never been better."

"What'll you name him?" Sarah asked as the baby curled a hand around her finger.

"I was thinking about Francis," Laura said.

"Absolutely not!" Frank and Shane said together.

"Why not?"

"That's an awful name to pin on a little guy," Shane said. He'd joined them at the hotel right before Christmas and had become an invaluable member of the renovation team. He was also helping Mac and Luke with the installation of new laundry and restroom facilities at the marina and had committed to staying on through the spring to help out with the new low-income houses they'd be building on the Chesterfield property.

"I want to name him after you," Laura said to her father.

"And I'm honored, honey. I truly am, but don't do that to him. Give him a good, strong first name, and I'll allow Francis as a middle name."

"He still thinks he's the boss of me," Laura said to Owen and Sarah, who laughed.

Sarah laughed more often now that her bruises had healed. Her husband was prohibited to have any contact with her as the case wound its way through the courts. Laura would've been lost without Sarah the last few months as the pregnancy made it impossible for her to do half the things that needed to be done at the hotel. Sarah had stepped in ably, throwing herself into the project with a passion Owen said he'd never seen from her before.

After growing up in the hotel, Sarah had many stories to share, such as the one about the second-floor guestroom where a young couple had spent their only two nights as a married couple before he shipped off to World War II. He'd been killed nine months later without ever seeing his young wife again. Laura had suggested they name the room after the couple, an idea Sarah, Adele and Owen had loved.

That had led to a mission to the basement, where Adele had told Laura she would find much of the original furnishings in storage as well as logbooks full of stories about other guests who'd come and gone over the years.

Laura and Sarah had spent many a cozy winter day in front of the fire, thumbing through the yellowed books, mining for nuggets they could use to tell the story of the fabled hotel. Each room now bore the name of a guest who'd celebrated a significant milestone there, along with a framed telling of the guest's story inside the room.

Enlisting the help of Evan and Grant, Owen and Shane had moved much of the original furniture out of the basement. After she returned from her honeymoon to the Bahamas in January, Syd had deemed some pieces salvageable while others were relegated to the junk pile.

As the winter unfolded, the renovation had progressed along with Laura's pregnancy, until Owen and Sarah had proclaimed her on maternity leave a week before the baby's arrival.

Since she was too big and ungainly to be of much use to anyone, she'd ceded to their wishes and allowed Owen to wait on her hand and foot, the way he had in their early months together when she'd been so sick in the mornings.

And now, looking down at her baby son, she was filled with gratitude for the many blessings in her life and apprehensive about the phone call she needed to make.

"I have to call Justin."

"Yes." Owen disentangled himself from her and got off the bed, stretching out the kinks from hours of supporting her through the most strenuous part of her labor. He rooted around in the bag she'd packed for the hospital, produced her cell phone and handed it to her. "We'll give you some privacy," he said, leaning over to kiss her and then the baby.

"Thank you."

Frank, Sarah and Shane kissed Laura and the baby before they followed Owen from the room.

"What do you think?" she whispered to the baby, who watched her every move with unseeing eyes. She'd read that it would take a while for his vision to become clear. "Should we call your other daddy and let him know you've arrived?"

Even all these months later, the idea of speaking to Justin filled her belly with butterflies.

He answered on the first ring. "Laura?"

"Yes, it's me, and a brand new baby boy calling to say hello."

"Oh. Wow. Are you okay?"

"We're great." She couldn't take her eyes off the miracle in her arms, who pursed his tiny pink lips as if engaged in deep thought. "He's got your dark hair."

"Is that so?"

"Don't get too excited. I read that the hair they're born with often falls out in the first few months."

"Will you send me some pictures?"

"Of course."

"What will you name him?"

"I was going to name him Francis after my father, but he won't hear of it. He says it's an awful name to give a little kid."

"I have to agree with him."

"I figured you might. Any suggestions?"

"I've always been partial to Matthew or maybe John."

"Matthew Francis Newsome?" Laura said, gauging the baby's reaction. "I don't think he likes it."

"It does sound kind of boring. What do you like? Didn't you have a list of names going from the time you were a little kid?"

"Yes," she said, touched that he'd remembered. "I like Holden and Austin."

"Both good strong names. What does he think?"

Laura smiled at the way Justin was accommodating her whimsy. They'd come a long way in the last few months and were trying to work out their differences amicably. Laura suspected he'd met someone new, which had facilitated his newfound willingness to compromise—that and the pressure the senior partner at his firm had put on him not to further irritate Judge Frank McCarthy.

"I got a gurgle on Holden but not much of a reaction to Austin."

"Then Holden it is. Holden Francis Newsome?"

"Holden Francis Newsome," she said to the baby and watched in delight as he tried to kick his legs within the tight confines of the blanket. "I think we've got a winner."

"Thanks for allowing me to be a part of that, Laura. I know I haven't done much to endear myself to you in the last nine months, but I'm glad to hear you and the baby are well."

"Thank you," she said, moved by the effort he was making.

"Your dad has something with him that I asked him to give you after the baby arrived."

"What's that?"

"Signed divorce papers."

Laura gasped. Despite the effort they'd both been making to be more civil, she'd thought they were still a long way from brokering a settlement in the divorce. "What changed?"

"You won't believe it, but my mom had a come-to-Jesus conversation with me," he said, sounding sheepish. "Apparently, she heard about what happened between us from Mrs. Harrigan."

"Ahhh," Laura said. Mrs. Harrigan's daughter Tamara had been one of the bridesmaids who'd set up the phony date with Justin.

"She was extremely disappointed, and by the time she was through with me, I was ashamed of myself."

Laura winced, imagining the scene. "Your mom is one to be reckoned with."

"Indeed." His tone sounded almost regretful. "She also reminded me that we've got a child to consider, and it's best for him if we make an attempt to be civil."

"I completely agree. Thank you—and your mom." Laura couldn't believe this was happening. "What about the custody arrangement?"

"I agreed to your request—occasional weekends when he's older, alternating holidays, two weeks in the summer. I want to be part of his life, even if I'm no longer a part of yours."

"As long as we share a child, you'll always be part of my life, Justin."

"I suppose you'll want to marry the surfer dude once you're free of me."

She smiled at the way he described Owen. If only he knew how much substance the "surfer dude" brought to their relationship. "We haven't gotten that far." As long as she was still married to Justin, there hadn't been much point in discussing their future.

"I'd like to come see the baby in the next week or so. Whenever you're up for it."

"Of course. I'll call you when we're home and settled."

"Thank you for giving me a son, Laura. I'm sorry for what happened between us. I regret that I hurt you—and I felt that way before my mother laid into me."

"Things work out the way they're meant to."

Owen stuck his head in the door, and Laura waved him in.

"I really believe that," she added to Justin.

"Don't forget to send pictures."

"I won't."

He paused for a moment before he said, "You may not believe this, Laura, but I did love you, and I married you for the right reasons. Afterward, I don't know what happened… I freaked out, I guess. I couldn't believe you actually *left* me."

Astounded, she said, "What did you think I'd do when I found out what you were up to?"

"I never expected you to find out. It was stupid. In hindsight, I wasn't ready to be married, but I was so afraid of losing you. And then when I did…I behaved badly, and I'm sorry about that. I really am."

"It's in the past now," Laura said, filled with relief that they were finally moving past the ugliness. "All that matters now is this beautiful baby who needs both his parents in his life."

"He'll have us both," Justin said. "Take care of yourself. And the baby."

"I will." Laura ended the call and realized she had tears streaming down her cheeks.

Owen's sunny disposition immediately darkened. "Did he say something to upset you?"

"Quite the opposite. Apparently, he signed the divorce papers. My dad has them with him."

Owen's mouth fell open, and his gray eyes went wide. "Are you kidding me?"

"Nope."

"He really signed the papers."

Laura laughed at his reaction. "That's what he said."

"And the custody agreement?"

"That, too."

Owen's whoop startled the baby, who'd been dozing in his mother's arms. He let out a lusty wail of dismay.

"Sorry," Owen said sheepishly.

"That's okay. He's probably hungry anyway." She shifted on the bed, and her entire body protested the movement. "God, everything hurts."

"Let me help you." He took the baby until she was able to find a more comfortable position.

Laura wiggled her way out of the hospital gown, freeing breasts that had become embarrassingly large in the final weeks of her pregnancy. When she was ready, she reached for the baby. "Let's give this a whirl, shall we?" It took several attempts, but the baby finally latched on.

"Would you look at that?" Owen seemed awestruck by the sight of the baby's tiny mouth tugging on her nipple. "Does it hurt?"

"No, but it feels kind of weird."

"I suppose it will until you get used to it." He brushed her hair back from her face and leaned in to kiss her softly. "You've never been more beautiful than you are right now."

Laura released an unsteady laugh. "You might need to invest in some glasses, Mr. Lawry."

Shaking his head, he stole another kiss and ran a finger over her breast, tracing a vein that stood out vividly against her pale skin. "Gorgeous." He turned his attention to the baby, letting his finger glide over the dampness on his little cheek. "What's his name?"

"Holden Francis."

"Holden. I like it. It suits him."

"I think so, too." The baby chose that moment to release her nipple. Laura lifted him so Owen could kiss the baby's forehead. "Holden, say hello to your second daddy." Knowing the role Owen planned to play in her child's life, the title of stepfather didn't seem appropriate, so Laura had long ago decided that her child would have two daddies, and that would be that.

"Very nice to finally meet you, Holden," Owen said, shaking his little hand gently. "So what brought on Justin's change of heart?"

"Apparently, his mother laid into him and told him to do what was best for the baby."

"Thank goodness someone finally got through to him."

"He was very nice just now." She glanced at Owen. "He told me he did love me but wasn't ready to be married. It was nice to hear that he married me for the right reasons."

"Of course he did, Princess. That's why he was such an ass when you left. I'd go batshit crazy if you ever left me, so I get that."

"No worries about me going anywhere. I'm afraid you're stuck with us."

Owen leaned in to steal a kiss. "Thank God for that."

Laura transferred the baby to her other breast. When he latched on like an old pro, she smiled up at Owen. "Check him out. He's clearly gifted."

"Clearly," Owen said, amused by her delight. "So when will this divorce of yours be final?"

"Six months."

He counted on his fingers. "August."

She nodded.

"That'd be a fine time for a wedding on our new deck at the Surf, wouldn't you agree?"

Laura could almost feel the soft summer breeze on her face and pictured the sun setting over the ocean. "I'd say that sounds about perfect."

"Consider it a plan."

"You don't like to make plans," she teased.

"That was the old me. The new me is all about making plans, as long as they include you and the little guy." Somehow he managed to get on the bed with them and arrange her so he was supporting her and the baby, surrounding them with his love. "This, right here, is about as close to perfect as it gets." As he spoke, his lips brushed against her forehead in a soft kiss.

She leaned her head on his chest, happier than she'd ever been in her life. "Yes, it is."

Turn the page for a special added extra short story: A Wedding on Gansett Island. . .

A Wedding on Gansett Island

Sydney Donovan

&

Luke Harris

invite you to join them as they
exchange wedding vows on Christmas Eve
at their home on Gansett Island

Ceremony at 7 p.m.
Reception immediately following

All day, Luke had expected to feel nervous. At thirty-seven, he was about to be married for the first time, to the woman he'd spent half a lifetime waiting for. Now, as he donned the jacket to the black suit Syd had picked out for him during a trip to the mainland, Luke still didn't feel nervous. He was ready to take this step with the only woman he'd ever loved.

The one thing that would've made this day completely perfect was if his mother had lived to see it. She'd always loved Syd and had championed their teenage romance, while the Donovans had disapproved. Her support had meant the world to them back then, and it would've pleased her greatly to know they'd ended up together after a long and winding road. He'd given Syd his mother's diamond earrings as a wedding gift and couldn't wait to see how they looked on her.

A knock on the bedroom door had Luke turning away from the mirror. "Come in."

Mac McCarthy stepped into the room, also dressed in a dark suit with a red tie in deference to the season. With him was his father, Big Mac, who'd been the closest thing Luke had ever had to a father of his own.

"You clean up well, Mr. Harris," Mac said.

"Same to you, Mr. McCarthy."

"You both look pretty good for a couple of ugly dudes," Big Mac said.

"Gee, thanks, Dad." Mac held up the red rose boutonniere that matched the one on his lapel. "I'm told it's my job as the best man to make sure your flower's on straight."

"Do your worst." Luke forced himself to stand still while Mac attempted to secure the stem.

"Step aside, son," Big Mac said. "Let an expert handle this." Big Mac had the flower in place ten seconds later. "There."

"I could've done that if you'd given me a chance," Mac muttered.

Luke looked up at the older man. "Thank you." There was more he wanted to say, but the words wouldn't come. Apparently, he didn't need words, because Big Mac understood. He always did.

Big Mac patted Luke's face and hugged him. "Congratulations, son."

Luke clung to him for a brief moment and then pulled back before he humiliated himself by bawling like a baby. His every emotion was hovering on the surface today, threatening to break free at any second.

Mac rested his hands on Luke's shoulders. "Are you ready?"

"Yep." Luke retrieved a jeweler's box from his dresser that contained both rings and handed it to Mac. "Don't lose them."

Mac laughed. "I'll see if I can hold on to them for the next twenty minutes."

"Thanks, Mac. For being my best man and for being such a good friend."

Mac replied with a back-slapping hug. "My pleasure. I'm happy for you, man." He straightened Luke's tie. "Syd will be here any minute."

"Let's get this bromance on the road to the living room, shall we?" Luke said.

"Lead the way," Mac replied.

In the bedroom where Syd had spent every summer of her childhood, she fastened the back of the diamond earrings Luke had given her. They'd belonged to the mother he'd loved and lost far too young. The slight tremble in Syd's fingers was the first sign of nerves she'd experienced all day.

In the full-length mirror, she took a final look at the simple cream silk gown she'd chosen for her second wedding. It was sleeveless with classic, elegant lines and no train. She'd gathered her hair into a loose knot at her nape that showed off the gorgeous earrings.

Wandering to the window, she looked out at the snowy landscape that led to the empty Salt Pond. In the summer, the pond was chockablock full of boats and activity. Today, it was desolate, and the view stretched unimpaired all the way to the Coast Guard station that guarded the entrance to the vast pond.

Sydney thought of all the summer nights she'd snuck out of this house as a teenager to make love with Luke on the beach. She remembered the fine art of sneaking back in before dawn and being so certain each time that she was going to be caught.

Those summers had been among the happiest days of her life. And then they'd grown up, and she'd gone off to college and met Seth, the man she'd married and had two children with. Though she'd been happy with Seth and wild about her kids, she'd never forgotten her first love or forgiven herself for leaving for college one September and never returning to him.

She hadn't seen Luke again until the previous summer, when she'd come home to the island to pick up the pieces of her shattered life and Luke had come to find her. They'd been together again ever since.

Wandering to the bedside table, she picked up one of the many pictures of Seth and the kids that her mother kept in the house. They'd been gone nearly two years now, taken by a drunk driver in an accident that had left her badly injured and her life in tatters.

Syd ran a finger over the three dear faces: Seth, so handsome and full of life and plans and ideas; Max, with his father's dark hair and eyes and intellect; and Malena, a girl from the top of her silky dark head to the tips of her polished toes. The kids had been seven and five at the time of the accident, their lives just getting started. She hoped they were looking down on her today and blessing this new union with Luke.

With a kiss to the cool glass that covered the picture, Syd returned the frame to the table and dabbed at the moisture collecting at the corners of her eyes. Today wasn't a day for tears. Today was a day for joy and new beginnings.

A light tap on the door stirred Syd from her musings. "Come in."

"Hey," her best friend, Maddie McCarthy, said. "Are you ready?" Maddie stepped into the room, gorgeous in a red silk gown that emphasized her extravagant curves. "Wow, look at you! Oh, Syd… You look amazing."

"So do you! That color is perfect on you. Not bad for a couple of old broads, huh?"

"Not bad at all." Maddie took a closer look at her friend. "Are you okay?"

"Yeah, I'm good." She glanced at the photo by the bed. "A little emotional, but I suppose that's to be expected."

Maddie reached for Syd's hand and gave it a squeeze. "Of course it is. I have to believe they're here with you today and they'd approve of what you're doing."

"I hope so. Life has a funny way of marching forward even when you think it's over."

Maddie blinked back tears of her own. "I'm so proud of you, Syd."

"Of me? Why?"

"It would've been so much easier to curl up in a ball and turn your back on what was left of your own life. You didn't do that. You chose to live, and that wasn't the easy path."

Sydney smiled. They'd been friends since a long-ago summer job at an ice-cream shop in town. "You all didn't give me much choice. You and Luke and everyone here dragged me out of my grief and gave me a reason to keep going."

"It was no hardship on our part, believe me. We're thrilled to have you here with us." Maddie gave her a quick hug. "Let's not keep your groom waiting."

"No, let's not. He's already waited long enough for me."

The home Luke had once shared with his mother was Sydney's home now, too. They'd decorated the outside with twinkling white lights that greeted Syd when she arrived with her parents and Maddie.

As they drove down the long driveway that was lined with cars, Syd's heart began to race with excitement and nerves and anticipation. She closed her eyes and imagined how handsome Luke would look in the suit they'd chosen on a trip to the mainland. His silky dark hair would be shiny from the shower, his handsome face freshly shaven, and his brown eyes would be steady and sure. He'd always been so sure about them, despite what she'd put him through.

She'd broken his heart when she left him without a word all those years ago, but he'd been good enough to forgive her, and their second chance had quite simply saved her life. Now they would get their forever, and she couldn't wait.

Luke had shoveled a path around the house to the kitchen entrance. Taking her father's arm, Sydney raised her skirt and traversed the path illuminated by the outdoor lights she and Luke had installed in the fall. They stepped into the kitchen to a roar of voices and laughter from the living room.

Syd's mom turned to her and helped to remove Sydney's cream wool cape. "You look absolutely lovely, honey."

"Thanks, Mom."

"I'll hope and pray for your every happiness."

Grateful for her parents' blessing of a union with a man they'd once disapproved of, Sydney hugged her mother. "Thank you for everything. I never would've made it through without you."

"Oh, honey," Mary Alice said. "Don't make me cry."

"Sorry," Syd said with a smile for her mom.

"I'll see you in there," Mary Alice said.

Maddie's caramel-colored eyes were bright with excitement when she handed Syd her bouquet of Christmas greens, fragrant white lilies and red roses. "Shall we?"

"Ready, Dad?" Syd asked.

"Whenever you are, my love," Allan Donovan said.

"Then let's do it," Syd said.

Maddie signaled to someone in the next room.

Luke had asked if he could be in charge of the music, so it was a total surprise to Sydney when their friends Owen Lawry and Evan McCarthy played the Firehouse song "Love of a Lifetime," the same song Syd and Luke had danced to at a party their first summer together.

The song and the memories it resurrected took Syd's breath away as she was transported back to the sweetness of first love, the heart-pounding excitement and the joy. She'd loved him from the very beginning, and he'd loved her just as much. He'd never stopped loving her, even during all the years they'd been apart. And now he waited in the next room, ready to bind his life to hers.

Sydney slipped her hand into the crook of her father's arm. "Let's go, Dad."

Every eye was on the doorway from the kitchen when Maddie stepped into the room looking gorgeous in a floor-length red dress and carrying a bouquet of red and white flowers.

Luke scanned the gathering of friends and family. Adam McCarthy, home on Gansett for the holidays, stood next to his parents, Big Mac and Linda. Next to them were Grant McCarthy and his fiancée, Stephanie Logan, Evan's girlfriend, Grace Ryan, and Owen's girlfriend, Laura McCarthy. Joe Cantrell and his wife, Janey McCarthy Cantrell, were home from Ohio for a couple of weeks during Janey's winter break from veterinary school. Standing behind his wife, Joe rested his hands on the small baby bump that rounded Janey's abdomen.

Sydney's new friend Jenny Wilks, the lighthouse keeper, was there, along with Seamus O'Grady, who ran the ferry company in Joe's absence, Joe's mom, Carolina, Maddie's sister, Tiffany, the island's police chief, Blaine Taylor, Luke's friend and the island's number-one pilot, Slim Jackson, and cab driver extraordinaire Ned Saunders and his fiancée, Francine Chester, who was Maddie and Tiffany's mom.

Sydney had debated about whether to invite her friends from Wellesley, where she'd lived with Seth and the kids. In the end, she'd decided against inviting them, since they were short on space and wanted to be able to include all their island friends. Syd planned to send an announcement to the rest of her friends after they returned from their honeymoon.

Luke glanced at Mac, who watched his wife come toward them with a look of unabashed love etched on his face.

Maddie sent her husband a flirtatious smile as she took her place across from Luke and Mac in front of the hearth that burned brightly behind them. Sydney had decorated the mantel with fragrant evergreens, pine boughs and candles. In the far corner, the Christmas tree sparkled with white lights and gold ornaments.

When Syd and her dad appeared in the doorway, every thought drained from Luke's mind except for one—he was a lucky son of a bitch. *Look at her. Oh my God.* For a moment, he stopped breathing until Mac nudged him.

"Breathe," Mac whispered, amused by Luke's reaction to his bride.

Luke had spent so many long, cold, lonely winters in this house after his mother died, wishing for everything he now had. As Syd came toward him on the arm of her father, she was the answer to his every prayer, the love of his lifetime.

The Reverend Joshua Banks, the new pastor of the island's nondenominational church, was performing his first wedding since arriving a week ago.

Allan Donovan escorted his gorgeous daughter the short way from the kitchen to where her fiancé waited for her. Before Allan left Sydney, he hugged Luke. "Take good care of my girl."

"I will, sir."

Allan kissed his daughter and stepped back to join his wife.

Luke felt like his heart would explode from the overload of emotion that hit him when his eyes connected with Syd's. He took her hand and brought it to his lips. "You're beautiful."

"You're not too bad yourself," she said with the grin that was so her.

"Dearly beloved," Joshua began.

The next few minutes passed in a blur for Luke. He'd never remember what Joshua said about marriage. He would, however, remember the vows—to love, honor, protect and cherish. He'd remember the slide of white gold as Syd put the ring on his finger. He'd remember the look in her eyes when he put the matching band on her finger, where it joined the engagement ring he'd chosen for her.

Most of all, he'd remember when Joshua declared her his wife and told him he could kiss her. Luke would never forget the moment when his lips met hers or the surge of love and desire that filled his heart and soul.

Finally, finally, *finally.*

Mac cleared his throat next to them, reminding Luke they had guests and a party to see to before they could be alone. Reluctantly, Luke stepped back from his wife and noticed the high color of excitement in her cheeks as he squeezed her hand.

She returned the squeeze and smiled at him, happier than he'd ever seen her. Nothing made him happier than her happiness.

"Ladies and gentlemen, I give you Mr. and Mrs. Luke Harris," Joshua said.

Their friends applauded as Mac said, "Let's party!"

They posed for pictures, they ate, they drank, they danced, they laughed, and when Owen and Evan picked up their guitars, they sang—loudly. It was the most fun Sydney had had in longer than she could remember.

And when she asked Owen and Evan to play "Love of a Lifetime" one more time so she could dance with her husband, they gladly complied.

"I can't believe you remembered this song," Syd said, looking up at her gorgeous husband.

"I remember everything." He'd removed his suit coat and tie as soon as he could, and Sydney had teased him about breaking his personal record for the most hours in a tie. He'd done it for her, he'd said. Looking down at her now, he said, "Are you happy?"

"So happy? You?"

"What's the word for beyond happy?"

"Thrilled."

"Yes," he said, kissing her softly. "I'm thrilled."

"Good."

As all the noise and laughter from the party faded away, they moved together with the easy grace they'd known together since the very beginning.

"When are they going to leave?" he whispered in her ear, making her laugh and shiver in anticipation.

"Soon, I hope."

"I told you we should've booked a room somewhere so *we* could leave."

"And I told you I wanted to wake up here, in our home, on Christmas."

"If you'd listened to me, we could leave right now."

"It won't kill you to wait another hour."

"It might."

The party broke up right after midnight. Mac and Maddie stayed a short time longer to help clean up the worst of the mess.

"We did what we could," Maddie said, taking a wary look around at the carnage in the kitchen.

"Don't worry about it," Syd said. "We'll deal with it tomorrow."

"I can come back to help if you want."

"Absolutely not! Have a wonderful Christmas with your family, and don't worry about us."

"Are you having dinner with your folks?" Maddie asked.

"Later in the day." Even though Syd would've preferred to spend the entire day with only Luke, she'd never leave her parents alone on Christmas, a day that reminded them all of what they'd lost so tragically. This year was a time for new beginnings, and Syd was determined to get through the holiday looking forward rather than backward. She gave Maddie a hug. "Thanks again for all the help with the wedding."

"It was so much fun. I couldn't be happier for both of you." She drew back from Sydney and reached for her husband. "Come on, Mac. The newlyweds want to be alone."

"Can we play newlywed when we get home?" Mac asked his wife.

The slight slur to his speech had Maddie rolling her eyes as she patted his face. "If you can stay awake while I drive you home, we'll see."

"I can stay awake, baby."

Luke closed the door behind them, locked it and waited until they were in their car before he turned off the outside lights.

"Well," Sydney said, eyeing the wreckage that was their kitchen, "that went well."

"Very well," Luke said, coming toward her with intent in his eyes. He took her hands and backed out of the kitchen, bringing her with him.

"We should do something about the mess."

"Tomorrow."

"But—"

He stopped her with a passionate kiss. By the time they came up for air, her arms were looped around his neck and his were tight around her waist. "Tomorrow," he said again, walking backward to the bedroom.

"Oh," she said at the sight that greeted them. Someone—probably Maddie and Janey, if she had to guess—had sprinkled rose petals on the bed and filled the room with candles. "Wow."

"What's in the bag?" Luke asked, pointing to a gift bag on the bedside table.

Sydney went over to look. "It's from Tiffany. The note says, 'A few things from my new store to get your marriage off to the right start. Much love and happiness, Tiffany.'"

"Why am I a little scared of what's in there?"

"Maybe because it's from Tiffany?" Syd said with a laugh as she withdrew a red silk nightgown, a bottle of massage oil and an object Syd couldn't identify.

"What the heck is this?" It was a purple piece of rubber with one wide end and another narrower end.

Luke busted up laughing. "Ah, it's a vibrator, babe."

"Oh." Sydney felt heat creep from her chest to her face as she dropped it back into the gift bag.

Luke laughed again at her reaction. "What kind of store, exactly, is Tiffany planning to open?" he asked as he pulled off his dress shirt and came around to her side of the bed.

"I think we just got a sneak peek."

"That ought to be interesting on this island."

"No kidding."

"Let me see that nightgown."

Sydney handed him the slinky red concoction.

He held it up for inspection, which was when she noticed the material that would cover her breasts was entirely sheer.

"Very nice," he said. "Put it on."

"I don't know. It's not really my style."

"Oh, yes, it is."

"How do you figure?" she asked, perplexed.

"It's sexy. That makes it your style. I want to see it on you."

"You're awfully bossy tonight, Mr. Harris."

"I'm your husband now, *Mrs.* Harris," he said with a sexy grin. "You have to obey me."

"That was *not* in the vows."

"Well, that was an oversight. How'd I let that get by me?"

She shook her head at his silliness. "Will you unzip me?"

"With pleasure." He kissed and nibbled her shoulder while he pulled down the zipper. "You were so beautiful tonight, Syd. Mac had to remind me to breathe."

"That's sweet of you to say."

With her zipper open, he slid his work-roughened hands over her back and around to her belly, making her quiver with anticipation. "I had this image in my mind of what you might look like as a bride, but you blew me away with the real thing."

"Was the wedding okay? You've never done this before—"

"It was perfect." He rested his chin on her shoulder. "Want to know why?"

"Uh-huh."

"Because you were the bride. That was the only part that mattered to me."

"Luke…"

"Go get changed," he said, his lips skimming her neck. "Hurry."

After he released her, Syd's legs were unsteady as she went into the bathroom to remove her dress and put on the scandalous concoction Tiffany had left for her. It was even more scandalous on. Sure enough, her breasts were easily visible through the sheer fabric, and the hem barely covered all the important parts, ending at the very top of her thighs.

"I look like a porn star in this thing," she said.

"*That* I've got to see. Come on out and show me."

"Patience."

"I have none left after this endless day."

Syd let down her hair and ran a brush through it. She washed off her makeup and brushed her teeth, all the while feeling like a trollop. What had Tiffany been thinking? *Well,* Syd thought, *here goes nothing.*

The moment she stepped into the bedroom where Luke reclined on the bed in his boxers Sydney got what Tiffany had been thinking. The look on her husband's face was positively lecherous.

"I think I'm having a heart attack."

"Do you need some mouth-to-mouth resuscitation?"

"Desperately." He held out his arms to her. "Revive me."

She eyed the significant bulge in the front of his underwear as she came down on top of him "One part of you is already revived."

"This thing was made for you," he said as he smoothed his hands over the silk that covered her back until he was cupping her buttocks.

"It's trampy."

"It's gorgeous. You're gorgeous. And all mine. Forever. Do you know how happy that makes me?"

"How happy?"

"The happiest I've ever been in my entire life."

"Knowing that makes me happy," she said, kissing him. He deserved nothing less. "So I've been thinking a lot about something we talked about a long time ago, and now that we're married…"

"Uh-oh. Is this the part when you become someone totally different now that you've gotten me to the altar?"

"Haha. Not at all."

"What've you been thinking about, love?"

"I might want to try to have another baby."

The hands that had been moving so seductively on her bottom stilled. "I thought you couldn't."

"I want to look into having the tubal ligation reversed."

"Really?"

She nodded. "What do you think?"

"I'm not sure. I'd made peace with the fact that we wouldn't have any children, and I'm fine with that."

"Don't you *want* kids?"

"The bigger question is whether you do. You once said you didn't feel like you could take that risk again. That you'd always be worried about something happening."

"I've thought a lot about that and about what you said then—that we don't know anyone else in the world who lost both their kids the way I did, so maybe I've had my bad luck. At least I hope so. I can't live in fear, you know?"

"You're so courageous, Syd. The most courageous person I know. If you want to try this, we'll try it."

"Really? You're sure?"

He nodded and brought her down to him for a deep kiss full of love and longing. His arms tightened around her as he turned them so he was on top. Looking down at her, his eyes skimmed over her face as if he were memorizing every detail.

"What?" she asked, reaching up to caress his cheek.

"I can't believe you're my wife."

"Believe it. You're stuck with me."

"I feel like the luckiest guy in the world tonight."

"I feel pretty darned lucky, too. I thought my life was over, and there you were to show me there's still so much more."

He gathered her up and held her so tightly she could feel his heart beating in time with hers. When he raised his head, the love she saw shining down on her made her lightheaded and giddy and so very thankful.

She smoothed her hands over his back and under the waistband of his boxers, edging them down as she went.

"Is there something I can do for you, wife?"

"Yes. You can love me."

"Already do."

She pressed her pelvis against his erection. "Prove it."

"Happy to."

"Hurry," she said as she helped him remove his underwear.

His erection lay heavy, hard and hot against her belly as she squirmed under him, trying to get him where she wanted him.

"I want you," she said, in case she was being ambiguous. "Now."

"So demanding. I never saw this side of you before I married you."

"Yes, you did. Now hush up and do what you're told like an obedient husband."

Laughing softly, he said, "Yes, ma'am," and slid into her in one smooth thrust.

"*Yes.*" She arched her back and curled her legs around his hips. "That's what I wanted."

He bent his head to nuzzle her nipple through the fabric of the nightgown, if one could call it that.

Syd was so ready for him that it took only a few tugs of his lips on her nipple and a few thrusts of his cock to get her primed and ready to fly. "*Luke...*"

"What, honey?"

"Faster."

Grasping her hips, he gave her what she wanted until they came together in a moment of perfection so sweet it brought tears to her eyes.

She descended from the high to find him placing soft kisses on her face and lips.

"So beautiful," he said reverently.

"Yes, it is."

"I meant you."

"I meant *us*."

"That, too," he said, smiling.

Syd wrapped her arms tight around her new husband, thrilled that she got to spend forever with him.

Thank you for reading *Season for Love*! I hope you enjoyed it. If you did, please help other people find this book:

1. Help other people find this book by writing a review.

2. Sign up for my new-releases e-mail by contacting me at marie@marieforce.com, so you can find out about the next book as soon as it's available.

3. Come like my Facebook page at *facebook.com/MarieForceAuthor.*

4. Join the McCarthys of Gansett Island Readers Group at *facebook.com/groups/McCarthySeries/*

5. Join the Season for Love Readers Group at *facebook.com/groups/SeasonForLove/*

Turn the page for a sneak peek at Longing for Love, available now!

Longing for Love

The McCarthys of Gansett Island, Book 7

CHAPTER 1

Tiffany Sturgil stood outside her new shop and watched two workmen secure the hand-carved sign over the display window. Drivers on Ocean Road slowed to take a look at what was going on, but there wasn't much to see yet. Tiffany had kept paper over the store's window in an effort to maintain the surprise until the last minute. But once the sign was in place, it would be time to unveil her beautiful new shop.

Her heart raced with excitement and anticipation and a tiny bit of dread. What if she failed? What if she'd poured every dime she had—and then some—into the store only to fall flat on her face? "I can't let that happen," she muttered, determined to believe in herself or no one else would. Still, she couldn't help but wonder what her mother and sister would think about the shop, not to mention her soon-to-be ex-husband, who'd definitely have something to say about it. Not that she cared about his opinion. Not anymore.

"Ready?" one of the men called to her.

"Absolutely!" At those words, insane excitement immediately trumped the insecurity. This was it—the moment she'd waited for since that horrible night with Jim, her soon-to-be ex-husband, the night she'd landed in jail and then let the island's insanely hot police chief get her off in the kitchen. A tingle of desire heated her core as she remembered that explosive moment. Tiffany shook off the memory, as she had every day since, to focus on the store.

"Here we go!"

The two men tore the paper cover off her sign and stared at it, dumbfounded.

"Seriously?" one of them said. "On Gansett Island?"

"What?" Tiffany asked.

"*Naughty & Nice?*" the younger of the two men said, snickering.

"It's catchy," Tiffany said.

"It's *raunchy*," the older one said to guffaws from the other.

Suddenly, she wanted them gone. No one was going to rain on her parade. Not today, not on the day when all her dreams were about to come true. "How much do I owe you?"

"Fifty bucks."

"I'll get you a check." She stepped into the space that had occupied most of her waking moments for months. Working long hours seven days a week in between her mothering duties, she'd painted and buffed and polished until the place gleamed. Scented candles burned throughout the store, sending a hint of spicy cinnamon apple into the air. Racks of luscious, frothy lingerie in every style, shape and color, bins of panties, baskets of bras, lotions, potions and candles... Everything she'd imagined and then some. Through a beaded curtain, other treasures awaited, designed to bring ultimate pleasure.

"What do you need, boss?" asked Patty, the nervous young woman Tiffany had hired to help her out a few hours a week. Her mousy brown hair was cut into an unfortunate style that did nothing to enhance her other unexceptional features. Tiffany had makeover plans for her Plain Jane assistant as soon as things let up a little.

"A check for fifty dollars, please." She handed Patty the business card the men had given her.

"Coming right up."

Patty had been the only one to apply for the job. Tiffany hoped she'd eventually be able to leave the store in the other woman's hands so she could take an occasional break to spend time with her daughter. Her mother and pseudo-stepfather Ned had been great about helping out with Ashleigh while Tiffany was getting the store ready to open and were willing to keep her whenever Tiffany needed help.

Once she got the store up and running, Tiffany also hoped to jumpstart her social life. If the explosive orgasm she'd experienced at the hands of Blaine Taylor had taught her anything, it was that she'd been missing out on far too much during her years with Jim. She was determined to do something about that as soon as she had some free time.

Tiffany leaned over to sign the check and tore it from the ledger. "Thanks, Patty." On her way back outside to pay the men, she pulled the brown paper off the inside of the store window and went out to find the two idiots ogling the nearly naked mannequins dressed in racy lingerie. She'd gone with a red theme for her first window—lacy teddies and silk nightgowns, bra and panty sets, a large bottle of massage oil and lube that heated on contact.

"Holy smokes, lady," the older one sputtered. "I don't know what you think you're doing here, but this ain't that kind of island."

Tiffany forced a smile when she really wanted to scream. "What kind of island is it?" she asked sweetly. "The kind where no one has sex?"

He stared at her as if he couldn't believe she'd said that. Snatching the check from her hand, he tilted his head to tell his partner to get in the truck.

Tiffany happened to glance down to find the younger man's cock at full mast. She smiled when his startled eyes met hers. "Come on back soon," she said in her best baby-doll voice, "and buy something sexy for your lady—and yourself."

Flustered, he bolted to the truck. They left rubber in their haste to get out of there.

Watching them go, Tiffany experienced a twinge of apprehension. What if everyone in the conservative island town reacted the same way?

***

The next morning, she got up early to shower. As she spent extra time on her hair and makeup, her heart pounded with excitement and anticipation. Opening day! She'd planned and prepared for this day for months, and everything was set. From ads in the paper beginning today, to balloons out front, to special events to tout her sensual offerings, Tiffany was ready to announce her arrival.

"Look out, world," she whispered to her reflection. She'd chosen a sexy red silk blouse over a black skirt with stiletto heels for the opening. Applying lipstick in the same shade of racy red, Tiffany took one last measuring look in the mirror before she grabbed her purse and headed downstairs. Ashleigh had spent the night with Jim, so Tiffany was free and clear to focus on her store on opening day.

Her heels sounded like shotgun blasts inside the empty house. In one of the more acrimonious moves in their divorce proceedings, Jim had shown up one day with a moving truck and taken all the furniture, leaving her and Ashleigh with their beds and not much else. Until he'd done that, Tiffany had retained some hope that they might patch things up. Now she couldn't wait to finally be free of him. Any day now, her lawyer, Dan Torrington, had assured her. Couldn't happen soon enough for Tiffany.

With all her money tied up in the store, it would be some time before she'd be able to replace the furniture. What did it matter? They had what they needed, although she'd been astounded by how fast her savings had disappeared once she started buying inventory, shelving units, a computer, a cash register and everything else she needed to open the store.

"It'll all be fine once the money starts rolling in," she reminded herself in a sing-song voice.

For the millionth time since their encounter in the kitchen, Tiffany thought of Blaine and how much she wished she could share her excitement with him. Why him? Well, why not him? If he could make her come like a cannon with his fingers, imagine what he could do with his tongue or that thick shaft he'd pressed against her. The thought of it made her tremble with need.

And the way he'd looked at her with such yearning, as if he wanted something he couldn't allow himself to have. Then there had been the encounter last fall at Luke and Syd's house when he'd cornered her on a dark deck and told her to call him the second she was free of Jim. For a brief moment, she stopped to wonder if he was still waiting for her to call. Who was she kidding? A guy who looked like he did could have his pick of women. He'd probably moved on a long time ago when he got tired of waiting to hear from her.

She took a deep, shuddering breath and closed the front door. No time for negative thoughts today. Although, spending months surrounded by lacy negligee and thick dildos had left her twitchy with unfulfilled desire. "Someday soon," she said as she approached her little red car with the new NAUGHTY vanity plate. If Blaine wasn't interested in her anymore, she'd find someone else who was. Tiffany was sick and tired of feeling down about herself in the wake of the disaster her marriage had become. The store was only one step in a whole new life, and she was more than ready to get started.

Tiffany smiled, thrilled with the sun, the cloudless sky, the fragrant late spring breeze. She couldn't have handpicked a day better suited to starting her fabulous new life and had to curb the urge to wave to everyone she passed on the road.

On the way to the shop (she loved saying that—*the shop*), she went through her to-do list before the noon opening. She'd chosen to open on a sunny Saturday in early May in the hope that people would be out, about and curious. It was also important to have all the bugs worked out before the Gansett Island Race Week festivities later in the month. The island would be overrun with people in town for the annual sailing regatta.

Driving through town, Tiffany thought about how much she loved Gansett Island and how happy she'd been when she and Jim returned home to the island after he finished law school—that was until everything went to crap between the two of them for reasons still unknown to Tiffany. Perhaps she would never know. Over time, she'd begun to make peace with that possibility.

The Gansett town center included the requisite New England white-steepled church, a large park next door to the redbrick town hall, and the combined police and fire station. Tiffany's shop was located down the hill from the police station, which she passed daily, hoping to catch a fleeting glimpse of the sexy police chief. But she hadn't laid eyes on him since the night on Luke and Syd's deck last fall. His elusiveness had led her to wonder—more than once—if he was intentionally avoiding her because he'd changed his mind about being interested in her.

She could still remember the gravelly tenor of his voice when he'd grabbed her by the waistband of her jeans and pulled her in close to him on the dark deck. A shiver went through her when she thought about what he'd said. "*The minute you're free of him, the very same second it's final, you're going to call me.*" Before that encounter, she never would've thought a dominant man would turn her on. Now she knew otherwise. But since he'd made himself scarce ever since, she was left to wonder if he still felt the same way.

She pushed that unpleasant thought to the back of her mind, and the last half-mile of the ride to work passed in a blur of plans and exhilaration and eagerness. As she pulled into the parking space she'd decided would belong to her as the owner and proprietor of Naughty & Nice, she hoped the women in town would be curious enough to come check out the latest thing.

Rounding the corner to unlock the front door, Tiffany came to a dead stop.

"Oh my God. *No.*" Multicolored paint, as if shot from a paintball gun, was splattered all over the white brick front wall of her store, on the window and splattering her beautiful new sign—the sign she'd paid a thousand dollars to have hand-carved. Viewing the damage, white-hot rage overwhelmed her. Who could've done such a thing?

A gasp from behind her had Tiffany spinning around to find Patty holding a dozen red balloons and covering her mouth with her hand. "Oh no. *No, no, no*!" Patty's eyes were shiny with tears. "I'm so sorry, Tiffany."

"So am I." Tiffany gritted her teeth to keep from shrieking and jammed the key in the lock to open the door. Marching to the storage room in the back of the store, she found an unopened can of white paint and a new roller. She glanced down at her expensive silk blouse and skirt. Since she was unwilling to ruin her gorgeous new outfit, she rummaged around, looking for the gym bag she thought she'd left there the week before.

"Damn it," she muttered when she couldn't find the bag or anything else to change into. Moving to the front of the store, she checked the clock on the wall. Two hours until opening. Just as she had decided it was worth it to ruin her good clothes to repair the damage, her eyes landed on a saucy French maid costume on one of the racks. Glancing to her scarred window and then back to the outfit, she knew exactly what she had to do.

"They want to screw with me? Well, two can play at that game."

"Boss?" Patty said warily. "Are you all right?"

"I'm fine." Tiffany grabbed the outfit off the rack and headed for the changing room. "Start getting the wine and cheese ready."

Patty watched her with wide, doe-like eyes caught in headlights. "We're still going to open?"

"You bet your booty we are."

Across the street in the grocery store parking lot, Blaine watched from an unmarked police vehicle.

"What are we doing here, Chief?" Patrolman Trainee Wyatt Alcott asked. "The place was hit by vandals. Shouldn't we take a report?"

"Hang on. I want to see what she does about it." Blaine tilted a neck gone tight with tension. When he first saw what some idiot had done to Tiffany's store, he'd ached with dismay and had to resist the urge to fix it before she saw it. That was what the old Blaine would've done. The new-and-improved Blaine kept his distance from "projects" and didn't get involved. From a police standpoint, there wasn't much he could do besides assign additional patrols in the area, which he'd done the minute he first saw the damage.

Watching Tiffany drive up, seeing the spring in her step and then the devastated curve of her shoulders, Blaine's heart had broken for her. Then he saw her get mad, and he was proud. Now he waited anxiously to see what she planned to do about it. Ten more tense minutes passed before the door swung open. A paint can and roller preceded Tiffany out the door.

"Oh. My. God," Wyatt whispered. "What does she have on?"

Blaine couldn't speak as he stared at Tiffany in a black lace bustier with fishnet stockings, stiletto heels and a bow tie around her neck. Her dark hair had been pulled back into a ponytail, and the lithe dancer's body that he remembered in vivid detail after the night he saw her naked was on full display. The skimpy outfit reminded him that she was made up of miles of creamy-white skin and long, muscular legs, dancer's legs. His cock pressed against his fly, letting him know it approved.

"She's not really going to *paint* in that getup, is she?" Wyatt asked, his tongue practically hanging out of his face.

As she bent over to open the paint can, Wyatt got his answer.

Blaine saw red. What the hell was she thinking, parading around like that? This wasn't that kind of town, and he could only imagine what the powers that be would have to say about it.

Right as he was about to cross the street to have a word with her, the squeal of tires and the crunch of metal connecting with metal snapped Blaine out of the stupor he'd slipped into.

"Holy shit!" Wyatt said, his voice high-pitched. "She caused a freaking accident!"

Blaine reached for his jacket in the backseat and threw open the door. "Go take statements at the accident," he said. "Call the paramedics if there're injuries, and get some backup over here to handle traffic."

"I could take care of her if you want to handle the accident," Wyatt said with a cheeky grin as they ran from the car to the scene.

Blaine shot the patrolman a look that succeeded in shutting him up. He noticed that Tiffany was watching the two drivers shriek at each other with a horrified expression on her face. She'd been so happy when she first arrived at the store, and now it was all going to crap. Well, project or not, he couldn't let that happen.

He and Wyatt reached the street and went their separate ways. Blaine darted through cars brought to a stop by the accident and approached Tiffany, who seemed frozen with shock. Wrapping his jacket around her shoulders, he tried to ease her toward the shop door.

All at once, she snapped out of it and pushed him away. "What do you think you're doing?"

"Taking you inside."

She shook him off, which caused her barely covered breasts to shake, too.

Blaine peeled his eyes off her jiggling flesh while trying to suppress the memory of how her skin had tasted, and the delicious raspberry-colored nipples that were threatening to break free at any second. He'd spent a ridiculous amount of time over the last ten months thinking about those nipples.

"I'm not going anywhere. I've got to get this mess cleaned up before I open at noon."

"Wearing *that*?"

Her green eyes shot fire at him, but mixed in with the anger, he saw desire. *Oh yeah, she's thought about me, too.*

"It's either this or naked." She tossed his coat back at him. "Take your pick."

Blaine swallowed hard as he remembered her naked and handcuffed to her scumbag of a husband. "I choose neither," he said through gritted teeth as he realized they were drawing a crowd of spectators who'd figured out that Tiffany's outfit had caused the crash. The two drivers were arguing with a red-faced and flustered Patrolman Alcott.

"You may not be aware that this town has decency laws," Blaine said.

"All the important stuff is covered," she retorted, bending over to fill the roller pan with paint.

At the sight of her rounded bottom, a surge of lust hit Blaine right in the groin. "It's not covered well enough."

"So write me a ticket and be on your way. I've got work to do and not much time to do it." Running the roller through the glossy white paint, Tiffany began applying it to the splotches of red, green and yellow paint that marred the front of her store. Up went the roller, down went the front of the black bustier.

Blaine wasn't sure what was going to happen first: either his head was going to explode or her boobs were going to bust free of that thing she called decent. "Tiffany, please. Come on. We'll get someone over here to do the painting."

"Who? Who will we get to come help the woman who had the nerve to open a sex-toy shop on this button-downed, sexless, freak-show island?"

He stared at her, his brain attempting to process the words as he began to sweat in earnest. "I thought this was a lingerie shop," he somehow managed to say. "You didn't say anything about, um, toys."

"I said lingerie and *other items*."

"Is that how you managed to get it past the town?" he asked, mesmerized by the sway of her breasts as she worked the roller. A bead of perspiration traveled from the base of her neck straight down to the valley between her bountiful breasts. Despite his best efforts to keep it under control, his dick surged to full hard-on status. He shifted his coat so it covered the front of him.

"They've been so busy trying to keep Jumbo Mart from invading their pristine island that they barely noticed me."

Blaine glanced at the knot of traffic, the mangled cars, infuriated drivers and his rookie attempting to bring order to the chaos. Relieved to see two more cruisers heading toward the scene, Blaine returned his attention to her. "I think it's safe to say they've noticed you now."

"That's the goal," she said with a saucy grin.

"You caused an accident!"

"Um, no, the person who wasn't watching where he was going caused the accident."

Blaine anchored his free hand to his hair to keep the top of his head from blowing off. "You need to put some clothes on, or I'm going to have to cite you." He couldn't charge her with anything other than creating a public nuisance, but she didn't need to know that. Besides, his threats of law and order had hardly stopped her from finishing the job.

Tiffany covered the last of the red splotches with a wide stroke of the roller. "You know, whoever decided to redecorate my shop has actually done me a favor."

"How do you figure?" Blaine asked, exasperated that she refused to take him seriously.

"Well, I needed to repaint and didn't have anything else to wear. Who knew this little number would get me so much free publicity? Maybe a little 'creative advertising' is what I need to make a name for my new shop."

Now Blaine was not only sweating but also wondering why the idea of her parading around half-dressed in the center of town made him so damned mad. It wasn't like she belonged to him or anything. But if she did—belong to him, that was—you could bet *your* ass that she wouldn't be showing *her ass* to anyone but him. "Sweetheart, it's safe to say you've made a name for yourself that'll be remembered on Gansett Island for years to come."

"Perfect."

"Listen, I'm trying to help you here." Once again, he tried to cover her with his coat, and once again she pushed it away.

"I appreciate your whole hero-to-the-rescue act, but I'm all set. Go do your job, and I'll do mine. I'm very busy, and you're going to scare all my customers away with that nasty scowl on your face."

Now that made him mad. "This isn't over." He was dying to ask about the status of her divorce, but this wasn't the time or the place.

Bending to pour the remaining paint from the roller tray back into the can, she gave him another view of her superb backside. When she stood upright again, she turned to him, her face red and flushed from heat and exertion. "*Sweetheart,*" she said in a mocking tone, "it was over before it started."

Longing for Love, available now!

Other Contemporary Romances Available from Marie Force:

The Treading Water Series

Book 1: Treading Water

Book 2: Marking Time

Book 3: Starting Over

Book 4: Coming Home

The McCarthys of Gansett Island Series

Book 1: Maid for Love

Book 2: Fool for Love

Book 3: Ready for Love

Book 4: Falling for Love

Book 5: Hoping for Love

Book 6: Season for Love

Book 7: Longing for Love

Book 8: Waiting for Love

Book 9: Time for Love

The Green Mountain Series

Book 1: All You Need Is Love

Single Titles

Georgia on My Mind

True North

The Fall

Everyone Loves a Hero

Love at First Flight

Line of Scrimmage

Romantic Suspense Novels Available from Marie Force:

The Fatal Series

Book 1: Fatal Affair

Book 2: Fatal Justice

Book 3: Fatal Consequences

Book 3.5: Fatal Destiny, the Wedding Novella

Book 4: Fatal Flaw

Book 5: Fatal Deception

Book 6: Fatal Mistake

Single Title

The Wreck

About the Author

Marie Force is the *New York Times, USA Today* and *Wall Street Journal* bestselling, award-winning author of more than 25 contemporary romances, including the McCarthys of Gansett Island Series, the Fatal Series, the Treading Water Series and numerous stand-alone books. Watch for the new Green Mountain Series, coming in 2014. While her husband was in the Navy, Marie lived in Spain, Maryland and Florida, and she is now settled in her home state of Rhode Island. She is the mother of two teenagers and two feisty dogs, Brandy and Louie. Visit Marie's website at marieforce.com. Subscribe to updates from Marie about new books and other news at marieforce.com/subscribe/. Follow her on Twitter @marieforce and on Facebook at facebook.com/MarieForceAuthor. Join one of her many reader groups! View the list at marieforce.com/connect/. Contact Marie at marie@marieforce.com.

What others are saying about Marie Force's books:

"With the McCarthy's of Gansett Island, Marie Force makes you believe in the power of true love and happily ever after. Over and over again." —Carly Phillips, NY Times Bestselling Author of the Serendipity series

"Maid for Love was a charming beach read that had you believing in the HEA." —Joyfully Reviewed

"Fool for Love was a treat to read with engaging characters and their deep love for one another. Marie Force writes wonderfully, romantic heroes that you just want to curl up next to!" —Joyfully Reviewed

"Ready for Love is a beautiful and inspiring love story. I was riveted to the pages of Ready for Love not only for this magical romance but for the outstanding secondary plot lines as well. This may be my first McCarthys of Gansett Island book but it will not be my last! I am in love with these people and the tiny island they live on." —Joyfully Reviewed

"Ms. Force has the ability to make you fall in love with her Island and all of the quirky and sweet characters that reside there. I can't wait to read the next story in this fantastic series! Falling For Love is another keeper in the McCarthy's of Gansett Island series!" —Joyfully Reviewed.

"Treading Water is a definite must read! Treading Water creates an emotional firestorm within the reader. It shines the light on the good and the bad in life and proves that one moment can change everything and it's never too late to find love. Marie Force grabbed my heart and squeezed every ounce of emotion out of it but most importantly her monumental story left me blissful. Treading Water may be fiction but it gives me hope; hope in everyday people and happily ever after. I cannot wait for the next book in this trilogy, Marking Time." —Joyfully Reviewed, a "Recommended Read" for November 2011!

"Georgia On My Mind" meets real life issues head-on. It will easily touch your heart with a variety of emotions. If you love a book, in spite of any flaws it may suffer, it's a keeper. This one meets that test. You'll laugh and you'll cry.

Most importantly, I'm betting you'll have a satisfied smile on your face when you reach the end." —Romance at Random gives Georgia on My Mind an "A."

"It's a rare treat that you get three gorgeous romances in one story but Marie Force has achieved that with Georgia On My Mind. Ms. Force has seamlessly woven these stories into one magical novel. Each couple is drastically different with their own issues and smoking hot chemistry. This story has a bit of suspense, plenty of humor and lots of romance. Georgia On My Mind is a keeper!" —Joyfully Reviewed.

"With its humor and endearing characters, Force's charming novel will appeal to a broad spectrum of readers, reaching far beyond sports fans." —Booklist on Line of Scrimmage.

"LOVE AT FIRST FLIGHT by Marie Force is most definitely a keeper. It is an astounding book. I loved every single word!" —Wild on Books

"This novel is The O.C. does D.C., and you just can't get enough." —RT Book Reviews, 4.5 Stars for Fatal Affair

"This book starts out strong and keeps getting better. Marie Force is one of those authors that will be on my must read list in the future." —The Romance Studio on Fatal Affair

"As Cole encourages Olivia's incredible talent for drawing and her love of adventure through a series of carefully planned dates, the two embark on the emotional roller-coaster ride of their lives in Force's steamy contemporary romance, a heartwarming Cinderella story set mostly in and around Washington, D.C." —Booklist on Everyone Loves a Hero

"Marie Force's second novel in the Fatal series is an outstanding romantic suspense in its own right; that it follows the fantastic first installment only sweetens the read." —RT Book Reviews, 4.5 Stars for Fatal Justice

CPSIA information can be obtained at www.ICGtesting.com
Printed in the USA
LVOW12s1642250214

375113LV00004B/902/P

9 780615 824376